FARISHTA

Patricia McArdle

RIVERHEAD BOOKS

NEW YORK

✦

RIVERHEAD BOOKS
Published by the Penguin Group
Penguin Group (USA) Inc.
375 Hudson Street, New York, New York 10014, USA
Penguin Group (Canada), 90 Eglinton Avenue East, Suite 700, Toronto, Ontario M4P 2Y3, Canada
(a division of Pearson Penguin Canada Inc.) • Penguin Books Ltd., 80 Strand, London WC2R 0RL,
England • Penguin Group Ireland, 25 St. Stephen's Green, Dublin 2, Ireland (a division of Penguin
Books Ltd.) • Penguin Group (Australia), 250 Camberwell Road, Camberwell, Victoria 3124, Australia
(a division of Pearson Australia Group Pty. Ltd.) • Penguin Books India Pvt. Ltd., 11 Community
Centre, Panchsheel Park, New Delhi—110 017, India • Penguin Group (NZ), 67 Apollo Drive,
Rosedale, Auckland 0632, New Zealand (a division of Pearson New Zealand Ltd.) • Penguin Books
(South Africa) (Pty.) Ltd., 24 Sturdee Avenue, Rosebank, Johannesburg 2196, South Africa

Penguin Books Ltd., Registered Offices: 80 Strand, London WC2R 0RL, England

This is a work of fiction. Names, characters, places, and incidents either are the product of the author's
imagination or are used fictitiously, and any resemblance to actual persons, living or dead, business
establishments, events, or locales is entirely coincidental. The publisher does not have any control over
and does not assume any responsibility for author or third-party websites or their content.

The opinions and characterizations in this book are those of the author, and do not
necessarily represent official positions of the United States Government.

First Riverhead hardcover edition: June 2011
First Riverhead trade paperback edition: June 2012
Riverhead trade paperback ISBN: 978-1-59448-578-7

The Library of Congress has catalogued the Riverhead hardcover edition as follows:

McArdle, Patricia.
Farishta / Patricia McArdle.
p.   cm.
ISBN 978-1-59448-796-5
1. Women diplomats—Fiction.   2. Americans—Afghanistan—Fiction.
3. Loss (Psychology)—Fiction.   4. Afghanistan—Fiction.   I. Title.
PS3613.C266F37   2011   2011003852
813'.6—dc22

PRINTED IN THE UNITED STATES OF AMERICA

10   9   8   7   6   5   4   3   2   1

Praise for *Farishta*

"*Farishta* opens a window into the challenging life of a diplomat. Patricia McArdle accurately portrays life in the northern regions of Afghanistan. Her written wealth of knowledge and experience enhances the reader's ability to understand and appreciate a complex career and multifaceted culture. An outstanding read!"

—Deborah Rodriguez, author of the
New York Times bestselling *Kabul Beauty School*

"A compelling and readable book about the challenges faced by soldiers and civilians stationed in Afghanistan—the constant fear of attack; the unforgiving landscape; the hostile and often corrupt warlords; the uncertain loyalties of Afghan colleagues; the efficacy of their mission; and the constant isolation. . . . But this book is more than a book about one woman and her desire to help Afghans find their own way. It is a well-told story of the daily dangers that Angela and her male colleagues face, the trauma that can accompany their work, and the difficulty they have reentering society."

—*The Huffington Post*

"Combining the emotional insight of *Three Cups of Tea* with the narrative intensity of a Jason Bourne story, *Farishta* is the gripping story of a female U.S. diplomat living and working in Afghanistan. Met with open hostility not only by the Afghan males, but also within her own all-male mission team, over the course of her year there, she has to overcome their antagonism and confront real danger and tragedy."

—Valerie Plame Wilson, author of the
New York Times bestselling *Fair Game*

"*Farishta* uses fiction to untangle the immense complexities of Afghanistan . . . and sheds light on how difficult it can be to achieve progress."

—*The Daily*

"The point *Farishta* ultimately makes is well taken: Afghanistan, as welcoming as it is hostile, has proved to be far more complex than we outsiders ever imagined."

—*The Washington Post*

Farishta is dedicated to the soldiers and civilians

who are risking their lives every day

to bring peace to Afghanistan.

✦

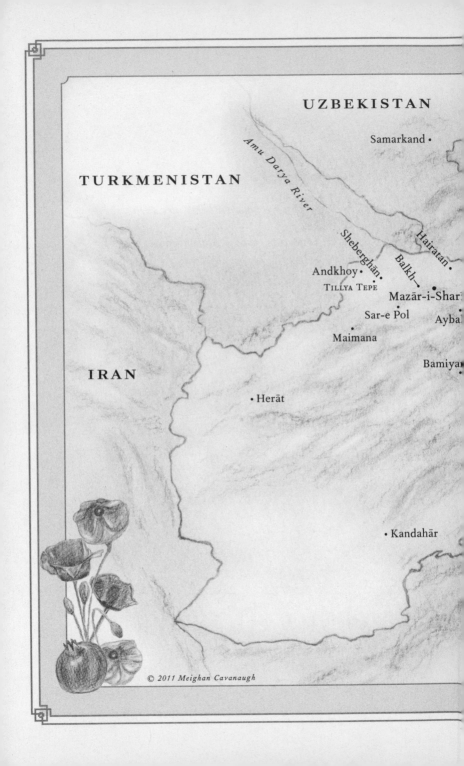

UZBEKISTAN

Samarkand •

Amu Darya River

TURKMENISTAN

Hairatan •

Sheberghān

Balkh

Andkhoy •

TILLYA TEPE

Mazār-i-Shar

Sar-e Pol •

Ayba

Maimana •

Bamiya

IRAN

• Herāt

• Kandahār

© 2011 Meighan Cavanaugh

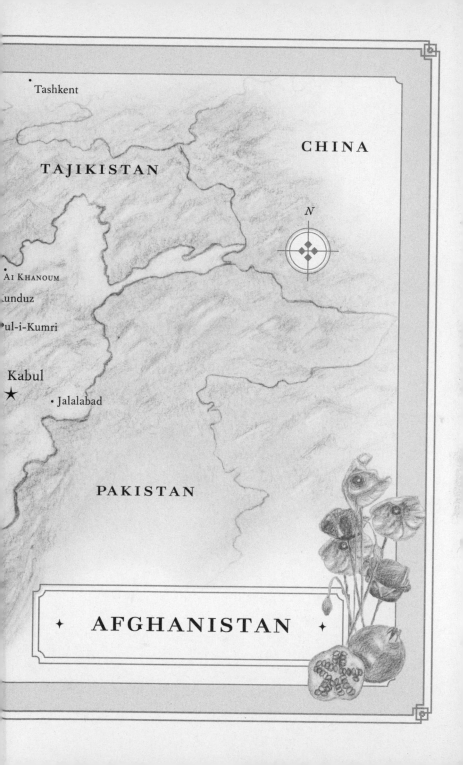

Tashkent

TAJIKISTAN

CHINA

N

Ai Khanoum

Kunduz

Pul-i-Kumri

Kabul
★

• Jalalabad

PAKISTAN

✦ AFGHANISTAN ✦

PROLOGUE

"Ange, I don't think you should be riding anymore until after the baby's born." My husband made this not unexpected announcement as we led our horses, still breathing hard, through the paddock and under the shaded archway of the old brick barn.

"You can't be serious, Tom. I'd go nuts if we couldn't get out of the city every Saturday for these rides."

Mohammed, the stableman who cared for the horses at the Kattouah Riding Club as if they were his own children, stepped out of an unused stall where he had been grilling his lunch over a small clay brazier. He had two lamb brochettes in his hand. He couldn't understand a word we were saying, but he sensed the tension between us and was planning to defuse it with food. *"Salaam aleikum,"* he greeted, flashing his gap-tooth smile, handing us the sticks of sizzling meat and taking the reins from our hands. "This good, you like!"

When Mohammed led the horses away, Tom wrapped one arm around me and tipped my chin up until our eyes met. He was right, of course. Our first child was due in less than four months.

The Lebanese ob-gyn I was seeing had assured me that as long as I took it easy, I would be able to work at the embassy until I was in my seventh month, then fly back to my parents' ranch in New Mexico to have the baby. Tom would pack us out and join me in Albuquerque for the birth. After a month of leave, we would all go to Washington, D.C., where Tom and I would start Russian language training for our assignments in Leningrad.

"I stopped galloping three months ago, Tom. What if I promise not to trot or canter?" I pleaded with a halfhearted pout.

"Ange, knowing how you ride, I'd say that would be an impossible promise to keep." He laughed as he popped a spicy lamb cube into my mouth.

The following Monday, just as my taxi driver swung onto the broad corniche facing the Mediterranean, he tapped the brakes on his ancient Mercedes to avoid ramming the seawall and turned to gaze at a large yacht anchored just offshore. His unexpected stop threw me slightly forward in my seat, and I instinctively placed both hands over my swollen belly in that protective gesture of all mothers-to-be.

"I'll get out here, driver," I said in rapid-fire Arabic as I handed him a fistful of Lebanese pounds. I had reluctantly agreed on Saturday to Tom's request that I stop riding my horse, but I still needed exercise. On this warm April morning, I would walk the final three blocks along the esplanade to the embassy.

For the past few months, our sector of Beirut had been relatively free of the sporadic bombings and gun battles that still raged in other parts of the city. A few American diplomats, including my husband, even jogged along the corniche before work.

My meeting with a group of Lebanese journalists had gone well, and I was planning to join Tom in his office for a lunch of falafel, hummus, and fresh pita bread I'd purchased from a street vendor. I grabbed the greasy paper bag of food from the backseat of the taxi and set off on foot for the embassy, absently patting my stomach and enjoying the fresh salt air. When I glanced out to sea for an instant to watch a flock of battling seagulls, my life suddenly ended—or should have. A blast of hot air, followed by a roaring in my ears, threw me hard against the cement seawall. The bag of food flew out of my hand, over the wall, and sank beneath the waves.

As I struggled to my feet, I could see a roiling black cloud rising into the air where the embassy stood just around the corner. Cars parked close to the compound had flipped over and were on fire. People were lying in the street. They were bleeding. Their mouths were open. They must have been screaming, but I could hear only a loud ringing in my ears. I began to run through the falling debris, one hand still on my belly to protect my unborn child. The entire front of the embassy had collapsed. Where Tom's office had been, there was nothing.

ONE

The first ring jarred me awake seconds before my forehead hit the keyboard. I inched slowly back in my chair, hoping no one had noticed me dozing off.

Narrowing my eyes against the flat glare of the ceiling lights, I scanned the long row of cubicles behind me. I was alone.

The second ring and the scent of microwave popcorn drifting in from a nearby office reminded me I was supposed to meet some colleagues for dinner and a movie near Dupont Circle at eight. It was almost seven thirty.

The third ring froze me in place when I saw the name flashing on the caller ID.

If irrational fear could still paralyze me like this after all these years, then perhaps it really was time to give up.

It wasn't only real danger that would accelerate my pulse and cause me to stop breathing like a frightened rabbit staring down the barrel of a shotgun. It was little things. Tonight it was a telephone call.

I forced myself to grab the receiver halfway through ring number four.

"This is Angela Morgan," I said, struggling to suppress the anxiety that had formed a painful knot in my throat.

My computer beeped and coughed up two messages from the U.S. Embassy in Honduras. I ignored them and began taking slow, measured breaths.

"Angela, you're working late tonight. It's Marty Angstrom from personnel."

Marty's chirpy, nasal voice resonated like the slow graze of a fork down an empty plate.

He was stammering, obviously surprised that anyone in the Central American division at the State Department would pick up the phone this late on a Friday evening. I had apparently upset his plan to leave a voice message that I wouldn't hear until Monday morning.

"Hello, Marty. It's been a long time." My heart was thundering. "Is this a good news or a bad news call?"

"It depends," said Marty.

"On what?"

"On what your definition of good is." He chuckled.

The wish list I'd submitted to personnel for my next overseas diplomatic posting had been, in order of preference: London, Madrid, Nairobi, San Salvador, Lima, Caracas, Riga, St. Petersburg, and Kabul. I'd thrown in Kabul at the last minute, thinking it would demonstrate that I was a team player and increase my chances for the London assignment. But they would never send me to Kabul, not after what had happened in Beirut.

"Marty, please get to the point. Did I get London?"

I could hear him breathing through his nose into the phone like an old man with asthma. He sounded almost as nervous as I felt.

Not a good sign. Was I being sent south of the border again just because I spoke Spanish? But why would that make Marty nervous?

Before I retired or was forced out of the Foreign Service for not getting promoted fast enough, I was hoping for just one tour of duty in Western Europe. Foreign Service Officers, like military officers, must compete against their colleagues of similar rank for the limited number of promotions available each year. Consistently low performers are drummed out long before reaching the traditional retirement age of sixty-five.

I desperately wanted an assignment in London, but I'd settle for Madrid. After all I'd been through—I deserved it.

"Well, you'll be spending a lot of time with the Brits," Marty replied eagerly.

"Meaning?" I put him on speaker and began to rearrange the stacks of papers on my desk. My pulse and breathing were returning to normal.

"Listen, Angela, I know you had some tough times a while back, but that was more than two decades ago."

Tough times—a dead husband and a bloody miscarriage. *Yeah, those were definitely tough times,* I thought, looking over at the small silver-framed photo of Tom and me. We were sitting on our bay Arabian geldings at the Kattouah stables near Beirut. Our knees were touching. His horse was nuzzling mine. We were laughing.

Tom and I had met for the first time in 1979 at a private stable in the Virginia hunt country, where we'd arrived separately to rent horses for a few hours on the weekend. Although we were both studying Farsi in preparation for our first assignments as junior diplomats to the U.S. Embassy in Tehran, we had different instructors at the Foreign Service Institute. Our paths had never crossed until that warm summer morning, when the New Mexico rancher's daughter and the southern prep school boy discovered the first of their many common interests.

"Ange, you're going to get kicked out of the Foreign Service in another year if you don't get promoted," warned Marty.

That was true. After the embassy bombing killed Tom, and I lost the baby a few days later, the Department had ordered me back to the United States to recover, but not for long. I stayed with my parents for three months, was given a low-stress desk job in D.C. for the following year, and was then expected to start Russian language training and take the assignment in Leningrad where Tom and I should have gone together.

During that two-year tour of duty in the Soviet Union, I had developed a taste for vodka—which became my painkiller and therapist of choice—an affinity that led to a series of less than stellar performance evaluations. After that disaster, I was exiled to Central and South American outposts where the Spanish I'd learned from my mother would come in handy and nothing I did would have serious policy implications for the U.S. government.

My father's prolonged illness and my frequent trips out west to see him had made it impossible for me to take any more overseas assignments for the past six years. My career had been dying a slow and painful death in a series of dead-end positions at State Department headquarters in Washington.

"Continue," I replied, growing weary of Marty's little guessing game.

"You really need this promotion, Angela."

This conversation was becoming unbearable. I focused on my breathing, willing my anxiety not to resurface.

"Marty, I'm going to hang up the phone right now if you don't tell me where the Department is sending me."

"Okay, you're going to Afghanistan in December."

Oh, God, this has got to be a joke. I laid my head down on the desk blotter and closed my eyes.

"Marty, I don't know a thing about Afghanistan," I whispered into the speakerphone. What I didn't add was that serving in another Islamic country, war or no war, was an experience I didn't think I could handle.

"It doesn't matter. Neither does anybody else. You put it on your bid list."

"It was the very last post on a very long wish list, Marty," I said, trying to maintain my composure.

"Listen, Ange, at this point we're filling positions in Afghanistan and Iraq with anyone remotely suitable who volunteers. We may eventually have to start forcing people to go, but you'll get more brownie points if you go willingly now. I know this was your last choice, but it's only for a year, and I promise to try and get you an onward assignment to someplace great . . . like London!"

In 2004, the United States was fighting not one but two wars. The one in Iraq, begun the previous year, was sucking most of the air out of the State Department. Meanwhile, the "forgotten war" in Afghanistan had been relegated to the back pages of *The Washington Post* and a few understaffed offices at the State Department.

I shared the sentiments of many of my Foreign Service colleagues, who believed we should have stayed out of Iraq and completed our mission in Afghanistan. A few brave souls actually spoke up and even resigned in protest. I'm ashamed to admit that I, like many, kept my head down, stayed focused on my less controversial part of the world, and tried hard not to think much about either war.

"Marty, I don't speak Dari or Pashto."

"Your personnel file shows you have an extremely high aptitude for foreign languages. It says you got the highest score ever recorded at the Foreign Service Institute when you took Farsi."

"That was twenty-five years ago, Marty, and no one in my Farsi class was ever sent to Tehran because the Iranians took everyone in the embassy hostage that year. You'll see in my file that my husband and I were put in Arabic language training, reassigned to Yemen for a year, and then sent to Beirut."

Marty ignored my comments and continued. "I am told by unnamed sources that you still read and are able to recite Rumi in the original Persian."

"Who told you that?"

How could this be happening? Rumi's poetry, which had given me such comfort in the months after I lost Tom and the baby, was now being used by Marty as a rationale to force me back into the same conflict-ridden part of the world that had taken them away from me.

"Is it true?" Marty asked.

My eyes were now brimming with tears, and the knot in my throat was returning. Fortunately, no one was in the office to witness my mini-meltdown.

"Ange?"

"So what? Rumi is the most popular poet in the United States."

"True." Marty chuckled, irritating me even more. "But most Americans read his works in English translation."

I was too upset to respond.

"The Department doesn't have many Farsi speakers left," Marty continued, "and they need someone up north who is fluent in Dari."

"I just told you I don't speak Dari, and what do you mean, 'up north'? I thought I was being assigned to the embassy in Kabul."

"Remember I said you'll be spending a lot a time with the Brits?"

"So am I being assigned to the British Embassy?" His question puzzled me.

"You won't actually be in Kabul. You're going to be spending a year with the British Army at a PRT in Mazār-i-Sharīf."

Me? At forty-seven, they were assigning me to a Provincial Reconstruction Team, a military outpost that conducted surveillance patrols in the northern provinces? And not even a U.S. camp, but one where I'd be doubly an outsider—as a civilian and an American.

"We're putting you in a one-on-one Farsi–Dari conversion course next month," Marti continued. "You should be fluent by December. They say Dari is just like Farsi, but easier. With your language aptitude, it shouldn't take you too long to pick it up. Your Arabic won't be very useful, but I hear your Russian may come in handy up there."

"My Russian?"

"Yeah, they say some of the warlords in the north speak Russian. And the Russians still have an interest in what goes on up there—even after all these years," he added with a conspiratorial flourish.

"Look, Ange, they want you in Mazār by early January, and you'll need a few days in Kabul for briefings before you head north. Will that be okay?" Marty was now sounding almost apologetic. "Is Christmas a big deal with your family? Will they be upset if you aren't home?"

"Not really," I said, glancing at a favorite old photo I had tacked to the cloth partition in my cubicle. Mom and I were halfway down our winding driveway at the ranch in New Mexico setting out *luminarias* for the annual Morgan Christmas fiesta. Her long, dark braid fell over her shoulder as she bent to help me light one of the candles.

I remembered how much I had looked forward to coming back to the States from my overseas postings for the holidays before she died—but that was almost ten years ago. After Dad's long illness and his miraculous recovery last summer, he had surprised my brother and me by marrying one of his nurses, a much younger woman from Albuquerque. The new Mrs. Morgan wasn't big on the whole family Christmas thing.

"Hey, Ange, watch out for those British officers," Marty added in an awkward attempt at humor. "I think you'll be the only female up there and with those big green eyes you're not too bad looking even at your age."

I winced, but let it roll off me. "Thanks for the kind words, Marty. Shall I file my sexual harassment suit now, or just let it simmer until Monday morning?"

"Sorry, I'm kidding, Ange, nothing serious, okay? So, have

you ever been in a war zone?" he asked, trying to change the subject.

"Does Beirut 1983 count?" I replied, gazing again at the photo of Tom and me. I recalled the moment just after the photo was taken when he had leaned over in his saddle to kiss me.

"Oh, yeah, of course. Sure it does. Sorry," Marty said, his voice softening. "You'll do fine in Afghanistan. They even give you two R and Rs, so you'll be able to come home twice. Hey! You could use one of your free trips to go check out London in case I'm able to get you that dream assignment. Have a great weekend, Ange."

My colleagues were not surprised when I called to say I wouldn't be joining them for dinner. It happened often. I walked home in a daze.

My apartment, a few blocks from the State Department, was still the only place I felt completely safe. Other than my solitary evening jogs through Foggy Bottom, I spent far too much time alone there.

Tom and I had shared this place for the first eighteen months of our marriage. It was a small one-bedroom, which we had leased to friends when we were sent to the U.S. Embassy in Yemen. Our plan had been to sell it when we came home after a few tours of duty overseas and buy something bigger for the three kids we were going to have.

I put on an old jazz album that Tom loved, kicked off my shoes, poured a glass of wine, curled up on the couch, and stared out the window at the diamond and ruby lights spinning around Washington Circle. This was not how I'd planned the final years of my diplomatic career. This was not how I'd planned my life.

Ever since Beirut, I hadn't handled stress—or living—very well. This evening's call from Marty had been almost more than I could bear. I walked barefoot into the bedroom, my toes sinking into one of the carpets Tom and I had bought in Yemen, which I had imagined in the living room of the Victorian townhouse we were going to own. The wall behind my bed was covered in photos of the two of us: Tom and me laughing with our arms around each other on the front porch at my parents' place in New Mexico; clowning with embassy friends in front of one of Sana'a's medieval mud-brick towers; Tom taking his horse over a triple bar jump at the stable in Beirut.

Although riding was the passion that had bonded us the instant we met, our styles could not have been more different. Tom's parents had enrolled him in lessons as a boy. By high school, he was competing in stadium jumping and three-day eventing for juniors. My brother and I had been taught to ride with English and Western saddles by our father but it was our no-holds-barred races across the high desert of New Mexico that had shaped my more aggressive riding style.

During our two overseas diplomatic assignments together, Tom and I sought out fellow horse lovers as soon as we arrived. Lebanon had been more problematic than Yemen because of the security situation, but we had discovered the Kattouah stables hidden in a valley just outside the Beirut city limits. The small group of regulars—expat and Lebanese riders—had welcomed us like family and had teased Tom constantly about his concern that I might harm the baby or even give birth during one of our Saturday rides. I had not been on a horse since I lost Tom.

I went to the bookshelf, pulled out one of his small, leather-bound collections of Rumi's poetry, and pressed it against my chest. When the tears began to flow and I dropped it on my pillow, it fell open to a well-read page. I curled up on my bed, whispering the words in Farsi until I fell asleep.

TWO

Ali's Afghan restaurant in south Arlington, redolent with sautéed garlic and the sweet charred odor of roasting lamb, thundered with the sounds of men talking and laughing above the tunes of a Bollywood soundtrack. Over the course of my four months of Dari language training with Ali's uncle, Professor Ahmad Jalali, this restaurant became like a second home to me. I wanted my language training and these lunches to go on forever—anything to put off my eventual year in Afghanistan.

The State Department had given me no choice: Learn Dari and go to Afghanistan or get ready to retire early if I didn't get promoted in 2005.

Professor Jalali was spending six hours a day, five days a week alone with me in a small windowless room at the Foreign Service Institute. Our weekly trips to his nephew's restaurant were essential for both our sanities. And it didn't hurt that the food was delicious.

When I reported for my first day of instruction, I learned that he would be my private tutor and that as few people as possible were to know how fluent I was expected to become in Dari. Jalali had been ordered by his supervisor not to discuss my language ability with anyone. Marty said it had something to do with a request that I quietly assess the accuracy of certain interpreters at the PRT who were rumored to be concealing information from the Brits. I was too despondent to make additional inquiries about the reasons for this secrecy.

My evenings were spent alone in my apartment studying Dari, reading Rumi, and flipping endlessly through the photo albums Tom and I had assembled during our few years together. I ran my fingers over his curly blond hair and laughing face in each photo where we were waving and smiling or wrapped in each other's arms for our obligatory "kissing shot"—each one with mountains, monuments, stables, or beaches in the background. I had almost thrown them all away in a drunken rage many years ago. Thank God I'd saved them. The only pages I still couldn't bear to look at were the ones with snapshots Tom had taken after we found out I was pregnant.

Professor Jalali, known to all as "Doc," was a diminutive Afghan of Tajik extraction. He had a thick gray crew cut, horn-rimmed glasses, a broad smile, and a Ph.D. in Persian literature from Kabul University. Doc had been a teacher in Mazār-i-Sharīf before fleeing Afghanistan after the Soviet invasion.

"Uncle, is this the woman who is going to live in our beloved city?" asked Ali as he rushed out of his steaming kitchen and wiped his hands with his apron on the first day Doc took me to Ali's restaurant. Where Doc was the complete image of a meticulous professor, his nephew was the total opposite. The loud, smiling, rotund chef stroked his short black beard and shook my hand vigorously when Doc introduced us.

"Hamid," Ali shouted in Dari to a tall young man leaning against the kitchen door, "bring *palau*, *ketfa*, and *bulonie* for my uncle and his guest and don't forget the *naan*."

As soon as the steaming trays of rice, lamb brochettes, savory pastries, meatballs spiced with cinnamon, and hot flat bread were placed before us, Ali stepped behind me and folded his hands over his broad chest. In a booming voice, he announced in English to his kitchen staff and the other customers eating lunch that his uncle Professor Jalali was teaching "his very best Dari to this brave American woman, this angel," who had volunteered to spend a year living near the city of his ancestors in their war-torn country.

Not exactly volunteered, I thought.

I shot a look at Doc, hoping he could find a way to rescue the situation. He knew that the degree of my language skill was not to be raised at Ali's restaurant or anywhere else. As well meaning as Ali was, someone that gregarious was bound to spread word of my fluency throughout the Afghan population in D.C.—and to his relatives in Mazār-i-Sharīf.

"Angela Morgan," Ali continued, "when you come to my restaurant, I will call you *Farishta*. This is our Dari word for 'angel'—like your American name."

Doc smiled at me, patted my hand, and said, "Farishta is a good Dari name for you. I should have thought of it myself." He looked up at his nephew and winked quickly at me. "Ali, you must always speak to my pupil in Dari, but very slowly or she will not understand what you are saying. She's only a beginner." Ali nodded gravely before returning to the kitchen.

———

There was little training available in late 2004 for American diplomats assigned to Provincial Reconstruction Teams in Afghanistan. Some of my colleagues were being sent out with no language instruction at all. Our only other preparation was a week of lectures on current Afghan history and politics, which raised my anxiety to new levels with its relentless focus on the conflicts that had led to the 9/11 attacks.

I soon discovered that there was far more to Afghanistan's past than the events of the last few decades or even the last few centuries. The faded tourist posters plastering the walls of Ali's restaurant reminded his customers that Afghanistan's violent and colorful lineage was thousands of years in the making. Alexander the Great, Darius, Zoroaster, Marco Polo, and Genghis Khan, all players in the endless cycle of conquest by invaders and their ultimate defeat, looked down on Ali's customers and inspired me to learn more about Afghanistan's ancient works of art, architecture, and literature.

"Look, Doc," I said, pointing at one of the faded posters, "your nephew likes Rumi!"

Doc snorted and shook his head.

When on the first day of class I had mentioned my love of Rumi's poetry and reminded Doc that Rumi had been born near Mazār, he had wrinkled his nose, straightened his glasses, and made it quite clear that we would be reciting a lot more of his favorite poet Hāfez than my man Rumi.

"Angela, my dear, you must understand that Hāfez sings. Rumi merely recites," he chided me gently.

Doc was persistent, but he could not change my mind about Rumi, whose every verse reminded me of Tom. Soon after Tom and I had met that morning at the riding stable in Virginia, we began reviewing our lessons together every day after Farsi class. We were so young and so idealistic—excited about being diplomats, representing our country overseas, and helping to make the world a better place. The attraction between us was growing, but we had both been too shy to do anything about it until one evening I hosted a study group at my apartment and Tom came. After everyone else had gone home, he recited one of Rumi's love poems to me in flawless Farsi and I wouldn't let him leave.

Before Doc and I could begin another argument about the merits of our favorite poets, Ali came bursting through the kitchen doors carrying a small laptop computer. "Uncle, my brother has just sent me photos from last week's *buzkashi* game. You must see them! Khan Cherik's horses won again, and my brother tells me that Governor Daoud is livid," he said, laughing.

Ali pulled a chair between Doc and me to show us his photos of the fierce riders on their rearing stallions. "Look," said Ali, touching the screen with a greasy finger, "there is your nephew Qais on my brother's favorite stallion. You see how well he sits?"

I was captivated by this game, which reminded me so much of the wild gallops of my youth across the high desert of New Mexico. As Ali showed me the photos, Doc explained the rules of the game. Hundreds of riders mounted on powerful stallions, bred only for this violent competition, battled one another for the privilege of dragging a headless calf around an enormous field at a full gallop. I was mesmerized by the power, beauty, and fierce courage of the *buzkashi* horses.

Ali, sharing his uncle's delight in my interest in the game, loaded a DVD of *The Horsemen* into his laptop.

"This, Farishta, is *buzkashi*," declared the be... "Watch closely, because I doubt you'll be able to see a real game while you are in Mazār. Afghan women do not attend these competitions."

Doc explained that the movie featured actual Afghan riders, some of whom he had seen compete in Mazār as a boy.

"Farishta," he said in his most professorial voice as the movie continued, "only if you understand *buzkashi* will you ever understand Afghanistan."

I threw up my hands. "But, Doc, how will I ever understand this game? It's too confusing. There are so many players, and they move so fast I can't figure out which rider is on which team."

"Precisely," he replied.

THREE

Language training was over. I had been deemed sufficiently fluent in Dari, and the dreaded departure date was only three weeks away. Every night, I was being shaken awake by stomach-churning, heart-thumping panic attacks and night sweats. Was this more menopause? Was my post-traumatic stress disorder resurfacing or was I now getting a combo package?

The term PTSD had been coined by the psychiatric community only three years before that April day in Beirut when the American Embassy exploded in flame-licked clouds and collapsed with Tom inside. Three days later, when my baby was stillborn, I almost bled to death before a Lebanese neighbor found me lying on the floor of my apartment and took me to a hospital.

I could have resigned at that point but I liked the travel and the prestige of being a diplomat. The pay was good and I really didn't know what else I would do. I needed serious help to cope with my trauma, but there was none available. The culture of the State Department was to deal with such events the British way—with a stiff upper lip and a stiff drink. Short of being hauled out in a straitjacket, Foreign Service Officers, like military officers, would never voluntarily consult with a shrink and risk losing their security and medical clearances. For years, I struggled without professional help to overcome the trauma and loss of that week—an effort that included significant amounts of legal self-medication and a string of disastrous relationships.

When the excessive drinking, which had started in Leningrad, the pills, and the parade of unsuitable men caught up to me and were about to drag me into a hole from which I would never emerge, I locked up my emotions, threw away the key, and buried myself in a series of inconsequential diplomatic assignments.

Intellectually, I knew that my anxiety about going to Afghanistan was irrational. Although it was technically a "war zone," the possibility that I would be wounded or killed was minuscule.

Mazār-i-Sharīf was on the north side of the Hindu Kush, where the only fighting in the past year had been between competing Afghan warlords and their militias. All U.S. and allied combat operations were in the south along the Pakistani border.

By December 2004, the flood of U.S. government employees and contractors going to Baghdad was getting most of the attention inside the Department of State. All Green Zone–bound volunteers were required to attend a security course, which included several days of first-aid training as well as weapons and explosives familiarization. There had not been any similar preparation available for civilians headed to Afghanistan. Hoping that some training—any training—would help to calm my fears about going, I managed to talk my way into one of the classes two weeks prior to my departure.

Despite the fact that even in combat zones American diplomats are not authorized to carry weapons, the Department of State had decided that its civilian personnel going to Baghdad needed practice firing some of the small arms used by our military. It was never clear to me what untrained civilians were expected to do with weapons they had handled and fired only once, but I was hoping the afternoon "shooting party" would help me overcome my predeployment jitters.

"All right, gentlemen—and lady," said our bearded instructor as we filed into the armory next to the firing range, "today we'll be loading, emptying, reloading, and firing an AK-5 assault rifle, a Sig Sauer pistol, an AK-47 or Kalashnikov—that's the one the bad guys use—a Colt M4 submachine gun, and a Remington shotgun. Any questions?"

There were none as we stared in silence at the well-oiled firepower arrayed on long metal tables before us.

"Have any of you ever fired a weapon?" he asked. Two of us raised our hands. The other fellow was a former Marine gunnery sergeant. The instructor turned to me, "Ma'am, would you like to share with us which weapons you have fired?"

"My brother and I used to go rabbit hunting," I said, regretting immediately that I had raised my hand, "with an air rifle."

I didn't mention that I was a pretty good shot. That became apparent when we filed outside with our loaded weapons and I began blasting away at the targets and ripping out their center circles. I channeled my fear about going to Afghanistan into each shot. My classmates were impressed.

The next three days of first-aid training had quite the opposite effect. Our instructor, Mike, a gruff but compassionate former Special Forces medic, had a genuine desire to prepare us for what we might face in a war zone. He also kept us in a moderate state of terror so we would pay close attention to everything he said.

Mike was a gentle giant, with skin the color of polished ebony and a shaved head that glowed like an eight ball under the fluorescent lights in our crowded classroom. He showed us how to assess swelling and discoloration, when and where to apply pressure, how to treat a sucking chest wound with a credit card and duct tape, and some very creative ways to use Super Glue.

On day two, we held a drill where groups of four practiced conducting triage after a bombing. Our job was to determine who would be given immediate first aid, who could survive for a while without treatment, and who would be left to die.

Carrying notepads, several of us followed Mike through a simulated disaster site, stepping carefully over the prone bodies of our moaning classmates in the auditorium of the training facility. The victims had covered themselves with realistic pools of latex blood and anatomically correct wounds.

I was moving along at a good clip, bending over each victim, and shouting, "Can you hear me?" before checking them for breathing, bleeding, pulse, and broken bones. The fifth victim was a man in his mid-twenties with shaggy blond hair and soft brown eyes. Just like Tom.

It was too much. I doubled over and broke into a sweat.

Mike was next to me in seconds. He knelt at my side, placed one hand on my back, and began to talk me out of the panic attack that had overwhelmed me. My eyes were closed and I was gasping for air. I bit down on my tongue to keep from screaming.

"Morgan!" he shouted. I whipped my head around and looked

him in the eyes. "Check the shadows. Do you see a second bomber hiding?"

I scanned the perimeter and saw only the walls of the auditorium.

"No," I responded, my breathing still ragged.

"Look again and tell me exactly what you see. Every detail!" He was shouting over the bedlam in the auditorium.

I began to describe the color of the walls, the shape of the windows, the size of the doors, and the length of the curtains. My breathing became more regular.

His hand was now resting lightly on my neck. He was subtly monitoring my breathing and heart rate.

"When did it happen?" he asked softly.

"Beirut, '83," I said, my voice barely audible.

"The Marine barracks?" he asked.

"No, the embassy, my husband. The building collapsed. I couldn't help him." I was sobbing.

"Jesus, Morgan," he said sitting down on the floor next to me. "And I'll bet you haven't talked to anyone about this." I shook my head.

"Are you sure you're ready for Afghanistan? You'll probably be the only civilian at that PRT, not like the rest of this bunch who are all headed for the overpopulated and well-stocked confines of the Green Zone in Baghdad."

"It's in the north—Mazār-i-Sharīf—there's no fighting up there. I'll be fine," I replied. "And yes, I'm ready."

"Okay. If this happens again, you'll know what to do?"

"Yes."

"You see someone else freeze, you'll know how to bring 'em out of it?"

"Thanks to you, I will."

"Morgan, you can't keep this bottled up forever. We are only as sick as our secrets, sweetheart, and this one's eating you alive."

"I know. I'll talk to someone when I get back."

"Good. Now, let's get the rest of these Green Zone weenies squared away."

FOUR

The State Department had ordered me to break my December trip to Afghanistan with a stop in London, where I was to meet with a desk officer at the Foreign and Commonwealth Office. Since I was being dispatched to a British PRT, it would be useful to hear their perspective on the political situation in northern Afghanistan. And I'd get to spend a few days pretending I had been posted to London instead of Mazār-i-Sharīf.

A colleague told me off the record that there had been a heated debate regarding the need to even assign another American Foreign Service Officer to the PRT in Mazār now that the Brits were in charge and had one of their own diplomats there. So why were they sending me?

Gray skies and a stiff breeze greeted me when I landed at Heathrow Airport, where the thermometer hovered just above freezing. After a cramped overnight flight in economy class, all I wanted was to crawl under several blankets and sleep off my jet lag.

I switched on CNN in my hotel room, programmed the TV to shut down in half an hour, and was beginning to doze off when a loud advertisement for the Royal Beirut Hotel shook me awake. Two minutes later, the timer hit the thirty-minute mark and the screen went black. As I lay awake in the darkened room, I remembered how excited Tom and I had been when we learned about the assignment to Beirut after our year in Yemen. It would be a great career move, and we were both relishing the challenge of another hardship post. Although the ongoing Lebanese civil war would restrict our movements, we knew there were still riding stables near Beirut and, of course, the extra pay would come in handy—perhaps to start a college fund for those three kids we planned to have.

It took several more hours of switching between CNN and BBC before I fell asleep.

Walking to my meeting at the Foreign Office, I tried to ignore the last-minute holiday shoppers, muffled against the damp cold and crowded into department stores that shimmered with lights and hummed with tinny Christmas carols. I had traveled to New Mexico the previous week for an early Christmas celebration with my father, brother, and their young wives. Unlike the days when Mom was alive, the house had no decorations except for a small tree my brother had festooned with a few of her homemade ornaments.

I had set my watch incorrectly when I arrived in London, and was an hour early for my appointment with Mr. Smythe, a British diplomat who monitored activities in northern Afghanistan. I'd been waiting for thirty minutes on a couch near his secretary's desk when at eleven fifteen she poked her head into his office and reminded him that I was here. She left his door wide open, promised me I would be seen in just a few minutes, and dashed out for an early lunch.

Mr. Smythe's phone was ringing nonstop. He concluded another call and stepped out to greet me. "Miss Morgan, so nice to meet you face-to-face. I have just one short meeting before ours. I hope you're not in a hurry." I assured him I was not.

"Please feel free to sit at my secretary's desk and use her phone to call the United States if you have the need," he said before rushing back to his office to take another call. It was much too early to ring D.C. or New Mexico and I really had nothing more to say to anyone stateside, so I settled into the secretary's comfortable chair to review the questions I had jotted down for our meeting.

"Excuse me, miss, my name is Davies, Major Mark Davies, is Mr. Smythe . . ."

I glanced up from my notes and into the electric blue eyes of a dark-haired man in a business suit. He tugged uncomfortably at his tie, which did not budge. Standing stiffly before me, he swallowed hard and cleared his throat.

Resting his fingertips on the edge of the desk, leaning forward and staring at me with his brow slightly furrowed, he began to study my face as though we'd met before but he couldn't quite remember where. The intensity of his gaze rendered me momentarily speechless.

He was younger than me, but it was hard to tell by how many years. He had olive skin with a thin tracing of lines around those intense blue eyes. He was clean-shaven, but a pale shadow already visible across his chin emphasized the hard sweep of his jaw.

It was our similarities that fascinated me—silky black hair—

although mine was loose and layered, his clipped and military. The planes of both our faces were angled with sharp cheekbones, and his nostrils, like mine, were slightly flared. And those incongruous eyes—mine so green and his so blue.

We had each inherited pale but permanent suntans from ancestors who had likely not fit well into polite western society. Mine had come from the Lopez side of my mother's family, and from my father's Comanche grandmother, who had married an Irish carpenter named Morgan. My green eyes, my last name, and a sprinkling of freckles across my nose were the only remnants I still carried of my Celtic heritage.

Our intense but wordless exchange lasted less than ten seconds. With his eyes still locked on mine, the major snapped to attention and his voice returned.

"I'm quite late for my appointment with Mr. Smythe. Is he in?" he asked, shifting his gaze to Smythe's open door.

"Yes, he's . . ."

Not waiting for me to finish my sentence, and without a thank-you, he spun around and walked toward Smythe's office.

"Mark," said Smythe, rising to greet him, "how nice to see you again. Thank you for stopping by. So sorry to disrupt your final day in town, but I wanted to speak with you in person before you left."

"Sir, shall I close the door?" asked the major, glancing back at me with a look that I could not decipher.

"No need," said Smythe. "This will be brief." I could see Smythe through the open door, sitting at his desk and tamping loose tobacco into his pipe. It was lunchtime in London and his phone had gone suddenly quiet.

"Sir, my apologies for being late."

"Not a problem. When are you leaving for Kabul?" asked Smythe, his unlit pipe clenched between his teeth.

"I leave tomorrow morning to spend the holidays in Brunei. I'll be reporting to NATO headquarters in Kabul in early January."

"Excellent. Listen, Mark, I'm aware that your preference was to return to Basra and continue the fine intelligence work you have been doing for our forces in Iraq, but as your commanding officer has hopefully explained to you, we need you right now in Afghanistan."

These remarks caught my attention. Was Davies someone I would be working with? As Smythe began to review with the major the overarching political concerns of the British government in northern Afghanistan, I was grateful that I had arrived early and that Smythe hadn't bothered to close his door.

"I presume you are aware the Americans have decided to post one of their diplomats to our PRT in Mazār for another year," said Smythe at the conclusion of his briefing.

"Excuse me, sir, I thought the Yanks had decided not to send any more diplomats to Mazār. Don't we already have one of our own up there? The U.S. Army turned that PRT over to us more than a year ago."

I sat without moving, my hands folded in my lap, hoping the phone would not ring and the secretary wouldn't return while I listened with increasing concern to Smythe's conversation with the major.

"Yes, they did, but . . ."

The major broke in, "Permission to speak freely, sir."

"Go ahead," said Smythe—a slight sharpness in his voice betraying his irritation.

"I really don't think at this point we need to muck up what is already a very delicate situation in Mazār-i-Sharīf with another Yank moving in and trying to tell our boys what to do. Is this a firm decision, sir?" asked Davies.

"Mark, if the Americans want to have one of their own up there reporting back to Washington, there's not a great deal we have to say about it. Also the State Department and our Foreign Office both want a diplomat in Mazār who is fluent in Dari. Neither our current diplomatic representative nor his replacement has sufficient fluency."

"But, sir . . ." Mark interrupted.

Smythe ignored him and continued. "We suspect that some of the interpreters may not be briefing our officers accurately on all the side conversations taking place during their meetings with the local warlords. Mind you, no one at the PRT, except for the commanding officer and his deputy, is to know about her language ability until she is able to spend a few months going out on patrols with our boys and assessing the accuracy of our terps' translations."

"They're sending a woman?" I could hear the agitation rising in the major's voice. "That camp is quite small and really, sir, with an all-male infantry company, it's no place for a woman."

"Regardless of what you think, Mark, Her Majesty's government, NATO, and the commanding officer of PRT Mazār-i-Sharīf have already expressed their full approval of and support for her assignment."

Smythe glanced at me through the open door, raised one eyebrow, then turned back to the major before continuing. "Even more important, however, the gender of the diplomat the Americans choose to send to our PRT should be of no concern to you whatsoever.

"The British Army has temporarily housed female soldiers and civilians in the past at PRT Mazār—medics, journalists, supply clerks. Just because there aren't any there at this time doesn't mean we can't accommodate the American for the next year."

The major shook his head and ran his fingers repeatedly through his short-cropped hair.

"You should also be aware that you won't be spending your tour in Kabul as initially planned, Mark. The Foreign Office intends to ask your commanding officer to release you for duty in Mazār-i-Sharīf for at least six months since your own regiment will be taking over there in April."

There was no reply from the major to this new information.

"You'll spend a few days being briefed at NATO headquarters in Kabul, but you are urgently needed to take over the running of the intel shop at PRT Mazār. It's a total mess. We also need someone of your caliber to begin organizing the smooth transition of the whole intel operation to the Swedish Army when they take over the PRT from us at the end of 2005 and our boys move south to Helmand. We have requested your transfer north but, of course, it's entirely up to your commanding officer to approve it."

"Yes, sir, of course," the major replied in a tone that failed to conceal his displeasure.

Smythe tapped his pipe on an empty ashtray and continued. "We also need a fluent Pashto speaker like yourself in Mazār for the same reason we need the American diplomat's expertise in

Dari. We understand that the Afghan government may be moving some Pashtun police officials from the south into senior positions in the northern provinces. Although these moves make no sense to us because there are so few Pashto speakers in that part of Afghanistan, we must be prepared since only one of the interpreters at the PRT speaks the language."

"Is this woman with the CIA, sir? It would not help our credibility if word got out that we are providing cover for one of their agents."

Smythe glanced at me through the door and saw me rolling my eyes at the major's comment.

"The State Department says she's one of theirs," he assured Davies. "She'll have a small private room in the officers' section at the PRT, and she's quite agreeable to sharing their shower and bathroom facilities."

"And how can you be sure of that, sir?" asked Davies.

"Trust me, Mark, she knows what she's getting into," replied Smythe.

"Yes, sir, but with all respect . . ." The major's voice was rising again.

"Mark, the decision has been made," said Smythe as he stood to indicate that the meeting was over. "Would you like to meet Miss Morgan?"

"Who is Miss Morgan?" Davies seemed momentarily confused as Smythe led him to the desk, where I rose unsmiling to greet him. My initial attraction had been replaced by the simmering anger I'd felt so many times during my career when faced with the unreasoning prejudice of men who couldn't imagine working with me as an equal.

The major's demeanor had also undergone a dramatic transformation. He took my outstretched hand briefly into his, muttered, "Pleasure to meet you," thanked Smythe with great formality for their meeting, turned, and was gone.

"Is this the reception I should expect when I get to Mazār?" I asked Smythe.

After twenty-five years in the Foreign Service, I had grown accustomed to this attitude on the part of certain older male diplomats, although things had slowly improved as each year's crop of new diplomats brought the Department of State closer to resembling the America whose interests it represented abroad. The major's chauvinistic reaction put him firmly in the old guard and told me I would have one less ally to count on.

Smythe thrummed his fingers on his secretary's desk as we watched the major exit his office. "Miss Morgan, please let me apologize for this unpleasantness. I deliberately left my door open, because I realized when Major Davies arrived that this was the best way for you to understand what you'll be facing when you get to Mazār.

"I . . . we have the greatest respect for our military forces and their contributions to our national security, but we struggle at times seeing eye-to-eye on matters of diplomacy. Major Davies is one of the finest intelligence officers I have ever met, but he is very much of the old school, like many of his fellow Gurkhas."

"Who are the Gurkhas?"

"They are a unique regiment composed of Nepalese soldiers and multilingual British officers—in my opinion the finest regiment in the British Army and perhaps the most feared fighters in the world."

As annoyed as I was by the major's dismissive attitude, I couldn't help but add, "Do you know where he's from?"

"He has some northern Indian blood. I was at Oxford with a first cousin of his. There's a Kashmiri princess on the mother's side. Of course, the whole family's been in the UK since partition." Smythe's secretary returned while we were talking, and he suggested we step out for a cup of tea. As soon as we got outside, he lit his pipe and continued our conversation with it clenched between his teeth.

Over a pot of Earl Grey and a tray of scones, I asked for more details about the British military personnel I would be working with at the PRT. Smythe's response was not encouraging.

"I'm sorry, Miss Morgan, I don't have many details on the UK military personnel currently assigned to Mazār. I do know that there's an infantry company and an operations team—more than a hundred officers and men in total. No women, mainly for privacy concerns. It's a very small compound, mind you. There are also a number of six-man Military Observation Teams—MOTs, they call them—staffed with UK, Romanian, and Scandinavian Army personnel. Some of them work from safe houses in other provinces. Our new diplomatic representative at the PRT, Richard Carrington, is still on holiday. He'll be arriving in Mazār a few weeks after you. I'm sorry there's so much ambiguity about your role there. I don't envy you this assignment," he said with a sigh.

FIVE

December 22, 2004 ✦ Dubai

To reach Afghanistan from London, I had to overnight in Dubai, where I'd been told to pick up an onward UN Humanitarian Air Service flight that carried aid workers and embassy personnel the last seven hundred miles into Kabul.

Dubai from the air took my breath away. Massive hotels and office buildings resembling cut-crystal perfume bottles were scattered across a swathe of green that stretched from the desert to the edge of the lapis blue Persian Gulf.

The U.S. Consulate in Dubai had made my reservation, assuring me that the perks of being a diplomat in the United Arab Emirates were impressive. My government per diem plus a diplomatic discount would allow me to stay at one of Dubai's finer hotels.

My destination, the Emirates Towers, was one of a pair of identical thin, angular, smoked-glass buildings. A smiling Filipino bellman took my bags from the taxi driver and led me into a soaring ten-story atrium. Glass elevators slid silently between the floors. Elaborate fountains splashed next to clusters of well-dressed men sipping tiny cups of coffee and conducting their business in discreet murmurs.

My clothes were wrinkled, I was tired and sweaty, and I felt totally out of place in the presence of these manicured customers being attended to by a very solicitous hotel staff.

I was taken to my room on the "women's floor"—where the hotel put females traveling alone. It was a suite, really, offering a spectacular view of the sea and a basket of fresh fruit on the coffee table. With nothing to keep me occupied until my nine A.M. flight to Kabul the following day, I decided to head down to the hotel restaurant for dinner. Going out at night on my own was something I generally avoided after my decade of debauchery following Tom's death, but tonight would probably be my last chance for a gin and tonic in the next twelve months and the restaurant had a bar—so what the hell.

Certain that my rumpled khakis wouldn't cut it at this hotel, I changed into a short black linen dress, the only knee-length item I had packed for my year in Afghanistan—perhaps to wear to an embassy party if I were ever invited.

Because air-conditioning kept the hotel's restaurants and lobby chilled to subarctic temperatures, I threw a light jacket over my shoulders and pinned on the brooch Tom had given me for my twenty-seventh birthday. It was a gold-plated replica of an ancient piece of Scythian jewelry depicting the goddess Artemis on a leaping gazelle. Except for my wedding ring, which I had stopped wearing years ago, it was my favorite piece of jewelry.

It had been many years since I'd entered a bar alone. I pulled myself up on a stool, briefly noting that I was the only unaccompanied female in the room, and asked the bartender for a menu.

"So what brings you to the emerald city?"

I turned my head and saw a tall blond man in tan slacks and an open-collared shirt sitting a few chairs down from me.

"Stefan Illyich Borosky, first secretary, Russian Embassy, Kabul," he said with a friendly smile.

Russian. I should have guessed from his accent. I had met a lot of men like him during my two years in Leningrad, but in the Cold War years, it would have been dangerous to respond to anyone who approached me like this out of the blue.

"Angela Morgan." I extended my hand. "I'm with the Department of State—on my way to a year at PRT Mazār-i-Sharīf. It looks like we're going to be neighbors," I said with a smile and the realization that I was engaging in a mild flirtation with a former Cold War enemy.

"I'm headed home for a few weeks of R and R in Moscow," he said, "but I've spent some time in Mazār."

"Maybe you can fill me in on some details I might not have picked up in my formal briefings."

"With pleasure," he replied with a broad grin.

With the instant camaraderie that often develops between travelers, we took our drinks and moved to a table in the restaurant. The conversation and wine flowed easily over dinner, although I was aware that we were both holding back, revealing only as much information as two strangers, who represented governments that were former and possibly future competitors for world domination, felt comfortable sharing—which was not much.

Stefan was fifty-three and divorced with three grown children in Moscow. He was planning to retire after one more overseas tour.

I was fairly vague about my professional background, leaving out my knowledge of Russian and the two years in the mid-1980s I'd served at the U.S. Consulate in Leningrad. I said nothing about Tom's death in Beirut, only revealing that I had been a widow for a long time.

We shared an interest in horses, although neither of us rode anymore. Stefan had taken a nasty fall years ago when his horse stumbled and put him in a body cast for six months.

After losing Tom, I had lost all desire to ride, but I invented a story for Stefan about being thrown off a horse in New Mexico when a truck backfired. Ever the gentleman, he did not probe for details when I began avoiding his questions.

"So what is Mother Russia doing in Afghanistan these days?" I asked as I fingered the stem of a glass of mellow Shiraz, which Stefan had ordered.

"We're watching you attempt what we failed to do thirty years ago," he said with a smile. "When you get up north, you'll see the rusting detritus of our futile and very expensive efforts to civilize Afghanistan." He took a puff of the Gauloises he was smoking and blew a thin stream of smoke into the air.

"Let's begin with the sad procession of derelict fifty-meter transmission towers, looming like lonely sentinels across the northern desert. They once carried reliable electric power from the USSR to Mazār-i-Sharīf and over the Hindu Kush into Kabul."

Stefan took a long swig of wine and closed his eyes. He was just getting started.

"If you have the good fortune to attend a *buzkashi* game in Mazār, you'll see just south of the field an abandoned multistoried structure. Locals call it the silo. It used to be a bread factory—built by us, of course. It produced thousands of loaves a day and provided hundreds of jobs."

Stefan raised his glass to the USSR's many development projects in Afghanistan, then continued with his litany. "We prepared women for professional careers, sent them to study in Moscow with the men, and told them they didn't have to leave their houses hidden under burkas. That did not go over at all well with the mullahs." He laughed.

After three shots of vodka and several glasses of wine, Stefan's voice began to lose its edge. I was intrigued by his frank assessment of Mother Russia's long and failed involvement in Afghanistan, and I wanted to hear more, but my eyelids and my brain were rapidly succumbing to the thick fog of jet lag.

"Am I boring you, Angela?" Stefan asked as I tried to stifle a yawn.

"No, not at all," I said forcing my eyes to stay open. "I hadn't realized the extent of your development work in Afghanistan."

"Yes, indeed," he continued after another long sip of wine, "but we didn't understand their culture. I'm not sure any outsiders ever will. The Afghans didn't take to our godless communism any more than I think they're going to accept your so-called egalitarian, democratic capitalism."

He leaned back into the jumble of multicolored cushions, closed his eyes, and took another drag on his cigarette. "So what are we doing? Watching and waiting, as your country repeats our mistakes one by one."

Stefan reached across the table with the wine bottle, and I held my hand, fingers outstretched, over the lip of my glass. He pulled back, offended that I had refused his offer of more wine.

"Are you afraid I'm trying to get you drunk?" he asked with a petulant frown.

I ignored his question. "So, Stefan, what would you advise the world's only remaining superpower to do in Afghanistan?"

He shook the last drops of wine into his own glass and rested his elbows on the table. "You can give up and leave with your tail between your legs like we did, and like the once mighty British Army did twice more than a century ago. Or your generals could adopt Alexander the Great's tactic of establishing permanent settlements. Marry your officers off to the daughters of the warlords, and leave them behind with a few thousand soldiers to breed with the locals for a few decades."

He chuckled to himself at that improbable image.

Stefan reached over and patted my hand in a gesture of sympathy. "I fear, my dear, that your country may be digging itself into a twenty-first-century version of Vietnam."

He called for the check, then chastised the waiter when he brought us the separate tabs I had requested.

"I must insist on paying for my own meal, Stefan," I said, handing my credit card to the waiter.

Stefan grumbled, but we concluded the evening amicably, agreeing to meet in Kabul for another dinner at an undetermined date. We parted in the lobby with a handshake. I had enjoyed his company far more than I should have. He was handsome, very handsome. Maybe this year wouldn't be so bad after all.

Although our initial encounter appeared to have been completely coincidental, I assumed that even with my inconsequential and ill-defined assignment to Mazār-i-Sharīf, Stefan would go back to his hotel room, dutifully write up an account of our conversation, and send it off to some office in Moscow.

I wasn't too concerned, but my guard was up, a remnant of my years in Leningrad when even a minor brush with an eastern bloc official had required a detailed memo to diplomatic security. I would definitely be reporting this encounter when I got to Kabul.

Despite my exhaustion, I had trouble falling asleep, but I was afraid to take one of my few remaining sleeping pills after all that wine. At three thirty A.M., I gave up and called room service for an early breakfast.

CNN was broadcasting grainy videos of a suicide bombing in Iraq from earlier in the evening. It was narrated by a distressed reporter, who explained that twenty-two of our soldiers dining in an Army mess tent in Mosul had been killed and sixty injured by a man in an Iraqi Army uniform. He had walked unchallenged into the tent and pulled his explosives cord. I switched off the TV.

After a five-hour wait at the airport the following morning, those of us taking the UN flight to Kabul were informed that it was snowing in southern Afghanistan. The UN plane was grounded until the following day. Exiting the air-conditioned airport into Dubai's eighty-degree weather, we shed our coats and sweaters and lined up for taxis. I was welcomed back like an old friend at the Emirates Towers reception desk. After a discreet inquiry, I was informed that Stefan had checked out. He was on his way to Moscow.

SIX

I am that rare grown-up who still gets a thrill from peering down at the earth from thirty thousand feet. I always ask for a window seat. The two-hour UN flight from Dubai to Kabul did not disappoint.

We traveled northeast through Iranian airspace under a cloudless sky. As we approached the Afghan border, I pressed my nose to the window.

The flat, dusky landscape of Iran's eastern desert began to rise and buckle under the pressure of the Indian subcontinental plate, which was pushing slowly northward as it rammed into and slid under the much larger Asian plate. Massive sheets of sedimentary rock sliced jagged gashes in the desert floor as these two colossal tectonic masses experienced the geologic equivalent of a slow-motion car crash, which had been under way for fifty million years. Further north, these slabs of what was once a seabed had been squeezed, shattered, and thrust skyward to create the massive Himalayan mountain chain.

The pilot took us higher, cresting the jagged white peaks of the Hindu Kush—an extension of the Himalayan range that stretches across western Pakistan and central Afghanistan. He circled once over Kabul before banking into a steep dive toward the airport. We touched down just before noon under an ice-blue sky.

Kabul's mud houses and gray government buildings were still coated with yesterday's snow. There were few trees left in or near this city, which had once been famed for its lush gardens and long shaded avenues but was now draped with rubble-filled barricades and tangled strands of razor wire. The snow-covered mountains surrounding Kabul like a pearl necklace provided the ruined capital with its only touch of elegance.

According to the Afghan solar calendar, which I had copied down under Doc's guidance with its Gregorian equivalents, it was the third of Capricorn 1383.

It was also Christmas Eve.

As our plane taxied down the runway, those of us arriving in Afghanistan for the first time stared silently out our windows at clusters of turbaned men huddled around fifty-gallon drums. Orange flames lapped over their rims into the dry winter air. Behind the men, dark skeletons of rusting airplanes lay half buried under the grimy layer of day-old snow.

Another group of men wrapped in thin gray blankets and wearing plastic face guards, walked shoulder to shoulder along barren patches of earth between the runways, swinging long-handled metal detectors back and forth in an endless search for stray land mines.

Unsmiling Afghan employees from the American Embassy collected our passports, loaded our bags into a truck, and herded us like a flock of confused sheep through perfunctory immigration and customs formalities in a bare wooden building far from the

main terminal. We climbed into bulletproof vans and were instructed by our armed American driver to strap ourselves in "for
Mr. Toad's Wild Ride" to the embassy in downtown Kabul.

As we sped along the narrow highway into the city, I had my
first glimpse of Afghanistan's female population, gliding down the
sidewalks in their burkas like silent blue ghosts.

Twenty minutes later, as we pulled up in front of the barricaded
embassy on Great Massoud Road, our driver barked out more instructions. "Get out of the vehicle here, walk through that door
single file, go through the security checkpoint inside, and show
the guards your passports. We'll unload your bags in front of the
admin trailer inside the compound. Someone will meet you there
and take you to your hooch."

"Hiya, I'm Carl Edgerton," said a pale middle-aged man with a
thinning comb-over. He walked up to where I stood next to my
suitcases. "Are you Angela Morgan?"

"Yes, I am."

"Hope your flight was okay. Bet you're tired, huh?" He inhaled quickly before continuing. "You won't have any trouble
finding your way around here. The dining hall is right behind us,
and there's a workout room next to the dispensary."

Waving expansively toward the white shipping containers laid
end to end in long rows, he announced with an oddly proud flourish, "Welcome to Containerville, Angela! Follow me, and I'll
show you to your hooch."

He turned to me as we approached container number thirty-
six. "Each shipping container is divided into two sections, or

hooches as we like to call them. Here's your key. If you're lucky, you might have this hooch to yourself until after New Year's. Generally, you transients have to share. Sorry about that." He paused for my reaction to this bit of bad news and seemed vaguely disappointed when my face remained blank.

"Any idea what you'll be doing up in Mazār?" he asked as I struggled with the lock.

"Not really," I said, pulling my door open and gazing into the sterile interior of my temporary residence.

A plane overhead drowned out Carl's chatter. He handed me an information packet and left me standing alone in front of my hooch.

The walls, floor, and ceiling of my room were of molded white plastic. The furniture—two single beds, two metal lockers, and one desk—was bolted to the floor. The whole place resembled a minimum-security prison.

I slipped into a T-shirt, sweatpants, and sneakers, spent an hour on the treadmill in the empty gym, and returned to my hooch for a long, stinging shower.

Night fell quickly in Kabul. The snowy mountains, which had cast a pale tangerine glow over the city late in the afternoon, vanished quickly moments after sunset. The hum of the embassy's generators seemed to grow louder as the rest of the city, much of it without electricity, shut down and locked itself in for the night.

Standing alone outside my hooch, I inhaled for the first time the smells I would forever associate with this country—a mix of cooking fires, grilled meat, crushed spices, mud, sweating pack animals, and the rusting detritus of Afghanistan's many wars.

I was hungry. It was time to find the dining hall even though I dreaded joining a room full of strangers for Christmas Eve dinner. No planes flew after dark, leaving the night sky to the millions of stars visible over Kabul. I picked out the Big Dipper, found Polaris, locked the door of my hooch, switched on my flashlight, and headed off to the cafeteria.

Bundled against the icy mountain air, I approached the door of the double-wide trailer Carl had pointed out when I arrived. The windows were dark and there was a CLOSED FOR THE HOLIDAYS sign taped to the door. A passing security guard told me there was another cafeteria near the old embassy building. He took me to an underground tunnel, which he promised led to the far side of the compound and a hot meal.

"It's just there," he said, pointing at a narrow stairwell and walking off to continue his patrol. I gripped the cold metal railing and stared with some trepidation at the concrete steps, which spiraled down into a dark passageway. This was a tunnel inside a well-guarded U.S. Embassy compound. What the hell was I afraid of?

I slowly descended the stairs and entered the tunnel. Halfway through, I heard the click of approaching boots and saw the hulking shape of an armed man approaching me. Behind the glare of a powerful flashlight, which was trained on my face, an unfriendly male voice demanded to see the embassy ID, which I had stuffed inside my jacket after showing it to the first guard. I struggled to untangle the badge on its metal chain from my scarf and zipper.

"Badges must be displayed at all times," he barked in heavily accented English as his flashlight flicked from my ID photo to my face. Releasing the badge, he walked away without another word, leaving me temporarily blinded, perspiring heavily, and standing alone in the tunnel.

Still shaking, I emerged into a poorly lit, rubble-strewn, and very muddy construction site surrounding the old and new embassy buildings. There were no signs and no people, just rows of darkened shipping containers. I briefly considered returning to my hooch, but hunger trumped fear and after five minutes of searching, I located a narrow path and a hand-drawn sign, which led me to another double-wide trailer strung with garlands of winking Christmas lights.

A Charlie Brown Christmas, broadcast from a wall-mounted TV set by the door, was competing with the Chipmunks' version of "Jingle Bells" on a portable CD player in the cafeteria kitchen. The room was overheated and the conversation subdued as the Marine guards and those embassy employees who had not gone back to the States for the holidays tried to make the best of a bad situation.

A large man wearing reindeer antlers and dishing up slices of turkey roll greeted me as I joined the serving line.

"You must be Angela," he said, wiping beads of sweat from his forehead. "Welcome and Merry Christmas. I'm Paul Plawner, Deputy Chief of Mission. The ambassador had the good fortune to go home for the holidays, but those of us who stayed behind are glad you're here." He dropped a slab of rubbery white meat on my plastic plate.

"There's plenty of food, so don't be shy," he said. "Take Christmas Day off, of course, but please call my secretary first thing

Sunday morning to set up an appointment. I'll try to see you in the afternoon."

Doc had explained to me during Dari language training that Afghanistan, like most Muslim countries, observes a Sunday through Thursday workweek. The U.S. Embassy in Kabul was officially closed every Friday, the Islamic holy day, and in theory it was also closed on Saturday. But I would soon learn that this being a war zone, most American Embassy employees were hard at work six and even seven days a week.

An excessively cheery personnel officer was passing out home-made Christmas cookies in plastic sandwich bags—three cookies per person.

"I didn't bake these myself, but I did put on all the sprinkles," she gushed as she offered me a bag, patted my hand, and said, "Come on, honey, it's not that bad here." I forced myself to smile until she turned her attention to the next customer.

I knew that alcohol, even a small glass of wine, which would have made this meal so much more bearable, was not permitted in this cafeteria because it was where the Marine guards ate. So I washed down my turkey, wilted broccoli, scoop of powdered mashed potatoes, and jellied cranberry sauce with one of the liter bottles of water that could be found stacked by the case in front of every building on the compound. Tap water, Carl had warned, was safe for bathing here, but not for drinking.

I sat down at a bare metal table with three young Marines and attempted without success to make small talk. They shoveled down their food, eyes glued to a football game playing on another Armed Forces TV set bolted to the wall near their table. As soon as their plates were scraped clean, they rose as one, explaining politely that they had to report for guard duty. I knew from my briefings in Washington that all but a few of these boys would soon be on their way to Iraq, replaced by a private security force that had been contracted to guard the embassy.

After picking at my food for a few more minutes, I grabbed the bag of cookies, switched on my flashlight, walked cautiously back through the tunnel with my badge out, and returned alone to my hooch.

SEVEN

December 25, 2004

At six A.M., I ate the three cookies and washed them down with a microwave cup of instant coffee from a jar left by a previous occupant. It was raining, my hooch was warm, and I couldn't face another walk through the rubble to the embassy cafeteria. Crawling back under the covers, I unwrapped the small package my brother, Bill, had made me promise not to open until Christmas morning. It was a plastic cube with six old black-and-white photos of Bill, Mom, Dad, Tom, and me on the ranch. I fell asleep with the cube on my pillow and didn't wake up until the sun was setting— just in time to throw on a pair of jeans, a sweater, and a jacket, switch on my flashlight, and force myself again through the tunnel and into a room full of strangers for leftover turkey roll.

There are many reasons for a diplomat to go unarmed and virtually untrained into a war zone—a sense of duty, an unhappy marriage, a big mortgage, or a less than brilliant career like mine that was about to crash and burn. Had I honestly added Afghanistan to my wish list because I thought it might help me get promoted?

One picture in the photo cube of me riding my pony Novio reminded me of the many times I had fallen off when Bill and I raced back to the barn. My strategy, which usually got me home first, was to jump over instead of walk through the smaller arroyos. When that plan failed, and I would arrive home limping, crying, and leading Novio, Mom would not let me in the house until I got back in the saddle and rode at a full gallop down to the main road and back. I had not been on a horse or in a war zone since I lost Tom. Perhaps it was time to remount.

I overslept and was late for my Sunday morning appointment with DCM Plawner, but he didn't seem to mind. The rules were apparently different here.

"I understand you speak Russian and Arabic and got the highest score ever recorded at FSI in Farsi years ago," Plawner said after welcoming me into his cramped office in the old embassy building. He remained behind his desk when I entered and motioned for me to take a seat on a worn leather couch.

"I was also told that you took a Farsi–Dari conversion course and reached fluency in Dari after only three months. Pretty impressive," he added as he stared out the window at the barricaded embassy grounds.

"It was actually four months, sir, and languages come fairly easily to me," I replied.

"Good, good," he said, nodding absently. "I understand that the DEA wants us to keep your fluency secret. They need to know if the interpreters at the PRT in Mazār are giving the full picture to the British Army regarding what's being said about the whole narcotics mess up there. We need accurate reporting on poppy production in Balkh Province and, of course, any evidence of government appointees' involvement in the opium trade."

"Excuse me, sir," I interrupted, "other than listening in on the interpreters and reporting on poppy production, what precisely will my role in Mazār be? I was given very few details on this assignment before I left Washington, and I know the Brits already have a diplomat there."

"Our biggest push right now is trying to convince local warlords to tell us where their hidden weapons caches are so the Afghan Army can confiscate them, but that's a bit of a hard sell. The Brits are working on that up north as well."

"I'm supposed to convince warlords to hand over their weapons?" I asked incredulously.

"Not exactly," he replied, still staring out the window, "but we do want you to report on any successes the British Army has in this regard and, of course, you and the British diplomat will be serving as political advisors to the PRT commander and his officers." Plawner ran through a laundry list of issues, droning on as though he were alone in his office and dictating into a tape recorder.

As I absently jotted Plawner's main points into my notebook, my gaze shifted to the wall behind his desk. Except for a faded map of Afghanistan bristling with red, green, and yellow pins, the wall was bare and in serious need of a coat of paint. The colored pins, which indicated U.S. PRTs and Forward Operating Bases, circled Kabul and Bagram Air Base, marched south toward Jalalabad and Kandahār, and merged into thick clusters along the border with Pakistan. There were few pins in the northern part of the map and none near Mazār-i-Sharīf. Perhaps Plawner would add one after I left his office.

He turned away from the window and leaned forward on his elbows, pausing until I had finished inspecting his map. "Most of the weapons and ammunition the Afghans have squirreled away were taken from the Russians during their occupation, but a number of these stockpiles also contain the remnants of some pretty nasty toys we gave the mujahideen back in the eighties.

"We certainly don't want all that firepower used against us in the future—especially the shoulder-launched Stingers. They can take out a helicopter or even one of our big transport planes. We're paying a pretty penny to get them back," he said, pausing to observe my reaction as he added, "up to a hundred thousand dollars."

I raised one eyebrow, scribbled in my notebook, and looked suitably impressed.

"You know, of course, that we're cooperating with the British Embassy on all these issues. You'll be working closely with your British counterpart up there. That should make things much easier for you," he added, having no idea how wrong that statement would prove to be.

"You might be interested in looking into the treatment of rural women," he continued. "It's appalling, and I don't know there's much we can do about it, but some reporting would be useful.

"No hostiles are shooting at NATO forces up north right now, Angela, but please do be careful. We expect political tensions to heat up as local strongmen start positioning themselves for the September parliamentary elections. That could be interesting," he added without much enthusiasm.

"You understand, of course, that the U.S. government's main focus is in the south where the fighting is," he said, motioning toward the pins on his map, "but we'll definitely be looking forward to reading your reports."

I nodded silently as he continued. "I do hope you'll be able to get out and explore some of the historic sites near Mazār. I understand they are quite remarkable. I've been here for almost a year, but I don't get to leave Kabul very often. The ambassador does most of the traveling while I stay back and mind the fort."

An alarm went off somewhere in the building. Plawner stiffened and grabbed the arms of his chair. We both froze, our eyes darting from the door to the window until the clanging ceased. This time, I noted silently, I wasn't the only one who had been spooked.

Plawner mopped his forehead with the back of his hand, took a deep breath, and continued with his lecture. "I've learned to my dismay that many Afghans, even the educated ones, have little appreciation for their country's remarkable past. A French archaeologist I met a few months ago at an embassy reception told me that many rural Afghans are taught a strange mix of historical facts and hero sagas by their village elders—legends of Alexander the Great blended with stories of Genghis Khan, King Amanullah, and the prophet Muhammad. Such a pity." His voice trailed off and his eyes focused again on the ceiling. I waited for him to continue.

"I'm no expert on this country. None of us are," he said, rubbing his forehead and shifting in his chair, which squeaked loudly. He leaned forward and looked straight at me for the first time. "We armed this place to the teeth, abandoned it fifteen years ago, and now we're paying a hellish price, Angela. We assign Foreign Service Officers like you here for one year at a time, the Afghans barely get to know your names, and then you leave, taking all your knowledge with you. It's an almost impossible . . ."

His secretary poked her head in the office. "Sir, your next appointment has arrived."

"I know your job description is a bit vague, but that's the nature of the game here. We're all sort of making things up as we go along. Please don't quote me on that. But seriously, if you have any problems, don't hesitate to call," he added with little enthusiasm as we shook hands.

"Do you have any idea when you will be taking your two R and Rs? We like people to space them out if possible so you're not all out of the country at the same time."

I shook my head. I had given absolutely no thought to when I would use my two free trips out of Afghanistan. "My father's had a lot of medical problems, so I'll probably be going back to see him, but I'm fairly flexible. I have no plans at this point."

"We can talk about that the next time you come down to Kabul," he replied. "Best of luck, Angela. I'm sure the Brits will take good care of you."

The man was clearly overwhelmed. I doubted we would ever meet again, but I wished him well, exited through his double cyber-locked doors, and headed down a poorly lit back stairway in the old embassy building.

Crates of bottled water blocked the battered metal door at the bottom of the stairwell. I would have to find another way out. I pulled a liter of water from one of the boxes that had already been torn open, unscrewed the lid, took a long drink, and checked my watch. Thirty minutes to find my way out of this place and get to my next appointment.

Having come from what should have been my most important briefing, I was at that moment unable to recall a single thing the DCM had just said to me. Sitting on the bottom step, sipping my water, and flipping through my notes, I briefly imagined an alternative scenario for my recently concluded meeting with Plawner.

"Miss Morgan, I have no idea why the Department wants you to go to Mazār since the Brits already have one of their own diplomats there. I suggest you hop on the next flight and get yourself back to Washington. You're not really needed here. You won't even be getting a pin on my map."

EIGHT

Dear Angela,

Please join me for a small dinner party Wednesday evening at one of the few restaurants we are still allowed to frequent after dark. I received a call this afternoon from the French archaeologist I mentioned during our meeting. He is working on a project at the Kabul Museum and will be heading to his dig as soon as the snow melts this spring. I thought you might enjoy meeting him and hearing about his excavation just a few miles from your PRT. Our embassy political counselor, an Afghan archaeologist from the Kabul Museum, and my counterpart at the British Embassy will join us.

Sincerely,
Paul Plawner
Deputy Chief of Mission
U.S. Embassy Kabul

Plawner's invitation, which had been slipped under the door of my hooch, was a pleasant and unexpected surprise after another long

day of the less than informative briefings I had been attending in
fortified compounds around Kabul. His request was a formality,
since one did not turn down an invitation from the DCM, but the
prospect of meeting the French archaeologist intrigued me, and I
would have gone in any case. I called his secretary and accepted
the invitation.

My first exposure to the endless internal debates about America's
efforts to pacify and rebuild Afghanistan had been at a disarmament strategy meeting at the embassy, which I attended as an
observer the day after I had seen Plawner. A U.S. Army colonel,
who had been trying for almost a year to defang illegal militias in
Kandahār Province, stood up and openly mocked a proposed national decree that would give warlords and their followers one
month to disband and hand over their stocks of weapons and
ammunition.

"Who the hell do we think we're we kidding here?" he snorted.
"The Afghans have been living in these mountains for thousands
of years. If I've learned one thing here, it's that these are a damned
patient people. Hell, they can sit on a rock watching a herd of
sheep eat grass all day and not get bored."

There were a few snickers around the table, but the colonel
wasn't finished.

"The Russian Army was here for ten years, but the Afghans
knew they'd leave eventually. They don't know how long we'll
be here, but they do know one thing for damn sure. We won't be
here forever. And when we get tired and pull out, they'll dig up
all those munitions they have wrapped, oiled, and buried in their

backyards or hidden in caves, and control of this country will go right back to the guys with the most guns."

People around the table nodded, but no one spoke up to defend the colonel's position.

At the embassy counter-narcotics office, I was told about plans to send in hundreds of Afghans to manually chop down poppy fields in the south the following spring. If that didn't work, another proposal under consideration involved the use of crop dusters to spray poppy fields from the air with herbicides. American military personnel did not like either of these ideas.

"You must understand, Miss Morgan," said a somber young Army captain, pulling me aside after another briefing, "those of us who work in PRTs down south are dead set against the poppy eradication programs. If the farmers think our soldiers are involved in destroying their crops, it won't be safe for my men to patrol outside the wire. I don't know what the answer is, but pissing off a few hundred thousand Afghan farmers is a really bad idea."

A cold drizzle fell on my third and final day of consultations, leaving Kabul awash in a sea of ashen mud. My grim-faced driver steered our armored embassy vehicle through the soggy streets, swerving aggressively around the endless security barricades that had turned the city into a rain-soaked obstacle course.

The weather added to my already gray mood, which was growing darker after every meeting. Each person I spoke with further reinforced my impression that I would be spending the next year in Mazār-i-Sharīf as a powerless and unwelcome bystander, writing reports that no one would read.

My last meeting was with a distraught young electrical engineer, who had been contracted by USAID to work on the design of Afghanistan's new electric power grid. He was as fiercely critical of the plans for electrification as the Marine colonel had been over efforts to disarm the illegal militias.

"Take a look at this, Miss Morgan," he said, unrolling a 1980s-era Soviet map of Afghanistan, Turkmenistan, and Uzbekistan across his battered desk. Plastic overlays with red and yellow dotted lines indicated where the new power grid and transmission towers were to be installed.

"We are about to fund the construction of an obsolete twentieth-century grid that will force the Afghans to purchase electricity from central Asia for decades to come!" Stefan had taken great delight in describing this very plan to me during our dinner in Dubai, calling it another move on the "Great Game" chessboard, which our side would eventually regret.

The engineer removed his glasses and swept them in a wide arc across the map. "Afghanistan has the potential to generate much of its energy requirements with renewable resources. We should be helping these people build a twenty-first-century distributed power system with wind turbines and solar thermal plants. Don't you agree?" he pleaded, as though I could have some effect on these decisions.

I knew little about energy and nothing about power generation, but his arguments certainly made sense to me. "So why aren't we doing it?" I asked.

"Vested interests, the fossil fuel industry, ossified, unimaginative development officials, greed, corruption," he replied, his voice rising in an angry crescendo.

I was fascinated by this man's passion for renewable energy, but his angst was making me increasingly uncomfortable. When he grabbed me by the arm and dragged me across the room to look at another wall map, I began to perspire under my sweater.

"It's criminal that we're doing this to a country where the sun shines more than three hundred days a year," he cried, wringing his hands in frustration.

I nodded in agreement and gathered my things to leave his office before he began another tirade.

"We're funding the construction of uninsulated cinder-block school buildings that are boiling hot in the summer and freezing in the winter. Sub-subcontractors are doing most of the construction work, so when the roofs fall in or their generators and ventilation systems break down, nobody is responsible."

I was exhausted and really didn't want to hear any more.

"I'm not sure what you're supposed to be doing in Mazār, Miss Morgan, but whatever it is, I wish you the best of luck. I'm leaving this place in one month, and I hope to God I never come back."

NINE

Plawner and his security detail picked me up just after sunset in front of the old embassy building. Unsure about appropriate evening attire for a night out in Kabul with the boys, I decided that warm, comfortable, and modest—a long-sleeved sweater, wool slacks, boots, a heavy jacket, and a plain white head scarf tucked into my purse just in case—would have to do.

The city after dark was more alive than I had imagined when gazing up at the night sky from behind the three-meter sand-filled Hesco barriers that surrounded the embassy compound. Taxis and horse-drawn vehicles moved through the city streets, although with much greater caution than during the day. Bearded, turbaned men, wrapped in blankets and walking hand-in-hand along the broken sidewalks, cast flickering Goya-like shadows across the streets as they passed in front of bare lightbulbs and kerosene lanterns hanging in tea shops and markets stalls.

Kabul at night was for men only. Women and children were all safely locked away.

Sealed inside the DCM's fully armored SUV, I could neither hear the sounds nor smell the odors of the city as we rolled through the darkened streets in our three-vehicle convoy. Unlike the rest of the embassy staff, who traveled around town in solitary armored vehicles, neither the ambassador nor his deputy ever left the compound without a protective security detail.

We pulled up in front of an unmarked mud-brick wall with a single wooden door set in a metal frame. *What kind of restaurant,* I wondered, *would be hidden behind such an uninviting exterior?* One of the security guards jumped out of the first vehicle with his weapon drawn. He knocked on the door, was admitted by another armed guard, and emerged after a few minutes motioning for us to follow him down a dimly lit corridor, which opened onto a warm, candlelit dining room, its walls and floors covered with Afghan carpets—a surprising hidden jewel in this post-apocalyptic urban landscape. Wide couches, set around low tables, were crowded with foreigners and a few Afghans in western dress. The room smelled of lemons and coriander. A Miles Davis album played softly in the background. The four men who were joining us had arrived early. They stood as we approached.

Plawner made the introductions and suggested that I sit next to the archaeologist, Professor Jean-François Mongibeaux of the Sorbonne's Department of Art History and Archaeology in Paris.

Mongibeaux was a tall, lean man with hooded brown eyes, thick white eyebrows, rosy cheeks, and a shock of white hair, pulled back in a short ponytail. He interrupted Plawner's lengthy introduction with a broad smile and a request to everyone at the table, "Please call me Jeef. It is so much easier than my excessively long name, and it's what everyone has called me for the past forty years."

A waiter appeared and handed out menus, wineglasses, and a

corkscrew. Most restaurants catering to foreigners in Kabul did not serve wine, but some did allow customers to bring as much as they could discreetly carry. When Jeef pulled three bottles of a 2004 Beaujolais Nouveau from his backpack, I offered a silent prayer of thanks that Plawner's archaeologist friend was a Frenchman. The evening began with a round of toasts in honor of Jeef's Afghan counterpart, Dr. Fazli, who had studied in Paris many years ago. Jeef explained to us that Fazli had been appointed to oversee preparation of the Afghan Museum's traveling exhibit of the Bactrian gold.

Fazli spoke fluent French, but his English was limited. As we raised our glasses in his honor and began to pepper him with questions, he gratefully deferred to his friend Jeef, who offered to recount in English the story of this remarkable find.

"The Kabul Museum has recovered almost twenty-one thousand pieces of this priceless Afghan treasure. For the past two decades, it was the object of a hunt worthy of the legendary Indiana Jones," Jeef began, with all eyes focused on his craggy, candlelit face.

"In 1978, Afghan and Russian archaeologists discovered a two-thousand-year-old Bactrian burial mound inside the ruins of a four-thousand-year-old temple in Jowzjan Province."

Jeef turned to face me. "Angela, that's only about two hours from Mazār-i-Sharīf, but it's too dangerous to visit the site now with all the land mines. I'll be working with an Afghan team much closer to you on a dig near Balkh just ten miles from your PRT. We started it several years ago and are slowly uncovering a Hellenistic-era settlement. I hope you'll be able to come over meet my team."

He turned back to face the others. "Sorry for the diversion, gentlemen. Now on with my story.

"As you know, Balkh and the surrounding region was for thousands of years a major trading center for caravans on the ancient silk routes across Asia. The Bactrian find that Fazli is cataloguing is unique because it was untouched for millennia." Jeef paused to refill our wineglasses.

"When the Russians invaded and the resistance fighting began, curators at the museum in Kabul became concerned about their ability to safeguard this and other priceless treasures in the museum's collection. They carefully wrapped every single piece— golden diadems, jewel-encrusted daggers, pendants, combs, sculptures, coins, and necklaces in squares of tissue paper—and locked it all away in trunks that were hidden in the presidential palace vault."

Fazli understood most of what had been said. He smiled proudly while Jeef continued to describe the vast treasure trove under his care.

"The vault was uncovered less than a year and a half ago when President Karzai authorized the locks to be broken, but the trunks were not unlocked until last spring."

A waiter arrived and set out steaming plates of tandoori chicken, grilled lamb, Afghan flat bread, yogurt, and bowls of scented rice. Jeef apologized for having monopolized the conversation, while Plawner, his British counterpart, and the political counselor immediately shifted the conversation back to the endlessly frustrating business of reconstructing Afghanistan.

Jeef sensed that I wanted to hear more about the Bactrian gold and the excavation near Mazār-i-Sharīf. He tilted his head toward the three men who were already deep into a discussion about the poppy eradication program and added so that only I could hear, "Angela, I promise you that Fazli and I will invite you to the museum for a private showing the next time you are in Kabul. And, of course, you are most welcome to visit my dig near Balkh this spring."

Fazli nodded in agreement, and the three of us turned our attention to the meal spread before us.

"Miss Morgan, when will you be going up to Mazār?" asked the British DCM as he poured himself another glass of wine.

"I'm leaving tomorrow morning, weather permitting. I've reserved a seat on your C-130," I replied.

"What good fortune. You'll be there for the New Year's Eve celebration," he said. "That should cheer the lads up a bit.

"Were you able to meet Richard Carrington while you were in London?" he asked. "I know he was looking forward to meeting you."

I shook my head. "I met your desk officer, Mr. Smythe, but Richard was on holiday." I didn't mention my encounter with Major Davies.

Although I was only passing through Kabul, I had received a relatively warm welcome from my peers at the embassy. At the PRT in Mazār, as an American and a woman, I would be doubly the outsider. If the other British soldiers there were anything like Davies, I wasn't going to have an easy go of it.

TEN

As unhappy as I was about leaving Kabul for Mazār, I had mentally steeled myself for the morning flight, and was sitting with my two suitcases, my helmet, my sleeping bag, and my Kevlar vest in front of the admin trailer an hour before our convoy was scheduled to depart for the airport.

When my driver didn't arrive at the appointed time, I called the motor pool and was informed by an apologetic Afghan dispatcher that no one was going to the airport since Jalalabad Road had been declared off-limits due to an IED threat. The following morning, my driver and I sat for two hours in a line of vehicles waiting to exit the compound, but the embassy's security gate could not be opened due to a short circuit in the wiring. By the time the gate was repaired, I had missed that flight as well and had resigned myself to spending New Year's Eve alone in Kabul. My anxiety had reduced itself to a quiet despair as I returned again to the hooch, which I'd had to myself since my arrival.

A tall, wiry redhead wearing tight-fitting black body armor and baggy cargo pants was unlocking my door. She had a black pistol strapped to her hip and an enormous black assault rifle slung over her shoulder.

"Hi, hon, are we sharing?" she asked with a smile. She identified herself as Sally Dietrich, a DEA agent, who was in-country to train the Afghan police drug interdiction forces. "We're not deploying until January the second, so I'm planning to ring in the New Year at the embassy bar tonight. Want to join me and my team? I'm the only girl in the group, so I'm sure the boys would love your company."

Sally was an old-timer. This was her fifth short-term deployment to Afghanistan, and she knew her way around the compound. She tossed her weapons and duffel bag onto one of the cots and headed off to eat lunch. The last thing I wanted to do was spend New Year's Eve in a room of complete strangers whom I would most likely never see again. I could do that just as well in D.C.

I declined her invitation and spent the evening alone in my hooch recalling the four New Year's Eve celebrations Tom and I had shared as husband and wife. Even in Sana'a and in war-torn Beirut, he would put on his tux and I would slither into the long, black-sequined dress I'd picked up at a thrift shop in D.C. We usually went out with friends, but that last year in Beirut, embassy personnel were under curfew after a car bomb had exploded near our neighborhood. It was the best New Year's Eve ever. We downed our last bottle of champagne, danced for hours to Sinatra, eventually disposed of the tux and the dress, and made mad passionate love until dawn.

I was disappointed that I couldn't start the New Year in Mazār-i-Sharīf, but was also so totally exhausted that I didn't hear Sally come in after her evening of revelry with the DEA boys.

ELEVEN

I finally made it to Mazār on a chartered flight with one of the embassy's two-engine, eight-seat contract planes piloted by a pair of young South Africans, who chatted amiably while looping around the jagged white peaks of the Hindu Kush. After a quick stop in Bamiyan and another in Herāt to drop off a Department of Agriculture veterinarian, we touched down in Mazār just after one P.M. following a stomach-churning, corkscrew landing.

The faded lime green airport terminal, a crumbling relic of 1960s-era U.S. foreign aid, looked abandoned. Across the southern horizon, the snowcapped mountains loomed like frozen sentinels. To the north, the flat, salt-encrusted desert rolled empty and featureless toward the Amu Darya River and the high steppes of central Asia.

There were no airplanes or equipment on the runway and no people except for two young British soldiers in camouflage uniforms, smoking cigarettes and lounging against a battered white Toyota Land Cruiser that was idling near the empty terminal.

Unlike the American soldiers and Marines I had seen on duty in Kabul, these men were not wearing helmets or body armor, just heavy jackets and floppy hats to protect their eyes from the intense glare of the winter sun.

The pilots cut the engine only long enough for me to deplane and unload my suitcases and equipment. They wished me well, closed the hatch, and taxied away, leaving me standing alone with my pile of gear at the far end of the runway.

Both soldiers took final drags on their cigarettes, crushed them under their boots, and climbed slowly into their vehicle. Long before my two-man welcoming party drove up to where I was waiting on the tarmac, the South Africans were in the air and on their way back to Kabul.

"Welcome to Mazār, ma'am, I'm your vehicle commander, Lance Corporal Franklin Fotheringham," said a tall, unsmiling, and very muscular young soldier with a large olive-green assault rifle slung over his shoulder. He had just the beginnings of a ginger beard, and his youthful face offered a stark contrast to the weapon he was carrying.

"That," he said, pointing at his equally young, but much thinner, dark-haired companion, "is your driver, Lance Corporal Peter Jenkins."

Jenkins nodded in my direction. "Just so you know, ma'am," he added in a thick Cockney accent, "the lads don't call your vehicle commander Fotheringham. Everyone calls him Fuzzy."

Fuzzy had nothing to add to this piece of information. He and Jenkins were clearly showing me only enough courtesy to avoid being accused of rudeness. While disappointing, this only confirmed my expectations about how I would be greeted upon my arrival at the PRT.

Fuzzy effortlessly tossed my suitcases and body armor into the back of the Toyota with his free hand. "You can leave your Kevlar and your helmet in the boot of your vehicle, ma'am," he said. "You won't be needing those things up here."

"This vehicle is mine?" I asked. No one had mentioned that I had my own Land Cruiser.

Fuzzy, I quickly learned, was a man of few words. He nodded toward Jenkins, who responded to the rest of my questions.

"Yes, ma'am, it's owned by your government, and it's been at the PRT since before we arrived. The American bloke who was here before you used it. As you can see, it's not in the best of shape. We've patched the seats with duct tape and the engine gets pretty loud when we go over sixty-five clicks, so we calls it the Beast."

I could hear the Beast growling as it idled next to us on the tarmac. I also noticed that one of its windows was partially open, something that would not be possible in the hardened vehicles they used in Kabul.

"Isn't it armored?" I asked, embarrassed at the slight quaver in my voice. I had grown accustomed to the protective bubble in which embassy personnel existed in Kabul. I didn't want these soldiers to see how nervous I was, but I found it impossible to conceal my anxiety.

"Oh, no, ma'am. We don't use them vehicles up here. No need. No one's shooting at us—at least right now," Jenkins added with a grin. Fuzzy did not smile at this remark.

"That's why we don't wear the Kevlar or the helmets, ma'am. The locals actually seem to like us, and the colonel, he wants us to drive around waving and smiling, weapons on the floor, passing out free newspapers in the local lingo. Can't do that in those armored buckets with the windows glued shut. And they're fucking heavy—impossible to maneuver on muddy roads in the mountains. Lord help us if we had to drive one of those two-ton fuckers through a river or near the edge of a cliff."

Jenkins stopped speaking and looked at me, his eyes wide, fingers pressed to his lips. "Sorry, apologies for the language, ma'am. We're not used to having the ladies around."

"Don't worry about your language, but I'd rather you didn't call me ma'am. It's Angela."

"Right, Angela," replied Jenkins as he waited impatiently for me to climb into the Beast, which was growing angrier and louder. I felt the knot in my throat pushing up, but I was not going to show any weakness in front of these young soldiers.

"Would you mind turning off the motor for a minute, Jenkins?"

Rolling his eyes at my request, he reached in and pulled the key out of the ignition. The Beast shuddered violently then grew still. I sucked in a lungful of icy mountain air, released it slowly, and began to focus on my surroundings the way Mike, the Special Forces medic, had shown me the day I'd lost it during first-aid class. A blanket of silence settled over the empty runway, magnifying the vastness of the place and making me feel suddenly, inexplicably safer.

The absence of machine-generated noise was having an equally profound effect on Jenkins and Fuzzy. They were both staring up at three raptors circling high above us, black chevrons against an impossibly blue sky. The only sounds were the rustling of the wind through the dry grasses along the runway and the raptors calling to one another overhead.

"Ma'am—Angela, we'll need to load up," whispered Jenkins, tapping me softly on the shoulder and bringing to a close my few moments of serenity. "We're driving back through town with vehicles coming from the Forward Support Base. They'll be arriving any minute."

As he switched on the ignition and the Beast began to protest like a camel struggling to its feet under a heavy load, a convoy of three PRT vehicles rumbled by us. We followed them off the airfield, leaving it as we had found it, silent and empty with the raptors circling overhead.

TWELVE

January 4, 2005 ✦ Provincial Reconstruction
Team, Mazār-i-Sharīf

Long before sunrise the following morning, I was startled out of
a deep sleep by three soldiers running down the metal staircase
outside my room. Their elongated shadows backlit by the security
lights on the roof of the PRT danced across the bedsheet I had
tacked over my window for privacy. I sat up, breathing hard, as
the clatter of boots on metal faded into the predawn silence. According to a thermometer nailed to the wall near my bed, it was
forty-five degrees inside my room.

Somewhere in the neighborhood, the quavering voice of a mu-
ezzin was summoning the Mazāri faithful to the first of their five
daily prayers. His singsong chanting took me back to that last day
in Beirut with Tom, who had awakened as he always did when the
first calls to prayer began drifting across the city. He brought me
a steaming cup of coffee and a croissant and greeted me with two
kisses—one on the lips and a second one on my swollen belly.
Already dressed in his sweatpants, T-shirt, and sneakers, he was
about to leave for his solitary morning jog along the corniche.

I showered, threw on my clothes, and ran out the door in a
rush, forgetting to put on the brooch Tom had given me for my

birthday. During my meetings that morning, each time my fingers moved absently to press against my expanding midriff, I would reflexively lift them to touch the spot where the brooch should have been pinned to my lapel—and grow anxious at its absence. Later in the day, when Tom's body was pulled from the smoking rubble, I held him in my arms sobbing and rocking him like a baby. Returning alone to our apartment that evening, I found the tiny golden goddess on her leaping gazelle lying next to Tom's coffee cup in the kitchen.

Hoping to banish the memories of my husband's body in the charred ruins of the embassy, I rose from the bed in my room at the PRT and peered out my second-floor window. Under the glare of a full moon, I could see across the street an old mullah in front of a tiny mosque. He was standing before his prayer rug under the bare branches of a gnarled tree that cast a lacy trellis of blue shadows across the snow in his courtyard. When his chanting ended, I crawled back into bed and stared at the ceiling.

The camp generators kicked into high gear, interrupting my momentary descent into melancholy. Somewhere in my suitcase was a box of earplugs, but it was too cold and I was too depressed to search for them. Wrapped in a fleece robe, flannel pj's, and two pairs of wool socks I burrowed deeper into my embassy-issued sleeping bag, and curled into a tight ball.

I had planned to take a shower the previous night before bed, but I couldn't bring myself to enter the British officers' steaming all-male redoubt.

"What the hell," I muttered, switching on my light, crawling out of my sleeping bag, picking up my towel, and marching down the darkened hallway into the empty men's shower room. Thirty minutes later, I returned to my room thoroughly parboiled. I dressed in the khaki cargo pants, hiking boots, and long-sleeved white shirt that would become my unofficial uniform, put on a down jacket, and sat at my desk with a volume of Rumi. He would have to comfort me until the sun rose over the eastern desert and breakfast was served.

During the first thirty minutes of our drive from the airport back to the PRT the previous afternoon, my two young escorts had not said a word. Jenkins was focused on keeping up with the convoy and maneuvering the Beast through the clogged streets of Mazār-i-Sharīf, while giving the right of way to every camel, donkey, and darting child we passed.

The British Army driving style contrasted starkly with the aggressive tactics I had experienced in Kabul, riding with American security details. This 'softly, softly' approach was a calculated risk taken by British forces to gain the trust of the locals. I gritted my teeth and wished I could put on my body armor without looking like a complete wimp—I had felt so much safer in the fully armored American vehicles. But I could tell from the smiles and friendly waves of pedestrians that the British tactic was having the desired effect.

As we rode, I felt my anxiety slipping away. Even though they were giving the illusion of casual openness, my two military escorts were on high alert. I watched Fuzzy scan the sidewalks, giving special attention to the long rows of rusted shipping containers, which had been converted into shops and decorated with hand-painted signs. Each one bustled with vendors and customers haggling over piles of merchandise that spilled from their dark interiors.

Fuzzy was also examining the shoes of the burka-clad women who floated by us hidden beneath their blue pleated shrouds. When I asked him what he was looking for, he explained tersely that the "shoe test" was his method of determining whether there was actually a female concealed under the yards of billowing cloth.

Jenkins swung the Beast around a busy traffic circle, and we headed down a wide boulevard into the city center. Ahead loomed Afghanistan's most revered shrine, the glistening, ceramic-tiled, five-hundred-year-old Blue Mosque, surrounded by broad walkways and expansive rose gardens. A low fence of filigreed wrought iron enclosed the entire plaza, and a bustling two-lane road funneled traffic around the sacred complex.

"Do you guys know the history of this place?" I asked, hoping to spark a conversation with my sullen escorts.

"I don't, ma'am," replied Jenkins, glancing quickly at Fuzzy. "What about you, mate?"

Fuzzy didn't respond. He continued to sweep his eyes slowly back and forth out the front windshield, while his enormous hands squeezed and released the barrel of his rifle. His eyes lingered briefly on the blue-tiled domes and arches of the mosque complex before he resumed his rhythmic scanning of the pedestrians and their footwear.

"Fuzzy?" I repeated. "Do you know?"

Silence.

"Why doesn't he answer?" I asked Jenkins.

"He's watching."

"Watching for what?" I asked.

"For anyone who might want to kill us."

"What do you mean?" I demanded as I looked in alarm at the suddenly menacing crowd. "You just said that you drive around up here with your windows down, waving and smiling."

"We do, ma'am—but Corporal Fotheringham, Fuzzy, he's a sniper, and he's had a tour of duty in Iraq. He says we can't ever be too careful," explained Jenkins as he steered the Beast through heavy traffic around the Blue Mosque plaza.

"So tell us the story of the mosque, ma'am," said Jenkins as he slowed to avoid hitting an old man dragging a wooden vegetable cart across the road, "we'll be at the PRT in a few more minutes."

"Would you please not call me ma'am?"

"Right, Angela. Now tell us the story."

"Okay. Legend has it," I began, "that Ali, the cousin and son-in-law of Muhammad, was assassinated in A.D. 661 and buried in Kufa, Iraq. Did you get to Kufa while you were in Iraq, Fuzzy?"

There was no reply, so I continued. "Many Shiite Muslims swear that Ali's followers, in order to protect his body from desecration, strapped it to a white camel, which walked to Mazār-i-Sharīf and dropped dead of exhaustion right where the shrine is today."

"Bloody hell, do they actually believe that?" snorted Jenkins.

"Many people do," I replied. "Just like lots of people believe Moses spoke to God hiding inside a burning bush."

"Point taken," said Jenkins.

"The name *Mazār-i-Sharīf* means 'tomb of the saint.' The first shrine to Ali was built in 1136, right where the Blue Mosque is today, but Genghis Khan's army destroyed it looking for buried treasure. Three hundred years later, one of the Timurid sultans rebuilt the shrine, and it has survived until today through all the fighting and occupations of the past five centuries. Quite remarkable," I said to my captive audience, "don't you think?"

"Yes, Angela, it really is remarkable," said Fuzzy, momentarily breaking his silence, but keeping his eyes on the pedestrians swirling around the Beast.

"Do you think I'll be able to visit the mosque?" I asked. "Has anyone from the PRT been allowed to go inside?"

"We always have to stay outside guarding the vehicles, but I'm sure you'll be going in for some of the ceremonies with the governor. He's a piece of work, if I ever saw one," Jenkins added without further elaboration.

We turned off the main highway, bounced down a deeply rutted dirt road, and entered the mud-walled PRT compound through a pair of corrugated metal gates. Two bearded Afghan guards with AK-47s slung over their shoulders dragged them open for us.

The Beast rattled to a stop next to a collection of weathered yellow buildings, each with a metal staircase leading to sandbagged guard towers. Jenkins explained that this crowded compound had housed the family of a local warlord before the U.S. and then the British Army moved in.

Fuzzy and Jenkins jumped out of the Beast, pointed the barrels of their rifles into a large bin of sand, and removed their ammunition clips.

While Jenkins parked the Beast, Fuzzy escorted me in silence to the small office—it was more like a closet—of the PRT's Sergeant Major, who greeted me with a brusque nod. He was on the phone and engaged in a heated argument with someone at the airport in Kabul. Although officially outranked by even the youngest commissioned officer, Sergeant Major, I would soon learn, was not a man to be trifled with. Aside from the colonel, who outranked everyone else in camp, he was the most feared and respected enforcer of standards, discipline, and order at the PRT.

I turned to thank Fuzzy, but saw only his broad back as he headed out the door. A rotund supply clerk motioned brusquely for me to follow him out of Sergeant Major's office.

"Pity there's no welcoming party for you, ma'am," announced the unsmiling clerk, as I followed him up the stairs to the floor where the officers' sleeping quarters were located. He hadn't bothered to introduce himself.

"The colonel's out at the safe house in Sar-e Pol for a few days, and the chief of staff has been behind closed doors since morning with some visiting German Army officers over from Kunduz. The rest of the men are out on patrol or in training. Frankly, ma'am, we were all bloody gobsmacked when they told us the Yanks were sending a female up here to live for a year."

I wasn't sure if "gobsmacked" meant they were surprised or angry, and decided not to ask.

"This will be your personal space, ma'am," he said, opening the door to a small room with a thin layer of dust on every surface and a view of the Hindu Kush obscured by a forest of communication antennas. A smaller window behind the bed faced a mud wall and a metal staircase. There were no curtains.

"It's not posh, but at least you'll have it all to yourself. Only you and the colonel have private rooms," he added, looking down at me with his head cocked to the side and one eyebrow raised. "Mr. Brooks, the American who was here before you, had this room, but he's been gone for a while and we've been using it for storage—all nicely cleared out for you now, as you can see."

He pulled a sheet of paper from his pocket, unfolded it, and placed it on the desk. "Ma'am, I'll need for you to sign this inventory after we identify all the items in your space." Tapping the paper with his pen, he rattled off in his most official voice: "One metal bed stand, one plastic-covered mattress, one standing locker, one dresser, one desk, one lamp, one pillow, two sheets, one pillowcase, one towel. Your Yank friend left the blankets, so we won't count them. You also have a wall heater, though that may need fixing. Please sign here, ma'am." He pushed the paper over to me, clearing a path through the dust, and handed me his pen.

"Please call me Angela, and would you mind telling me your name?"

"Right, ma'am—I mean, Angela," he replied, pursing his lips. "It's Wickersham, Corporal James Wickersham. Wick will do," he said, extending his hand briefly to shake mine.

"One more thing, Angela." He opened one of the desk drawers and pulled out a battered cell phone attached to its charging cord. "This is also yours. The other Yank left it here.

"The loo's right outside your room," he added, pointing to an unmarked door that led to a communal toilet in the hallway. "You'll be sharing it and the showers on this floor with the officers and noncoms. There are curtains in the shower room, so you'll have some privacy. Ship showers only, of course."

I opened my mouth to ask a question, but he wasn't finished.

"The men all know you arrived today, and everyone's under strict orders from the colonel to keep a towel over their—private parts," he elevated his left eyebrow again, "when they leave their rooms. No worries there."

"What's a ship shower, Wick?"

"Right. A ship shower, Angela," he said, carefully pronouncing each syllable of my name, "means you do like the sailors do on a ship. You turn on the water and get wet. You turn off the water and soap up. You turn on the water again and rinse yourself and then you turn the water off. There are more than a hundred of us living in this camp right now, and when the Swedes start showing up in a few months, we'll be almost a hundred and fifty. When the Americans set this place up in 2003, there were only seventy of them. Our self-contained water and power systems are now stretched to the bloody limit."

Wickersham led me through a maze of passageways and up a flight of cement stairs to my "office," a long, narrow room that I would share with military liaison personnel from France, Finland, Romania, Norway, and Estonia. They, like me, had been sent to PRT Mazār by their governments with loosely defined roles and responsibilities. Only the two young Estonians had real jobs at the PRT. They were explosive ordnance demolition technicians, EODs, who spent their days defusing the occasional IED and blowing up the tons of ammunition and explosives that were being uncovered in caves all over northern Afghanistan.

My new colleagues looked up from their computer screens when we entered the crowded room, which they referred to as the bullpen. They rose to their feet in unison and greeted me with handshakes and broad smiles.

"Here's your spot, Angela," announced Wickersham, pointing

his stubby finger at a battered typing table barely large enough to hold a computer monitor, a keyboard, and a satellite phone. It had been shoved against the wall just outside the PRT commander's office door. My foreign military colleagues sitting behind their large desks smiled wanly and shrugged their shoulders in mute apology at the newest member of the bullpen who had drawn the short straw in the desk lottery.

THIRTEEN

"Last stop before I let you unpack and wash up for supper will be the interpreters' room," said Wickersham, trotting down the stairs as fast as his bulky frame would allow. I followed him along a narrow sidewalk bordering an overgrown patch of rosebushes in serious need of pruning. A few shriveled flowers still clung to their thorn-covered stems.

"Here we are," he said, rapping his knuckles against an unlocked door and pushing it open without waiting for a response.

"Hello, boys. Here's the lady we've all been waiting for. Rahim, I believe you've been assigned as Miss Morgan's interpreter." A broad-shouldered, square-jawed young man in his early twenties, with close-cropped black hair, sideburns, and a five o'clock shadow stood up to greet us. He wore a white T-shirt, pressed blue jeans, and held what appeared to be a large textbook in his left hand. His dark eyes met mine briefly, then shifted to Wickersham.

"Rahim, this is Miss Morgan. She's replacing Mr. Brooks as the U.S. government representative in these parts. We haven't had any females at this PRT permanent-like, as you know, but I'm sure

8

you and your mates will treat Miss Morgan with all proper respect." He seemed to say the last bit more as a warning.

The interpreters' room was sparsely furnished with threadbare red cushions around the walls, a prayer rug in one corner, a glowing electric space heater in the center of the room, and an ancient black-and-white TV set, which one of the interpreters had switched off as soon as we entered.

Rahim remained standing, his empty right hand tightly clenched, as his fellow interpreters began to discuss me and tease him. Their comments tumbled out in rapid fire. They had no idea I could understand every word they said.

"So this woman will be your master, eh, Rahim?"

"She's not bad looking. Could pass for a Tajik."

"No, her hair's too short!"

"I like those big green eyes, don't you, Rahim?"

Rahim had not moved. His cheeks were burning with humiliation.

"I wonder how old she is. Thirty-five maybe? Not quite old enough to be your mother, Rahim, but old enough to . . ." The others began to laugh. I forced myself not to smile at this flattering but bawdy comment.

"Maybe you can teach her something about Afghan architecture on your long trips," another added, pointing toward the book in Rahim's hand, which he immediately released. It hit the floor with a thud and a rustle of pages. Both his hands were now balled into tight fists as though he were preparing for a fight.

"Rahim, you'd better not try any funny business when you're out on patrol with your American woman."

I understood that the very presence of an unaccompanied

female was making the interpreters nervous and that they were diffusing their tension by teasing poor Rahim, but there was nothing I could do or say without revealing my knowledge of their language.

Rahim glared at his companions, then stepped forward and said to me in English, "It is an honor to meet you, Miss Morgan. It will be an honor to work as your *tarjoman*, your interpreter." He did not extend his hand, but as was the custom in Afghanistan, waited for me to extend mine. When we shook hands, the whispered comments of his colleagues began again.

"At least she's not taller than you, Rahim, but she's dressed like a man."

"Maybe people won't know she's a woman. They'll think she's a shaggy-haired American boy whose beard hasn't grown in."

"Look at her. No one will mistake that one for a boy."

They all laughed again except for Rahim, whose eyes remained fixed on the floor. I felt an overwhelming desire to defend my new interpreter and had to fight the urge not to lash out at his companions. Although he was obviously less than thrilled about being assigned to work for a woman, his refusal to join in his comrades' jeers had earned my immediate respect.

"Rahim," I said, addressing him in English, "It is an honor to meet you. I look forward to working with you this year. Please call me Angela."

"Yes, Angela," he replied as our eyes met briefly. My new interpreter—whom I didn't actually need—and I—whom he was ashamed to be working for—were off to a terrific start.

"Right," interrupted Wickersham. "Let's get you back to your room, Angela. Carry on, boys." He held the door open for me and we left the interpreters still teasing Rahim about his new assignment.

I followed Wickersham past the sad little rose garden and through another low archway festooned with multiple strands of razor wire. He stopped in front of a small patch of ground, surrounded by a low white picket fence and filled with an assortment of round and rectangular metal objects half buried in mud.

"This is our very own land mine garden," he announced with a flourish. "The Estonian EODs give briefings here every few days for the new arrivals, just so you'll know what to look out for. Don't want you tripping over one of these bastards when you're out on patrol," he added with a wide grin. "I'll let you know when they have the next session."

When I edged cautiously back from the display of land mines, Wickersham laughed again. "They're all duds, ma'am. No worries."

"Right," I muttered between clenched teeth, as I wiped away the beads of perspiration that had appeared on my forehead despite the frigid temperature.

"It's getting late and you must be tired. I'll take you back to your room. The PRT compound is, as you can see, ma'am—sorry, 'Angela'—not too large. I'm sure you'll be able to find your way around the rest of the camp tomorrow. There are a few exercise machines and treadmills in the hallway next to the laundry, which you are welcome to use any time of the day or night. No jogging outside the wire, of course. To get to the machines, you'll have to walk through our little pub. It's open every night for the officers and men—and for you, of course—from eight until ten. Beer and cider—but you should know that a two-can limit is strictly enforced. One more thing," he added with a look of concern, "don't forget your morphine pen. The doc will be here next week. You can stop by his office to pick one up."

"My what?" I asked.

"It's a little spring-loaded injector the lads carry on patrol. Looks like a regular writing pen," he explained. "Just jab it hard against your leg, and it will shoot enough morphine in to keep a smile on your face until someone can get you to a hospital. You know, just in case. When you're up in the mountains, you'll be a long way from any serious medical care. If you're badly injured, that little pen makes the trip back to camp so much more pleasant."

A forced smile concealed my discomfiture at this new bit of information.

"The German Army has a helicopter base across the river in Uzbekistan," continued Wickersham. "They're supposed to come get our boys if there's trouble, but they won't land anywhere that hasn't been cleared, secured, and swept clean with a toothbrush— which pretty much eliminates any situations we might get ourselves into in Afghanistan, so don't leave camp without your pen."

"I won't," I replied nervously as I braced for Wickersham's next bombshell.

"The doc has to sign the pen out to you. If you don't use it while you're here, you have to turn it in before you go home. It's a controlled substance, y'know."

He stopped in front of my room and pressed a key into my hand with a knowing wink. "Best to keep your room locked when you're out, Angela."

FOURTEEN

January 6, 2005

"Miss Morgan, is that you? Please do come in," called the colonel from inside his office when he heard my chair scraping the floor under my typing table. I stepped through the doorway and a short, rosy-cheeked man with a thinning blond crew cut rose to welcome me. His greeting was warm and genuine and not what I had expected to receive from the commanding officer of the PRT. At last, a friendly face. I liked him already.

"Harry Wilton, pleasure to meet you and welcome to our little camp," he said with a lilting Welsh accent. As we shook hands, he lowered his voice and added, "Would you mind terribly closing the door?"

"Not at all," I replied, shutting out my NATO colleagues who were watching me from behind their desks in the bullpen. "Please call me Angela."

"And you shall call me Harry," he said. "As you'll soon discover, Angela, our NATO colleagues in the outer office do not like it when my door is closed, but there isn't much privacy at this PRT, and you and I have some issues to discuss that can't be shared with anyone else at this point. Before we begin, may I offer you a cup of tea?" he asked, reaching for a small metal pot on a tray with two cups.

"No thanks," I replied, "I had my fill this morning."

"Excellent. It's already gone cold in any event. So sorry I wasn't here to greet you when you arrived. I try to get out at least once a week to one of our safe houses in the provinces. That's where most of our six-man Military Observation Teams—MOTS, we call them—are based. The round-trip travel alone takes more than eight hours to Sar-e Pol and several days to Maimana if the weather's decent.

"Have the men in ops shown you where to find all the briefing books?"

I inhaled deeply, wondering how to best answer Harry's question. My first visit to the ops room on the day after I arrived at the PRT had been an awkward affair. I'd stood for thirty minutes in a chilly basement hallway next to the shredders outside a locked metal door with a large sign that said DO NOT DISTURB—MEETING IN PROGRESS.

A cipher lock allowed only cleared personnel into the ops room where classified materials were processed and stored. While I waited, several soldiers rushed down the stairs, punched in the code, entered the ops room, and quickly latched the door behind them without even acknowledging my presence.

I had a top-secret NATO clearance, but that didn't seem to hold water with the men who worked in the communications and intel offices inside the vault. When the ops officer finally let me in after the meeting, he explained that it would take several weeks to validate my clearance. Until then, he could not provide me with the cipher lock codes, allow me to open a NATO e-mail account, or read the sensitive intel files where the profiles of local power brokers and warlords were kept.

"Yes, everyone's been very helpful," I said to Harry without much conviction, "but there appears to be a problem about my access to classified materials. I have the required clearances, but your officers want more proof, which they say will take weeks."

Harry puffed his cheeks and blew out a stream of air. "I'll get the chief of staff to sort that out for you. Do you have everything you need in your room?" he asked.

"Everything except heat," I said with a smile.

There was a loud knock at the colonel's door, and a young lieutenant barged in. His face was flushed. "Sir, the phones in the ops room are out of commission for the moment, and I wanted to warn you that the Estonians will be detonating a large cache of ammunition in . . ."

A tremendous explosion shook the building and rattled the windows in their frames. A small photo of Harry's wife and children crashed to the floor. I gripped the arms of my chair to keep myself from bolting out of his office and diving under the nearest desk.

"Well, just now it appears, sir," the lieutenant said with a grin.

"Thank you, John, and get those phones fixed," said Harry, bending down to pick up the photo in its unbroken plastic frame. He looked up at me with concern. "Miss Morgan—Angela, are you feeling all right? You've gone quite pale."

My hands were trembling, my heart was about to crush my ribs, and I was breathing hard. "I'm fine," I replied in a tone that made it obvious to Harry I was not fine at all. "It's just been a long time since I've heard such a loud . . . noise."

"I'm afraid these are a regular occurrence around here," Harry said, still observing me closely. "We're trying to track down all the ammunition and explosives caches in this area so our Estonian friends can blow them up."

As soon as the lieutenant shut the door behind him, Harry leaned forward on his elbows and cupped his round chin in his hands. My pulse was beginning to return to normal, but Harry's office still felt painfully warm.

He noticed my damp forehead. "Are you quite sure you're feeling all right, Angela?"

"I'm okay," I repeated, although it was obvious I wasn't. "Please continue."

"Right. I understand you are fluent in Dari, and have been tasked with helping us sort out whether our interpreters are giving us accurate translations especially regarding the matter of the ubiquitous poppies."

Harry explained that opium poppy cultivation in Balkh Province was expected to reach an all-time high in the spring despite the governor's claims to the contrary. Although local warlords, who were also allies of the governor, were known to be major growers and traffickers, it had so far been difficult to prosecute any of those who had "connections." He admitted it was possible that some of the PRT's interpreters were concealing information, but he remained skeptical about the allegations despite the fact that life was cheap in Afghanistan, most of the interpreters were young and without powerful patrons, and it would have been fairly easy for the traffickers to co-opt a few of them.

Harry despised the cultivation of opium poppies. A nephew of his in Cardiff had been addicted to heroin before committing suicide several years ago. Watching that young man's descent into hell, said Harry, had been the most painful experience of his life, but the safety of his soldiers patrolling the northern provinces was now his paramount concern.

He had made it quite clear to the British and American embassies in Kabul that an active poppy eradication program in the north, especially aerial spraying, would make it far too dangerous for the MOTs to safely patrol the remote sectors of our provinces. Afghan farmers, he argued, as had the American lieutenant in Kabul, would not differentiate between foreign contract eradication teams and his young soldiers.

"I do hope that with your language skills you'll be able to help us resolve these allegations, Angela."

"I'll do my best, Harry," I replied.

"I was also told that no one is to know about your fluency in Dari—with a few exceptions."

"Exceptions?"

"Yes, my chief of staff, of course, and our incoming intel officer, Mark Davies, who speaks Pashto. I believe you and Davies met at the Foreign Office in London."

"We did."

"He should be arriving at the end of next week."

"Great," I replied with forced enthusiasm. I was in fact dreading the arrival of this man who had objected to my assignment here on all possible grounds—that I was a woman, an American, and a diplomat.

It was difficult enough trying to fit in with this all-male group of soldiers and officers, but at least none of them seemed to be openly hostile to my presence.

"It will be important to keep both of your foreign language skills quiet until we sort out this issue with the interpreters," Harry continued.

"Yes, of course," I said, forcing myself to stay focused on our conversation. "But according to my embassy, I'm also to serve as a political advisor to you and your officers."

"Right. Just as your predecessor, Mr. Brooks, did." Harry pressed his lips together before continuing. "There is one small complication, Angela. Brooks arrived when the U.S. Army was still running this PRT. Since they turned the camp over to us in 2003, Her Majesty's government has also assigned British diplomats to serve as political advisors and reporting officers here."

"I know that, Harry. What is the complication you're referring to?"

"Brooks was deeply involved in overseeing the many U.S.-funded reconstruction projects in this area. I'm not sure what they were exactly, because he was rather reluctant to share that information with us. It's my understanding that after he left, your embassy assigned a contractor in Kabul to manage all U.S.-funded development work in the five northern provinces covered by this PRT."

It was now clear why Plawner hadn't said anything about my role in monitoring the reconstruction under way in the north. I had no role.

"Are you saying that I'm not needed here?"

"No, no. Of course, you're needed here, Angela," Harry continued. "I'm delighted you've come and I fully support your assignment. I'm sure that with your language skills you'll bring a great deal to the PRT team."

Harry looked at me with a mix of sadness and relief as he continued. "My opinion matters little at this point, however, because I'll be leaving at the end of next month. Colonel Jameson, my successor as PRT commander, and our new Foreign Office diplomatic representative, Richard Carrington, will hopefully arrive a few days before I depart."

My heart dropped at this news. Finally, I had met someone at the PRT who didn't treat me as an inconvenience, who even welcomed me, and now he was telling me he was leaving.

Harry stood up and began pacing on his threadbare carpet. "Angela, how would you like to accompany me next week to a weapons handover ceremony? We hold these little events whenever a local warlord collects enough rifles and rockets from his men to make a credible claim that his people are disarming."

He returned to his desk and scribbled something into his calendar. "We'll leave at 0630 hours sharp a week from Saturday. And let's take Rahim since the old professor, my head interpreter, is still on medical leave in Kabul. You can listen in on the side conversations and brief me later on how accurately Rahim is telling us what's being said. What do you say to that?"

"Sounds great," I replied with little enthusiasm.

"Excellent. You can get started on sorting through Brooks's papers and weeding out unnecessary materials. He left several filing cabinets stuffed with old maps, brochures, UN reports, and God knows what else. I believe there may even be some State Department cables in there.

"You might also want to get your driver to take you out to the local Afghan Army base so you can meet the American military personnel who are working as embedded trainers there. A new National Guard unit arrived from the United States just a few weeks ago. I haven't met their commanding officer yet, and I'm sure he'll be making a courtesy call here very soon, but it might be useful for you to meet him on his own turf."

"I'd like that," I said. No one at the embassy had mentioned the fact that there were American soldiers working in this part of the country.

"Please feel free to sit in on our various staff meetings, Angela, and, of course, the debriefing sessions with our Military Observation Teams. Ask as many questions as you wish," added Harry, as he paused and looked at me with concern. "Oh, yes, and get plenty of rest. Many of the men seem to come down with a nasty virus a few days after arriving, so you'll need to keep up your strength."

Harry was right on that count. The day after our meeting, I was hit with a miserable stomach flu. I spent the next two days in bed and in the loo next to my room. Fuzzy, Jenkins, and even Wickersham surprised me by taking turns bringing me trays of soda, broth, tea, and crackers from the field kitchen. Harry stopped by several times to make sure I was still alive. I heard nothing from Rahim.

When I had fully recovered, I arranged to have Fuzzy and Jenkins take me out to meet the American soldiers. They and their commanding officer, Colonel Hugo Tremain, were with the Texas National Guard. This lantern-jawed American officer, a long, tall Texan and devoted family man, was in real life the chief of the fire department in his small East Texas town. Tremain was respected by the Afghans and adored by his own men, who welcomed me into their drafty plywood offices and immediately offered me all the Diet Coke, blueberry muffins, and Snickers bars I could carry back to the PRT.

Tremain was a soldier's soldier with one serious aversion. "Man dancing, don't like it, won't do it, Morgan," he would remind me whenever we got into discussions about his Afghan counterpart, General Raisul, who occasionally invited him on overnight military exercises, where the soldiers would dance around the campfire in the evening.

"Sweet Jesus," Tremain said on more than one occasion, "every time they break out the drums and the flutes and those fiddles and start dancing, Morgan, I want to crawl into my tent and hide in my sleeping bag."

He further clarified his position on "man dancing" one afternoon when he had just returned from another patrol with Raisul. "Morgan, I will sit for five hours on a cold dirt floor with the general and his officers, drink twenty cups of green tea, and eat every speck of food I am offered with my bare right hand, including a sheep's eyeball, but dancing should be like marriage— between a man and a woman. Period!"

FIFTEEN

After recovering from my bout of flu and making my initial call on Colonel Tremain, I spent the next few days in the bullpen getting to know my NATO colleagues and sorting through the thousands of documents Brooks had left stuffed in his filing cabinets.

I tried to find out more about my mysterious predecessor's activities from the NATO officers, but they had little to add to the few details I'd gleaned during my week in Kabul. Brooks had kept his activities and his contacts to himself.

He had not learned Dari and had departed the PRT without warning, following a hasty transfer to Bangkok a month before his tour in Afghanistan was up. The rest of my queries about him were met with shrugs and apologetic grins from the bullpen crowd. I finally gave up asking questions about Mr. Brooks.

Friday, the Islamic Sabbath, was the only day of the week that PRT personnel not on duty were allowed to sleep in. I had many more of Brooks's files to sort through, but it was time to give myself a break. Late in the morning, I was stretched out on top of my sleeping bag, basking in the winter sun that streamed through my window. Sipping my second cup of tea and deep into a favorite Navajo detective novel, I was able to forget for a blissful few hours that I was in Afghanistan—until someone began pounding on my door.

It was Jenkins. "Miss Morgan—Angela, Sergeant Major is letting us use two PRT vehicles to take some of the lads to the *buzkashi* game. Can we use the Beast so more of the fellows can come?"

"Of course, you can." The look of excitement on his face reminded me again that this wiry young soldier was also barely out of his teens.

Jenkins walked to the end of the hall, then turned to face me as I was about to close my door. "Would you like to come? It is your vehicle after all."

As tempting as it was to stay cocooned, I knew that Doc and Ali would be terribly disappointed if they found out I had turned down the chance to see a real *buzkashi* game. "I'd love to."

Jenkins, who seemed less than thrilled that I had taken up his offer, told me to meet him and the others at the front gate in ten minutes.

The day was bright, cloudless, and freezing cold. I dressed quickly in heavy boots, cargo pants, two sweaters, and my winter jacket. Tucking my hair into a black knit cap, I hoped the Afghans at the *buzkashi* field wouldn't look too closely and would assume I was a male civilian working for the soldiers. As Doc and Ali had reminded me numerous times, women did not attend or participate in these games.

The British soldiers parked on the northern end of the field near the towering silo of the abandoned Soviet bread factory. They were careful to keep a low profile at the games and always stayed as far as possible from the cement viewing stands at the south end of the field. That was where Governor Daoud and other provincial dignitaries gathered to watch the hundreds of horsemen who swirled in churning equine scrums as they chased one another across this broad tract of high desert.

As I began taking photos, some of the younger noncompetitive riders and a few curious elders approached us to pose for pictures on their prancing steeds. They cantered back and forth in front of our vehicles as their horses shook their heads and arched their thick necks.

One of the young men asked if any of the soldiers wanted to ride his horse, a huge black with a red tasseled bridle, dark liquid eyes, a thick tail that brushed the ground, and oiled hooves on long slender legs. The stallion chomped on its bit and scattered flecks of white foam in the air each time it tossed its enormous head. Its silky hindquarters, tendons flexing under a glossy black coat, were damp with sweat despite the frigid winter air. This horse was all power and muscle and yet full of beauty and grace. Its wild spirit reminded me of the mustangs that still roamed northern New Mexico. The boy pulled the reins tight as he paraded in front of us, daring the soldiers to accept his challenge.

"You no want ride? Soldiers afraid?" the boy taunted as his horse snorted, bucked, and chomped on its bit. There were no takers.

Without being quite conscious of my movements, I handed my camera to one of the soldiers, stepped forward, pointed at the stallion, and then at myself.

"Angela, are you out of your mind?" cried Jenkins, who grabbed my arm as I started walking toward the horse.

"Probably," I answered, pulling out of his grip.

The young man jumped down from his saddle, a huge smirk on his face.

"You not soldier," he said, examining my clothing as I took the long leather straps from his hand and looped my fingers through a hank of tangled black mane.

"Ney," I said, shoving my left boot into the wooden stirrup, swinging into the saddle and digging my heels into the stallion's flanks. It was a rush to feel a horse beneath me again. I felt suddenly invincible, as though this animal were transferring some of its strength to me.

"Angela, you're insane!" The voices of Jenkins and a few others trailed off as I thundered down the field clinging like a burr to the back of this magnificent stallion. It took the bit between its teeth, flattened its ears and, as it had been trained to do, charged right for the center of the *buzkashi* scrum, where the *chapandaz* were battling one another for possession of the headless calf.

I did have enough sense to know that I had to keep far away from that roiling mass of riders, who were brandishing leather whips and urging their kicking, biting steeds into the fray. The discovery of a woman anywhere on the field would be scandal enough, but a woman in the actual game would bring shame on all the players and their patrons. I could feel the stallion's muscles tense as we approached the other horses, and I used its momentary hesitation to shift my weight and jerk its head to the left. It worked.

It was still fighting me, but I'd thrown it off balance enough to force it to turn and accept my control. As I slowed it to a canter, I realized how dangerously close I had come to the governor's viewing stand.

The stallion made one last effort to overpower me. When it reared, I shifted my weight again, spun it on its hind legs, and turned the horse north, coaxing it into a gentle lope back toward the bread factory. Two more PRT vehicles had pulled up next to the Beast, and I could see more soldiers climbing out and joining the crowd.

I slowed the black stallion to a trot and then a walk, just before I jumped down and tossed the reins back to the stunned young rider.

"What a fucking brilliant ride!" cried Jenkins, slapping me on the back. "I got some great shots of you in full gallop. Take a look," he said as he handed me my camera.

Fuzzy stood next to Jenkins, scratching his head and grinning broadly. "Angela, do you have any other surprises for us?"

"I'm sure I do," I replied with a laugh.

"Is that one of our civilian contractors from the PRT?" said a voice that I recognized but could not immediately place. It was coming from the newly arrived group of British soldiers. "What's his name?"

"Well, you see, Major Davies, that 'he' is actually a 'she,'" shouted Jenkins. "That's Miss Morgan. I'm her driver, sir. Rides like a bloke, don't she?" I could hear this conversation over the heads of the soldiers who had clustered around me, but I still couldn't see Mark Davies, who had not been expected at the PRT for several more days.

"You should give it a go yourself, sir," added Jenkins. "I heard you played number three on the polo team at Sandhurst. That true, sir?"

"Yes, but that was years ago, Corporal, and I don't think it's appropriate for us to interfere with the Afghans' game. Who gave the American woman permission to ride?"

"Why, no one, sir. One of the Afghans rode up to us and asked if anyone wanted to ride his horse. None of us did, but he kept asking and Angela finally stepped up to the challenge. We tried to talk her out of it, but she was up on that horse and gone in a flash."

"Major Davies," I said, pushing through the crowd and extending my hand. "Welcome to Mazār-i-Sharīf. I see you arrived earlier than expected."

"Miss Morgan, you could have been killed out there," he replied, ignoring my outstretched hand. "How would your driver have explained that to the colonel and to your embassy?" he demanded, narrowing his eyes against the glare of the late afternoon sun.

"Nice to see you, too," I replied, shoving my hands into my pockets and returning his gaze without further comment.

He spun around and walked back to his vehicle, which his driver had kept running. As soon as Davies climbed in, they pulled out and headed for the PRT.

"Looks like you're off to a great start with our new intel chief, Angela," observed Jenkins.

"Are all the officers like this?" I mumbled under my breath.

SIXTEEN

January 15, 2005

The following morning, I rose before sunrise. Since my arrival, my dread of encountering any officers on my way to the shower room had kept me tiptoeing through the hallways in the predawn darkness to take a speedy ship shower before any of them were awake.

My luck ran out that morning. As I rounded the corner to the hallway where the showers were, I ran into Daniel and Ross, who both worked in the ops center. Bundled against the cold in robes as thick as mine, with blurry eyes, spiky hair, and unshaven chins, they surprised me by smiling and greeting me by name as we entered the shower room together, slipped into our curtained stalls, and waited for the icy water to warm up. When I came out ten minutes later, Daniel was shaving over the sink.

I was headed for the door with my head down, when I heard the click of his razor on the sink and his voice addressing me.

"Angela, I didn't realize we had an expert equestrian in our midst."

"Oh, I'm not an expert," I stammered. "I used to ride, but it's been years since I've been on a horse."

"Until yesterday," he said.

"Yes, until yesterday."

"Word is you impressed the hell out of the Afghans," Daniel said with a laugh.

"I hear they all thought you were a bloke!" added Ross as he stepped out of the shower stall and rubbed his short blond hair with the edge of his towel. "Well done."

This was the first time any British officers except for the colonel had engaged me in friendly conversation. I turned to face them, my wet hair wrapped in a towel and cold water dribbling into my robe.

"Thanks," I replied, not certain whether I should continue this conversation or make a quick exit before any more officers came in for their showers.

"Look, Angela," said Daniel with a sigh, "I know some of the fellows have been a bit standoffish since you arrived, but I hope you haven't taken it too personally.

"Truth is, we were all bracing for another stuffy, secretive American like Mr. Brooks. When we heard the Yanks were sending in a female diplomat, we feared the worst."

"You were worried about having a schoolmarm in your midst?"

"No, not that," said Ross. "Younger officers are actually quite comfortable with women around. Many of us trained with them at Sandhurst. My ex-girlfriend was a helicopter pilot, for Christ's sake. It's more the senior officers, noncoms, and some of the skinhead squaddies who still have trouble accepting a woman in their midst."

"Don't forget the older ones from regiments like the RGR," added Daniel.

"The RGR?" I asked.

"The Royal Gurkha Rifles. They'll be here in a few months to replace our regiment. Many of them still have that South Asian cultural hang-up about being commanded by a woman. They're about a century behind the rest of us."

"That bloke you had a bit of a row with at the *buzkashi* field was a Gurkha," added Ross.

"You've heard about that, have you?" I said, blushing.

"Not to worry, Angela. You'll find that nothing stays secret for long at this PRT," Ross added with a wink. "By the way, good luck with that weapons handover this morning. Those ceremonies are a bit of a joke, but we're chuffed the colonel's taking you with him."

"You are?" I was stunned since I was pretty certain that "chuffed" meant happy.

"We need much better reporting on those meetings. The colonel doesn't give us enough details. He's a fine commander, but sussing out political nuances is not his strong suit. The officers leading the MOTs on their peacekeeping patrols aren't trained political analysts, either."

"Since you fellows are so anxious to read my reports, how long will I have to wait before I'm allowed into the inner sanctum to read yours?" I asked.

"Right," Daniel replied. "Isn't the chief of staff sorting that out for you?"

"So I'm told," I said as I turned to leave, "but nothing's happened yet."

"Angela," called Ross.

"Yes?"

"Why don't you ever eat in the officers' mess?"

"No one has invited me."

"Consider yourself officially invited," he shouted as I pushed through the swinging door.

"Thanks," I shouted back as the door swung shut behind me.

Since Harry had asked me to be ready at 0630 hours sharp for our trip to the weapons handover ceremony, I came down for an early breakfast. The door to the officers' mess was open when I walked by with my tray of eggs, toast, and orange juice. I could see Harry, Major Davies, and the chief of staff with their plates of food balanced on their knees, deep in conversation. The very sight of Major Davies, who along with the other two men was oblivious to my presence in the doorway, made me inexplicably uncomfortable. I decided this might not the best day to eat my first meal with the officers.

I spotted Fuzzy and Jenkins in the soldiers' dining area, wolfing down enormous plates of rashers, eggs, potatoes, and toast. On my first night in camp, they had taken pity on me and invited me to sit with them when I walked alone into their dining hall with a tray of food. Given my initial frosty reception by the PRT's officer corps, I had since taken to eating alone with a book in the soldiers' dining hall or joining Fuzzy and Jenkins at their table.

"Morning, Angela," said Fuzzy, nodding toward an empty spot next to him on the bench.

"We'll be following the colonel's car in the Beast to provide you with some extra security this morning," announced Jenkins, still chewing a mouthful of food. "Some of those mujahideen blokes aren't exactly over the moon about giving up their weapons, and you don't want to get stuck out there with only one vehicle. You'll ride with the colonel, and Rahim will ride with us. The colonel wants him to do the interpreting since Professor Sayeed is still sick."

"Who's Professor Sayeed?" I asked.

"The head interpreter at the PRT. Used to teach English at Balkh University, so everyone calls him the professor," said Jenkins.

Fuzzy and Jenkins stood up together. "We've got to kit up and get the Beast topped off for our trip. See you outside in twenty, Angela," said Jenkins as they carried their trays to the kitchen.

By six forty, our two-vehicle convoy was bouncing out the gates and splashing through a long ribbon of gray mud in front of the PRT. Pools of water concealed deep holes in the road, which Harry's driver and Jenkins behind us did their best to avoid. By the time we pulled onto the pockmarked asphalt road leading to the Sholgara Valley, our Land Cruisers were spattered with so much mud that the green NATO insignias on the sides of the vehicles were no longer visible.

The British officers and soldiers had informed me they did not wear seat belts so they could swiftly exit a vehicle in case of an emergency. I didn't feel safe without a belt and was glad I had strapped myself in when Harry's driver began to dodge potholes and speeding trucks at fifty miles per hour. I was comfortably secured on my side of the backseat, while Harry gripped the handle of his door and struggled to keep from bouncing into my lap. We rode in silence past fallow wheat fields, mud-walled villages, and large earthen mounds, rising fifty feet or more into the air and dotted with circular openings—the ancient and mysterious stupas, which Jeef had described at our dinner.

Harry was dozing even as he clung to the door handle, his head bobbing with each bump. His driver and vehicle commander, the most spit-and-polish pair at the PRT, were silent—keeping their eyes on the road that under a sudden downpour was now only visible through the triangles made by their thumping wiper blades. When the rain ended and the sky brightened from dark pewter to gunmetal gray, we crossed a narrow bridge spanning the Balkh River and pulled onto a remarkably smooth dirt road. I was asleep within minutes.

"Angela." Harry was tapping my arm. "We're almost here. You've been out for the past hour."

Our convoy rolled to a stop before a large assembly of bearded men in snowy white turbans. They all wore the traditional pajama-like brown and beige *shalwar kameez* topped with gray blankets or dark wool overcoats. Despite the cold, they had leather sandals strapped to their bare feet.

The men stared at me briefly when I got out, but quickly turned their attention to the British colonel, who was holding the certificates, printed on one of the copy machines at the PRT, that would confirm their compliance with the Interior Ministry's orders to hand over excess weapons and ammunition to the government. A blue UN truck, idling nearby, would cart their munitions off to a cantonment, where they would be inventoried and destroyed or turned over to the Afghan Army.

Rahim barely acknowledged my presence as he climbed out of

the Beast and moved to Harry's side to translate his remarks into Dari for the assembled mujahideen. The Afghan men had formed tight clusters around the grenades, rocket launchers, machine guns, and boxes of ammunition that were laid out in orderly rows on three blood-red carpets spread on the dirt in front of the local commander's walled compound.

"Honorable Commander and heroic fighters." Harry scanned the men's faces to be sure he had their attention. "I would like to thank you on behalf of your president and the PRT for your willingness to hand over your weapons and ammunition to assure a peaceful future for your country." Rahim's translation of Harry's remarks was clear and precise. The men nodded gravely.

Harry paused to allow Rahim to finish, then heaped more praise on the men for driving out the Taliban in 2001 and for their willingness to hand over their tanks and armored personnel carriers to the UN the previous year.

I was observing the ceremony a few yards away from Harry and listening to the men around me discuss their hidden caches of weapons—the ones we would never see. Their other conversation was about me.

"Who is this woman?"

"She must be one of the British officer's wives, but why would he bring her here?"

Rahim trailed Harry as he strode slowly down the neat rows of munitions, hands clasped behind his back, brow furrowed, and lips pursed. Suddenly, Harry stopped and turned in my direction. "Good gracious, Angela, I have completely forgotten to introduce you. Please join us over here and allow me to present you to the commander and his men."

As I stepped forward, Harry introduced me to the silent, staring crowd.

When he mentioned the millions of dollars the United States was spending on reconstruction in the north, the old man who had speculated about my marital status spat in the dirt and grumbled, "What reconstruction? The American money is going to the Pashtun friends of the president and rich foreign contractors." Rahim did not translate that remark.

After Harry handed out the certificates, we followed the commander into a room inside his compound. Thick cushions lined the walls of this narrow space that was lit only by small openings in the mud walls.

A worn green oilcloth unrolled in front of us, covered the length of the room. As soon as we were seated, barefoot young men padded down the oilcloth, placing cups, bottles of soda, and large warm rounds of fresh baked *naan* in front of the guests. More men pushed their way into the crowded room and squeezed onto the cushions.

Hot platters of meat and rice were set before the guests. The men kept their eyes on Harry and as soon as he dipped his fingers into the great pyramid of greasy rice, tore off a chunk of tender lamb, chewed it, and smiled, they began ripping the *naan* into small pieces and devouring their own trays of *qabale palau*.

The conversations about me continued and I listened, amused.

"So this woman is from the American government?" growled a young man, licking his fingers and pulling another strip of lamb from a bone buried in the rice. "Is she a soldier?"

"She looks like one of our women, but for those clothes."

"Why is she dressed like a man?"

"Why would her husband let her do this?"

Rahim did not translate any of these comments for Harry or for me.

Cleanup was fast and efficient. Three of the barefoot youths collected the bottles and cups. Four others picked up the half-eaten trays of *palau*, while the remaining two rolled up the oilcloth, which still contained large uneaten pieces of bread, bits of rice, and portions of lamb. They carried the cloth into the next hallway, where thirty more men were waiting to eat. It was unrolled, and the used cups and half-eaten food trays set in front of the second string of diners who devoured our leftovers and drank from our cups with gusto. The unseen women and children in the kitchen, who had prepared the food, would be given whatever scraps the men did not eat.

Harry suggested I ride back to camp in my vehicle with Fuzzy, Jenkins, and Rahim. "I won't be very good company, Angela, since I'm certain to be sound asleep for the entire trip."

Fuzzy and Jenkins, who had remained with the Beast while we ate, were anxious to get back to the PRT before the cooks stopped serving dinner. I was too drowsy to talk to Rahim, who sat stiffly on his side of the backseat staring out the window. Jenkins had turned up the heat, adding to my lethargy. I dozed off as soon as we pulled onto the dirt road and headed for home.

Just before sunset, I was startled awake by the horn and headlights of an approaching truck. Jenkins swerved violently, narrowly avoiding a collision with the brightly painted and dangerously overloaded vehicle.

"Fucking asshole!" he muttered. "Oops, sorry, Angela," he added as he forced the Beast back into our lane. Fuzzy glared at him but said nothing.

Rahim ignored Jenkins's outburst and still had his back to me. We rode in silence until we passed another one of the stupas.

"Rahim," I said, formulating a question I hoped would break through his wall of silence. "Do you know anything about the origins of these mounds?"

He surprised me by responding to my question immediately. "They're the remains of ancient mud-brick and earthen temple complexes," he replied in a weary monotone. "Grave robbers long ago removed everything of value, but most of the mounds have never been excavated by professional archaeologists. They were Buddhist temples almost two thousand years ago, long before my country became an Islamic nation. Some are even older."

"Have you met the men who are excavating the Greek ruins near Balkh?" I asked, wishing that Professor Mongibeaux were here to help me reach out to this sullen young man.

"I have heard about the work of the French archaeologists there, but I have not met them," said Rahim in a disinterested voice.

"Fuzzy, we've seen that dig, haven't we?" asked Jenkins.

Fuzzy nodded. "It looks like one of them tomb-raider movies."

"It's bloody amazing," added Jenkins. "Greek columns and Buddha heads all dug out of the same pit!"

All conversation ceased when the sun briefly set fire to the Hindu Kush and plunged into the western desert. Ahead of us, in the blood orange eastern sky, lightning pulsed inside an expanding thunderhead.

"Beautiful," I said aloud.

"Yes," replied Rahim, turning his head in my direction to look at the mountains.

"Rahim, have you spent your whole life in Mazār?"

He sighed and shook his head. "No. My sisters and I were born here, but my parents took us to Karachi when the Taliban came to power in 1996. I finished high school and started university there, but my father wanted to come home in 2001. We are Tajik and he thought he should support the Northern Alliance in their fight against the Taliban. He died of a heart attack a few weeks after our return, so now I must work as an interpreter to support my mother and three sisters."

"Your English is very good. How long have you worked at the PRT?"

Fuzzy turned around and looked at Rahim. "Tell Angela how the U.S. Special Forces blokes recruited you."

"Right," said Jenkins, laughing. "He had to get his mother's permission, Angela! No offense, Rahim, but you're the only one at the PRT who's seen any combat up here. It's a great story."

"Okay, no offense taken, Jenkins. I'll tell it." Rahim began to relax in my presence for the first time. He curled one leg up, stretched his arm over the back of the seat, and faced me directly.

"For several days after the fighting started in Mazār, my mother wouldn't let me leave the house. Parts of the city were being bombed, but we didn't know who was doing it since the Taliban had cut the phone lines and they controlled the only radio station. Nobody had cell phones then. We knew from BBC shortwave reports that there was fighting in the south, and that the Americans had sent soldiers and airplanes to attack the Taliban at Tora Bora, but there was no reporting on the fighting up here.

"One morning when the shooting and bombing stopped for a few hours, my mother told me to go downtown and find some food for our family. I was buying bread near the Blue Mosque, still concealed under my scraggly teenage, Taliban-required beard, when a truck with American Special Forces soldiers drove up. One soldier jumped out and came over to buy *naan*. He greeted me in Dari, and I replied in English. His Dari was terrible," Rahim said, laughing softly.

"I had studied English in Mazār and for four more years in Pakistan. When I answered him in his own language, he immediately asked me if I wanted a job as an interpreter. He told me I would have to shave my beard."

Rahim closed his eyes and leaned his head back on the seat. "I needed the work, but I told him I'd have to ask my mother's permission, so he and his men drove me to my house. They told my mother how much they would pay me. At first, she said no, but I insisted that I wanted to do it and reminded her that we had no more money for food. She finally said yes if the soldiers promised to keep me safe. They promised.

"I was nineteen years old. By late the next afternoon, I was pinned down by machine gun fire inside Qala-i-Jangi fort, where the Taliban were making their last stand against the Northern Alliance and the Americans. The soldiers had already broken their promise to my mother." He laughed.

"I crawled around in the mud behind your soldiers, eating their revolting MREs, translating instructions to the Northern Alliance fighters, and praying to Allah that my mother's son would not be brought home to her wrapped in a sheet. I am not a soldier, Angela, and I was very afraid," he admitted with surprising candor.

"The next day, the Northern Alliance and your soldiers flooded the tunnels and drove out the remaining Taliban, including an American. It was horrible. I have never told my mother about this battle. One of the Northern Alliance generals captured several thousand Taliban in Kunduz, brought them to our province in shipping containers, and left them to die in the desert. Some of them were only boys!"

Rahim was so young to have experienced such horrors, although I had to admit he was the same age as most of the soldiers. He seemed to have survived it all without serious residual trauma, but I felt a strong desire to shield him from anything like that in the future.

"Many, many people were killed during those days of fighting, Angela. If my mother found out, she would have forbidden me to work for the soldiers after that, but I liked being an interpreter and my family needed the money. We still need the money," he added with a heavy sigh.

"I would like to return to the university, but I must support my family so I stay with the PRT."

The sky was now almost dark, and Mazār was about thirty miles away. When rain began to pound the Beast with fat drops, Jenkins and the colonel's driver ahead of us slowed for a procession of small children crossing the road. Each little boy and girl was bent under an enormous bundle of sticks and brush.

"Where are these children going?" I asked Rahim.

"They are bringing fuel back to their village so their mothers can cook," he replied. "As you can see, we Afghans have cut down most of our trees for firewood. Long ago, much of my country was covered with forests of cedar, pine, oak, and fir. We had wild animals living in the mountains. Now even many of our fruit or-chards and vineyards have been chopped down for cooking fuel."

I watched the sad parade of children disappear into the darkness.

"We used to export dried fruits and nuts all over the world, Angela. Now all we export is opium paste," said Rahim bitterly.

"I still don't understand why these little children are out gath-ering firewood so late," I replied. "Isn't it dangerous?"

"Angela, Afghan men do not do this sort of work, and the women are not allowed out in public, so it is the village children who must perform this task every day. Sometimes they go onto the property of other farmers to find fuel. They do it in the evening so they won't be caught and beaten."

"But if there are no trees left, what are they collecting?" I asked.

"They cut down bushes and reeds that grow along the irriga-tion ditches. Unfortunately, the more of these bushes the children remove, the more erosion our farmers suffer. It is a vicious cycle, but how can they stop it? Their mothers need fire to cook."

"We see kids like those little ones every time we go out on patrol," said Jenkins.

Fuzzy nodded. "Yeah, poor buggers should be in school."

"You're right about that, Fuzzy," said Rahim.

"Rahim, how do you think the handover ceremony went today," I asked, changing the subject. I wanted to take advantage of this temporary break in his wall of silence.

"It was just like all the others," he said. "The khans order their men to put out their oldest and most useless weapons for the colonel to admire. Everyone makes a speech. I translate. The muj collect their certificates, the colonel reports their compliance to Kabul, and the major weapons caches remain concealed."

I was stunned at his sudden burst of candor, although it confirmed what I'd overheard when the men standing near me had been discussing their hidden weapons caches. "So this has happened before?"

"All the time," he replied. "Right, fellows?" he asked Jenkins and Fuzzy.

"I'm afraid it's true," said Jenkins.

We were now driving in the dark, with only oncoming headlights visible through the rain. There was no shoulder on this road. Overloaded trucks, many with only one headlight, continued to speed by us with inches to spare.

I was growing to like this quiet young Afghan, no matter how unwilling he was to like me. He was direct and honest—and though I hated to think it, he was about the age my son would have been.

"What did you study at university?"

"Architecture," he replied. "I had a wonderful Afghan professor in my first and only year at university in Pakistan. He wanted to start a renaissance in traditional building practices, using the earthen wall and mud-brick designs of our ancestors with a few modern alterations. He teaches in Germany now, but he has many followers in Pakistan and Afghanistan. I continue to study his writings on my own," he added, patting a worn textbook on the seat next to him.

"Today in my country, only farmers still build the old way, but it is our way. It uses our Afghan earth and dung and chopped straw, it is beautiful, and it is perfectly adapted to our climate. City people stupidly have great disdain for traditional architecture. They want so-called 'modern' cement and cinder-block buildings, which require heating and air-conditioning.

"Someday when I get my degree, I will design beautiful buildings that respect our ancient architectural customs. I will make my people proud again," he said in a voice that resonated with determination.

Jenkins turned off the main highway, and we bounced down the last quarter mile to the PRT. The Beast's headlights glinted off the deep pools of water ahead of us.

"The power must have gone out while we were away," I said, noting the darkened buildings on both sides of the road. This was the first time I'd been outside the PRT at night.

"Angela," snapped Rahim, "we have not had electricity in Mazār for weeks."

"What do you mean?" I said. "The power was on when we left the PRT this morning."

"The PRT runs on electricity from generators, Angela. Can't you hear them roaring day and night?"

He was right, of course. I heard the generators all the time. They had kept me awake my first night at the PRT, but had rapidly become background noise, which I no longer noticed. It had never occurred to me why the PRT would have power when the rest of Mazār did not.

Rahim wasn't finished. "Only the wealthy in Mazār can afford their own generators and diesel fuel. Look around you, Angela. Where do you see lighted buildings?" he demanded.

It was then I noticed for the first time that only the PRT, a few sprawling compounds owned by warlords in our neighborhood,

and the Kefayat Wedding Club several blocks away with its illuminated plastic palm trees, were lit up and visible through the
rain.

"Why is there no power?" I asked. A flush of shame rose in my
cheeks. Was I so cosseted in the PRT that I hadn't noticed the
darkness that surrounded us every night?

"Angela, do you not know that most of Mazār's meager supply
of electricity comes from across the river in Uzbekistan and Turkmenistan?" asked Rahim, as though he were addressing a child.

"If the governor doesn't pay the bill, or the lines break, or our
northern neighbors don't have enough power to sell to us, there is
nothing we can do." He turned his back on me and stared silently
out the window at the dark shadows of men drinking tea in the few
shops illuminated by flickering kerosene lamps.

SEVENTEEN

January 18, 2005

"You seem to be picking up far more information than I ever have," Harry said, handing me the report I'd written on the weapons handover. "I'd appreciate it if you don't mind coming with me to all my meetings outside of camp."

"I'd love it, Harry. That's why I'm here."

Much to Rahim's relief, Harry and I didn't need him for the frequent disarmament discussions with local UN officials since everyone at those meetings spoke English. Despite our friendly conversation on the trip back from Sholgara, Rahim had made it abundantly clear that he wished to spend as little time as possible in my presence.

Since my language skills had to be kept secret, we brought Rahim along to translate the first time Harry and I went to see Governor Daoud, the former warlord who controlled Balkh Province. Rahim made a point of sitting as far away from me as possible.

Harry frequently saw the governor to convey complaints the PRT received from delegations of Hazara men. Under the Taliban, the Hazara, a minority sect, were brutally massacred. Tens of thousands had fled to Iran and Pakistan, leaving behind their land and possessions.

At least once a month, small groups of Hazaras bundled against the cold in their gray blankets appeared at the gates of the PRT to deliver handwritten requests for help in recovering their lands. Their letters, always written by a scribe in elaborate Perso-Arabic script and marked in purple ink with the fingerprints of the illiterate petitioners, detailed their repeated accusations of land theft against Daoud's sub-commanders. We could offer no help other than our useless promises to hand their petitions over to the very Afghan authorities they believed had taken their property.

The first time I arrived at Daoud's office with Harry and Rahim, a member of the governor's staff escorted us with much bowing, scraping, and fluttering of hands into a large reception hall. It was a garishly furnished room with high ceilings, crystal chandeliers, and overstuffed brocade chairs on gilded legs—a stark contrast, I would soon learn, to the cramped, musty offices of governors in the other northern provinces.

Daoud had led thousands of mujahideen against the Russians and then against the Taliban. After the expulsion of the Taliban, he had been engaged for several years in combat for control of the northern provinces with his former Northern Alliance ally, General Kabir. Both men had voluntarily given up their tanks and heavy weapons and agreed to an uneasy truce in late 2004. Harry was convinced that the presence of the PRT in Mazār was the sole check on both men's desire to wield absolute power in the north.

With great fanfare the governor swept into his office, followed by his entourage, thirty minutes after we had already consumed several cups of tea awaiting his arrival. I was prepared for such behavior. Traditional displays of power in this part of the world required that supplicants be kept cooling their heels for at least this long. With his tardy arrival, Daoud had indicated that he considered us to be the "supplicants."

Despite walking with a severe limp, this stooped, white-haired man radiated an aura of unquestioned power. The governor greeted us with a slight bow and brushed an invisible piece of lint from his green silk cape. His beard was neatly clipped and, like the other men in the room, he wore a snowy white turban.

Harry presented me to the governor, who regarded me silently while Rahim translated. The governor greeted me in Dari and awaited my response.

I replied with a simple Dari greeting and extended my hand, which he took briefly, then dropped. "So you speak our language?" he said, adjusting his glasses and staring at me with unreadable black eyes.

When I hesitated Rahim jumped in, "*Wali Sahib,* the woman only speaks a small amount of Dari. I am here to interpret for her and the colonel." The governor's eyes remained trained on mine.

"Do you not use her name?" he asked Rahim sharply.

"Yes, sir, I call her Angela," Rahim replied, lowering his eyes in apology.

"Angela. What does this mean in our language?" the governor asked Rahim, who was now watching me.

As I held the governor's gaze, I heard Rahim answer, "It means 'angel,' *farishta* in Dari."

"Farishta," the governor repeated slowly. "Well then, please be seated, Farishta-*jan*, and let us begin this meeting."

I could see that Rahim was uncomfortable with the governor's reply. He knew, as did I, that I had just been insulted. What little authority I had as a representative of the U.S. government had been casually dismissed by the governor's use of the familiar *jan*, a Dari term of affection among friends and family members. One did not use *jan* with strangers, especially in an official setting, and I knew Daoud would never use it with Harry. In this case affection was not the governor's intent. By daring to address me in public with such familiarity, he was ensuring that everyone in the room knew he did not consider me to be on an equal footing with the British colonel.

Male servants entered silently to refill our cups with tea and replenish cut-crystal bowls with the pistachios, green raisins, and sugar candies we had been munching while waiting for the governor. Electric heaters blasted warm air from the ceiling.

While the governor sat stiffly in his throne-like chair, Harry presented the PRT's current list of complaints. The governor responded, as Harry had predicted, with vague promises to create a committee that would investigate the latest charges of land theft from the Hazaras. He assured us that we would be summoned to meet again at an unspecified future date to receive his committee's report.

Sitting on the governor's left, in a dark blue uniform with red epaulettes and three silver stars on each shoulder was his new chief of police, a senior Pashtun policeman from Jalalabad, whose scraggly beard and beaked nose reminded me of Fidel Castro. The police chief traveled everywhere with a Pashto interpreter since he did not speak a word of Dari, which made him an odd choice by the central government to lead a Dari-speaking, provincial police force in northern Afghanistan.

The requirement for Rahim to interpret everything from Dari into English for Harry, back into Dari for the governor, and then for the police chief's personal interpreter to repeat everything one more time in Pashto, tripled the length of our meeting. This, along with the endless pouring and drinking of green tea and the governor's thirty-minute absence from the reception room to say his afternoon prayers, stretched what should have been a one-hour meeting into three and one-half hours with no bathroom breaks for the governor's captive audience. To say it was taxing would be an understatement.

Nothing concrete was accomplished, and neither Rahim nor I had any idea what the Pashtuns were saying to one another. That, I presumed, would be one of Major Davies's responsibilities.

I had seen little of Davies since his arrival five days ago. He had spent all of his time behind closed doors in the intelligence cell to begin the task of sorting out the mess his incompetent predecessor had left behind.

After that first meeting, and to Rahim's great relief, Harry began rotating interpreters each time we met with the governor or any other official, so I could start assessing the accuracy of each one's translations. They all appeared to be providing correct accounts of what was being said, and I hoped that soon I would be able to end this ruse and start using my Dari. There was still no word from the PRT's head interpreter, Professor Sayeed, who remained in Kabul recovering from his illness.

"Angela, did I mention that Edwin Trumbull, the British diplomat who was based here last year, will be coming up to Mazār from Kabul next week to make his official farewell calls?" asked Harry as we returned to the PRT from another meeting with the governor.

"No, you didn't. How did he and Brooks get along?" I asked.

"Not well," Harry said with a shrug. "Brooks had been at the PRT for more than six months before Trumbull arrived with the first British regiment. There were some territorial issues, which I don't believe they ever really resolved. For the most part, they functioned independently."

"So what's Trumbull like?"

"I'll reserve my comments on Trumbull and let you make your own judgment when you meet him, Angela," Harry replied with a sympathetic smile. "I'll be in Kabul for meetings while he's here, but you must definitely arrange to go with him on his calls. It will be an excellent opportunity for you to get to know some of the key political players in the region."

"That would be terrific," I said, embarrassed by my lack of solo appointments outside the wire after several weeks at the PRT.

It was not to be.

The day after Harry left for his meetings in Kabul, I was standing in the chow line when I spotted an unfamiliar civilian pulling a tray from the cart. I walked up and introduced myself to Edwin Trumbull.

"A pleasure to meet you, Miss Morgan," he said. "I heard you arrived a few weeks ago and that you've been ill. Hope you're on the mend," he added, adjusting his glasses to examine the steaming trays of roast pork and lamb chops.

"I'd love to join you this week on your farewell calls," I said as we moved together through the chow line.

"Right," he said with a pained look on his face. He set his tray down and removed his glasses. "Unfortunately, Miss Morgan, I'm afraid that's just not in the cards. I have worked very hard to develop contacts for Her Majesty's government, and I don't want these people to think that I'm now handing them off to an American. Nothing personal, mind you, but I am planning to introduce my replacement in absentia, and I don't want any confusion about which governments you and I are representing. I'm sure you understand."

He held my gaze and awaited my reaction. With a lump in my throat and my pulse suddenly in high gear, I took a deep breath and fought to suppress the tears that were about to betray my vulnerability. I was speechless, stunned, and offended at his blunt refusal to my very reasonable request.

Trumbull scooped boiled potatoes onto his plate and continued to stare at me, his raised eyebrows forming thin arches over his drooping lids. "I'm confident your predecessor, Mr. Brooks, whom I remember with great fondness, left you with detailed notes and letters of introduction, which you can use to make your own calls."

I was ashamed to admit that Brooks had left me nothing but a cell phone with abbreviated names that I couldn't decipher and stacks of documents that were going to take me months to sort through. I had no ready reply to Trumbull's withering sarcasm and finally lowered my eyes in embarrassed silence.

Trumbull grabbed his tray, took a few steps toward the officers' mess, then turned to hurl another dart in my direction. "Oh, by the way, I've been invited to a reception tomorrow for the Mazār consular corps. I'm not officially a consul general, and neither I presume are you, but they have always included me in their little gatherings. I forgot to mention it earlier. It's at the Turkish Consulate. I'll take you along as my guest unless, of course, you've received your own invitation."

I had not. My face reddened as I struggled but failed to come up with some response to Trumbull's barbs.

"No need to wear a head scarf, my dear," he added with a simpering grin. "With the exception of the Iranians, this is a fairly secular Islamic crowd. Most of our consular colleagues will be in business suits. I'm not quite sure what you should wear since you'll be the only woman, but I'm sure you'll sort that out. Be ready at 1800 hours sharp."

He vanished into the officers' mess and left me standing alone in the hallway with a tray of food I no longer wanted to eat.

EIGHTEEN

February 8, 2005

The Turkish Consulate was one of the largest and most heavily guarded compounds in Mazār-i-Sharīf. Its rooftop, bristling with almost as many communications antennas as the PRT, left no doubt about the Turkish government's intense interest in northern Afghanistan.

As soon as the British military escort dropped Trumbull and me at the entrance, the Turkish consul stepped forward to greet us. I braced myself to be ignored, insulted, or both.

"Edwin, so good to see you again. I hadn't planned it this way, but you must consider this gathering as your official farewell party."

Trumbull returned his greeting and introduced me with a perfunctory nod. The Turkish consul had much better manners. He turned to me with a broad smile and extended his hand. "Miss Morgan, for you, our modest consular officer assemblage will have to serve as your welcoming party. Please go in and help yourself to drinks and food. No Afghan guests this evening, so the bar is open."

Edwin stayed on to chat with our host, while I took a deep

breath and walked alone through a curtained doorway into the main reception room. Although I kept reminding myself that this gathering was just like the hundreds of others I had attended during my diplomatic career, I found myself suddenly immobilized by a sensation that could only be described as stage fright. Small clusters of men, talking, drinking, and eating—the Mazār-i-Sharīf consular corps—all stopped speaking and turned to stare at me, the first woman to invade their all-male domain. I remained frozen in place until I heard a familiar voice.

"Angela! Welcome to Mazār!" It was Stefan in an expensively tailored gray suit, waving at me with a drink in his hand. The other men glanced at Stefan and then at me to observe my response.

"You are looking lovely as always, although slightly more concealed than when we met in Dubai," Stefan said taking in the black slacks and shapeless gray tunic I had worn in deference to my Islamic colleagues. Seeing that many of them had availed themselves of the bar, I regretted that I hadn't dressed with a bit more western flair.

"Stefan, what a wonderful surprise to see you here," I gushed, trying to suppress the grin that was spreading far too quickly across my face.

"Prepare yourself to be invited to these rare but very stuffy little gatherings from time to time," he said, with a look of mock pity on his broad Slavic face. "There's certainly not much else going on in Mazār that you could or even would want to attend. Except, of course, for the Mazār Social Club, which this crowd would never be invited to and probably doesn't even know about." He waved his hand dismissively at the Central Asian diplomats in their ill-fitting black suits, thin black ties, cheap shoes, and white socks.

"I'm so glad to see you, Stefan. What are you doing in Mazār?" I asked, my voice catching slightly. It wasn't wise for me to be feeling this thrilled about running into a Russian diplomat whom I barely knew and whom I certainly shouldn't trust. I could feel my cheeks burning and hoped Stefan hadn't noticed. I hadn't realized until now just how lonely I'd been feeling.

"I was sent up here for a few days to audit the consulate," he said, "and our consul general invited me to come with him tonight. I was secretly hoping you would be here, and here you are! What can I get you to drink?" he asked, his pale blue eyes lingering for an uncomfortably long moment on mine.

"A glass of white wine would be wonderful."

Stefan returned with another tumbler of vodka for himself and a chardonnay for me.

"So what's the Mazār Social Club?"

"Hasn't Mr. Trumbull told you about the Mazār Social Club?" Stefan laughed. "He certainly spent enough time there during his year at the PRT."

I shook my head and took a long sip of the chilled wine. It felt so good to be having a civilized drink that I had to remind myself to slow down. I was already dangerously close to losing myself in front of Stefan.

"It's at the UN residential compound where a lot of expats live. It's the only place in town where those foreigners who like to drink alcohol and party a bit after work can safely gather a few nights a week to—how do you say it—let our hairs down." He laughed again.

"Do you know all these men, Stefan?" I asked, looking at the consuls, who had resumed their conversations with one another.

"I was acting Russian consul general up here for a few months last year, and yes, I do know them. Finish your drink, and I'll do the introductions," he said, steering me toward a window that looked out over the garden. He lowered his voice again and added, "I don't suppose Trumbull has been very accommodating. You'll find he's not one to share information unless it's to his benefit."

"He's made it quite clear that I'm on my own."

Trumbull ignored me for the entire evening, but Stefan, his fingertips resting lightly on my elbow, steered me around the room introducing me to the consuls general from Turkmenistan, Tajikistan, Uzbekistan, Pakistan, India, and finally to his Russian colleague.

The older man smiled, shook my hand, then looking intently at Stefan whispered in Russian, "This is the woman you met at the Emirates Towers? You must . . ." Stefan cut him off with a sharp glance, then said to me in English, "Angela, you must be thirsty. May I get you another glass of wine? I don't want to bore you any longer than necessary with old Mr. Alexandrov."

Although I didn't think Stefan knew I spoke Russian, I was careful to show no reaction to the unexpected comment of his colleague or to Stefan's abrupt change of subject. It was clear that he had reported our meeting in Dubai to his superiors. Stefan led me back to the bar, where our Turkish host joined us and insisted on presenting me to the Iranian consul general, an elderly, gray-bearded gentleman, wearing a black turban and a floor-length white robe. He was standing in the far corner of the room with his assistant, drinking an orange soda.

When we approached and I greeted him in deliberately halting Farsi, he stiffened and handed the soda to his assistant. I extended my hand in greeting. He nodded curtly, kept his eyes on the floor, and folded his arms tightly across his belt. After a mumbled reply, he turned away and walked to the other side of the room. Apparently, not everyone in this crowd was prepared to accept a woman. His nervous assistant approached me several minutes later to explain in hushed tones that it was my gender and not my nationality that had prompted the consul's diplomatic brush-off.

Trumbull continued to avoid me until a two-vehicle convoy of British soldiers pulled up in front of the Turkish Consulate at nine P.M. to escort us back to the PRT.

Stefan walked me to the door and gave me a farewell peck on the cheek, which I wanted to return but did not. An unsmiling Trumbull had been observing us closely throughout the evening and I was not going to provide him with any ammunition to use against me later.

"Remember to call me the next time you are in Kabul, Angela," said Stefan as I climbed into the truck with Trumbull.

I was sad that the evening was over. It had been such a delight to spend a few hours talking, drinking, and laughing with an attractive, intelligent diplomatic colleague who actually seemed to enjoy my company. Stefan waved again as we pulled away from the consulate. I hoped we would be seeing each other again very soon.

Trumbull said nothing about Stefan on our ride back to camp. He departed for Kabul two days later and never returned to Mazār.

After Trumbull's refusal to share his contacts with me, I accepted the fact that I was going to be on my own in Mazār, at least until my new British counterpart arrived.

It remained unclear to me what I could accomplish with no formal introductions, virtually no instructions or guidance from the embassy, and no specific tasks to accomplish in this corrupt, chaotic, male-dominated culture.

Accompanying Harry to his meetings was useful, but I had to establish my own identity. Charging across the *buzkashi* field on that stallion without getting thrown off had boosted my confidence, despite Major Davies's harsh reprimand, but it did not make me feel any less alone at this PRT. After my panic attack in first-aid class, Mike had urged me to start conquering my fears by focusing on the reality around me. Getting on that horse had been a huge first step. Step number two would be getting myself outside the walls of this camp on my own terms.

NINETEEN

"Angela Morgan? My name is Bob Donovan. I'm with the ambassador's security detail at the embassy," announced a brusque voice on my cell phone. I was standing outside in the rose garden, where I'd gone for a few minutes to recover after another Estonian demolition had rattled the windows in the bullpen and sent my pulse into overdrive. These neglected bushes were in desperate need of pruning. Next time I'd bring some scissors.

"Yes, how can I help you?"

His reply came back like machine gun fire. I held the phone away from my ear. "The ambassador may fly up in a few weeks to meet with General Kabir and his followers at the general's residence in Andkhoy. We need you to arrange with the general for the loan of some of his SUVs and places to sleep for our five-man security advance team.

"They'll land at a nearby airstrip our guys built a few years back. Kabir's men can pick them up there. The old man likes Americans, fought with us against the Taliban after 9/11, so there should be no problem. Think you can handle that?"

"Of course," I said, trying to sound confident but wondering how I was supposed to convince this powerful warlord, who was also Governor Daoud's sworn enemy, to provide sleeping accommodations for an American security detail. At least it would give me an excuse for a meeting.

When I explained my travel plans at our daily ops briefing, Harry was agreeable to my request to meet with the general. Major Davies was not.

"Sir, General Kabir is the most notorious and brutal warlord in northern Afghanistan," he said, avoiding my eyes. "We believe he is guilty of serious war crimes. I don't think it's advisable for Miss Morgan to make this trip."

"Mark, neither we nor any of our diplomats have had contact with Kabir for months, and he is not one to be ignored. We all know he has close ties with the American Special Forces, so I don't believe Angela will be in danger. I can't spare any officers to go with her, but we'll send her with two vehicles, an interpreter, and four soldiers. Do you think you can handle this on your own, Angela?" Harry asked with a slightly worried look on his face. "I'm sure you'll bring back some useful intel for the major and his staff."

"Absolutely," I replied, looking defiantly at Davies.

Early the next morning, Rahim, Fuzzy, Jenkins, and I were off to Faryab Province in the Beast. Another PRT vehicle followed close behind.

Halfway to Andkhoy, I spotted across a weed-covered field near the road the three-meter-high, hundred-meter-wide excavated mound of Tillya Tepe, which Jeef had mentioned at our dinner in Kabul. Two decades ago, local inhabitants had dug small pits all over the site in their search for gold coins and jewelry that the archaeologists had missed. Now the entire area was off limits due to the thousands of unexploded land mines and ordnance that had been scattered across the landscape by the endless parade of warring factions.

"Do you know about the Bactrian gold they found at Tillya Tepe?" I asked Rahim. He hadn't said a word since we left the PRT, and I thought this might be a good way to draw him out.

"No, Angela," he replied, his voice annoyingly flat. "Where is Tillya Tepe?"

"It's right out there," I said, pointing north toward the flat earthen mound, "the legendary 'hill of gold.'" I told him the story of the discovery, which had taken place only a few years before he was born.

"When the French archaeologist comes up this spring, I'll take you to meet him. It's your heritage and you should know about it."

"All Afghans should know these things," Rahim said, staring out at the pockmarked field.

General Kabir's deputy Abdul had taken my call the previous afternoon as soon as I got off the phone with the embassy security officer. According to Rahim, Abdul spoke fluent English so I wouldn't need an interpreter to make the call.

"The general would be happy to provide accommodations for the ambassador's security detail." After a long pause, he added, "Why don't you come to Andkhoy tomorrow to confirm the arrangements? The general is in residence and would like to meet you."

"Thank you," I said. This was going to be easier than I expected.

"General Kabir has been good friends with your American soldiers since he fought so bravely to drive the Taliban from the north in 2001," continued Abdul breathlessly. "He has never met a female American diplomat. It would please him. You are invited for lunch, then you can join us for a celebration of the first day of Id al-Adha, when the people of this province will pay their respects to the general at our town soccer field."

Rahim's presence was not strictly necessary for this trip, since Abdul spoke English, but Harry insisted he go with us. "If you break down or have any trouble with the locals during your eight-hour round-trip, you will need a Dari speaker, Angela, and it can't be you. I'm afraid Rahim will have to go along. I'm aware that he hasn't completely accepted his role as your interpreter, but he has to start getting used to it."

Kabir's compound was hidden behind massive walls that towered over the houses surrounding it. Three heavily armed guards wearing expensive ski jackets and sunglasses waved us through a set of ornate iron gates and into an enormous courtyard dotted with elaborate fountains and a large, empty swimming pool.

Fuzzy, Jenkins, and the two soldiers in the other vehicle stayed outside with their engines running. They were already digging into their sack lunches as Rahim and I followed one of the guards toward Kabir's pool house where the general's interpreter waited to greet us.

"Welcome, Miss Angela," said Abdul, standing in front of the glass-walled atrium. As he motioned for me to follow him, Abdul approached Rahim and hissed in Dari, "Why did the woman bring you today, when she knows I speak English?"

"I don't know," replied Rahim, who towered over the wiry aide, but had assumed a submissive posture in his presence. "I certainly had no wish to accompany her on this trip."

"The PRT commander could have at least sent your senior interpreter, Professor Sayeed, as a sign of respect for the general," Abdul huffed.

Rahim ignored Abdul's insult. "The professor is ill and has been staying with his family in Kabul," he said wearily.

"You are not really needed at this lunch," Abdul continued, "but since you are here, we must let you join us. You may follow."

Switching to English and smiling at Rahim, he added for my benefit, "Rahim, old friend, how nice to see you. Please join us for lunch."

The meal was as surreal as it was delicious. Kabir, who had already settled into a throne-like chair at the head of his long, elaborately laid table, greeted me politely but without standing. The table had been placed next to an Olympic-size indoor swimming pool. To Kabir's left and right were his robed and turbaned commanders, who glared at me and fawned over their general.

Hanging on the wall directly behind Kabir was a large flat-screen TV, displaying a National Geographic special on the mating habits of primates. The sound was off, but the images of copulating gorillas flashing on the screen just above the general's narrow, balding head were hard to ignore. Rahim, who had been placed next to me to provide a buffer between the general's male guests and the "woman," could not keep his eyes off the TV. As world-weary as he often seemed, I was reminded again just how young and innocent he really was.

Servants padded quietly around us, filling our glasses with Coca-Cola and setting out steaming plates of roast lamb, fragrant rice, boiled eggplant, yogurt, *naan*, dumplings, and other Afghan delicacies. There were gold-plated forks and spoons at each place, but once Kabir began eating with his fingers, everyone, including me, followed suit.

Chewing a mouthful of lamb, Kabir turned to Abdul and said, "Ask her why the Americans decided to send a woman instead of a man to Mazār."

"Miss Angela, General Kabir welcomes you to Andkhoy," said Abdul with a forced smile. "He asks how a woman came to be chosen for this very important position at the PRT in Mazār-i-Sharīf."

"Please tell the general that all the men they asked to come were afraid, so my government sent me instead," I replied, suppressing a grin and curious to hear how Abdul would translate my flip reply.

As Abdul repeated the literal if not figurative meaning of my words in Dari, the commanders stared at me in silence. Kabir was watching me for another reason.

I had pinned Tom's Scythian brooch to my tunic for today's lunch, and Kabir had been staring at it throughout the meal. He stroked his drooping white mustache and turned to Abdul. "Tell the woman her gold pin is very beautiful," he commanded from his end of the long table. "Tell her it reminds me of the photo from my presidential campaign posters where I am riding my favorite chestnut stallion—my best *buzkashi* horse."

I could hear Rahim gasp. In this part of the world, custom dictated that an overt compliment from someone as powerful as Kabir required the admired object to be handed over immediately as a gift.

"Angela," said Rahim, his voice quaking, "the general wants your pin." He looked genuinely worried, and I was touched by his concern, but there was no way I was letting that man take my brooch. I also knew that such a blatant request was the general's way of testing how far he could push me.

I waited for Abdul's translation, then rose to my feet, praying that the trembling in my knees wouldn't be too obvious when I started to speak. In my best Russian—which I knew Kabir understood well—I began. "General, with all respect . . ." His eyes narrowed. I had his full attention. "It has been an honor to dine with you and your brave followers in this magnificent guest house. Thank you for inviting me."

Abdul and the commanders, who had no idea what I was saying, stopped eating to watch the general's face for his reaction to being addressed by a woman.

"As the senior U.S. government representative in northern Afghanistan, I would also like to thank you on behalf of my ambassador for your generous offer to assist his security detail with vehicles and sleeping quarters if he should decide to make a trip north later this month to meet with you."

Kabir continued staring at my brooch and licking the grease

from his fingers while I spoke. Rahim lowered his eyes and was slowly moving food around his plate with one of the golden forks.

Kabir's comment about my brooch had awakened emotions buried so deep, I had all but forgotten them. I now used these feelings to add strength to my speech. "General, the United States is very much looking forward to your leadership in the northern provinces as the Afghan government begins to disarm the illegal militias. You have the power and the influence to make this effort a success by convincing all of your commanders to turn in their weapons and ensure a peaceful future for Afghanistan." *Fat chance*, I thought.

"I am honored that you find my pin so beautiful. Just before my husband was killed by a terrorist bomb in Beirut in 1983, he gave me this brooch and told me to keep it close for good luck. I swore to him I would do just that." Kabir nodded gravely. "I am certain you will understand my deep attachment to something as worthless as this small piece of costume jewelry."

Kabir rose from his chair, cleared his throat, and replied in Russian, "Angela Morgan, I am deeply sorry for your tragic loss. We are united with you and your country in fighting all terrorists and other enemies of our nation, and we fully support our president's disarmament plan. Please send my highest regards to your ambassador."

I acknowledged his statement with a silent nod and remained standing. Despite Kabir's reputation for drunken rages and the mass exterminations of his enemies, his charisma and influence were palpable. I felt no fear as we eyed each other from opposite ends of the table. At that moment, I felt only the small satisfaction of having made an important point about disarmament to an

Afghan leader who actually had the power to convince his followers to start turning in their "real" weapons. Whether he would do so was another matter.

Kabir stepped away from the table, signaling to all that the lunch was finished. Over the scraping of chairs on the tile floor, his voice boomed out once again in Russian, "I hope you will be able to join us for the ceremony downtown." It appeared that my refusal to hand over Tom's brooch had not totally soured our relationship.

"It would be an honor, General," I replied with a deep sigh of relief that the lunch was finally over.

Kabir continued to stare at me with narrowed eyes and added, "My compliments on your excellent Russian."

Rahim and I were the last ones out of the pool house. I was lost in thought, trying to analyze what had just happened. Should I have made that joke about men being afraid to take my job? Probably not, but I couldn't resist. Was it wise to address Kabir in Russian? Definitely. Was I glad that none of the officers from the PRT had accompanied me to this meeting? Yes. But best of all, my self-confidence had soared to new heights after I had faced down Kabir in front of his men.

Rahim followed me without speaking to the parking lot, where Fuzzy and Jenkins were sitting in the Beast with the engine on and the heat blasting. They were laughing hysterically at a bootleg copy of *School of Rock*, which they were watching on Jenkins's battery-operated DVD player. The other two soldiers had driven over to the PRT's Andkhoy safe house to wait for us.

As we climbed into the Beast, Rahim finally spoke. "Angela, I didn't know you spoke Russian." He didn't mention the brooch.

"Rahim, there are many things about me that you don't know, and I am sure there's still a lot about you that I don't know," I replied with a smile that he immediately returned. Standing up to Kabir, and doing it in Russian, had impressed him far more than I'd imagined.

We followed Kabir's convoy of six black Mercedes with dark-tinted windows into the soccer field downtown, where the excited crowd parted for the general like the Red Sea for Moses. The motorcade stopped ten yards from the center of the field, and Kabir climbed out with his entourage in tow.

Fuzzy started to follow me when Rahim and I began to wade in behind the general, who was being welcomed loudly by his cheering followers.

"I think it would be better if you stay back here with the vehicle, Fuzzy," I said to my grim bodyguard. "I'm afraid your uniform and loaded weapon may not be appreciated by this crowd."

"Angela, I'm supposed to provide you with close protection at all times."

"I know that. But look at the women in this crowd."

The few adult females who were standing with their husbands, all political supporters of General Kabir, were bundled against the cold in long dark coats and head scarves. The cultural influences of the former Soviet Republics just across the northern border had filtered down to some of the more educated ethnic Uzbek women in this province, where a small but growing number of them no longer wore the all-enveloping burka at public gatherings.

"With Rahim at my side and my hair wrapped in this black scarf, I'm going to blend right in," I argued.

"All right, Angela, but I don't like it," muttered Fuzzy as he turned and headed slowly back to the Beast.

The speeches by provincial and local officials had already begun, with each man heaping ever-greater praise on Kabir's leadership. His dark, narrow face beamed with pride and the rows of medals on his ancient olive drab uniform jangled noisily as he approached the podium.

I had been invited at the last minute by Abdul to stand next to the general during the ceremony, but I had declined, arguing that it would not be appropriate for me to usurp the place of one of Kabir's loyal supporters. In truth, I didn't want to be seen in public standing next to a man whom many in the international community considered to be a war criminal.

Abdul told me that the general would be very disappointed if I didn't accept, but I stood my ground and positioned myself next to Rahim behind several rows of the party faithful, who were anxiously waiting for the general to begin his speech. The sky was clear, but a cold wind blew across the soccer field where the general's audience huddled together and tried to stay warm.

Surrounded by the attentive crowd wrapped in their dark coats and blankets, my attention was suddenly drawn to a small girl in a red cloak near the stage. She was tugging on her father's hand and raising her arms. She wanted him to pick her up, but he was ignoring her pleas. She had the blond hair that occurred from time to time in this part of the country and with her apple cheeks and tight curls she reminded me of a young Shirley Temple. She caught me looking at her and offered me a wide smile before darting into the crowd.

While the general was taking his position with the other dignitaries, Abdul whispered something into his ear and pointed in my direction. I presumed that he was conveying my refusal to join them on the stage. As soon as Kabir glanced my way with an angry scowl on his face, I saw his eyes grow suddenly wide. A voice in the crowd shouted, *"Allahu Akbar."* Then came the explosion and the smoke and the screaming.

The blast sent shock waves but little shrapnel into the crowd. Rahim threw me to the ground and covered my body with his. I could feel him bracing for a second explosion, but none came. Images of the black cloud over the embassy in Beirut flashed through my mind, but I forced them out and replaced them with the memory of Mike, crouched at my side in the auditorium, talking me through my panic attack.

Rahim tried to stand up, but people kept tripping over us as they fled the site of the blast. I glanced toward the stage and could see Kabir looking strangely calm as his bodyguards whisked him off the field.

The crowd thinned out rapidly, with only the injured and their families forming small clusters around the smoking and mutilated body of the suicide bomber.

"Angela-*jan*, are you hurt?" cried Rahim as he helped me to my feet. I was shaken but uninjured and surprised at how calm I felt. I was also secretly thrilled to hear Rahim addressing me for the very first time using the familiar term *jan* after my name.

"Angela, Rahim!" I could hear Fuzzy's and Jenkins's voices as they pushed their way toward us through the fleeing survivors. There were no medical personnel on the field.

A few yards in front of me, I saw a red bundle on the ground. With a gasp, I realized it was the coat of the little girl. Her father

was crouched over her, scanning the crowd desperately for someone to help him. Blood was gushing from a gaping wound in
her leg.

Mike's first-aid training kicked in, and I went into autopilot.
Femoral artery, I thought running to her side, pulling off my head
scarf, stuffing it into the wound, and applying pressure. The blood
continued to pulse from her leg. I pressed down hard on the artery
and grabbing the end of the head scarf used it to make a tourniquet
around her thigh.

"Rahim, tell this man we must get his daughter to a hospital
immediately or she will die," I shouted. "Fuzzy, Jenkins, pick her
up. Keep her head lower than her legs, and I'll keep pressure on
the wound.

"Rahim, tell her father to come with us, and tell Jenkins how
to get to the nearest hospital. We're taking this little girl and her
father there now."

Fuzzy, Jenkins, Rahim, and the girl's father reacted quickly
and without further discussion. Jenkins called the soldiers waiting
for us at the safe house and told them to follow us to Sheberghān,
where there was another PRT safe house and a small hospital. We
arrived an hour later at the poorly equipped hospital, where the
little girl and her leg were saved.

By evening, Harry and Major Davies had driven over from
Mazār with a convoy from the Forward Support Base to join me in
meetings with the local police.

Harry was relieved that none of us had been hurt in the blast,
and although I could tell how awful he felt about what had happened, he stood by his decision to allow me to make the trip. Major
Davies felt otherwise. He grabbed me by the elbow as I exited one

of the meetings behind Harry. "Miss Morgan, I admire your quick thinking, but you wouldn't have been in any danger if you had taken my advice in the first place. You're going to get yourself killed."

"Thanks for your concern, Major, but I fully intend to meet with any officials in the northern provinces who are willing to see me. I believe that's why I'm here," I snapped as I pulled out of his grip.

An international criminal investigation team flew in from Kabul to view the mangled body of the unidentified suicide bomber and gather evidence. Only a few bystanders, like the little girl who had been near the bomber when he pulled the cord on his belt of explosives, had been hurt by the blast. Kabir was unharmed, and none of his deputies seriously injured. No one had died except for the bomber. According to the investigators, the explosives, which had eviscerated the bomber but left his shoulders, neck, and head untouched, were unusually compact.

Over the next few days, evidence and witnesses began to vanish mysteriously. The identity and motives of the bomber and any possible accomplices were never uncovered, leading some to conclude that Kabir might have arranged the attack himself to build sympathy and support.

After the incident in Andkhoy, I silently vowed never again to leave the PRT without my tiny golden goddess and her leaping gazelle pinned to my jacket.

The ambassador's trip north was postponed indefinitely.

Surviving the bombing along with my quick action in getting

the little girl to a hospital had profoundly altered my standing with the few officers at the PRT who still questioned my presence, except, of course, for Major Davies.

When our convoy returned to Mazār the next afternoon, Jenkins breathlessly recounted to a very attentive Sergeant Major how I had taken command of the situation. That night, I received a round of applause as I walked through the pub on my way to the treadmill. When I returned an hour later and the chief of staff offered to buy me a beer, I accepted and enjoyed my first drink in the pub.

Early the following morning, when Harry saw me attempting to squeeze my legs under the typing table that served as my desk in the bullpen, he took pity on me and offered to let me use one of the two empty desks in his office. The larger one was reserved for the British diplomat who would soon be arriving, but the spare one for official visitors, he admitted, was rarely occupied.

Much to my regret, these men, who would soon be rotating out with the rest of their regiment, would be replaced by the far more conservative soldiers and officers of Major Davies's Royal Gurkha Rifles. I was especially disappointed that Harry, with whom I had established a great working relationship, would be leaving in three weeks.

At least Fuzzy and Jenkins would still be here. Both were scheduled to complete their military service at the end of the year. They had been asked and had agreed to stay on at the PRT as my designated driver and vehicle commander until I left in December.

Major Davies, who would be around for another six to eight months, seemed indifferent to the fact that I had survived the Andkhoy bombing. I was growing increasingly uncomfortable with

his silent brooding stares during every meeting we attended together.

And then there was Rahim. After the suicide bombing, he and
I had begun to bond in a way that remained unspoken between us,
but which I hoped would survive my coming months of linguistic
deception.

TWENTY

TO: MorganAL

FROM: PlawnerRP

SUBJ: Possible human rights abuse

Ambassador was approached at a reception in Kabul yesterday by the minister of women's affairs. She has received complaints about ill-treatment of females in Mazār central prison. Investigate and submit report with recommendations. Thanks for reporting on your meeting with Kabir and the suicide bomber's attempt on his life. Glad you're okay.

I was equally thankful that I hadn't been injured or killed in that bombing. My coolheaded reaction continued to astound me when I recalled the chaos of the moment. The Estonians' demolitions still caused me to jump, but when faced with an actual crisis, I had been able to draw on reserves of strength I though I would never regain after Beirut. Was it Mike's swift intervention when I panicked during the triage exercise that had improved my ability to handle stress? Would it last?

"Sergeant Major, I'm going to need my vehicle today," I said, walking into his office and waiting politely for him to finish another profanity-laden conversation with his counterpart at the Forward Support Base. "My embassy has asked me to visit the central prison to check on reports of abuse of female prisoners."

He looked harassed as always, but his attitude toward me had done a complete 180 after the suicide bombing in Andkhoy. Where before he was the soul of obstruction, he now bent over backward to accommodate all of my vehicle requests, even at the last minute.

"Angela, I'm terribly sorry to disappoint," he said, "but I don't have a single spare driver. Jenkins and five of his mates are at the Forward Support Base for a day of training. The others are all out on patrol."

"I can drive myself," I replied. "I only need one vehicle to go into town, I know how to use a stick shift, and Rahim knows the way to the prison. All I need is a vehicle commander to ride shotgun."

"Sorry, luv, officers aren't allowed to drive," he said, tilting his closely shaven head to one side and raising an eyebrow.

"Sergeant Major, I'm a civilian and the State Department allows us to drive our own vehicles. My Foreign Service colleague at the German PRT in Kunduz drives himself alone all the time." What I didn't add was that most Afghan men considered it culturally offensive for a woman to drive. It was not against the law for females to have driver's licenses here, as it was in Saudi Arabia, but only a few brave women in Kabul had taken the plunge after the Taliban fell from power. As far as I knew, there were no lady drivers in Mazār-i-Sharīf.

When two of the three phones on his desk began to ring, he

furrowed his brow, reached into a metal locker, and handed me the keys to the Beast. "When do you want to leave?"

"Fourteen hundred hours, if that would be possible."

"For you, Angela, anything," he said with as much of a smile as he would allow anyone to see. "I'll send Fuzzy to protect you from the bad guys."

Rahim had such a look of distress on his face when he saw me in the driver's seat that I had to force myself not to laugh. Even I had to admit that the image of me in the shaking Beast, its keys jangling in the ignition, could not have been the most comforting sight for this young man, who had never seen a woman drive anything in Afghanistan. He climbed warily into the backseat.

"Angela-*jan*, do you know how to drive this?" he asked.

"My question was slightly different, Angela," interrupted Fuzzy, as he wedged his rifle between his leg and the door and began the longest sentence he had ever uttered in my presence.

"Have you ever driven anything as big as this Land Cruiser in a city like Mazār-i-Sharīf, where no one has a license, women do not drive anything, there are no stoplights, there appear to be no rules of the road, and drivers completely ignore the few aging policemen who are attempting to direct traffic?"

"Calm down, both of you. I've driven in New York, Los Angeles, Mexico City, and Moscow. Mazār will be a piece of cake," I said, laughing to conceal my own nagging unease about driving the Beast into town. Adjusting my head scarf, buckling my seat belt, and swallowing hard, I hit the clutch and shifted into reverse. I could see Rahim in the rearview mirror. He was mumbling something to himself—probably prayers.

I did attract a lot of attention as I steered the Beast cautiously into town. "Angela, you're going to cause an accident," Fuzzy said nervously. "Every driver who sees you is doing a double take."

I kept my eyes on the cars, camels, and pedestrians ahead of us, grinding the Beast's gears and white-knuckling the steering wheel. What happened next made up for everything I'd missed.

Traffic had come to a complete standstill when we entered the boulevard that circled the Blue Mosque. Directly in front of us was a rusting yellow taxi with a mottled paint job that resembled the skin of an overripe banana. It was packed with young men. Inside the trunk, its lid propped open with a piece of wood, were two women concealed under white burkas.

Women riding in the trunk of a car was not an unusual sight in Mazār-i-Sharīf. A woman driving a car was unheard of.

The two leaned toward each other, their heads bobbing in animated conversation, their exposed fingers pointing in my direction. When the traffic jam cleared and we began to move, both women lifted their burkas, revealing two young, heavily made-up faces. They smiled at Fuzzy and me and gave us an enthusiastic thumbs-up before dropping their burkas as the taxi sped away.

"Beautiful girls." Fuzzy whistled. "I guess you gave them something to talk about when they get home tonight." There was no comment from Rahim in the backseat.

When we arrived at the prison, Fuzzy reluctantly stayed behind to guard the Beast while Rahim and I crossed a muddy plaza and walked through the heavily guarded front entrance.

"Why are we coming to this prison, Angela-*jan*?" asked Rahim as a guard escorted us through several locked gates.

"My embassy wants me to investigate reports of abuse of female prisoners."

"There are women in here?" Rahim seemed surprised. We had passed several corridors of cells filled with sullen young men, but had not seen a single woman.

The guard pulled open a metal gate and motioned for me to go through. When Rahim tried to follow, the guard shoved him back.

"No men in the women's quarters," he said in a menacing voice.

"But the American woman does not speak our language. I am her interpreter," said Rahim, explaining to me in English the guard's objections, which I had already understood.

"No men," the guard repeated.

"He won't let me go in with you," said Rahim, glaring at the guard in frustration.

I had been dreading just such a moment for weeks and hadn't worked out a solution. I couldn't reveal my knowledge of Dari, but I was loath to leave the prison without completing my assignment—especially when I finally had the opportunity to do something constructive.

I was about to give up and leave with Rahim when a striking young woman poked her head around the corner from inside the female wing of the prison. "Does someone need translation?" she asked in heavily accented English. Her glossy black hair was uncovered and tumbled long and loose over her shoulders.

"Hello, madam. I am Nilofar. May I be of service?" Her liquid brown eyes flicked from me to Rahim, who seemed to have taken root where he stood.

"Do you work here?" I asked after I had introduced myself.

Her eyes continued to jump between my face and Rahim's.

"No, madam," she answered, smiling at me with the straightest, whitest teeth I had ever seen. "I am a law student and I come here to help women accused of marriage crimes."

"Marriage crimes?" I asked.

"All of the women in this prison are here for marriage crimes," she said grimly. "Come with me. You can meet them and their children. They will tell you their stories."

There had been no mention during my many meetings in Kabul about women being thrown into jail for violating their marriage vows. Perhaps that was because all of my briefers had been men.

"There are children in here with them?" I asked.

Rahim stood silently in the doorway, watching the two of us talk as the guard continued to block his way.

"Your son must wait outside," said Nilofar, flashing her radiant smile at Rahim. He blushed and looked away. "I will take you in to see the women, madam."

"He's not my son, he's my interpreter," I told Nilofar. Turning toward Rahim, who now looked like he was in actual physical pain, I added, "I guess you'll have to wait with Fuzzy. I'll be out in an hour."

The poor boy had been struck dumb by the unexpected appearance of this beautiful young woman, but I could see he was also upset that she would be taking his place as my interpreter.

Rahim parted his lips to speak, but pressed them together again as his eyes darkened. He turned and walked away from us without a word.

I followed Nilofar into the cell while an unarmed male guard closed the door behind us and flipped the bolt to seal us in.

Faded blue carpets covered the cement floor. There were twelve women sitting on threadbare cushions that lined the four walls while their children played in the center of the room.

A female warden in a gray uniform was sitting on the cushions, talking with two prisoners who were breastfeeding their babies. Some of the women looked old enough to be grandmothers. It was freezing. A small charcoal brazier in the center of the room provided the only warmth. But even with these deprivations, the women looked clean and well fed.

Nilofar explained to me that the Afghan judicial system, even under the new constitution, did not favor women. Legally, they could marry without parental consent after their sixteenth birthday. In reality, local custom and traditional Sharia law dictated that parents choose the husband, negotiate the bride-price with the groom and his family, and hand their daughter over at any age in a contractual arrangement—a virtual sale euphemistically referred to as a "marriage." Even an educated woman like Nilofar was subject to these customs, she told me with a grim smile.

"I study law at Balkh University in Mazār-i-Sharīf," said Nilofar as she took a seat on an empty cushion and motioned for me to sit next to her. "One of my professors told us about these women. They have no lawyers and no family to help, so I come each week to talk to them and try to find a way to get them out or at least make their life in this prison a little better."

"Do other law students come?" I asked.

"No, they are afraid to anger the women's families. Fathers and husbands can have their daughters and wives convicted and sent to prison if they believe they have shamed the family by refusing to marry or running away. They don't like it when others interfere."

"Aren't you afraid?" I asked.

She looked up at me with her luminous dark eyes. "My grand-mother says if you are afraid to do what is right, you might as well be dead or in jail yourself. She is right, and no, I am not afraid," Nilofar said defiantly.

"I've been told that some of the women in this prison are being mistreated. Do you know if this is true?"

"Madam, these women are not mistreated. The female guards try to help them, but they have little to give." Nilofar told me that although the female wardens were paid only twenty dollars per month, they often used their own money to buy fresh fruits and vegetables for the imprisoned women and children, who rarely had visitors.

"This girl," she said, gesturing toward a young woman in a green head scarf, watching listlessly as her infant son chewed on a worn rubber ball, "has been accused not of killing her husband, but of knowing who the killer is. Her husband was forty-five, and she was fifteen when her parents forced her to marry. The man beat her frequently.

"She thinks her twin brother came to her house in the night and killed her husband, but she wants to protect him from her husband's powerful clan, so she will say nothing. When her baby turns three, her husband's relatives will claim the child because it is a boy. They will take it from her. She has threatened to kill her-self when they do."

A toothless old woman snored loudly as she dozed open-mouthed on her back in a far corner of the room. The long veil covering her head and arms had slipped off, revealing a horribly disfigured face and stumps where there should have been fingers on both of her hands.

"This woman was given by her parents in marriage to a commander in Chahar Bolak when she was thirteen," Nilofar continued, her eyes glistening. "They say she was very beautiful. Her husband was fifty and had three other wives. One of his men brought home stolen jet fuel for the women to cook with. They thought it was kerosene. It exploded in their faces, setting them all on fire. Two of the wives were killed. This woman's two young children, who were standing next to her, also died. She burned her fingers off trying to get them away from the fire. Her husband accused her of murdering his wives and his children. Once she left the hospital, she was brought here. That was three years ago."

"How old is she, Nilofar?" I asked, looking at the woman's raw gums and scarred lips.

"That one is twenty-eight years old," she said.

These women were not being mistreated in prison. The whole system was rigged against them. Without a powerful patron who could bribe the appropriate officials, they had no way out.

"Nilofar-*jan*, I wish to speak with the American woman," said the elderly warden, easing her bulk onto the cushion next to mine. Nilofar hovered nearby to provide the translation, which I did not need.

The warden launched into a plea on behalf of the silent staring women who lined the walls of their prison home. "Madam, I have worked as a guard in the Mazār-i-Sharīf prison for seventeen years. Under the Taliban, most women were only kept here for a few days until they were taken to the soccer field and stoned to death. Anyone could accuse them and there were no courts or trials.

"The women in here have had their trials and they are safe

under this government, but most will never leave or they will be sent to the prison in Kabul. Can't you help them? They are not criminals."

"I'll be reporting what I've learned to my embassy in Kabul and . . ." The words felt empty to me and I struggled to say them with any conviction. A male guard rapped his baton loudly on the bars of the women's cell and put an end to my conversation with the warden. He insisted that we leave immediately.

Nilofar walked with me to the parking lot, where Fuzzy and Rahim were entertaining an excited gaggle of little boys next to the Beast.

As soon as we exited the prison, she casually draped a loose head scarf over her hair. She was making a silent but courageous statement by refusing to cover herself with the burka, which was still worn in public by almost every woman in Mazār. While her boldness would not result in any formal punishment, as it would have under the Taliban, it nevertheless exposed her to constant harassment and to the simmering anger of traditional Afghan men who still preferred their women hidden from view.

"Now you see the hopeless legal problems these women face," she said as we approached the Beast. "Perhaps you will be able to help them."

"You're a good woman," I said, squeezing her hand. "The embassy will receive my report tomorrow, but I honestly don't think there's much my government will do for them."

The query from the minister of women's affairs had been only about the possible mistreatment of female prisoners, not about the much broader issue of basic rights for Afghan women or jail cells filled with marriage "criminals." My report that there was no evidence of abuse would close the case as far as Plawner and the minister were concerned. I looked down with a sense of shame and regret at this determined young woman, who continuously put herself in harm's way when all I had to do was type out another report and hit the SEND button.

Fuzzy had climbed into the passenger seat of the Beast and was tapping on his watch to remind me of the time. Rahim remained standing outside, his hand on the open car door, trying not to stare at Nilofar.

"Do you need a ride home?" I asked Nilofar.

Her somber mood vanished as she glanced up at Rahim with a mischievous smile. "I was going to take a taxi, but if the young man would not mind to drop me at the university, I am most grateful." Rahim, whom she thought would be driving us back to the PRT, looked away in embarrassment.

"Hop in and let's go," I said, climbing into the driver's seat. Fuzzy wedged his rifle below the window so it was out of sight, and Rahim, his eyes downcast, held the rear door open for Nilofar.

"You are driving?" she asked me with a puzzled laugh. "Is this allowed?"

Rahim looked at Nilofar and said in Dari, "With Angela-*jan*, everything is allowed."

TWENTY-ONE

March 7, 2005

"This will sadly be my last meeting with all of you," said Harry to those of us who had taken our assigned seats for his weekly five P.M. staff meeting in the officers' mess. Sergeant Major had decided in late February to print out our names and titles on pieces of construction paper and place them on the chairs he thought we should occupy.

There were always visitors and new arrivals and never enough chairs. He wanted to ensure that the regulars were able to sit down quickly and avoid the endless dance of musical chairs that delayed the start of every meeting. His plan had met with some resistance, but it worked.

My designated location was between the ops officer and the quartermaster. With our new seat assignments, I found myself at every meeting directly across the room from Major Davies, whose staring made me painfully self-conscious. He radiated disapproval at what I'm sure he felt were my brash American ways, and he continued to avoid my presence outside the confines of these formal meetings.

"My replacement, Colonel Robert Jameson, will be arriving

with our new Foreign Office diplomat, Richard Carrington, next Monday," said Harry. "We, unfortunately, won't have a formal handover, but I'm sure you'll make them both welcome," he added, before extending his usual request that each of the "regulars" spend a few minutes telling everyone what they were working on. It was going to be a long meeting. I raised my eyes and met the major's expressionless gaze.

The meeting dragged on until supper. I ate quickly with Fuzzy and Jenkins in the soldiers' dining hall, which still felt more welcoming to me than the officers' mess, and rushed back to Harry's office to lock up a sensitive report I'd left on my desk. He was packing for his morning departure.

"Angela, please feel free to keep using the extra desk in my office," he said as he sorted through his personal effects. "I'm certain Carrington and Colonel Jameson won't mind."

Harry stopped digging through his file cabinet and looked up. "Angela, it's been a real pleasure working with you. Brief—but I hope as useful for you as it has been for me. I heard from one of the officers about Trumbull's refusal to take you on his farewell calls with the local officials. I'm sure things will be better with the new lot now that you're a bit of an 'old-timer.'"

"Harry, I've been here less than three months."

"Yes, but that's longer than either of the two newcomers," he replied. "None of us spends very long here. With more than two months under your belt, you may now officially be considered an expert."

"Hardly." I laughed. His words touched me. I was going to miss this man.

"One request before I go?" he added as he removed the photo of his wife and children from the wall behind his desk and stuffed it carefully into his briefcase. "I agreed to represent the PRT at a provincial council meeting in Aybak the day after tomorrow. Since I won't be here, I was wondering if you would be able to attend in my place.

"It's a three-hour drive one way, but the canyon road through the mountains is spectacular and it will give you a chance to meet the governor of Samangan Province. You should take an extra hour after the meeting to visit the Buddhist caves outside town. They are remarkable. Our guards at the safe house will be able to tell you how to get there."

Early Wednesday morning, our two-vehicle convoy quickly covered the first thirty miles to Aybak on the newest paved section of the ring road that cut a dark gash through the pale salt flats east of Mazār. The only time we had to slow down was for the ragged processions of children crossing the road near a sprawling displaced persons camp where the road forked north to the Amu Darya River.

This camp had sprung up after the fall of the Taliban. Hundreds of returning families lived here under flapping sheets of blue plastic that did little to protect them from the icy winds gusting off the Hindu Kush. Little girls and boys who could not have been more than five years old dodged trucks and buses as they sprinted across the highway to sort through piles of trash near a cluster of shipping containers that had been turned into roadside market

stalls. The children were beginning their daily trek into the foothills in search of brush for their mothers' cooking fires, but since
garbage could also be burned, they collected that as well.

"Rahim, is there nothing else for these families to cook with?"
I asked as Jenkins braked for another group of children dragging
a recalcitrant donkey across the road.

"No, Angela," he said. "Look around. There is nothing but
desert brush and soon that will be gone, too. These refugees have
very few animals, so there isn't enough dung for them to burn and
none of them can afford bottled gas," Rahim added.

Rahim, Fuzzy, and I waved at two little boys who had stopped
by the side of the road to watch us pass. Barefoot and dressed in
rags, they smiled and lifted their tiny clenched fists in the univer-
sal thumbs-up gesture of greeting that thousands of Afghan children had learned from western soldiers.

As we left the children behind, I could see in the distance a line
of abandoned electric transmission towers. These were the giant
rusting sentinels Stefan had described—the skeletal remnants of
Mother Russia's failed attempt to pacify and electrify this uncon-
querable land.

Ahead of us, the morning sun lifted above a cloudbank sitting
low on the horizon and temporarily blinded all eastbound drivers.
Jenkins donned his sunglasses, but removed them five minutes
later, when our convoy turned south into a shaded, marbled canyon that cut through the foothills of the Hindu Kush.

The contrast between the blazing desert landscape and the alpine scenery inside this canyon was stark. The sides of the road
were dotted with thick clusters of rockroses and trumpet flowers,

which grew in profusion among the boulders and even over the treads of abandoned Russian tanks. Long lines of camels, loaded with boxes and bags of cargo, padded with studied indifference through patches of melting snow.

An hour later, Jenkins dropped Rahim and me at the entrance to the governor's faded gray headquarters on a litter-strewn plaza at the center of this small provincial capital. He and Fuzzy waited in the Beast just across the street, while the follow car went on to the safe house.

Rahim and I entered the dimly lit hall and took our seats just as the meeting began. The large room held the standard arrangement of wooden chairs tightly packed around the walls.

The issues raised by the aging governor to the assembled NGO representatives were seemingly hopeless and of almost Biblical proportions—too few wells to provide water for the thousands of refugees who were returning from Pakistan and Iran, a tuberculosis outbreak in one village, a plague of locusts in a nearby valley, no medical care available for the injured from last week's earthquake.

The meeting had dragged on for two and a half hours when I saw the door crack open. Fuzzy, a worried look on his face, poked his head in and scanned the room to make sure Rahim and I were still alive. Once we had made silent eye contact, he pulled the door shut.

After the meeting, we headed up to see the Buddhist caves carved out of a hillside just above town. Rahim knew the way, but he had no idea who had fashioned the caves out of solid limestone many centuries ago. As our two vehicles bumped up a winding dirt road to the site, I could see an unmarked Range Rover idling next to an enormous rock dome. An Afghan driver sat in the vehicle smoking a cigarette.

"Looks like some tourists beat us up here," observed Jenkins. "Probably some of the expats who were at your meeting with the governor."

We parked and headed toward the massive six-meter sphere that had been hewn from a solid block of yellow limestone. A small hut was carved in stone at the top of the polished dome. As three European men emerged from the shaded entrance of the structure, one began waving in my direction.

"Angela, what a delightful coincidence," he shouted in a thick French accent, cupping his hands around his mouth. It was Jean-François Mongibeaux, the archaeologist I'd met at Plawner's dinner in Kabul.

"We meet again, Jeef," I shouted back while stepping gingerly onto the wooden walkway that led over a deep chasm to the top of the dome where Jeef stood with his companions.

"We came to Aybak this morning for a provincial council meeting. The PRT commander said we shouldn't leave without a visit to the Buddhist caves," I said after he introduced me to his colleagues.

"I have passed by here many times over the past thirty years, but my colleagues visiting from Paris wanted to have a look since we were so close," Jeef explained, nodding at the other men.

"We drove over the Salang Pass yesterday and spent last night at a guesthouse in Pul-i-Kumri. We're on our way to see how my dig in Balkh has survived the winter. I had actually planned to stop by the PRT to see if you were in. But here you are!" He laughed, clapping his hands together.

Rahim was watching this reunion with great interest. Here was the archaeologist I had been telling him about. He was clearly bursting with questions, but too shy to be the first to speak.

"So, young man," said Jeef, stepping forward to shake Rahim's hand, "you probably know far more about this remarkable site than I do."

Rahim shook his head and smiled at the gregarious white-haired Frenchman. "Sadly, sir, like many of my countrymen I know very little about Takht-i-Rustam or any of the historic locations in northern Afghanistan. Angela has told me about you and your work in Balkh. I was hoping you would be able to teach me something about my country's ancient history."

"Then let me be your tour guide today," said Jeef, setting off at a brisk clip toward the caves. In a rapid-fire mix of English—and French for the benefit of his colleagues from Paris—he explained that Buddhist monks had carved the earliest of these caves into the hills of Samangan Province almost two thousand years ago.

"Much of the story behind these caves is still pure conjecture," added Jeef as we followed him through a small nondescript opening in the side of the barren hill and entered a vast hand-sculpted complex of cool, naturally lit corridors, market stalls, and domed temples.

"You know, of course, Rahim, that your country was a major crossroads of ancient eastern and western cultures for centuries. Are you also aware of the fact that your ancestors prayed to Buddha for more than a thousand years under the Kushan Empire and then under the Persians?"

"I have heard that tale before, and everyone knows about the great Buddha statues of Bamiyan that the Taliban destroyed, but they didn't teach us about this in school," he replied.

"Why do you think that in the Dari language, 'God be with you' translates as *Khuda hafiz* instead of *Allah hafiz*?" asked Jeef with a twinkle in his eye.

"Perhaps you are right, Professor." Rahim laughed. "Even after thirteen hundred years as an Islamic people, we may still be hoping for the blessings of the great Buddha."

Jeef led us into the first of two enormous domed temples with natural skylights carved into the smooth curved walls. Dusty beams of sunlight illuminated the elaborate but fading lotus leaf murals at the apex of the thirty-foot ceiling.

The voices of our little group of soldiers and archaeologists echoed along the wide corridors as we scattered to explore the caves and niches that burrowed deep into the mountain. Rahim and I stayed close to Jeef, fascinated by his stories.

"The first modern explorers to find these long-abandoned caves were the British officers Maitland and Talbot, who wrote about their discovery in 1886. They claimed that these caves were grander than any they had found surrounding the colossal Buddha statues at Bamiyan.

"It's shameful what the Taliban did to those irreplaceable statues," Jeef said with bitterness in his voice.

"Yes," agreed Rahim as he ran his fingers over the dusty stone niches where jeweled statues of Buddha had once stood.

"We have no idea why or when these caves were abandoned

and we can only speculate about what they looked like in their heyday." Jeef gazed up at the smoke damaged lotus frescoes. "We're going to lose it all if it's not restored, but," he added, "that takes money . . ."

When we had finished our tour, Jeef led us out of the caves and into the blinding afternoon sunlight. "Did you know, Rahim, that the foothills of Samangan Province used to be covered with pistachio groves?" he asked as he pointed toward the barren hills to the south and east of Takht-i-Rustam.

"Yes, Professor," Rahim replied. "My father told me that when he was a boy, northern Afghanistan was famous for these orchards. I know there is one pistachio tree left in Mazār-i-Sharīf. It is in the courtyard of the mosque across the street from our PRT."

I had seen this tree from my bedroom window, although until now I hadn't been aware of its significance. The first buds of spring had only this week begun to cover its gnarled branches.

Jeef lowered his head in thought and closed his eyes briefly, but his sparkle returned and he motioned to Rahim.

"Come, my boy, let's show my friends the monks' sleeping quarters and their waterworks at the foot of the dome," he said, clapping his hand on Rahim's shoulder and marching him back up the hill to the base of the polished limestone stupa. The rest of us trailed behind them, amused at the instant bond that had formed between the elderly Frenchman and his eager Afghan pupil.

Late that afternoon, when our convoy exited the shaded confines of the canyon, we were again blinded by the sun, which had made its daily transit across the sky and was now a circle of molten gold plunging into the western desert.

Jenkins and Fuzzy donned sunglasses and lowered their visors, while Rahim and I looked out our windows or dozed. The freshly poured asphalt on the Mazār–Kabul road allowed Jenkins to maintain a good clip until we reached the shipping-container shopping mall where the road forked north to the Amu Darya.

Jenkins slowed the Beast to allow another ragged parade of children, balancing bundles of brush and cardboard on their heads, to cross the road.

A slender whirlwind danced toward us across the desert, flinging everything in its path high into the air and raining bits of roadside trash onto the hood of the Beast.

"Roll up your windows!" shouted Jenkins as he pulled over, temporarily blinded by the blowing sand. Small cardboard boxes and juice containers with torn foil liners glinted in the sunlight and bounced across the windshield, landing in the dirt near the plodding children.

At that moment, for reasons I will never understand, the answer to a question I had not even asked popped into my head. I gasped in surprise at my sudden epiphany.

"Of course," I shouted, staring out the window at the receding dust storm.

Rahim, Fuzzy, and Jenkins all turned and stared at me with worried looks on their faces.

"You all right, Angela?" asked Jenkins.

"I'm fine. I'm just thinking," I replied. It had not occurred to me until now that there was plenty of fuel for cooking in Afghanistan, an endless, free supply. It was the sun—beating down on these poor kids and their families almost every day of the year!

Memories flooded back of a long ago summer in New Mexico when I had earned a Girl Scout cooking badge. Our troop leader suggested that I build a primitive solar oven with a cardboard box and aluminum foil. I had never thought about solar ovens again—until now.

"Rahim," I said as he stared out the window at the children on his side of the road. "Does anyone in this country use solar ovens?"

"What is that, Angela-*jan*?" he replied, looking puzzled at my question.

"It's an insulated box painted black inside with a piece of glass on top and aluminum foil reflectors. It cooks food with sunshine."

"How can you cook food with the sun, Angela?" asked Jenkins, who could never resist joining a conversation. "Is that like the panels people are putting on their roofs to make electricity?"

"No, those are photovoltaic cells. Solar ovens are much simpler than that, and they're really cheap. They turn plain old sunlight into heat and trap it inside a box," I replied. "I made one years ago, but I think I'll do a little research tonight. If I can find some plans on the Internet, maybe I'll build one and show you boys how it works."

TWENTY-TWO

March 12, 2005

Three days after the arrival of Colonel Robert Jameson, the PRT's new commanding officer, and Richard Carrington, the young diplomat who would represent the British Foreign Office, I was politely asked by the colonel to vacate the desk Harry had allowed me to use in his office. I packed my things immediately, deeply embarrassed at this unexpected request. Richard watched impassively from his desk next to the colonel's as I carried my boxes out of their office and returned to the bullpen. My NATO colleagues, who had been using my typing table for storage, quickly cleared it off and welcomed me back without comment. The colonel's door was now frequently shut.

Before Richard's arrival, I'd been hoping he would become an ally as Harry had. I was sorely disappointed. Since his first day at the PRT, he had through word and gesture marked his territory, making it clear to the colonel, the other officers, and especially to me that he and only he would provide political guidance at this PRT. He had even taken me aside to inform me I was no longer welcome at senior staff meetings. Much to my disappointment, Colonel Jameson, who was focused completely on his military mission and the welfare of his soldiers, had decided as soon as he arrived to leave all things political to Richard.

And then there was Major Davies. Now that my security clearance had come through, I had access to everything coming out of his shop. As unpleasant as he seemed to be, I had to admit that his detailed reports were reason enough to be grateful he had arrived. The tangled power relationships that existed among the warlords, mullahs, and government officials in the five provinces we covered were beginning to make sense, and I was at last feeling confident enough to spread the word among the MOT commanders that I was interested in going on an overnight patrol.

My first invitation came from the Romanian MOT. It was for a three-day trek into the northern desert that was exhausting and bone-chilling, but endlessly fascinating. The illiterate, poorly armed, and often shoeless border policemen we met in remote outposts along the Amu Darya River were underequipped, underpaid, and surprisingly candid about their allegiance to the warlords who controlled their districts. At the end of each day of meetings, the Romanians, their interpreter, and I would drive deep into the desert, pitch our tents in the lee of a massive sand dune, build a huge bonfire, and cook pots of spicy chicken goulash. I hoped this patrol would be the first of many during my year in Mazār.

TWENTY-THREE

March 16, 2005

"I'm going to need a burka, Rahim," I said when he stopped on his way to breakfast to watch me pruning the rosebushes after an early morning Estonian demolition. Rahim, who still put on his best gruff face when the other terps saw us together, had begun to seek out my company.

"Angela-*jan*, why do you need a burka?" he asked with a puzzled half-smile. "No one expects an American woman to cover herself like Afghan women do. Why, even that law student Nilofar does not wear a burka when she goes out in the street."

He said her name with such feigned disinterest I almost laughed. Although he would never ask a direct question about Nilofar, Rahim managed to work her name into our conversations whenever he could.

She seemed equally interested in him. A few days after our encounter at the prison, Nilofar called to invite me to dinner at her family's home in Mazār. "My father said you can bring your cousin along, and he can eat with the men," she added in a loud voice.

"Nilofar, Rahim is neither my son nor my cousin. He's my interpreter," I said, laughing. "You know that."

"Yes, Angela-*jan*," she said, lowering her voice to a whisper, "but the only way my father would allow him to enter our house is if he thinks you are a relative. I told him you are Rahim's distant cousin from America and that you can't travel in the evening without him. After my family gets to know him, we can sort these details out as a mistranslation on my part."

"Fine with me," I said, wondering what I was getting myself into.

Our dinner conversation had been awkward but the food was wonderful. Nilofar's mother had prepared steaming trays of *qabele palau*, the lamb, rice, pistachio, and raisin dish that seemed to be the primary fare served at all special occasions in northern Afghanistan.

Rahim and I ate in separate but adjoining dining rooms where the men and women could see each other but not speak. I had warned him in advance about Nilofar's little white lie concerning our relationship. It pleased him immensely.

Lounging with Nilofar, her mother, and sisters on the overstuffed cushions surrounding the trays of food in the women's dining room, I allowed her to control the conversation since she had to translate everything we said to one another.

In the other room, Rahim limited his discussion with Nilofar's father and brothers to sports. We were thus both spared the need to elaborate on her innocent deception. Nilofar's father, who like her mother was Hazara, did not seem bothered that Rahim was Tajik, but then again, he didn't realize he was talking to a potential suitor for his daughter's hand.

"The reason I need a burka, Rahim, is so I can have some privacy when I go on patrol with the soldiers," I said, adjusting my bloodstained woolen gloves that were providing little protection against the thorny rosebushes. "Since I survived the three-day trip with the Romanians, the other MOTs have started inviting me to join their patrols."

"I know that, Angela-*jan,* but do the soldiers expect you to wear a burka?" he asked, still confused by my response.

"No, of course not," I said. "But when the soldiers stop out in the desert or on a treeless mountain pass to, well. . . . to relieve themselves next to their vehicles, there is no place I can go where they or a passing Afghan shepherd won't see me. The burka will make me virtually invisible to Afghan men, and it will save me the trouble of having to walk so far away from the soldiers and our vehicles."

"So you want a burka to use as a portable loo?" asked Rahim, trying to suppress a grin.

"Correct," I replied.

That afternoon, with Jenkins driving the Beast, Rahim and me in the backseat, and Fuzzy in the passenger seat, grinding his teeth and kneading the barrel of his assault rifle, we were off to the crowded market stalls of Mazār-i-Sharīf. This was a route we had taken dozens of times before, so Fuzzy's hypervigilance didn't make sense to me.

"Fuzzy, you seem upset. Is everything okay?"

He stared straight ahead, while Jenkins jumped in with a response. "Fuz just got word this morning that one of his mates was killed in an ambush in Iraq. They were childhood friends."

I breathed in sharply. It was so easy for me to forget how young these guys were.

"I'm sorry," I said, leaning forward and placing my hand on Fuzzy's shoulder.

"Thanks, Angela."

The heating/air-conditioning system in the Beast had finally given out and been declared unfixable by the camp mechanic. Now that the weather was starting to warm up, we always drove with the windows rolled down. This made us a tempting target for young men selling phone cards, who would rush our vehicle every time Jenkins had to slow down for pedestrian and animal traffic.

They were aggressive salesmen, but always friendly as they shoved their fistfuls of cards through our windows. Fuzzy grew increasingly agitated with each new onslaught of vendors that surrounded the Beast. Jenkins sensed his concern and tried to avoid slowing down, but it was impossible.

When we pulled up to the market entrance, Fuzzy was clearly agitated. He climbed out of the Beast with his assault rifle, and for the first time ever, insisted on accompanying me.

I wanted to humor him, but I knew his presence would attract unwanted attention inside the covered market. "Fuzzy, I don't think it's such a good idea for you to go in there with us. Your uniform, red hair, and loaded weapon are going to really stand out," I said, hoping he would agree and wait in the Beast with Jenkins.

Fuzzy stared down at me, clenching his jaw and squeezing the stock of his rifle. "Listen, Angela, I'm the vehicle commander, and I'm also supposed to provide you with close protection whenever we leave the PRT. I should never have let you go alone into that crowd when the suicide bomber blew himself up in Andkhoy," he said, his voice catching.

"We were just damned fortunate that nothing happened to you or Rahim. I was also bloody lucky that Sergeant Major agreed with your decision that day to leave me behind in the vehicle. But goddamn it, Angela, this is not a political rally, and I am under strict orders never to let you go off alone again. Is that understood?"

"Okay," I said, submitting reluctantly to his demand.

The three of us left Jenkins sitting in the Beast in front of the Blue Mosque as we vanished into the milling crowd of turbaned men and covered women.

It bothered me to be buying a burka, knowing what it symbolized in this part of the world. Nilofar put herself at risk every time she left her house without a burka, and I, who enjoyed a level of freedom she would never know, was about to purchase one. But the very thing that made the burka so loathsome—its ability to make a woman invisible to men—made it perfect for my need to provide myself with some privacy when I went out on patrol.

A deeply embarrassed Rahim asked one male shopkeeper after another where we could find a burka shop. None of them seemed to know, and it was forbidden for Rahim to ask the women floating by under their shrouds. Since I had to maintain my sham ignorance of Dari, I couldn't ask them, either. Rahim's face reddened as the amused vendors listened to his questions and suggested possible locations for the burka store.

"This way, Angela-*jan*," Rahim ordered as the three of us waded deeper into the covered bazaar. I followed him around another corner and through a narrow door into a shop that re-sembled a giant blue pillow with burkas covering all four walls. Fuzzy remained just outside and was quickly surrounded by a gaggle of curious young boys.

"And why does the English lady want a burka?" asked the owner.

Rahim melting with shame responded without bothering to translate the question for me. "She is American, not English, and she wants a burka because she thinks they are beautiful. She would like to take one back to her country to show her family."

"A souvenir, of course," said the smiling merchant as he eye-balled my height and removed a burka from the rack on the wall. "This might be a little short, but it should do. Would she like to try it on?"

"*Ney, ney,*" Rahim snapped. "How much is it?"

"Fifteen hundred Afghanis," said the shopkeeper with a straight face. Although the thirty dollars that translated to was reasonable from my perspective, I remained silent and poker-faced while Rahim began the obligatory bargaining.

"Are you trying to rob her?" Rahim shouted, waving his arms in the air. "The woman will pay you five hundred Afghanis for this inferior piece of workmanship."

"Did you know, my young friend, that every one of the hun-dreds of pleats in this cloth is pressed by hand?" The shop owner lifted the hem of the burka to reveal its workmanship. "Do you think I can simply give it away for what I paid for it?"

Their verbal jousting continued for several more minutes until Rahim turned to me. "The man wants to be paid in U.S. currency, Angela-*jan*. Give him ten dollars and let's go."

"We need to make a few more stops before we go back to the PRT," I announced as we left the burka shop. Rahim and Fuzzy did not reply, but their muffled sighs made it clear they wanted this shopping trip to be over.

"I've printed out the plans for several solar ovens from a site I found on the Internet. I need supplies to build them so I can test them on the roof," I informed my unhappy escorts.

"The kitchen staff at the PRT gave me a roll of aluminum foil, which they don't sell in Mazār, but I need a few cooking pots, a can of black paint, a few sheets of glass, and some glue."

It took another hour to find, bargain for, and purchase my supplies, but Rahim and Fuzzy humored me and insisted on carrying my packages back to the Beast.

"Fuzzy, this is the first shopping trip I've ever taken with an armed guard," I said as he took another plastic bag from my hand.

"The first of many for both of us, I'm sure, Angela," he replied, trying but failing to suppress a smile.

TWENTY-FOUR

March 17, 2005

While I never achieved the level of rapport with Colonel Jameson that Harry and I had so quickly developed, I did appreciate Jameson's objectivity and his sense of fairness. Although upon his arrival, he had made no overt efforts to ensure that I was included in his staff meetings, he never objected to my presence, and as soon as he learned of Carrington's machinations to have me barred from command team discussions, he had leaped to my defense. Even Major Davies, who had by no means welcomed me, spoke up on my behalf when Carrington tried to keep me from attending the senior staff's strategy sessions.

Despite this slight improvement in my relationship with the PRT's new crop of senior military officers, I still felt marginalized and was shocked when at the end of a weekly all-hands meeting the colonel announced that the major and I would be representing the PRT at the Afghan Nauroz or New Year's Day celebration at the Blue Mosque.

My pen slipped from my fingers and rolled under my chair at the colonel's words. As I bent down to pick it up, I sneaked a glimpse at Major Davies, whose eyes had widened in surprise.

Richard glared at me but said nothing. He would be at a meeting in Kabul with the colonel over the New Year's holidays. Had they been in Mazār, they would have represented the PRT at this major event.

Nauroz was the annual celebration of the spring equinox, which dated back to pre-Islamic times and derived from the Persian zodiac calendar. March 21, the first day of Aries, was also the beginning of the Afghan New Year. People came to Mazār from all over the country to witness the annual raising of the *janda,* an enormous flag-decked and beribboned pole, which would stand for forty days in front of the Blue Mosque. Many believed it had curative powers if touched.

"I believe that after the ceremony you will both be expected to join the governor and his guests in the viewing stands at the *buz-kashi* field for the final match of the season," the colonel added with a suppressed smile.

He turned to the major, who was still digesting this unwelcome news. "Mark, I'm counting on you to make sure that Angela does not gallop off on one of their horses again," he said to a burst of laughter and applause, which did not include the stony-faced Major Davies.

The night before the celebration at the Blue Mosque, I decided to skip my evening workout and finish assembling one of the cardboard solar ovens I'd been building. I planned to test this one and several others on the roof of the PRT to determine which design would heat water most efficiently.

After dinner, I headed up to the atrium to get to work. This large, rarely used, and empty room with a balcony overlooking the distant Hindu Kush offered a perfect space for me to spread out my materials. The evening was mild, and I propped the balcony doors open. Shoeless and dressed in jeans and a T-shirt, I knelt on the cool concrete floor surrounded by cardboard boxes, a can of paint, pots of glue, scissors, marking pens, a ruler, and rolls of aluminum foil. As I worked, I had an English-language tape of Rumi's poetry playing in the background.

The sound of footsteps in the stairwell interrupted my reverie as the uniformed figure of Major Mark Davies appeared in the doorway. I hit the STOP button on the cassette player.

"Excuse me for the interruption, Miss Morgan," he said, clearing his throat.

Pushing back my increasingly unruly hair, and looking into those cobalt blue eyes, I swallowed hard and felt my pulse begin to rise. I was in too good a mood to deal with this man, who still insisted on calling me Miss Morgan.

"Mark, we attend meetings together almost every day and, although we've yet to engage in an extended conversation, we have known each other now for almost three months. I very much appreciate the fact that you spoke up on my behalf when Richard tried to stop me from attending your meetings, and I think it's time you start calling me by my first name."

"Of course, you're absolutely right," he said, stiffening in the doorway.

"The reason I'm interrupting your—whatever it is you're doing, Angela, is to inform you that the governor's office just called. We've been asked to arrive at the Blue Mosque tomorrow morning by seven A.M. We'll have to leave the PRT by six fifteen sharp."

He turned to leave, then spun around and faced me again. "Are you certain you want to do this?"

"I can't wait, Mark."

When he continued to stare at me without speaking, I decided to provide him with a subtle opening to offer me some assistance. "I suppose I'd better start clearing up this mess, then."

He ignored my unspoken request for help. "I want to assure you, Angela, that I for one am not looking forward to our little adventure tomorrow."

"Is that so? I think it's a unique opportunity."

"May I ask what you're doing?" He stepped into the atrium and let the screen door swing shut behind him. "It looks like you're constructing some sort of junior school science project."

I looked up at him without replying, annoyed at his tone of voice. Setting my scissors on the floor, I stood up and brushed bits of cardboard from my jeans. He was at least half a foot taller than the five feet six inches I stood in my bare feet.

"I'm building solar ovens," I said without further elaboration.

"And what, may I ask, is a solar oven?" he replied, his brow furrowing slightly.

"It's an insulated box painted black inside, topped with a sheet of glass and an aluminum foil reflector. It cooks food with sunshine."

"And why are you building these—solar ovens? Don't you like the way our cooks prepare food at the PRT?" He smiled, but I refused to give him the satisfaction of laughing at his little joke.

"I love PRT food, Mark, but I'm not building these for myself. I'm building them because of what I've seen in the short time I've been traveling around northern Afghanistan. If you left that locked vault of yours in the basement once in a while, you'd know what I'm talking about."

His head tilted slightly and his eyes narrowed. "If you are implying that I don't know what's happening in northern Afghanistan, you are flat wrong, Angela. With the masses of information we're collecting, my staff and I probably know more than anyone else about what's going on up here. Except for you, of course."

If he was trying to provoke me, it was working. Leaning forward with my hands on my hips and rising up on my toes, I shot back, "Have you and your staff noticed that the Taliban, the opium traffickers, and the warlords aren't the only threat in this region?"

"Are you saying that we've missed something?"

"I am." I was straining to keep my voice steady. "You might have observed that the five provinces our soldiers patrol are completely barren in places where there used to be orchards and forests. None of the MOT commanders mention this in their reports. If you got out once in a while, you'd see young children, who should be in school, leaving their villages every day to harvest and carry home enormous bundles of brush for their mothers to burn in smoky cooking fires. They're stripping the land of its remaining groundcover, causing massive erosion around the irrigation ditches and destroying productive farmland."

"And what does that have to do with the security of this region?" he asked, his arms folded defensively over his chest.

"Once erosion depletes their fields, and once their remaining orchards—which took decades to grow—have been chopped down for firewood, farmers start planting opium poppies to replace their lost income. You must agree that the growing threat of an Afghan narco-state is a serious security risk."

"I do," he said, nodding gravely.

"The most urgent energy requirement these people have is for some kind of fuel to generate heat so they can cook their food. Afghanistan's most plentiful source of free fuel is the sun, but these people don't know how to access it. If they don't start using renewable energy soon, their economy will never recover."

Mark looked down at the materials I had spread out on the floor with a new seriousness. "Continue," he said.

"The U.S. government is about to spend tens of millions of dollars on a new power grid for this country, Mark. But before any money is used to provide rural villages with electricity for lights, these people need a sustainable way to cook their food. I'm hoping to show a few Afghans in this part of the country a cheap and simple way to do just that."

"A worthy endeavor, I'm sure," he said. "Saving the country and winning the war on terrorism without firing a shot."

"Diplomats don't carry weapons, Mark."

"Of course," he said training his eyes on mine again. "So your plan is to defeat the Taliban and revive the Afghan economy using cardboard boxes lined with aluminum?"

I couldn't tell if he was being sarcastic or making another lame attempt at humor. "I don't expect to win any wars or even reduce the production of opium poppies, but I may be able to help a few women and children."

"Is this a new task you've been given by your embassy?" he

asked, bending down on one knee to look at a square of foil-lined cardboard I had just finished gluing.

"My embassy has no idea I'm doing this, but I'll tell them if I'm actually able to get one of these things to work and demonstrate it in a few villages," I said, brushing damp strands of hair from my face.

"During almost three months at this PRT, my sole accomplishment has been to write endless reports, e-mail them to my embassy, and wait for responses that never come."

"Angela, I seem to recall that you saved the life of a little girl in Andkhoy last month. Certainly, that counts for something," he said gently.

"Yes, I suppose it does."

I held up another box for his inspection. "I have to do something useful while I'm here."

"And for that I commend you," he said, taking the box to examine it more closely.

"I believe I heard you listening to Rumi when I came in."

A bolt of electricity shot through me at his mention of Rumi.

"Yes, I . . . like Rumi very much," I stammered.

"So do I. My mother used to read his poetry to me when I was a child. May I?" he asked holding his finger over the PLAY button on my cassette recorder.

Defending my project to Mark had been frustrating, but I was heartened by his support and was beginning to relax in his presence. The next poem on the cassette was one that had given me enormous comfort after Tom's death. I must have let it carry me too far away because I suddenly felt Mark's hand on my shoulder and noticed tears running down my cheeks.

"Miss Morgan, Angela, is there . . . ?" He pulled back at the sound of someone running up the stairs.

Wiping my eyes with the back of my hand, I hit the STOP button and faced the door.

It was Jenkins. "Angela, we're leaving at 0615 hours instead of 0700 hours," he announced breathlessly as he bounded onto the landing and flung open the screen door.

"Oh, excuse me, Major, sorry to interrupt, sir," he said, snapping to attention when he saw Mark kneeling at my side and noticed my red eyes.

"Stand easy, Corporal," Mark replied, rising quickly to his feet and stepping back several paces. "I came up just before you to deliver the same message to Miss Morgan."

Mark turned to me and bowed his head slightly. "You'll forgive me for the disturbance," he said, walking quickly around Jenkins and out the door.

"Are you all right, Angela? Did I interrupt something?" Jenkins asked with a worried look on his face.

"Not bloody likely," I said with forced laughter. "Now get in here and help me clean up this mess."

"You know that Fuzzy won't be joining us tomorrow," Jenkins said as we began stacking my supplies in the corner. "Sergeant Major has him working in the supply room for the next few days."

I nodded. I had witnessed Fuzzy's meltdown in the pub Saturday night. "How is he?"

"I've seen him better."

BBC TV had begun running a series of retrospectives in anticipation of the second anniversary of the U.S. invasion of Iraq.

Many of the soldiers at our PRT who had already served in Basra were growing increasingly agitated at the graphic footage being shown on news reports between soccer games.

Fuzzy, who had not recovered from the loss of his mate, went over the edge that evening and tried to drown his sorrow in beer.

"If the bloody politicians had given our boys the right kit, Billy would be alive. If I'd been there . . ." he muttered through clenched teeth, "but no, I'm here in bloody fucking Afghanistan riding around the desert in that fucking rattletrap Beast, assigned to guard a bloody Yank woman who doesn't even want my protection."

I watched silently from the table behind him where I was having a beer with the French and Finnish liaison officers. Every man in the room studiously avoided making eye contact with me.

"What the fuck are we doing here, lads?" Fuzzy asked the soldiers at his table. "No one's shooting at us and there's no one for us to shoot back at.

"Fucking terrorists, we should brass up and bomb the lot of them," he mumbled. "Billy and me was best mates since we was six years old."

Fuzzy grabbed a full can of beer and threw it hard at the television. It smashed against the wall a few inches from the screen, spraying beer and foam over the men seated nearby. Jenkins and another soldier grabbed him under the arms and hoisted him to his feet.

As they led him out of the pub, one of the other sharpshooters clapped his hand on Fuzzy's back and shouted, "We hear you, lad.

We'll be going to Helmand in just a few more months. We'll give it to those choggie terrorist cunts."

All the soldiers in the room, fully aware that Fuzzy's outburst could mean Sergeant Major might close the pub for several days, nevertheless rose to their feet in unison, lifted their beers, pounded the tables with their fists, and shouted, "On to Helmand!"

TWENTY-FIVE

March 21, 2005

At six fifteen the following morning under a cloud-streaked salmon sky, Mark and I climbed silent and unsmiling into the backseat of the colonel's vehicle. The Beast was in the shop for repairs. Rahim was wedged unhappily between us.

Jenkins was assigned as our driver, and the colonel's spit-and-polish vehicle commander had replaced Fuzzy in the passenger seat.

Only the governor's official vehicles and those of his invited guests were permitted to enter the city center that morning, but it still took Jenkins almost an hour to maneuver through the crowds to the designated drop-off point near the mosque.

Thousands of New Year's Day pilgrims arriving on foot had jammed Mazār-i-Sharīf's broad boulevards overnight. Everyone wanted to be as close as possible to the beribboned *janda* and its magical powers when it was hoisted into place in the courtyard of the Blue Mosque.

Leaving the two soldiers with our vehicle, Mark, Rahim, and I followed an Afghan policeman along a narrow path into a fenced area near the mosque where VIP guests were being served steaming glasses of green tea.

Hundreds of nervous Afghan policemen, their arms linked to hold back the frenzied pilgrims, did not hesitate to bring their wooden batons down on the heads of anyone who pushed too hard against their human phalanx.

Just below the VIP viewing stand was the fifty-foot ribbon-draped *janda*. It lay on its side, tied down like Gulliver and looped with the ropes and pulleys that would be used to hoist it into position.

We took our seats, which were still shaded from the heat of the rising sun by the dome of the mosque. Several members of the Mazār consular corps and a few of the governor's ministers, whom I had met previously, recognized me and nodded in my direction, but the din of the crowd made conversation impossible.

A loudspeaker blared prayers and religious music, while an announcer shouted futile orders to the hundreds of thousands of pilgrims to move back. Mark and Rahim sat stiffly in their chairs, staring straight ahead.

There was not a cloud in the sky as the sun rose higher and the shadow of the Blue Mosque slid slowly away under our feet. The heat became instantly oppressive, and the restive crowd pressed ever closer against our heavily guarded enclosure.

"Angela, there's Nilofar," shouted Rahim, jumping to his feet. He grabbed my arm and gestured toward the crowd, where the young law student was trying to support an old woman. They were both about to be trampled by the crowd behind them.

"She is close to the *janda*, and one of the policemen is trying to force her back. She is with her grandmother. May I leave you and the major here to help them? I can get to them through the VIP gate."

I looked at Mark. "You're in charge. May he go?"

Rahim pointed Nilofar out to Mark. She was arguing with a very agitated policeman and was struggling to keep her grip on the old woman.

"Go help her, Rahim," Mark ordered. "Angela and I will be fine. If we're still separated after the ceremony ends, meet us back at the PRT vehicle. Go, man! Quickly!"

I watched anxiously as Rahim fought his way through a sea of blue burkas and turbaned men to reach Nilofar's side. She was surprised to see him, but clearly relieved as he supported the old lady, pacified the policeman, and shielded both women from those behind them who were straining to reach the *janda*.

"Is that young woman a relative of Rahim's?" asked Mark.

"No, she's a law student we met when we visited the women's prison last month. Rahim and I had dinner with her family a few weeks ago."

"Her family?" he said, sounding surprised. "She's an unmarried girl, and they invited him into their home?"

"It wasn't quite like that, Mark," I replied. "Nilofar wanted to see Rahim again, so she invited us both to dinner. The men and women ate separately. She told her parents I was Rahim's American cousin and said I had insisted he come with me."

"And you went along with this?"

"It was perfectly harmless, Mark."

"Angela, in this country, there is little we foreigners do that can be classified as 'perfectly harmless' especially when it involves interfering with the Afghans' strict codes of conduct."

I rolled my eyes at this latest reprimand and turned to watch as Rahim struggled to hold back the crowd that threatened to crush Nilofar and her grandmother.

"Her male relatives may not be very happy to see him getting so close to her," Mark mused as he observed the unfolding drama below.

"I don't think the normal rules apply under these circumstances, Mark."

"Is Rahim involved with this young woman?"

"I have the distinct impression he'd like to be. Unfortunately, she's Hazara and he's Tajik, which would present a big problem for both of them if things actually get serious."

"Let's hope they don't," he said before lapsing again into silence.

Moments after Rahim arrived at Nilofar's side, the governor finished his remarks. At his signal, a group of heavyset men wrapped thick ropes around their hands and began hoisting the *janda* into place. As the top of the pole rose skyward, people showered it with fistfuls of paper money and extended their arms to be the first to receive its magic.

Cannons boomed while a group of men blew their horns and pounded their drums. When the line of policemen nearest the mosque dropped the barriers, the crowd, no longer restrained, surged with a deafening roar toward the *janda*.

Mark and I watched helplessly while people swarmed around the pole. The old woman extended her trembling fingers, rested them for an instant on the *janda*, raised both hands in victory, then collapsed into Rahim's arms.

"Good God, how will he get them out of there?" cried Mark.

Nilofar stumbled, and Rahim, who was already carrying the old lady in one arm, reached out to wrap his other arm around Nilofar's waist to keep her from being trampled.

As I watched Rahim battling to protect the two women, I felt ashamed that one of us had not offered to go with him. There was nothing I could do now. Policemen were shoving us and the rest of the VIPs through a narrow enclosure that had been held open for the governor and his entourage.

Once the governor's black Mercedes sped away, the police melted into the crowd and hundreds more chanting worshipers surrounded us in their desperate quest to get close to the *janda*.

Mark's hand grabbed for mine, but I was already being sucked into the swirling mass of pilgrims. Our fingers laced together briefly before the crowd closed in and forced us apart. I was start-ing to panic as men, who had suddenly noticed the presence of an uncovered woman in their midst, began to press their bodies against mine. Slapping them away and shouting at them in Dari to back off, I forced my way into the midst of a group of women.

Enraged but also frightened by the anonymous men who had violated me with their groping hands, I remained hidden inside the sea of blue burkas, trying to regain my composure. Thirty minutes later when the crowd had thinned and I found my way back to the PRT vehicle, Mark and Rahim were waiting with Jenkins.

"Thank God you're safe, Angela," cried Jenkins.

It was impossible to read the look on Mark's face as he walked up and took my hand in his.

"I didn't mean to abandon you in that crowd, Angela. There was nothing I could do."

"It's all right, Mark. I'm fine," I said, pulling my hand out of his and hoping that neither he, Jenkins, nor Rahim could tell how terrified I'd been just a few minutes before. "How's Nilofar?"

My young Tajik interpreter could barely suppress his elation after the daring rescue, which had put him in direct and forbidden contact with Nilofar.

"Angela-*jan*, her brothers spotted us right after Nilofar's grandmother touched the *janda*," he said breathlessly. "Both her brothers thanked me for protecting the women since they had become separated from them in the crowd, just like you and the major."

He was beaming and wanted to recount every detail of his adventure.

"Nilofar's grandmother is fine and she is so happy. She had to touch the *janda* to cure her arthritis. She has invited the three of us to come to dinner. You, too, Major Davies," said Rahim, making no effort to conceal his delight at the prospect of another evening at Nilofar's home, even if it meant only speaking with her father and brothers.

Still out of breath with excitement, he turned to Mark and added, "Thank you, Major Davies, for allowing me to go and help them."

"Of course, Rahim, you did the right thing," replied Mark with a mixture of disapproval and relief. He glanced at his watch and turned to Jenkins. "Right, Corporal, let's see how quickly you can get us back to the PRT without flattening any camels. They'll be serving lunch for another forty minutes, and I for one have had enough excitement today. Any objections if we skip the afternoon's festivities? I really don't think the governor will notice our absence. Angela, I'd hate to deprive you of another *buzkashi* game, but . . ."

"No problem here, Mark," I said as we climbed into our vehicle.

An hour later, I was sitting in the officers' mess with a plate of spaghetti balanced on my knees, regaling three young officers with tales of our morning's adventure at the Blue Mosque. I looked up and smiled at Mark as he appeared in the doorway holding his lunch tray. He hesitated for a moment, turned away, and walked alone into the soldiers' dining hall.

TWENTY-SIX

April 3, 2005

By early April, the PRT had been without its senior interpreter for more than four months. The ailing professor was still staying with relatives in Kabul and recuperating from a series of surgeries. None of the interpreters knew exactly what was wrong with him or when he was coming back, but they didn't seem to miss him and seldom commented on his absence. Rahim, the most proficient English speaker after the professor, was called on with increasing frequency to accompany Colonel Jameson to his meetings with the Afghans.

Richard had been more absent than present lately due to the British Embassy's constant requests that he come to Kabul to fill in for officers on R&R. He was also traveling on a regular basis to the American PRT in Helmand Province, where preparations were under way for a handover to the British Army in early 2006.

When Richard was not available, Colonel Jameson expected me to join him at all meetings outside the PRT. This meant that Rahim and I were spending even more time together.

I was growing increasingly fond of this passionate, intelligent young man who brimmed with ideas for his country's future.

Since meeting Jeef, Rahim had developed an intense interest in
archaeology. On our lengthy day trips to meet with officials in the
neighboring provinces, he often carried along stacks of books
about his new favorite subject. When I asked him about the piles
of reading material on the backseat of the Beast, all stamped with
the faded crest of Balkh University, he replied with a satisfied
smile, "I am learning about the ancient and amazing history of my
country, Angela-*jan*."

"Where are you getting these books?"

"I have a friend at the university who is checking them out of
the library for me," he replied, pressing his lips together to avoid
providing additional details about his "friend."

"Do I know this 'friend'?" I asked.

"You do, Angela-*jan*, but I can't discuss that with you right
now," he said as his face reddened. He lowered his dark lashes to
hide the excitement his eyes.

"Be careful, Rahim," I warned, "both of you."

The following afternoon, Rahim arrived breathless and grinning
at the door of the bullpen. "Angela-*jan*, Nilofar is outside waiting to see you. She says her grandmother has finally invited us
for dinner to thank me for rescuing them at Nauroz. They want
the major to come as well. Do you think he will?"

"You'll have to ask him yourself, Rahim."

Nilofar had been stopping by the PRT on a fairly regular basis.
She normally had a women's rights issue to discuss with me, but
her arrivals and departures seemed always timed to coincide with
Rahim's duty schedule.

Our little walled compound was the only place in all of Mazār-i-Sharīf where the two of them could safely steal a few minutes alone in the shaded archway that led to the outer gate.

Rahim had pleaded and Mark had reluctantly agreed to accompany us to Nilofar's home for dinner despite his disapproval of the little white lie about Rahim being my distant cousin.

This minor ruse bothered me far less than the much greater deception I was involved in—the embassy's continued insistence that I conceal my Dari language ability. Over the past three months, I had attended meetings with and monitored every one of the interpreters at the PRT. I found their translations accurate even when we were asking warlords and known corrupt officials about opium poppy production. The ailing professor, whom I had yet to meet, was the only one I had not monitored.

I was growing weary of this subterfuge. And because I was worried that when the truth came out it would damage my relationship with Rahim, I could never completely relax in his presence. My requests to the embassy continued to fall on deaf ears.

The only useful side-chatter I was picking up from the Dari-speaking men seated near me at meetings were grumblings of resentment about the continued presence of foreign troops in the northern provinces. Mark, who had been asked by the colonel to join him at meetings attended by Balkh's Pashto-speaking chief of police, was reporting similar comments.

"Angela, may I have a word with you?" Mark had followed me into the hall after a long staff meeting.

"Sure, Mark, what's up?" I attempted as always to lighten the tone of our conversations. His was so annoyingly formal for a person I had seen almost every day for more than three months.

"It's about your observation today that we are ignoring rural Afghan females at our peril."

"Go on," I replied, placing my hands on my hips and bracing for another argument.

"How can our patrols interact with females when the MOTs are all composed of men from infantry companies? And what could a woman possibly tell us that would be useful in any event?"

"Perhaps the British Army should try recruiting a few female soldiers from other regiments to join the patrols. You're missing out on a lot of information when you ignore half the population, Mark."

He stared at me in silence as I walked away, satisfied that I had made my point.

TWENTY-SEVEN

After testing my homemade solar ovens on the balcony of the atrium, I was ready for a demonstration. I had been invited by the Romanian MOT to join them on a day trip to Marmol, a small village in the foothills of the Hindu Kush. It was only thirty miles from Mazār-i-Sharīf, but a bone-crunching three-hour drive up a winding, rocky, dry riverbed.

This was my second day-trip to Marmol with the Romanians. In late March, their young captain, his interpreter, and I had sipped tea for two hours and listened patiently in a chilly room while the Marmol district chief explained his village's need for a new road, shortwave radios, and motorcycles for his policemen. When our meeting ended, the bearded and bespectacled young chief took us on a walking tour of his village. It was still dusted with snow and as silent as only a place free of machinery can be.

Each footstep, each scrape of boot on rock, even the soft rustling of our host's woolen robes was magnified as we climbed toward the upper village. He led us along a steep trail and around melting clumps of snow to a cliff overlooking a tiny stand of cedar trees in a narrow canyon above the village.

"Here is our forest," he announced proudly. "It used to fill the entire canyon, but this is all that remains." It was less than an acre.

"The Russians destroyed part of it with their bombs, but wood thieves have tried to take the rest. Two men must stand guard here every night. If someone cuts down the remaining trees, our village will be washed away in the next big storm.

"Marmol has been here for more than two hundred years. I will not allow it to be destroyed," he said defiantly. At this altitude, we could see for miles in every direction. There was not another tree in sight.

The Romanians and I followed the chief back down the trail until he stopped before a rough wooden door surrounded by high earthen walls. He turned to our interpreter. "Ask the woman if she would like to visit one of our families."

I waited patiently for his translation, and quickly nodded my agreement. The chief rapped hard on the door. An elderly man with a gray beard cracked it open and peered out. As soon as he saw the chief, he swung the door wide and bowed his head. A rough mud partition directly behind him shielded the rest of his family from prying eyes. The chief motioned for me to enter and the man stood aside.

"Only the woman and I may go in," the chief said to the soldiers when they tried to follow us.

Inside the compound, two women squatted in the dirt before a smoking pile of twigs, fanning it rapidly as they cooked a pot of rice. Their children, who had just returned from a foraging trip, were stacking a large pile of reeds and bushes against the far wall. The chief said nothing, but his message was clear. His village was running out of fuel.

When we arrived in Marmol on our return trip, the district chief greeted us like old friends. Just before we went in for our meeting, I poured a liter of water into a black pot and put it inside my home-made solar oven. Placing it on a patch of dirt in front of the chief's compound, I rotated the oven to face the sun and left it to heat the water. The chief and a few men loitering nearby watched me with great interest, but did not ask for an explanation. They all stayed far away from the strange device.

When the Romanians and I stepped outside with the chief an hour later, the pot was boiling and the crowd of men had grown to more than forty. They had formed a circle around the box and were craning their necks to locate the hidden fire they believed was making the water boil.

I stood next to the chief and with the help of the Romanian's interpreter explained to the incredulous men how this box was able to trap the heat of the sun. "It is not magic," I assured them.

"Sahib, can this box make water hot enough for tea?" asked a heavyset man tugging on his thick black beard. "There is no fire." The water was steaming, but he and the others still couldn't believe what they were seeing.

The chief nodded. "Yes, and your women could cook food with this box," he added, motioning for the man to approach.

I lifted the glass lid and invited the man to touch the steaming pot. When it burned his fingers, he shook them dramatically in the air and laughed in surprise.

After the chief had taken his turn touching the pot, the rest of the men stepped forward one by one to scald their fingers and prove to themselves that neither their eyes nor I were deceiving them.

"We have cardboard," said a young man, "but where do we get that shiny paper?"

"Madam Angela," said the Romanian's terp, who was also astounded to see water boiling inside a piece of cardboard, "these people do not have aluminum foil. What can they use to make such an oven?" He was right about the foil. In my excitement, I hadn't thought that far ahead.

I was searching for a reply, when the chief reached into the pocket of his *shalwar kameez* and extracted a pack of cigarettes. He tore off a strip of the thin foil wrapper and waved it aloft like an offering to the gods.

"We can use this for our shiny paper," he announced triumphantly as other men removed their own cigarette packs and flashed slivers of sunlight at each other with the small foil squares.

When we left the village that afternoon, I gave the box to the district chief and promised to send him rolls of foil so the men in his village wouldn't have to smoke themselves to death to build their own solar ovens.

My report to the embassy on my solar cooking demonstration received no response, but I was hooked.

A few weeks later, I wrote up a proposal for a U.S.-funded solar oven project in a displaced persons camp a few miles from Mazār. I handed a copy directly to the ambassador when he came up for a two-hour meeting with Governor Daoud. The only reply I received from the embassy that time was a reprimand for jumping the chain of command by giving my proposal to the ambassador. If I did anything more with these solar ovens, it would have to be on my own.

The morning after my triumphant demo in Marmol, I was making a cup of tea in the soldiers' dining hall when Mark appeared behind me to draw his own hot water from the urn.

"I hear the locals thought you were a sorceress yesterday when they saw you boiling water with a piece of cardboard."

"They did have a little trouble believing what they were seeing," I said, laughing, "but after they'd all burned their fingers on the pot they got it."

"So will they be setting up a solar oven factory in Marmol any time soon?"

"Not likely, Mark, but I would love to get out and show these to some women's groups."

"I doubt that will be possible," he replied. "Other than weddings, I don't believe there are any occasions when grown women are allowed to gather in public."

"There must be someplace I can demonstrate them," I argued.

"Even if there were, Angela, you aren't at liberty to go off organizing ladies' groups without a military escort," he said with a shrug as he headed back to the ops room with his tea.

"Thanks for your support," I muttered as he left the room.

TWENTY-EIGHT

April 16, 2005

It had seemed like a joke when I first read Plawner's message. Citing my knowledge of Russian and my driving skills, he wanted to know if I was willing to make a six-hundred-mile round-trip by road with a U.S. cotton expert to a meeting in Tashkent, Uzbekistan—in the Beast, with no military escort. Just the two of us! I had accepted immediately, of course, but now, strapped into the cavernous, vibrating hold of a C-130 military flight on my way to meet the cotton expert in Kabul, my old insecurities came creeping back.

The United States and the UK were desperate to find replacement crops for the burgeoning fields of opium poppies that were spreading across the country like an out-of-control virus. Several senior Uzbek cotton experts, who had worked with Afghan farmers during the Soviet era, were apparently anxious to return to Afghanistan and share their knowledge. The U.S. agricultural expert who wanted to meet with them in their capital city of Tashkent had to be back in the States in less than three weeks. According to Plawner, the fastest way to get him to and from Uzbekistan was by road.

By late afternoon, I was settled into my temporary hooch on the embassy compound in Kabul. I confirmed my meetings with the ag official and called Jeef at the museum to arrange for the tour of the Bactrian gold collection he and Fazli had promised me. As soon as I hung up, my phone rang again.

"Angela, I found you at last," said a familiar voice.

"Hello, Stefan. I didn't know you were looking for me."

"I heard you were flying down for meetings at the Ministry of Agriculture and thought we could get together for drinks tomorrow evening. I have an appointment with an old Bulgarian friend of mine at NATO headquarters at five. I could join you in the bar around six. What do you say?"

It was wonderful to hear his voice, but tiny alarm bells started to ring in my head. Why was Stefan tracking my movements so closely? Should I be flattered or concerned? I decided to be a bit of both.

"I'd say that's the best invitation I've had in months, Stefan. I'd love to join you, but my schedule the next few days is pretty packed. Who told you I was coming to Kabul?"

"My dear, we are all working together to help the Afghans," said Stefan, gently reproaching me. "You must remember that those Uzbek cotton experts you are going to meet in Tashkent were trained in Moscow and sent to Afghanistan thirty years ago by my former government, the late great Soviet Union. Your embassy's agricultural representative and ours have been discussing the need to coordinate with the Uzbeks for the past several weeks."

So far, his story seemed completely plausible.

"When I learned from one of your colleagues that you spoke fluent Russian—naughty girl for keeping that little detail from me," he chided, "I suggested that you and your USDA man drive up to Tashkent for the meetings. Your British military escort will have to abandon you at the border, but you'll be quite safe driving on your own in Uzbekistan."

Although he seemed to be making light of the fact I had not told him about my fluency in Russian, I cringed when Stefan mentioned it, and said nothing while he continued with his story.

"We passed the idea to your embassy and apparently they liked it. I also thought you would appreciate the opportunity to see how we have restored the great Timurid monuments of Samarkand, which is on your route to Tashkent."

This made sense and seemed completely aboveboard. In my relief, I sighed a bit too heavily into the phone.

"Angela?"

"Yes, Stefan, I'm fine, and I suppose I do owe you a big thank-you. I've always wanted to see Samarkand. Why don't we meet for drinks the next time I'm in Kabul. I'll give you a call when I get back."

"Why do I have to wait that long? You can at least have one drink with me while you're in town. No?"

After another pause, I replied, "*Da* . . . sure, I'd love to join you."

Stefan switched immediately to Russian. "My dearest little Angela, it will be a delight to see you."

"You, too, Stefan."

"Don't hang up yet. I'm not finished," he said suddenly. "When will you be taking your R and R? I'll be coming up to the consulate in Mazār a few times this summer, and I don't want to miss seeing you."

I hadn't thought about taking any time off. I was busy and starting to enjoy myself. "I don't really know, Stefan. It depends on my father's health, but you'll be the first to know when I decide."

"Excellent. Until tomorrow evening, then."

I reluctantly admitted to myself that I was anxious to see Stefan, perhaps too anxious. His sharp intelligence and sardonic wit made him fun to be around, and I couldn't deny that I found him attractive. I stretched out on the bed in my hooch and reviewed the details of that one delightful evening we'd spent together in Dubai. Too bad I couldn't wear my little black dress to the NATO bar tomorrow night. It would have to be my usual trousers, tunic, and long-sleeved shirt.

TWENTY-NINE

April 17, 2005 ✦ KABUL

Wednesday afternoon, an armored embassy vehicle dropped me at the heavily guarded Kabul Museum compound where the Bactrian gold and other treasures from Afghanistan's distant past were being cleaned, restored, and catalogued for eventual display. Jeef bounded down the steps and wrapped his weathered fingers around mine.

"Angela, what a delight to see you. I'm so sorry Rahim couldn't join us. How is my star pupil doing?"

"He's reading everything he can get his hands on about the ancient history of Afghanistan," I said, smiling at the sight of this energetic Frenchman. "I fear you may yet convince him to run off and join your dig."

Jeef led me through the dim, musty corridors of the museum and into a brightly lit but windowless room filled with Afghans and foreigners in white lab coats working quietly over trays of gold ornaments.

Fazli waved us over to his table. Speaking in French, he began to explain the history of the delicate silver-and-gilt ceremonial plate he was cleaning. It would be so much easier to converse with him in Dari, but I waited patiently while Jeef translated his French into English.

Fazli placed the fragile, two-thousand-year-old plate into my outstretched hands. It was less than ten inches in diameter. Carved in bas-relief were two women wearing flowing gowns and riding a gilt chariot pulled by a matched pair of black lions with thick golden manes. A robed guard held a feather canopy to shelter the women from the glare of the sun god, who stared down from his perch in the sky.

"Who do these figures represent?" I asked.

Fazli nodded at Jeef, who proceeded to respond to my question.

"Cybele, the Greek goddess of nature, is the main figure in this plate. She greatly resembles the goddess Artemis on your pin," he said, glancing at the tiny Scythian princess on Tom's brooch, which I wore almost every day.

"Some used to believe that Cybele and Artemis were one and the same," he added.

"Where was it found?" I asked.

"It's from Ai Khanoum, a city built by Alexander the Great near Kunduz," said Jeef, tracing the delicate folds of the princess's gown with a small brush, "but we've found similar artifacts at Tillya Tepe very close to Andkhoy. I understand you and Rahim were almost killed there."

He drew in a deep breath and for an instant rested the tips of his fingers on my wrist. "You must be careful, Angela," he said, avoiding my eyes, as I returned the plate to Fazli.

An hour later, an embassy driver let me off in front of the heavily fortified NATO headquarters, on the same street and less than three blocks from the entrance to the American Embassy. The streets of Kabul were so dangerous for American diplomats that we were not permitted to walk on public sidewalks even for this short distance.

The cozy officers' bar with its dark wood paneling, overstuffed chairs, and crackling fire had the sweet tobacco-scented atmosphere of a gentleman's club, which it essentially was. There were very few women.

Stefan had reserved a table for us. He waved when he saw me enter the room, and my heart jumped when I saw him. I liked feeling this way about a man again. After months in Mazār, I had almost forgotten that being feminine could actually be an asset and not a liability. I should have known then how dangerous such feelings could become if they caused me to drop my guard.

"Your hair is getting a bit shaggy, my dear. I'll have to get you the name of a good hairdresser in town from one of our secretaries," he said, rising from his chair as I approached. "So good to see you, my dear."

"It's wonderful to see you, too, Stefan," I replied as my pulse quickened and my throat went suddenly dry.

"I ordered you one of those Bombay gin and tonics with a twist of lime you said you like." His cell phone rang and he looked down at the display. "You'll have to excuse me briefly."

Although I was feeling like a nervous adolescent on her first date, I had carefully covered my bases before having drinks this evening with Stefan. I had mentioned my two prior encounters with him to our economic counselor during yesterday's meeting about my trip to Uzbekistan. I also told the security office we were getting together for drinks tonight. So far no one seemed bothered by my friendship with Stefan, so neither, I decided, would I.

The bartender was playing one of Tom's favorite Sinatra albums. I sank back into the soft leather chair to enjoy a few quiet moments listening to Ol' Blue Eyes and was about to take a long sip from my first iced gin and tonic in months, when I saw Mark walk into the bar with two other British officers. What was he doing here?

I had last seen him in Mazār, three days before, poring over the intelligence briefs that covered his cluttered desk in the int cell. Several of his men had been teasing me about my upcoming drive to Tashkent with the cotton expert, and Mark had joined in. He had said nothing about traveling to Kabul.

Mark was in a tense discussion with the officers when he spotted me across the room and stopped speaking just long enough to irritate one of his companions. Their voices were raised. I could hear enough to know they were discussing Helmand Province, where the British Army was headed in early 2006.

Mark left his companions and walked quickly to my table. "Hello, Angela. What a surprise to see you here!" Since I considered him no more than a friend and colleague, it bothered me how much I didn't want him to know I was here with Stefan.

"I'm more surprised than you, Mark," I stammered. "As you know, I'm in town to meet my cotton expert. What are you doing here?"

"Last-minute intel brief for some visiting senior staff. I flew down today." He glanced at the single tumbler of gin and tonic on my table.

"You should know that I plan to bring up your point about the consequences of cooking fuel shortages in the rural areas when I brief them tomorrow. With your permission, I'd also like to mention your experiments with the solar ovens," he added, taking a step closer to my chair.

"Mark, we need you over here," called one of the officers.

"Don't go anywhere," he said as a slow grin spread across his face. "I'll be back shortly." He turned and walked toward the other officers before I could reply.

Their discussion was growing quite heated as Stefan re-entered the bar looking pleased with himself. He squeezed around the three officers who were partially blocking the doorway, returned to our table, and kissed me lightly on the cheek at the very instant Mark broke away from the group and turned again in my direction.

"So sorry, dear girl, I didn't greet you properly when you arrived," Stefan said, sitting down across from me. "Let me order myself a vodka so we can catch up on our various adventures."

Mark watched in silence a few paces behind Stefan, who remained oblivious to his presence. My eyes and Mark's met briefly but with such intensity that even Stefan noticed. He turned around to see whom I was looking at, but Mark had already left the room.

At that moment, all I wanted to do was run out the door and find Mark, although I had no idea what I'd say if I actually caught up with him. I worried that seeing me here drinking with a stranger would give him the wrong impression, that he would again think I was being irresponsible. Since under the circumstances, chasing after him would have been not only undiplomatic and impolite but difficult to explain to all concerned, I sipped my gin and tonic in silence.

Stefan began to regale me with the story of his fresh victory—which he had resolved with that final phone call—over a fellow diplomat who had tried to beat him out of an assignment to a senior foreign ministry position in Moscow. "Just because I'm retiring in a few more years doesn't mean I can be stepped on," he huffed.

After a few minutes, Stefan had me laughing again with tales of his bureaucratic triumphs. I tried hard not to think any more about Mark.

THIRTY

May 2, 2005

My six-hundred-mile round-trip to Uzbekistan's capital city was a fiasco from start to finish, although I did get a kick out of driving the Beast without a military escort for a few days. The Uzbek agronomists were unable to obtain permission from their government to travel to Afghanistan, and the whole project was cancelled on our last day in Tashkent. Our planned one-day visit to Samarkand was cut short after my ag expert got food poisoning, and when I headed south for the Afghan border with my ailing passenger, the Beast had three flat tires, delaying our scheduled arrival at the border by eight hours.

I'd been unable to reach the British soldiers waiting for us on the Afghan side of the Amu Darya River to notify them about our late arrival, and they were about to leave when I finally rumbled across the dark and empty Friendship Bridge at seven P.M., honking my horn and flashing my headlights. After transferring my very ill traveling companion into one of their vehicles where a medic could look after him, I followed them back to Mazār in a two-hour, rain-soaked convoy.

I was never so happy to see a building as I was the PRT that night, glowing brightly in all its *Fawlty Towers* splendor on our unlit and muddy road. Lights blazed from the atrium on the top floor, which thundered with music and conversation. The six-man Romanian MOT had invited me to this party weeks ago, but by late that afternoon, I'd given up hope I would make it back to the PRT in time. They were going home after completing their six-month tour of duty in Mazār and tonight they were throwing a farewell bash for themselves and welcoming their replacements, who had just arrived from Bucharest. I parked the Beast in the back lot of the PRT, thanked my military escorts profusely, and dashed upstairs.

"It won't be a war in Helmand," said Sergeant Major, leaning against a doorjamb and waving his beer at an attentive young lieutenant as I passed them on my way to the shower room with a towel and a bar of soap. "It's going to be a bloody swamp that will suck our boys in and piss them out in jagged little pieces. Oh, sorry, Angela," he said, jumping out of the way.

"What happened to you?" asked the lieutenant, staring at my filthy clothes and hair.

"It's a long story. Right now I need a hot shower, a meal, several glasses of wine, and I'll be fine," I replied.

When I entered the atrium thirty minutes later, clean body, clean clothes, wet hair pulled back, the highly charged atmosphere of the all-male party had electrified the room. This normally empty space was vibrating with the energy of forty drinking, laughing men who greeted me with the familiarity of an old friend. Mark stood as I passed and nodded politely.

He and I had not spoken since that evening in Kabul when Stefan had unknowingly kept him from joining me for a drink. My feelings at this moment were, to say the least, confused. Although I owed Mark no explanation about my relationship with Stefan, I still felt the need to assure him that the Russian diplomat and I were just good friends.

The Romanians were dancing in a tight circle, their arms locked around one another's shoulders. Every light in the atrium had been switched on, and the doors at either end of the room propped open to keep fresh air circulating. I poured myself a glass of red wine, filled a bowl with lamb curry and rice, and found a chair. Before long, I was surrounded by three sweating, laughing Romanians.

"Angela, we have been waiting for you. You must come and dance with us."

They led me to the center of the room and pulled me into their pulsing circle. I'd forgotten how much I loved dancing. Like horseback riding, it was something I had given up after I lost Tom.

The Romanian captain plucked me from the circle, grabbed my waist, and spun me around the room in a vigorous polka. He passed me to his first sergeant, who pulled me back into the raucous swirl of dancing men.

As the entire Romanian military team linked arms with some of the less inhibited Brits who had joined them, they began to stamp and shout in time to the quickening tempo of their traditional *sarba*.

I was the only woman present, and yet I felt completely safe as I was passed from soldier to soldier for a twirl around the room and pulled repeatedly back into the expanding circle of dancers. The atrium vibrated with the clapping of callused hands and the thunder of military boots hitting the cold cement floor.

"Good God, man," said one of the British officers standing next to Mark as I flew past them in the arms of the Romanian sniper, who had extracted me from the circle for another polka, "someone should rescue the poor girl before the Romanians accidentally fling her off the balcony."

"I'm not tempted," sniffed Mark. "She seems quite capable of taking care of herself."

When I approached Mark and his companions again, this time in the arms of the Romanian medic, one of the Brits called out to me, "Angela, you're actually enjoying this?"

"You have no idea how much!" I shouted as another hand snaked around my waist. "By the way, don't anyone dare rescue me," I added, looking directly at Mark.

The Romanians dragged me back into their pulsing circle and one by one jumped alone into the center, fingers snapping over their heads, boots pounding a staccato beat.

Someone tossed a long red scarf to the dancer in the middle and turned the music even louder. He whistled in short bursts as he swung the scarf over his head in widening circles. Without warning, he flipped the scarf over my head and pulled me into the middle of the circle. Knotting the scarf around my hips, he left me alone surrounded by the laughing, stamping soldiers. They began to clap in unison urging me to dance.

This normally silent, cold, and empty room had completely

seduced me with its wine, its heat, the music, and now the men circling me and begging me to dance for them. It was hard to believe that only five hours ago, I'd been standing in a freezing rain arguing with Uzbek customs officials about the stamps in the passport of the very sick man lying in the backseat of the Beast. I raised my arms over my head, bringing my hands together in time with the music, and began to move my hips in a slow circle.

Through the spinning ring of soldiers, I could see Mark watching me. Feeling exhilarated, possessed, and momentarily without inhibition—I allowed my movements to become slower and more seductive and the men louder and more insistent until at last I pulled the scarf from my hips and tossed it around the neck of another Romanian soldier. I dragged him into the center of the circle before I escaped and collapsed, perspiring, into a chair.

Mark took three steps in my direction, set his wineglass on a table, then turned abruptly and walked out the door. As he left the room, he brushed by Rahim, who had just entered.

The interpreters were generally not invited to these parties because alcohol was served. Rahim had a large manila envelope in his hand. He was staring at me with a look of shock and puzzlement that had frozen his innocent young face into a mask of disbelief. He handed the envelope to the colonel. Although he saw me wave at him, he turned without responding and followed the major down the stairs.

I had momentarily forgotten that I was in Afghanistan. Now I began to worry that this moment of spontaneity might have cost me Rahim's respect.

THIRTY-ONE

May 3, 2005

Rahim was waiting for me in the rose garden early the next morning. He looked sad and confused. I knew why.

"Angela-*jan*, you have told me I can ask you almost anything."

"Yes, I have, Rahim."

"Last night, I saw you dancing with the soldiers. This is not allowed in my country. An Afghan woman would never dance in front of men." He gazed down at me with his impenetrable dark eyes, begging for a response that would restore my reputation according to the rigid standards of his culture.

"Rahim, you told me a few weeks ago that you and your friends listen to American music. Have you ever seen films of Americans dancing?"

He nodded gravely.

"Did you see men and women dancing together?"

Another nod.

"So you know that's how we dance?"

"Of course I do. The Taliban have been gone from Afghanistan for almost four years. People my age watch TV and DVDs.

We have access to the Internet and cell phones. We listen to your music and some of us even like it," Rahim replied, sweeping his arms in the air to indicate the breadth of his exposure to the outside world.

"So why are you asking me these questions?" I said, probing gently.

"Because I think of you like I do my mother, and I could never imagine her doing such a thing as you did last night with the soldiers," he said, choking imperceptibly on his own words.

His response stunned me. My innocent dancing with the soldiers had deeply embarrassed this gentle young man, who was already the unwitting recipient of the motherly affection I'd never been able to give to my own child.

"Rahim, what I did last night would be considered completely acceptable and harmless in my country. I did nothing wrong and I had a wonderful time. I hope you won't judge me too harshly."

"It's not just me," he replied, still distressed. "What about the other soldiers?"

I was touched by his concern that my reputation might have been damaged after my wild romp in the atrium.

"Rahim, I promise you that the soldiers will not think any less of me because I danced with them last night."

"And the terps? What about them?" he asked, his voice rising.

"I'm really not worried about this, Rahim. Unless you tell the terps yourself, they probably won't even know. It's just not a big deal for Americans and Europeans."

"Thank you for explaining this to me, Angela-*jan*," he said with a relieved sigh. "Perhaps someday this sort of dancing will be allowed in my country."

"Is there anyone in particular you'd like to dance with, Rahim?" I asked, a smile slowly spreading across my face.

"Angela-*jan*, there are some questions I should not ask you, and there are some questions you should not ask me," he replied, returning my grin.

"Touché," I said, gathering up my gardening tools.

"Angela-*jan*, what does this 'touché' mean?"

"Let's save that conversation for another day, Rahim," I replied with a laugh. "It's a French word. Perhaps you can ask Professor Mongibeaux the next time you see him."

THIRTY-TWO

May 5, 2005

The newly arrived Gurkha Sergeant Major tried hard to be as accommodating as his predecessor when I had last-minute vehicle requests, but after my disastrous return trip from Uzbekistan, he had vowed he would never again allow me to drive the Beast.

I put his ultimatum to the test one morning when Nilofar stopped by the PRT to invite me to join her for Ladies' Day at the Blue Mosque. Rahim had told me about Ladies' Day, one of the rare opportunities for large groups of Afghan women to gather in public without wearing their burkas.

"Not on my watch, Angela," grumbled Sergeant Major, folding his beefy arms over his chest and frowning when I came to his office to ask for the keys. "If you need to go somewhere in your beloved Beast, a British soldier—and not you—will be at the wheel."

"You're the boss, Sergeant Major," I replied with a shrug and a smile.

"Corporal Fotheringham and Corporal Jenkins will be ready to take you to Ladies' Day at the Blue Mosque in twenty minutes," he added with a twinkle in his eye.

Rahim, who knew he wasn't needed for this trip, walked Nilo-far and me to the Beast and waved us out the gate. His eyes never left Nilofar, who leaned out the window and waved back at him until Jenkins swung the Beast onto the main road.

On the way into town, Nilofar placed her hand on my arm. Her normally bright eyes darkened. "Angela, I want us to have a good time today, but I must tell you about something that has happened before we get to the mosque."

"What's wrong, Nilofar?"

"Last week, I helped an eleven-year-old girl in Sheberghān escape an arranged marriage. She is now safe in Kabul with a women's organization. Her father was using her to pay a debt to an opium dealer. He and the man she was to marry have threatened me."

"Does your family know about this?"

"No, I don't want them involved, and you must not tell Rahim."

"Why are you telling me this, Nilofar?"

"If anything happens to me, I want someone to know," she said ominously.

As soon as we parked at the western entrance to the Blue Mosque and climbed out of the Beast, Nilofar's dark mood vanished and she said no more about the threats against her life. "You're going to love this, Angela!" she laughed as she walked toward the mosque.

Fuzzy jumped out, shouldered his rifle, and started to follow us.

"Fuzzy, I know we've agreed that you'll accompany me everywhere, but today has to be an exception. The only men allowed in the inner courtyard of the mosque on Ladies' Day are the mullahs. You'll have to stay here with Jenkins."

My hulking, ginger-haired bodyguard did not put up a fight. "Right, Angela," he said with downcast eyes.

Since losing his childhood friend in Iraq, Fuzzy no longer smiled and he spoke even less than before. He stood next to the Beast and watched me walk with Nilofar through the filigreed iron gates and into the vast gardens that led to the interior plaza of the Blue Mosque complex.

"Have fun, ladies," called Jenkins, who was already slipping a movie into his portable DVD player.

"Look, Angela, no burkas!" cried Nilofar, flinging her arms wide as we passed under an arch of pearl white marble and entered the sunny inner courtyard.

Other than large family weddings, Ladies' Day at the Blue Mosque was the only occasion for Mazāri women to gather in large numbers freed from the restrictive confines of their burkas. But even this small social exception was observed only once a week during the forty days following Nauroz.

Several hundred women were clustered around picnic baskets, or walking arm in arm and reveling in their few precious hours of secluded freedom. Their burkas, piled in shapeless blue heaps on the grass, no longer hid their heavy makeup, ankle-length robes, gold earrings, necklaces, and bracelets that sparkled in the afternoon sun. Flocks of white turtledoves circled overhead. A few of the bolder birds swooped down to feast on bits of *naan* and rice tossed to them by the chattering women.

Nilofar spotted a few friends from the university, who tsked over my unfeminine clothing and complete lack of makeup. I longed to engage them in a deep discussion about their lives, but I could only do it through Nilofar.

"Does she really live with men who are not members of her family?" asked one of the young women.

"She must be a prostitute to be staying with all those soldiers!" shouted an old lady, wagging her finger in my direction.

Nilofar laughed. "She is not a prostitute. She is an American diplomat who is here to help our people."

We were now completely engulfed by chattering clusters of women who offered to share their lunch with us while Nilofar's friends peppered me with questions about life in America. I regretted not having brought one of my solar ovens.

I could have stayed for hours surrounded by this joyous crowd as they reveled in their few hours of freedom, but Sergeant Major had made me promise to get Fuzzy and Jenkins back to camp by two P.M.

Many of the young university students described to us how excited they were about the opportunity to make real contributions to the rebuilding of their country. I hoped they would be able to realize their dreams. If the Taliban ever retook the government and imposed their draconian laws, the potential of these young women and that of half the nation of Afghanistan would once again be locked away and hidden from view.

THIRTY-THREE

May 24, 2005

Colonel Jameson squeezed awkwardly around my typing table and entered his office. He looked worried. "Angela, would you mind stepping in for a minute?"

"I'll be right there," I replied, logging off and grabbing my notebook.

"And would you mind closing the door?" he asked. I did, smiling apologetically and shrugging my shoulders at the unhappy faces of my NATO officemates. They hated it when the colonel shut his door.

"I'm sending a patrol tomorrow morning to meet with the leaders of a Pashtun village that's fairly close to Mazār. It's isolated from the surrounding districts by a winding branch of the Balkh River that cuts through their valley. We've been keeping an eye on that village from a distance and are concerned because we're not sure where their sympathies lie. We need to have some visible and positive presence there."

"Have Colonel Tremain's men led any Afghan Army patrols through that area?" I asked.

"No, they haven't, and apparently none of our MOTs have been there since early 2004, when they got a very chilly reception."

The windows in the colonel's office suddenly rattled and the floor shook violently. The Estonians were blowing things up again. I continued taking notes and silently congratulated myself on having finally overcome my fear of these explosions.

The colonel continued, "Tomorrow's *shura* should be fairly benign. Our main purpose is to find out if the farmers need any assistance. We've had reports of extensive poppy cultivation in that valley. The warlord who controls the area is a known trafficker and a pretty nasty fellow. We also suspect that villagers may still have links to Taliban family members in the south.

"How would you like to go along with the patrol tomorrow?"

"You know I would," I replied with a smile.

"Of course," he said. "Your observations will be useful, especially any Dari side chatter you pick up during the meeting. Are you up for this?"

"Absolutely."

"I've asked Major Davies to go along, since we're not sure if Dari or Pashto is the lingua franca in the village," he added. "Rahim will accompany your patrol as interpreter. I was hoping that the old professor, whom I've yet to meet, would have returned from Kabul by now so he could accompany you, but I'm told he's still recuperating."

The colonel leaned forward in his chair and pursed his lips. "One more thing, Angela. The Estonians dismantled a large IED earlier this week on Route Five, where you'll be traveling tomorrow. We have reports that there may be another, so everyone will have to wear helmets and body armor."

"Great! Another new experience," I replied with false enthusiasm. I wondered silently and with a creeping uncertainty just how my oversized Kevlar vest and ill-fitting helmet would protect me if a bomb went off beneath one of our unarmored vehicles. My body armor had sat unused in the back of the Beast for the past four months—right where Fuzzy had tossed it the day I arrived. I had felt completely safe riding around in the Beast with the windows rolled down until this unsettling announcement.

The sudden need for a bulletproof vest after all these months, along with my certainty that it would provide no protection at all if we hit an IED, triggered a minor anxiety attack, which I managed to conceal from the colonel. The room became much brighter as my pupils dilated and my heart began to race. The colonel continued to speak, and I nodded attentively, but his words had temporarily lost their meaning. When his phone rang and he took the call, I pressed my fingers hard into the arms of my chair, breathed slowly, and stared out the window until the sensation passed.

In the end, I survived the trip to the Pashtun village and sweated off a few pounds bouncing along in full body armor for six hours in our un-air-conditioned vehicle. There was no IED, but I was surprised to learn on that trip that the terps did not wear body armor. If it was necessary for my safety, then it should be necessary for theirs as well. I raised this with Rahim on the ride back to the PRT but he seemed unconcerned. "It's too hot to wear body armor today, Angela-*jan*." He was right about that.

"Angela, will you be coming to the camel races tonight? I believe you have a mount in race four," said the colonel with a wink as he passed me in the bullpen working on my Pashtun-village trip report after dinner.

"Your report can wait," he added. "You don't want to miss this."

"I'll be there," I promised.

There were no actual camels in these races, which were held every few months at the PRT. The colonel explained that they were the "afghanized" version of horse racing night, which British troops often staged during deployments in other parts of the world.

The Afghan carpenters in our maintenance shop had fashioned meter-high camels out of sheets of plywood and decorated them with red, blue, yellow, and green racing stripes. The floor of the pub served as the racetrack. The quartermaster and his staff wrote up elaborate tip sheets for the six camels in each race. Betting was in U.S. dollars, and the speed of each camel was determined by the toss of an enormous pair of sponge dice, which the designated jockeys tossed into the air or threw at their opponents, to the roaring approval of the crowd.

Everyone who was not working that night had gathered in the pub by eight thirty for the PRT Mazār Grand National spring camel races. The tip sheets were a closely guarded secret, which no one was allowed to see until they were handed out minutes before the first race, when bets were placed. Each race had a title, with detailed descriptions of the competing camels.

I flipped through the booklet, laughing at the descriptions of the camels, each of which referred obliquely to one of the officers or soldiers at the PRT. As the colonel had warned, my "camel" was in the fourth race, The Commander's Cup. Number 3: American Beauty. "A solar-powered camel from the United States, descended from the original Irish breed with the stamina to win, but will have to fight since this is her first race."

Fuzzy's camel was also in my race. Number 2: Staffordshire Knot. "A huge, well-armed camel, speed unknown, who doesn't say much, but if you try to pass him will spit bullets at you—and this camel never misses."

In race number five was Number 6: Davies Delight. "An imported polo camel from the famous Hertfordshire stables in Brunei. A quiet and highly intelligent animal that could sneak up from the outside and surprise some of the favorites."

The evening was raucous, with Fuzzy and me concluding our tie for last place by pummeling each other with the sponge dice. It was wonderful to see him smiling again. To my great surprise Mark showed up during my race and stayed until the end. He bet twenty dollars on his camel, tossed the dice with exaggerated seriousness, and won, using his prize money to buy a round of drinks for everyone in the pub.

"Strongbow?" he asked, handing me a can.

"Thanks, Mark. Congratulations on your win. You're the most popular man in the pub right now."

"A rare occasion for me," he observed with a wry smile. We chatted about our trip to the Pashtun village and shared our frustration at the lack of reconstruction assistance for the rural people who most needed it. When Mark dropped his guard, he was actually quite pleasant to be around. Although this was the first time I'd seen him totally relaxed, it didn't last for long. When he finished his beer, he excused himself with his usual formality—more intel reports to write before the morning staff meeting. I was sorry to see him go.

THIRTY-FOUR

May 29, 2005

Spring is the time of year when young boys released from the confines of school or field or workshop gallop through the back streets of Mazār-i-Sharīf and every other Afghan city, laughing and squealing as they battle for aerial supremacy with their multicolored kites.

These spring winds, which give such delight to the kite runners, descend cold and heavy from the melting mountain snows and are swept aloft by the warm air rising from the northern steppes and southern deserts. They also pose a serious hazard to aircraft flying low across Afghanistan's treacherous mountains between the months of March and May.

I had cleared my schedule for two days, anticipating the arrival of counter-narcotics officials from the British and American embassies. They were coming in response to a series of urgent e-mails I had sent reporting that it was already too late to stop the bumper crop of opium poppies expected to be harvested this year in Balkh Province.

I'd been asked to accompany the two men on a helicopter tour of the thousands of acres of poppy fields that had burst into deadly and colorful bloom. They were scheduled to arrive by Afghan Army helicopter—a risky way to travel over the mountains even in the best of times.

"The trip has been cancelled, Angela," said the operations officer when I entered the vault for our morning briefing. "One of your American choppers went down yesterday in a dust storm in Khost. All survived, fortunately, but the Afghan Air Force have wisely decided not to make the trip north today—if ever. It looks like you have no excuses left to skip the wedding tonight," he said with a malicious grin. Ahmad, one of our interpreters, was getting married in the largest wedding hall in Mazār-i-Sharīf.

"Great," I moaned. This was the third wedding I'd been invited to in the past six weeks.

"Don't worry," he reassured me, "you're not the only one from the PRT who's attending. The colonel, the chief of staff, Major Davies, and several other officers will be joining you."

"Don't get me wrong," I said with a laugh, "I don't mind attending, but the other officers won't really be joining me. They'll go together to the men's party while I'll spend the evening alone in a separate hall with three hundred women I've never met."

He rolled his eyes in mock sympathy.

"I do enjoy the Bollywood music and the dancing, at least for the first hour or two," I admitted, "but aren't weddings supposed to come with champagne?"

"All the weddings I go to," he agreed.

Since my language skills were still a state secret, I couldn't tell the ops officer how frustrating it was not to be able to talk to the women at these events when I was perfectly capable of doing so. Listening in on conversations about their hopes for their daughters was fascinating, but there were so many questions I wanted to ask them. It was torture to remain mute.

Layers of mascara, glitter-encrusted hair, glossy red lips, matching fingernails, impossibly high heels, and floor-length gowns were the standard attire at these events. I was always seriously underdressed, but tolerated as the odd foreign woman at the gathering.

Almost two hours had passed when I spotted Nilofar on the other side of the cavernous room, speaking to a group of young women. Nilofar saw me approaching and ran up, grinning broadly. Her eyes were dark with kohl, and her fitted pale green dress glittered with sequins. She had skipped the customary lacquered coiffure, allowing her lustrous hair to fall loose down her back. I smiled imagining the expression on Rahim's face if he could see her looking like this.

"Angela," she cried, kissing me on both cheeks, "I didn't know you were coming to this wedding."

"And I didn't know you would be here." I was thrilled to have my young friend to talk to for the next few hours.

"Ahmad's new wife's mother is my father's second cousin." She laughed. "We are Hazara, and that cousin is one-quarter Hazara from my great-grandmother. The rest of her family is Tajik. They don't like to talk about their Hazara blood, but my father does business with their family, so they had to invite us. All Mazāris are related to one another somehow. That's why our weddings are so big."

Her voice dropped to a conspiratorial whisper as she took my hand and led me across the room to a thick velvet curtain that separated the men from the women. "Do you want to see the men's party? I have been watching Rahim dance, and now one of your soldiers is also dancing."

"But women aren't allowed to be with the men, Nilofar." I worried that her impetuous nature would draw attention to her budding relationship with Rahim, which I feared was becoming too serious. The consequences for her if it got out of hand would be far greater than for Rahim. A young man could be forgiven such a transgression. A young woman's reputation would be tarnished forever, and no man would want her for his bride.

"Don't worry; no one will see us," she said, leading me to a couch that had been pushed against the thick floor-to-ceiling drapes. She nodded at an elderly woman dozing in an overstuffed chair near us. She had been assigned as a sentry, but despite the noise was snoring quietly.

Nilofar sat on an arm of the couch and poked her finger through a hole in the curtain. "Here it is," she said, peering quickly through the opening. "Look! The major and Rahim are both dancing!"

This I had to see. It was hard to picture the straitlaced major doing anything as rash as dancing at an Afghan wedding, especially given his reaction to my little romp around the atrium with the Romanians. I pressed my eye to the narrow slit in the curtain and had a panoramic view of the other half of the hall, where several hundred men were eating, talking, and dancing in clusters.

At the center of a group of laughing, swaying men was Mark, arms raised over his head, hands clapping. His eyes were closed and his head was thrown back. Rahim, whistling and shouting, was in the circle of men that surrounded him. Mark's sinuous body in his camouflage uniform swayed to the beat with a wild abandon that even the Romanian soldiers did not possess. Just then, I felt Nilofar's hand pulling me back.

"Angela, the old lady is waking up," she warned as she dragged me away from the curtain. "We have to go back to my table before she sees us. All the girls do this; you just can't look for too long."

"You're an early riser," said Mark as he strolled by the rose garden on his way to breakfast at six thirty the following morning. I was waging a losing battle against a massive invasion of aphids.

"So are you," I replied. "Did you enjoy last night's wedding?"

His crisp uniform and formal demeanor contrasted starkly with the man I had seen dancing with wild abandon the evening before.

"It was tolerable," he said. "I know the interpreters like us to attend, and I don't really mind."

I'll say you don't!

He stared at the bottle of noxious brown liquid I was spraying on the buds and stems of the bushes. There were no garden stores in Mazār, and after the first wave of aphids had attacked my adopted rose garden, Fuzzy, whose mother was the head of her garden club in Nottingham, had suggested removing and boiling the tobacco from a few packs of cigarettes.

"Is that your famous tobacco tea?" Mark asked with a hint of a smile.

"It is, but I think the aphids are starting to like it."

"Don't give up, Angela. Never give up."

I looked up from my spraying to reply, but saw only the back of Mark's uniform and his dark short-cropped hair as he headed for the officers' mess.

THIRTY-FIVE

June 9, 2005

In early June, Nilofar and I began slipping quietly out of the PRT compound under our burkas to demonstrate my solar ovens at a nearby Hazara displaced-persons camp. It was only a few blocks from the PRT, but so well concealed by the towering mud walls of the family compounds in our sector that I had not been aware of its existence until she mentioned it.

Nilofar had heard about my solar-cooking experiments on the roof of the PRT from Rahim, and had come at lunchtime several weeks earlier to see what I was making. On the day of her visit, I was preparing a traditional Afghan dish using ingredients I'd purchased in town.

"This is incredible!" She wiped her lips and laughed with delight as I spooned more of the tender spiced lamb and rice onto her plate.

While we ate, she told me about a Hazara camp near the PRT, which she had visited a number of times with her classmates from law school. They were helping the refugees document their land claims against Governor Daoud's Tajik followers. Her eyes suddenly brimmed with tears.

"Angela-*jan*, Rahim is Tajik, but he is a good Tajik. Did you know that there are many bad ones who hate the Hazara people? They call us dogs. I even heard bad things being said about us at Ahmad's wedding."

"Yes, Nilofar, I do know," I replied, avoiding her eyes and growing silent. I didn't know what to say about this absurd prejudice, which was forcing these two young Afghans to hide their love for each other.

We ate for a few more minutes without speaking until Nilofar grabbed one of my solar ovens and lifted it into the air. "Angela, you must show these amazing boxes to the Hazara women in the camp," she said before scraping the final bits of *qabele palau* from her plate.

"I would love to," I replied. "I'll see if Sergeant Major will let us have a vehicle tomorrow."

Nilofar objected immediately to my plan. She was certain that arriving at the Hazara camp with a British military escort would frighten the women.

"Angela, let's put on burkas and walk over without the soldiers," she said with a conspiratorial grin. "It's very close to the PRT and no one will notice, I promise you. I will tell Rahim to let us in when we return."

Inside the PRT, I enjoyed an extraordinary amount of freedom. Officially, I reported to no one, not even the colonel, although as a courtesy I consulted with him on almost everything I did. No one at the embassy in Kabul had the slightest interest in what I was doing on a daily basis. My weekly reports and an occasional memo were all they wanted.

This level of independence was restricted to life behind the mud walls that surrounded our compound. For good reason, no one was allowed to leave camp without a security escort. Despite the relative calm in the north, and even with the required force protection, we were still exposed every time we went out the gate to the possibility of suicide bombers, ambush, or IEDs.

I knew that some of my male diplomatic colleagues assigned to NATO PRTs elsewhere in Afghanistan had given up trying to get military escorts for their trips outside the wire. At least one, who had grown a beard and occasionally carried a weapon, drove himself to meetings, alone and unescorted—not a viable option in this country for a female diplomat.

It would be a risky move to leave camp on my own. I certainly couldn't ask anyone's permission. But it was just too tempting. I agreed to Nilofar's suggestion and met her at the gate the following morning.

We pulled the burkas over our heads while still hidden inside the covered archway and stepped into the street carrying the solar ovens in burlap bags. Unable to see anywhere but straight ahead through the tiny square of netting, I immediately stumbled into a large pothole. Nilofar laughed and helped me up. Although I always took my burka on overnight patrols, I would only put it on for my bathroom breaks. Walking along a dirt road, carrying a large bundle, and trying to keep up with my young friend while draped in this shroud turned out to be far more difficult than I had imagined.

Nilofar assured me that when we left the PRT carrying parcels with our faces and bodies concealed under the burkas, the Afghan guards and the British sentries in the watchtowers would all assume we were the laundry ladies and ignore us. She was right. It was as though we were invisible.

Our first demonstration was met with astonishment by the women whose children wandered daily through our neighborhood scrounging for fuel.

We cooked a pot of rice and answered their questions.

"How long will it take to cook the rice?" asked one of the women.

"One hour," I replied as Nilofar translated.

"That's too long," shouted another, who was sitting in front of her tent.

"How long does it take your children to gather fuel for your cooking fires every day?" I asked.

"It takes all day, but they are children. What else can they do?" she answered.

"They could go to school," I said as I watched her six- and seven-year-old daughters depositing scraps of paper and bundles of twigs in piles near her makeshift tent.

Each time we arrived in the camp, a few more curious women would gather to watch us cook and demonstrate the construction of the cardboard-and-aluminum-foil boxes. Everything needed to make a solar oven was available in Mazār-i-Sharīf, except for the aluminum foil.

In April, I had mailed a check to my brother, Bill, who purchased forty-five rolls of heavy-duty Reynolds Wrap and mailed them to my APO address. With a huge supply of foil stashed under my bed at the PRT, I inaugurated what I called Operation Sunshine, taking solar ovens on every patrol I accompanied and giving demonstrations whenever we stopped in a village. Enthusiastically supported by the colonel, who remained unaware of my clandestine visits to the Hazara camp, I recruited a few of the soldiers to help me build more solar ovens in the atrium a few nights a week. My unauthorized day trips with Nilofar would remain secret for a while longer.

THIRTY-SIX

June 29, 2005

"Sir, eleven trucks filled with men and equipment have just pulled up in front of the PRT. There's an American bloke at the gate says he wants to speak to you." The duty NCO was out of breath after running from the ops room, through the bullpen, and into the colonel's office. "Our internal phone lines are down again, sir."

"Damn, I wasn't expecting them until next week," groaned the colonel. "Take the American to the officers' mess and give him a cup of coffee. I'll be over in a minute.

"Angela, would you come in here, please?" called Colonel Jameson after he had dismissed the sergeant.

"I'm so sorry I didn't discuss this with you earlier," he apologized, "but I was under strict orders from our headquarters in Kabul to keep it close hold. I had planned to tell you before they arrived since your government is funding this activity."

"What activity would that be, Colonel?" I asked dryly. I walked over to his window and gazed down at the long line of white trucks idling in the road.

"Poppy eradication," he said with a sigh.

"It's a little late for that," I replied. "The biggest poppy harvest in Balkh's history has been under way for the past month."

It was not surprising that a U.S.-funded operation of this scope was about to take place in my area of responsibility and I knew nothing about it. The embassy was well aware of my objections to the poppy eradication program. Perhaps Plawner had decided not to tell me ahead of time because he knew I'd lodge a protest.

I felt embarrassed and betrayed to have been left so completely out of the picture by my own embassy. "There are thousands of hectares under cultivation, although it doesn't matter much at this point where they go since a good portion of the opium paste has already been scraped from the bulbs and packaged for transport. All this will do is piss off the locals."

"You're right, Angela, but it's out of our hands."

"Why won't those idiots in Kabul listen to reason?" I fumed. "Isn't there any way to stop this?"

"No, there isn't," the colonel said grimly. "I know full well the danger this presents for our boys. We'll just have to keep the MOTs out of the eradication areas for a while. We're not expecting much violence, but there are certain to be some very angry farmers."

On the second day of the operation, I approached the liaison officer for the eradication team after dinner. He was bunking at the PRT. "How are you determining which fields to destroy?" I asked.

"Ma'am, I don't decide what gets cut, and I am not at liberty to discuss my activities with you. My head office said you should send your questions to the people in your embassy who are managing this contract, and they'll relay the questions to my supervisor.

"Sorry, ma'am," he added as he headed into the pub for a beer and left me standing alone in the dining hall, wondering if I should even bother to report this.

THIRTY-SEVEN

July 2, 2005

Any time there was a lull in my increasingly busy schedule, I would haul a few hundred more pages of my predecessor's outdated but still confidential reports and cables into the basement of the main building, feed them into the shredder, and grind them into confetti. I resented having to waste my time disposing of classified material that Brooks should have chucked as soon as he read it. But it was now my responsibility, and I was determined to complete this task before the end of the month.

"Destroying more state secrets?" Mark asked as he exited the ops room, which was always kept cool to protect the communications equipment. His uniform was crisp and he carried a steaming cup of coffee. I was in jeans, sandals, and a tank top—and drenched in sweat. It was at least 110 outside and more than 90 degrees in the open hallway outside the ops room.

"I can't answer that question, Mark, or I'll have to kill you," I shot back with a grin, dropping another bundle of paper into the howling maw of the shredder and brushing my hair out of my eyes.

"Angela," he said as he made a discreet sweep of my dripping torso, "I could ask one of the men to help you with that."

"Thanks, Mark, but I'm responsible for cleaning up the mess left by Mr. Brooks."

"Why are you torturing yourself?" he asked.

"What do you mean?" I demanded as I pulled another sheaf of papers from the folder.

"Well, look at you," he began, "you're never . . ."

"Yes, look at me," I interrupted, shoving so much paper into the shredder that it shuddered to a halt.

"I've been shredding these damned papers for months, and I'm still at it. No one in Kabul is responding to my reports, and I'm still lying to the one person in this place who respects me and who I really care about."

I threw the shredder into reverse, showering us both with a hail of torn paper.

"You mean Rahim?" asked Mark as he stooped to gather up the scattered remains of Mr. Brooks's documents.

"Yes. But I don't know how much longer I can stand it, Mark," I said, still avoiding his gaze. "I've attended meetings with all the terps, filed endless reports stating that their translations are accurate, and my embassy still insists I keep my Dari a secret."

"Angela, Rahim is not the only person at the PRT who respects you," he said softly.

"Thank you for saying so," I replied, clenching my jaw and raising my eyes to meet his.

"It's just that Rahim and I have developed a real bond, Mark." I took a deep breath and continued. "I'm sure you know that I'm a widow."

He nodded, unsmiling.

"I lost my husband when our embassy in Beirut was bombed years ago, but I was also pregnant. The concussion from the bomb caused me to lose the baby a few days later. My son would be twenty-three now—Rahim's age—and Rahim has told me several times that he thinks of me almost like a second mother. Yet here I am still spying on him and lying to him."

Mark put his hand on my shoulder. I was trembling. "Someday soon, Angela, you'll be able to explain this all to Rahim. I'm sure of it."

I shook my head mutely and wiped my eyes with the back of my hand.

"Listen, a few of us are gathering in the colonel's conference room this evening to try out his new projector. We'll be showing *The Beast*."

Noting the quizzical look on my face, he smiled and continued, "No, it's not a movie about that rattletrap Toyota Land Cruiser of yours, it's an American film made in the late 1980s—the story of a Soviet tank crew trapped in a remote Afghan valley and pursued by a group of angry villagers. It's become quite a cult classic among war film buffs."

"A guy movie," I said, laughing.

"Yes, but you might enjoy it. Why don't you join us? The Swedes are bringing the beer, and the room is air-conditioned. What do you say?"

"I'd like that. Thank you, Mark," I replied, mopping my brow and resuming my shredding.

THIRTY-EIGHT

Cup after cup of green tea, which turned icy during frigid winter meetings in unheated rooms and tepid as spring moved into summer, had lost its novelty after seven months in Afghanistan. Our endless and often fruitless meetings with Afghan officials were beginning to wear me down.

I looked forward to Sunday lunch at the PRT as a much-anticipated respite each week. Say what you will about British cuisine, but the food prepared by our Nepalese Gurkha military cooks was superb. While their daily fare often had curry powder or hot sauce worked into most recipes, Sunday lunch was always British comfort food at its best. Every Sunday afternoon, they carved up steaming slabs of traditional English roast beef and lamb, accompanied by crisp roasted potatoes, mint sauce, and Yorkshire pudding. Even the boiled cabbage and broad beans were cooked and seasoned to perfection in the PRT's cramped field kitchen.

Jeef had sent a message that he was coming north to visit his dig in Balkh and I invited him to join me for lunch since he would be passing through Mazār on a Sunday.

The previous year, his team of archaeologists had uncovered a jumble of Hellenistic columns and their delicately carved capitals. Their trenches were more than six meters deep, but his Afghan crew had reburied the site for the winter to protect it from looters. Now that it was uncovered, Jeef had promised to show me "something remarkable" his men had discovered only a few days before.

"Angela, what a delight to see you," cried Jeef with his characteristic enthusiasm as he bounded from his vehicle and took both of my hands into his.

He had let his hair grow longer since we last met at the museum in Kabul. His one visible eccentricity, a snowy white braid held in place by a knotted red cord, now reached below his collar. He seemed much younger than his sixty-five years, and radiated the infectious energy of a man who loved his work with a passion.

"Will my young protégé be joining us for lunch?" he asked. "I do hope so. I want to quiz him on some of the books I have assigned him to read. Rahim told me he has a friend at the university who is checking them out of the library for him."

"Yes," I replied, worrying silently about Rahim's deepening relationship with Nilofar. I knew she was continuing to provide him with books on archaeology and architecture from the university during their brief meetings in town and sometimes at the PRT. I also suspected that neither of their families knew about it or would approve if they did.

Rahim was waiting for us in the dining room. His tray was piled high with this foreign food, which he ate in enormous quantities because it was free—but admitted he didn't really like.

Mark, who usually took his meals in the officers' mess, approached our table. "May I join you?" he asked, addressing the colonel. "I've heard a great deal about Professor Mongibeaux's excavations near Balkh from Angela. I was hoping to learn more about what his workers have found there."

"Of course, Mark, please sit down," said the colonel, motioning to an empty seat next to me and making the formal introductions.

Mark and I had finally developed a real friendship. He still thought I was rash and impetuous, and I sometimes found his formality stifling, but more and more, when his fellow officers had drifted away after dinner, we would linger over coffee to talk shop. Our discussions were never personal, but we genuinely enjoyed each other's company. I was glad he'd decided to join us for lunch with Jeef.

"Colonel, as a Frenchman, I don't normally have many positive things to say about your English food, but this meal is really quite good," Jeef said, scraping the last bits of Yorkshire pudding off his plate. He had regaled us over lunch with tales of the ferocity of his Afghan crew of former antiquity thieves who now zealously guarded his dig year-round.

As promised, he also quizzed Rahim on assorted details of the Hellenistic and Kushan civilizations that lay buried beneath the soil of northern Afghanistan. Mark and the colonel were both impressed with Rahim's newly acquired, encyclopedic grasp of his country's ancient past.

"You must all come to Balkh to see what we have found," said Jeef, his eyes sparkling. "I have promised to show Angela something quite amazing which my men have just uncovered."

"I have no appointments this afternoon and neither does Mark, I believe," said the colonel. "How about now?"

"With pleasure," said Jeef.

An hour later, Mark, Rahim, the colonel, and I were peering over the edge of Jeef's terraced excavation just outside the ancient walls of Balkh City. Below us a parade of perspiring Afghan men in ragged turbans and soiled trousers were passing buckets of earth up rough-hewn ladders.

Jeef waved his hand in the direction of the towering ochre walls that had completely surrounded the city of Balkh two millennia ago when it was known as The Mother of All Cities and had served as a transit point on the great Silk Road. He explained that this city, one of the world's oldest, had been a major commercial center as early as the third century B.C., when traders from Mesopotamia traveled here to purchase lapis lazuli mined in the Hindu Kush.

"It is generally accepted that Zoroastrianism originated and flourished in Balkh between 1000 and 600 B.C.," he said.

"We also have definite proof that Alexander the Great established a colony here around 328 B.C., but we're still sorting out the precise progression of the cultures that supplanted his armies and colonists."

Jeef stepped onto a narrow wooden ladder and began his descent into the multilayered pit. "Follow me, everyone. I want to show you our latest find," he said, vanishing over the edge.

"If I had the money to steal you away from the PRT, I'd have you stay here and work with me," Jeef said as he winked at my strapping but shy interpreter, who had followed behind him down the first ladder.

This well-intentioned comment made Rahim extremely nervous. He loudly assured the colonel that as fascinating as he found Jeef's work, he had no intention of giving up his job at the PRT.

"Of course, we know you won't leave us, Rahim," replied Colonel Jameson, who had sensed the young man's need for reassurance. "I'm certain even Professor Mongibeaux knows that we have the more pressing need for your skills."

The PRT's aging senior interpreter, Professor Sayeed, had returned from Kabul the previous week after his long illness and had resumed his position as the colonel's personal interpreter. Since Colonel Jameson no longer needed Rahim, he would now be expected to accompany the MOTs on their patrols when he wasn't traveling with me. But Rahim was a skilled linguist, and I knew the colonel wanted to keep him at the PRT.

Mark had descended the third ladder ahead of me and was standing at the bottom when one of the wooden rungs snapped under my boot and I tumbled backward. He caught me under both arms to break my fall. I braced for a mini-lecture on the proper way to climb down a ladder.

"Are you all right, Angela?" was all he said.

"I'm fine. Thank you, Mark," I muttered, hoping that no one else had seen me fall.

At the bottom of the pit, we gathered in a tight circle as Jeef knelt in the dirt before an elaborately carved Indo-Corinthian capital still half embedded in thick red clay.

"The skill of the carving and the realistic design of the foliage has most of us convinced that this work was done by Greek craftsmen, but look at what is in the center!"

Sculpted into the granite capital and still crusted with bits of rust-colored earth was a rotund seated Buddha. "This is the first of these we have found so far north," Jeef exclaimed.

Rahim bent down and ran his fingers over the tiny figure. "*Khuda-hafiz,*" he murmured. "God be with you."

THIRTY-NINE

A message from the U.S. Embassy had arrived informing me that Afghan customs officials in the northern border city of Hairatan were reportedly skimming off a portion of the U.S. jet fuel destined for Bagram Air Base as soon as it came across the bridge from Uzbekistan. Afghan women who bought the stolen fuel on the black market thinking it was kerosene were suffering terrible burns. I remembered seeing one of those women at the prison in Mazār. The embassy wanted me to do something about it.

"Angela, I'm delighted that your government is taking action on the missing jet fuel," said Colonel Jameson when I told him about the request and the documents I had received from my embassy.

"I'd like you to take the professor instead of Rahim with you to Hairatan tomorrow for your meeting with the customs officials."

"Good idea. He's the only terp I haven't observed in action."

"I want Mark to go with you as well."

"Mark? Why? This is a U.S. issue," I said, sounding more upset than I had intended. As much as I had grown to like Major Davies, he still made me nervous. I didn't want him hovering in the background while I undertook this awkward negotiation on behalf of my government.

"Because, Angela," the colonel replied, peering at me over the top of his glasses, "some of the new police officials being sent to Hairatan are Pashtun. You have monitored every one of our terps since you arrived in January, and they have all passed with flying colors. As you noted, the professor is the only one you have not observed, but since he speaks both Dari and Pashto, I want Mark to be with you listening in as well."

"Of course, Colonel," I replied, surprised and embarrassed at my outburst. "It makes perfect sense."

The formerly bustling port city of Hairatan was a major smuggling center in northern Afghanistan. Although its riverside loading docks sat silent and abandoned next to the lumbering Amu Darya, rail and truck traffic flowed in a steady stream across the Soviet-built Friendship Bridge, where three months earlier, I had made my frantic after-dark dash back into Afghanistan with the ailing agricultural specialist curled up and moaning on the backseat of the Beast. This border crossing was a cash cow for corrupt government officials and for the Afghan warlords who controlled the surrounding districts in Balkh Province.

Professor Sayeed accompanied me in the lead vehicle the following morning. He tugged nervously at his clipped gray beard and spoke little until after we left the Mazār city limits. The old man was clearly not thrilled about having to ride with "the woman" instead of with Major Davies in the follow car, but he knew I represented the U.S. government, which made me almost the major's equal in his eyes. He started to relax after our first hour on the road when I inquired about his time in Kabul. My efforts succeeded.

By the time we reached Hairatan, we were both laughing at his stories about the antics of his grandchildren during the long months he'd been recuperating at his son's home in Kabul. He seemed like a nice guy, and after today's meeting I looked forward to finally being able to check the last PRT interpreter off my list of suspects.

The meeting dragged on well into the afternoon. The first hour was routine. I made my points in English about how the jet fuel should be accounted for, and the professor translated my words into Dari with great precision. I handed over the documents from the minister of the interior, which the three customs officials and the Pashtun-speaking police chief read carefully, assuring me they would do their best to comply. Mark and I, on our fourth or was it our fifth cup of tea, began exchanging silent glances of desperation—would this meeting never end?

Well into the third hour, the conversation took a stunning turn. The meeting seemed to be winding down, when Mark and I watched in astonishment as the professor, having no idea we understood both of his languages, began to negotiate a deal with the four men to help them conceal their continued theft of fuel if they would give him a cut. The professor explained to us in English that he was telling the men how important the jet fuel was for fighting the Taliban in the south.

Confident that local warlords would protect them, the men plotted to continue sharing in the profits and completely ignore the documents I had just handed over to them.

The crafty old interpreter's belief that we ignorant "foreigners" had not a clue what he was doing was about to come crashing down. It was clear that this was not the first "deal" struck by the professor during his years at the PRT, even though we had no proof he'd ever been involved in drug trafficking. The colonel sent him packing as soon as Mark and I returned and made our report in the afternoon.

Mark joined me upstairs for a cup of tea after the ops room briefing the following morning. "Angela, your draft memo on yesterday's meeting in Hairatan is excellent, but you're looking quite exhausted this morning. Did you stay up all night writing it?" he asked.

"No. I called the embassy when we got back yesterday and gave them the unclassified version, then typed up the first draft as soon as I got off the phone. They've finally authorized me to start speaking Dari," I added with little enthusiasm.

"You don't sound very pleased," he said. "I thought you'd be over the moon about it. The colonel has also authorized me to start using my Pashto."

"That's great, Mark, and I am thrilled that the mystery of the unreliable interpreter has finally been solved, but I'm worried about the terps' reaction when they find out how we've been concealing our language skills."

My voice cracked, betraying the exhaustion I felt after having lain awake most of the previous night wondering how I would explain these months of deception to my young friend without losing the trust I had worked so hard to build.

"I'm sure Rahim will understand," Mark assured me. He knew exactly which terp I was referring to.

"The colonel seemed quite relieved at our morning briefing when he announced that the good professor was already on his way back to Kabul," Mark added as he poured milk into his tea.

"Yes," I replied wearily, "I think he was right to get him out of here immediately and leave him to the mercy of the Afghan authorities."

Mark took a deep breath before continuing. "Angela, you know that the Friendship Bridge may someday soon become a much more strategic choke point for NATO supplies coming into Afghanistan."

I nodded.

"I know that yesterday's meeting was at the request of your embassy, but I do hope you won't mind if I insert a few points on military security into your report before comms sends the classified version to Kabul."

I had no reason to object and was too exhausted to discuss the matter further. "Put in whatever you want and send it off. Leave a copy in my READ file. I have to go up to my room and lie down."

"Right," he said, looking concerned.

"Thanks for coming with me yesterday, Mark. I'm glad you were there."

"Anytime, Angela."

FORTY

Colonel Jameson saved me the trouble of explaining my sudden fluency in Dari to Rahim by summoning him to his office and offering him the position of head interpreter. The colonel left his door ajar so those of us in the bullpen could listen in on their conversation.

"Sir, I am most grateful for your generous offer," said Rahim. "We were all saddened and ashamed to learn about Professor Sayeed's deception, but, sir, I have always interpreted for the Americans, and I have been working with Miss Morgan for more than six months. It will be very difficult for her to start again with another interpreter."

I was stunned to hear Rahim turning down this promotion so he could continue working with me. His incredible loyalty was about to be rewarded with the news that I had been deceiving him all these months. My heart sank.

"Rahim, Miss Morgan doesn't need an interpreter."

"I'm sorry, sir, I don't understand."

"She speaks Dari almost as well as you," the colonel replied.

"Oh, no, sir. I know she took lessons in America, but she still needs me with her to translate when she goes to meetings."

He was defending me while still insisting that I needed him. What a wonderful kid. I cringed at what the colonel was about to tell him.

"Rahim, Miss Morgan has been under strict orders since she arrived at this PRT to conceal her knowledge of your language. Before anyone could know this, we had to make sure that none of our interpreters was providing inaccurate translations," explained the colonel as gently as possible to the stunned Rahim.

"She gave all of you glowing reports months ago, but until she and the major discovered the professor's deception yesterday, she was forbidden by her embassy from revealing her fluency in Dari. It's been difficult for her, but our long efforts have paid off and we have been able to rid the PRT of the one interpreter who was deceiving us."

Rahim was silent.

"So what do you say to my offer?" asked the colonel.

"Thank you, sir. This is a great honor and I accept."

Rahim stepped out of the colonel's office and into the bullpen, where my office mates stared at us both in amazement.

"Angela, may I speak to you alone?" whispered Rahim as he squeezed around my typing table. I nodded and followed him into the rose garden, which had exploded into a riot of red, yellow, pink, and white blossoms.

Rahim looked at me with an expression I could not read. His silence was providing unspoken confirmation of the one thing I feared most—that no matter what I said to him in the future, he would never trust me again.

"Does this mean that we were never really friends after all?" he asked, staring down at me. "I can't believe you've been spying on me all these months. How could you possibly think that I would lie to you or the colonel about what was being said during your meetings?"

His deep brown eyes glistened, and his jaw muscles flexed while he waited for my response.

"Oh, Rahim-*jan*," I said, speaking to him for the first time in his native tongue and unable to control my tears, which were now flowing freely. "I always trusted you, and it has hurt me terribly to have to lie all these months, but as the colonel explained, I had no choice."

"Does this mean we can no longer be friends since you won't need me to translate for you?" he whispered in Dari as he struggled to maintain his composure.

"Of course, we'll still be friends," I said taking his hands into mine. "We can be better friends than ever. I've hated this deception. I only hope you'll forgive me."

A single tear trickled down his cheek, and he wiped it away as a broad grin spread across his face.

"I will forgive you under two conditions," he said.

I swallowed hard and nodded.

"Since we can now speak to each other in Dari, I want to start calling you by your real name," he announced.

"My real name?"

"Yes, your Afghan name. Governor Daoud calls you Farishta and so will I."

"That's fine with me, Rahim," I said, relieved at his modest request.

"One more thing, Farishta-*jan*, before I forgive you for deceiving me."

"Yes?" Perhaps I had relaxed too soon.

"Nilofar's family has invited me and my American 'cousin' to dinner again on Saturday. I can only accept if you come with me. Will you?" he asked.

"Of course, I will!"

"Then, Farishta-*jan*, all is forgiven," he said with an enormous sigh as he turned and ran to the interpreters' room to share his surprising news.

FORTY-ONE

July 23, 2005

"Angela, I was just informed by the boys at the airport that you have several kilos of letters and magazines and a hell of a lot of aluminum foil waiting to be picked up in your mailbox," said Sergeant Major when I passed him in the hall.

"I've authorized an airport run in your vehicle. The ops officer has instructed Jenkins to take 'route blue' south of town since we've had reports of a possible disturbance on the main road out of Mazār," he added, looking mildly concerned. "Jenkins and Fuzzy are leaving in thirty minutes if you want to go along."

As the Beast churned up thick clouds of summer dust and Jenkins struggled to keep its fenders from scraping the mud walls that lined the narrow village roads south of Mazār, my cell phone began to vibrate in my pocket.

"Hi, Angela, it's Marty. How ya doin'?" My favorite personnel officer was calling from Washington, perhaps with good news about the elusive London assignment.

"Marty! What a surprise! I'm fine, but I can't hear you very well. Is there something urgent or can we continue this conversation via e-mail?"

"Don't worry, Ange, it's not a collect call. The Department's paying and I'll make it quick."

I gritted my teeth. The Department might be paying for his end of the call, but it wasn't paying for mine. Every minute we talked was using up one of the cell phone cards that I bought on the street in Mazār. But I had to keep this civil. Marty was my lifeline if I ever had any hope of getting to London—which after six months in Afghanistan felt as far away as Xanadu.

"What's up?"

"I've got two males and one female candidate bidding on your position at the PRT for next year. Only six months to go, Ange! I'll need a two-page description of your living conditions ASAP."

"Any word on my next assignment?" I asked hopefully.

"I'm working on London, assuming that's still your first choice but I . . ." Marty was fading and difficult to hear over the urgent voice that began crackling on the Beast's two-way radio.

"Delta two zulu, delta two zulu, this is Hotel one zero. Report received of BBIED your route. Return my location immediately. Repeat, return my location immediately!"

I had lost the signal with Marty, and presumed we were in some sort of danger, but I hadn't understood the message. I unclipped my seat belt in case I had to exit the vehicle quickly. Gripping the front seat, I scanned the street in front of us. I could see only a young boy riding his bicycle a few blocks away.

"Fuzzy, what's a BBIED?" I asked as Jenkins hit the brakes and shifted the Beast into reverse.

"Bicycle-borne improvised explosive device!" shouted Jenkins before Fuzzy had even opened his mouth. The innocent youth who was now riding in our direction looked suddenly menacing.

"How the fuck am I supposed to turn the Beast around in this fucking tunnel?" Jenkins fumed as he looked behind us at the narrow road lined with towering walls.

Three children suddenly appeared in front of us and two more jumped out in back, blocking our way. Jenkins began honking and shouting out his window. This had the effect of summoning even more children into the street.

The boy was now pedaling fast.

Fuzzy released the safety on his rifle and took aim at the approaching cyclist. "Jesus, Jenkins," he shouted, "can't you get us out of here? I don't want to shoot a kid."

"Let me get out and speak to the children," I said. I could feel the bile burning my throat. I was scared, but I was also determined not to curl up into a useless ball. "I can explain why we need them to move."

"Angela, I want you down on the floor, now!" shouted Fuzzy. I obeyed without further discussion and resigned myself to the fact that my life was now in the hands of two young men who weren't even old enough to buy a fucking beer in the United States of America.

Jenkins leaned on the horn and maneuvered the Beast down the road in reverse. The children jumped out of the way when it became clear that these soldiers would not be passing out candy or free NATO newspapers.

As soon as the road widened, he spun the Beast around. I climbed back into my seat and we drove as fast as the Beast would carry us back to camp. Neither the reported disturbance on the

Mazār road nor the bicycle bomber ever materialized, but we were safe and no children had been harmed in my failed attempt to pick up my mail.

With no new magazines to read, I composed a long e-mail reply to Marty that afternoon with a description of our mud-walled compound, my Spartan living quarters, coed bathroom, typing table, the Beast, and my still undefined but increasingly active role in the PRT command structure.

It really didn't matter what I wrote, however, because soon after my replacement got here at the end of December, the Swedish Army would take over the running of PRT Mazār from the Brits and would abandon this ramshackle collection of buildings for their far more secure compound under construction near the airport.

FORTY-TWO

July 24, 2005

I'd overdone it at Sunday lunch and had gone up to my room for a
little snooze before returning to the bullpen. Today was a work-
day, but I knew no one would notice my absence for an extra hour.
The AC had been fixed in my room, and it was a comfortable
eighty degrees. My nap was cut short by a knock at the door.

"Farishta-*jan*, I need to speak with you!" It was Rahim, whose
whispered voice and soft tapping were barely audible.

As soon as I saw his face, I knew something was wrong.

"Come in, Rahim."

"No, it would not be right for me to come inside your room,"
he insisted as he planted himself in the doorway.

"Shall we go downstairs?" I asked.

"No, no. We must talk here," he insisted. "It's Nilofar."

"Did something happen to her?"

"We've been talking about getting married. She went to her
mother and told her about us last night, and her mother went right
to her father, who ordered her not to see me anymore. You know
that her family is Hazara and I am Tajik. Her mother told her they
had only been inviting me to their house for dinner because you

came with me. They still think you and I are cousins, and they may let her visit you at the PRT, but she has been told never to see or speak to me again." He pressed his fingers against his forehead and closed his eyes.

"Her father is a merchant, but he lost most of his savings and all of their land during the years of fighting here. Nilofar's mother told her that a Hazara businessman in Mazār has already asked their permission to marry her.

"She called me this morning. She was crying and threatening to run away. What should we do, Farishta-*jan*?" he pleaded.

I exhaled slowly. What could I tell him? He and Nilofar were headed for heartbreak or exile from their families—or worse. I cursed myself for having encouraged their flirtation. How could I have been such a Pollyanna?

"Rahim, perhaps with time, her father's heart will soften. You must be patient," I replied, knowing that such a response would provide no comfort to my distressed young friend.

"I love her. I will not stop seeing her," he vowed through clenched teeth.

Rahim remained for almost an hour in the doorway of my room, baring his soul about his love for Nilofar. All I could do was listen since I had no solutions to offer. Marriage for love was still a rare occurrence in Afghanistan.

"Farishta-*jan*, will you still invite Nilofar to the PRT for meetings if her parents allow it?" he begged.

"Of course, I will."

I knew this was a mistake. It would only prolong their suffering and make it even more difficult for them when Nilofar's parents made good on their threat to marry her off.

It soon became clear that Nilofar was far more headstrong than I had imagined. She and Rahim continued to meet secretly at the university, and whenever she came to see me at the PRT, she made certain it was Rahim who let her in the gate and escorted her out at the end of our meetings. I so wanted these two young people to be together, but if I'd been honest with myself, I would have admitted that there could be no happy ending to this story.

FORTY-THREE

July 25, 2005

An angry swarm of bees was chasing me across an open field. I ran barefoot toward a faceless man whose singsong chanting grew softer the closer I got. Tom appeared next to me, grabbing my arm and pulling me to the ground. We both crouched and braced for the explosion. "Tom, I can't breathe," I cried, but he was gone. The bees surrounded me, and my arms flailed as I tried without success to brush them away.

I awoke with a start, gasping for breath in the rose-hued darkness of early morning Mazār-i-Sharīf. My cell phone, tethered to its charging cord, was vibrating loudly on my desk. Sunrise was still thirty minutes away, and the mullah across the street was completing the final verses of his first call to prayer.

I jumped out of bed and grabbed the phone. My heart, thundering as it always did when calls came at odd hours, felt like it was about to explode. Peering through the cluster of communications antennas just outside my room, I could see the old mullah below, partially concealed under the thick summer foliage of his pistachio tree. I watched him slowly rolling up his prayer rug. I was still out of breath from my dream.

"This is Angela Morgan."

"Ange, it's Bill. Dad's in the hospital and he's pretty bad off. He was riding the mare when something spooked her. She threw him, and the doctors aren't sure he's going to make it. If you want to see him before he checks out for good, you'd better get back here pronto." Bill's words were as clear as if he were in the next room. I could hear the anxiety in his voice.

After providing the gory details of Dad's possible cerebral hemorrhage and multiple fractures, he made me promise I'd get home as soon as possible. As hard as this news was to hear, it wasn't unexpected. I'd put off taking my R&R for just this eventuality.

The colonel, Sergeant Major, the embassy—everyone— jumped through hoops to get me booked on the eight separate flights that would take me from Mazār to Kabul to Dubai to New York to Albuquerque and back again in the space of two weeks.

Three days later, with my mind numbed by twelve time zones of jet lag and thirty hours of sleepless travel, I walked right by my brother, who had been waiting for me in the baggage claim area at the airport.

"Ange, where are you going?" Bill's familiar voice soared above the airport din like a well-aimed arrow and pierced the fog that shrouded my brain. I was still searching the crowd for his leathery face when two rough hands grabbed my shoulders and spun me into the biggest, tightest hug my brother had given me since grade school.

As Bill's embrace lifted me from the stupor of that long trip, the sights and sounds of home began flooding in—starting with Roberta Flack purring out of the airport's Muzak system. Two fresh-faced, giggling teenage girls in jeans and tank tops walked by us, trailing their parents through the terminal, dragging their roller bags and fiddling with their cell phones.

It was all so wonderfully normal and unremarkable. No one stared at them because of how they were dressed, no one was carrying a rifle, and there were no blast walls.

"God, I'm glad you're here, Ange," Bill said. "It looks like Dad's going to pull through. He's awake and sore, but as ornery as ever. There's been no more bleeding, thank God. The doctors want us to put him in assisted living, but he said if he can't go back to the ranch, they might as well just shoot him and dig a hole."

"So what are we doing?" I asked my brother, who was still gripping me tighter than a drowning man in a stormy sea. Although Bill and I had drifted apart after I'd joined the Foreign Service, the potential loss of that final link to my childhood was summoning emotions I thought had faded long ago.

I remembered how much Tom and I had enjoyed visiting Bill and my parents at the ranch. My mother adored Tom, while Dad in his own gruff way had made him feel like he'd always been a member of our family.

One of our favorite things to do when we went to the ranch was ride the fence line. On those daylong mounted treks, we would walk our horses through miles of prairie short grass, checking for breaks in the barbed wire and rescuing stranded heifers. The last time we had visited the ranch together was right when we were starting to try for a baby. As we rode, Tom and I spent hours talking about the day when we would be able to share all of this with our own children. I had imagined lazy afternoons in years to come when I would send Tom off with Dad and the kids to check the pastures while Mom and I made fresh tortillas and roasted chili peppers for supper.

It was still painful to acknowledge that my dream of a large and loving family gathering at the ranch to celebrate the holidays was never going to happen. Bill had been running the business side of Dad's spread for the past few years, but since he also worked part-time in Albuquerque as an accountant, he had already leased most of the land out to neighboring ranchers.

Bill's wife, who also worked in Albuquerque, had been nagging him since they got married to give up their long-distance commute and move into the city. The thought of no Morgan family members on the ranch saddened me, but since I hadn't lived there full-time for almost thirty years, I had little say in the matter.

Dad's young wife, who clearly hadn't planned on becoming the nursemaid to an invalid old man, was sitting near his hospital bed when we arrived. She was the saddest-looking person in the room, but it wasn't because of Dad's injuries. Bill told me she had just learned that although Dad's estate would provide her with a comfortable living when he was gone, he had left the ranch to Bill and me.

Our ever-practical father, who knew that his young wife wouldn't be willing to nurse him back to health and who didn't want to bother Bill or me, had also with great reluctance arranged for the sale of fifty prime acres of his ranch to a developer in order to cover the expense of round-the-clock nursing care at home.

Six days after I arrived, we took Dad home and settled him into his rented hospital bed. The nursing assistants started their rotations, fussed over Dad, and pretty much took care of everything, to the great relief of the young Mrs. Morgan, who spent most of her time watching soap operas and doing her nails.

Bill and I went on a few rides together, but we didn't go far and didn't talk much while we rode. He asked very few questions about my life in Afghanistan.

On my last day at the ranch under the blazing New Mexico sun, I cooked an Afghan meal of lamb, rice, and dumplings in a solar oven Bill helped me assemble out in the barn with an old cardboard box, a windowpane, and aluminum foil. Even Dad, a meat-and-potatoes man, seemed to enjoy the food.

"This solar box stuff is pretty neat, Ange," he said, smacking his lips.

"So tell us what it's like over there in Afghanistan."

"It's beautiful, Dad, confusing and heartbreaking," I began.

"Are you really the only woman with all those foreign soldiers?" asked Dad's wife, grimacing at the thought.

"I am for the moment," I replied. "There were a few women at the PRT before me, but none lived there full-time, like I do."

"I assume they all speak English," huffed my father.

"Most of them are British, Dad. Their English is better than mine."

"Why didn't they put you with some of our American boys?" he asked with a hint of anger in his voice.

"Most State Department officers are assigned to U.S. PRTs, but I really don't mind being with the Brits. They're great guys, and there's a camp about fifteen miles from us with a unit of Texas National Guard soldiers who are training the Afghans. They treat me like family whenever I go out there for meetings."

"Texans," he harrumphed. "Too bad it wasn't a New Mexico

unit." Dad paused to chew and swallow another mouthful of rice. The mention of Texas had reminded him of his favorite subject. "The Lobos are going to crush Texas Tech this fall, don't you think, Bill."

"Not unless UNM finds a new quarterback before the season starts," Bill said with real concern.

The subject had changed, and I knew we would not be talking about Afghanistan anymore this evening. But I didn't mind. Listening to Dad and Bill blather on about football was strangely comforting, despite the fact that I had not the slightest interest in the sport. Even the conversation between Dad's wife and Bill's wife about a TV show I'd never heard of made me feel oddly at home.

Bill offered to do the dishes that night and suggested I take the dogs for a last walk. In the star-spangled blue dark of a balmy New Mexico summer evening, I strolled down our long dirt driveway with Dad's two border collies bounding ahead of me.

As the moon rose over the Sandias, casting the same long silvery shadows that crept every night over the ragged peaks of the Hindu Kush south of Mazār, I was overwhelmed by an intense and inexplicable desire to be back in Afghanistan. I missed the sights, sounds, and smells of that distant land, but I also missed the feeling of purpose and camaraderie that comes from being thrust into a dangerous situation with a group of dedicated people. And, yes, if I thought about it long enough, I missed my conversations with Mark.

As I followed the dogs toward the main road, I wondered what these feelings meant for my return. How could that country I'd been so sure would destroy me have cast such a spell over me?

And why was I so anxious to get back to a place where there were people who might actually want to kill me and where I encountered professional and personal frustrations on a daily basis?

Halfway down to the highway, the dogs almost tripped me as they scooted underfoot chasing a rabbit into a clump of chaparral. An approaching truck backfired once, then louder the second time as its headlights flashed by our gate on the unlit road.

I froze after the second explosion. My pulse went into overdrive. My palms and forehead grew clammy with sweat. The familiar wide-open spaces of my youth suddenly terrified me. I braced for another blast and irrationally reassured myself that it was just the Estonians conducting one of their demolitions.

Crouching in the dirt, my hands covering my face, I waited for the panic attack to subside. The dogs, sensing my fear, crowded around me, whining softly and pressing their cool noses against my neck.

After seven months of living behind the guarded walls and razor wire of the PRT, and leaving that confined space only when accompanied by armed soldiers or hidden under my burka, I felt suddenly naked, vulnerable, and terrified on this narrow dirt road I had traveled a thousand times in my youth.

The dogs helped, but it was the memory of Mike's shouted instructions from first-aid class that pulled me out of what I vowed would be the last panic attack of my life.

"*Morgan, check the shadows. Look around and tell me exactly what you see. Every detail!*"

The intense rush of adrenaline had ampified my senses, making it easy to scan my surroundings and describe to myself the sand verbena, black brush, and desert holly that grew in thick clumps to the western horizon. The dogs circled me until I stood up. When they were satisfied that I was okay, they lowered their noses to the ground and resumed their search for rabbits and field mice. My breathing became more regular. I whistled for them to follow me and walked back to the house. I would discuss this incident with no one.

Four days later, as the embassy plane circled for a landing at the empty airfield in Mazār-i-Sharīf, I was thrilled to see Fuzzy and Jenkins lounging against the Beast on the shimmering hot runway. They welcomed me with hugs. Although I knew my presence here was temporary—that these young soldiers and I would be leaving Afghanistan in less than six months—I felt at that moment as I climbed into the backseat of the Beast far more like I was coming home than I had in New Mexico.

We drove slowly into town and around the Blue Mosque, with the hot dusty summer air blowing through the Beast's open windows. Fuzzy scanned the crowds as usual while Jenkins updated me on the comings and goings at the PRT.

"Are you guys hungry?" I asked. They had missed lunch waiting for my plane.

"I'm starving," replied Jenkins. "We'll get some leftovers when we get back to camp."

"Let me buy you guys lunch in town," I said. "Turn left up here, Jenkins, and we'll make a stop at the open market where they sell food."

"Are you sure this is a good idea?" asked Fuzzy with a worried frown.

"Trust me, Fuz."

"Stop here, Jenkins," I said, jumping out of the vehicle and waiting for Fuzzy. He hoisted his rifle over his shoulder and followed me reluctantly to the smoking grill of a brochette seller, where I bought half a kilo of roasted lamb kabobs. At nearby stalls, I purchased three rounds of fresh-baked and still warm *naan*, three liters of Coca-Cola, and a sweet, ripe Mazār melon. Fuzzy helped me carry them back to the Beast.

"Dig in, fellows," I said. "You'll love it."

I was silently disappointed to learn that Mark had been sent south to Helmand for several weeks, but the familiar faces of the other soldiers and the terps, who greeted me warmly as I hauled my suitcase up to my room, wrapped me in a blanket of familiarity as comforting as that first cup of tea I made for myself when I entered the main PRT building.

I remained tied to my desk until an invitation arrived a few days later from one of the MOT commanders to accompany him and his men on a ten-day patrol into a remote corner of Sar-e Pol Province.

FORTY-FOUR

August 12, 2005 ✦ Sar-e Pol Province

A late afternoon breeze sweeping down the canyon rustled the tamarisk bushes next to the stream where I had knelt to wash my hair. It was day six of our patrol through the most remote mountain districts of Sar-e Pol.

We had stopped to make camp for the evening, and I was taking advantage of this opportunity to wash my hands, feet, face, and hair with running water. I leaned over, dipped my head into the stream, and was rinsing shampoo from my hair and eyes when I heard splashing and shouting.

"Angela, stay down and don't move!" It was Captain Tim Baker, the commanding officer of our three-vehicle patrol. The splashing was now accompanied by barking. I froze into a crouched position, and turned my head just enough to see a gigantic earless dog, his teeth bared, splashing over the rocks in the stream and coming fast in my direction. I took a deep breath, recalled the promise I'd made to myself in New Mexico, and stayed still.

Behind the approaching dog, I could see three bearded, turbaned Kuchi nomads carrying large staffs. They were trailed by six camels loaded down with supplies and three women wearing

indigo gowns, their arms, ears, and noses jangling with gold jewelry. Small children chased one another around the camels. None
of them seemed at all concerned about the huge dog that was
about to attack me.

Glancing over my shoulder again, I could see Fuzzy standing
near our campsite. His rifle was trained on the dog, which he was
about to shoot, when a sharp whistle from one of the nomads
brought the animal to a sudden halt. The dog was less than three
meters away from me, and the thick ruff of its matted brindle coat
was raised in anger. It bared its teeth, swung its earless head, the
size and shape of a bear's, in my direction and let loose a final low
growl before trotting back to the herd and resuming its job of
guarding the sheep.

Fuzzy lowered his weapon and went back to helping the others
set up their tents and communications equipment in the shade of
the massive orange-streaked slab of granite that loomed over our
campsite.

"All clear, Angela. Back to your shampooing," shouted Baker,
his laughing voice echoing off the steep canyon walls.

As the caravan lumbered by on the opposite side of the stream,
I sat on a flat rock, dangled my toes in the water, and greeted
the women in Dari while I dried my hair. They smiled and waved
back, but their men stared at me in silence— as though I were an
alien species—neither male nor female, or perhaps a bit of both.
They did lift their long wooden staffs to wave at the soldiers, who
returned their greeting.

This journey had taken us into valleys—Hazara, Pashtun,
Uzbek, and Tajik—that hadn't been visited by NATO soldiers for
more than a year. In each village where we stopped, Captain Baker

and his second-in-command would go off with their interpreter to meet with the district chief or local warlord.

Now that I no longer had to hide my language skills, I used these opportunities to speak with the women. As soon as our convoy rolled into the center of a village, I would cover my hair with a head scarf, put on a knee-length tunic, and stand in the road next to our vehicles. Within minutes, curious women would crack their heavy wooden doors just wide enough to peek out. As soon as they spotted a female with the soldiers, they would poke their fingers out and invite me to enter their walled compounds, where they could remain hidden from prying male eyes.

It was always a challenge explaining to them who I was and why I was traveling alone with so many men. The cultural chasm between us was almost too vast to bridge, but they still seemed anxious to share with me stories about their children's schooling, local opium trafficking, and the real power brokers in their districts.

The biggest concern for these women was that their husbands or their sons might have to go into battle again—against other warlords, the Taliban, the Russians, or a new foreign invader. They did not yet include us in that last category.

It didn't really matter to them who the enemy was. Many of them didn't even know the name of Afghanistan's current president. All they wanted was to have their husbands at home, cultivating their crops and tending their animals. They were terrified that if there was renewed fighting in the north, more land mines would be scattered across their fields, the irrigation ditches would be bombed from the air, and their men wouldn't be able to produce enough food to last through the winter. They wanted to be left in peace to raise and educate their children. They wanted access to medical care and, of course, they all wanted cell phones.

Whenever we stopped in a village over the lunch hour, I'd pull out one of my solar ovens and gather a few women inside a compound to show them how I could boil water with sunshine.

On the seventh day of our patrol, we pulled into a small dusty village, dominated by a hulking mud-walled fortress on a cliff just above town.

"This is the territory of Khan Hussein Cherik," said Zalmay, the young PRT interpreter who had accompanied us on this patrol. "That is the khan's home," he added, pointing with great solemnity up at the medieval walls and imposing guard towers of the massive mud structure.

"He is a great friend of General Kabir. The khan's granddaughter was the little girl who was almost killed by the suicide bomber in Andkhoy. The one you took to the hospital." Zalmay's eyes widened to indicate that Khan Cherik was clearly a powerful and important man and that I was very fortunate to be in his good graces.

"I'd love to see how she's doing, Tim," I said to Captain Baker. It was hard to believe that I might actually know someone in this isolated corner of Afghanistan. It seemed that years rather than months had passed since that cold February afternoon in Andkhoy when I'd first seen the little girl with her father.

"If she's there, you should be able to see her this evening, Angela. We'll be camping near the village, but we're all invited to the fort for a meal later this afternoon with the khan and the male members of his family."

Dinner was a lavish affair. The khan's son Farhad recounted to the assembled male diners the entire story of the bombing in And-khoy, portraying me, much to my embarrassment, as a cross be-tween Wonder Woman and Florence Nightingale.

As we prepared to return to our camp, Farhad insisted that his wife and mother wanted me to spend the night with them in the women's quarters. I shot a quick glance at Baker, who was looking extremely unhappy at this idea. Before he could stop me, I told Farhad that I would love to accept their invitation.

"Please be careful. Call us if you need help for any reason, Angela," Captain Baker told me as he pressed a radio into my hand before walking through the gate that was about to separate me from the rest of the MOT. Fuzzy turned around and shot me a final worried glance as the tall wooden doors were pulled shut and bolted by the khan's men.

"*Honum,* come with me, please," said a servant who led me into a spacious room with arched windows that looked out over a long, irrigated valley. She reappeared, carrying a basin filled with warm water, a folded towel, and a simple blue robe. After I had bathed and put on the robe, a movement at the door caught my eye. It was the little Afghan Shirley Temple peeking shyly around the corner.

When her mother and another woman, whom I presumed to be her grandmother, urged her to approach me, she began to walk in my direction, supported by a tiny crutch under her arm and limp-ing as though she were still in pain.

"Thank you for saving my daughter," the child's mother said. She began to weep and kiss my hands. The little girl grabbed her mother's skirt and looked up at me with solemn eyes.

"I was happy that I could help her. It was a terrible day." I looked down at the little girl who was now standing in front of me. She was beautiful.

"Why does she limp?" I asked.

"Part of the metal from the bomb is still in her leg. The doctor said she does not feel pain, but she will always walk this way. Her life comes at a cost. The wounds have left terrible scars. No man will ever want to marry my wonderful child. But my sons will protect her."

"What is your name, child?" I asked.

"Farishta," she replied.

"Farishta is my name, too!" I said. "We are both angels!"

She laughed and pressed her small hands together. "Mama, we have the same name!"

More female family members entered the room followed by their children. We slept early and rose at first light. After we were served tea and fresh warm bread, Grandmother, who had expressed serious concern about me traveling with the soldiers and wearing boots and trousers, stood and walked to my side.

"You are a very bad woman to live with those foreign men, Farishta," she said, slapping my hand gently, but with a twinkle in her eye. "It is even worse that you dress like them! At least your eyes should look like a woman's eyes." She extracted a silver vial of kohl from a pocket in her robe and waved it in the air.

"This will make your eyes beautiful." The other women nodded.

Grandmother led me to the window where the light was best. She dipped a thin silver applicator into a saucer of water and then into the vial of dark kohl, tapping it to loosen the excess powder.

"This will make a man lose himself when you look at him, but you must be careful not to look at any of those soldiers you are traveling with. They will not be able to control themselves." The other women laughed hysterically.

"Don't you have a husband, Farishta?" asked little Farishta's mother when the laughter stopped.

"I lost my husband many years ago," I replied.

The women lowered their eyes and fell silent until Grandmother announced matter-of-factly that many women who lose their husbands are still able to find another one.

"You are still young, Farishta," she chided.

"I'm not as young as you think, Grandmother," I replied.

When I told them my age, which was only twelve years younger than Grandmother, there was much astonishment and chattering among the other women until Grandmother called everyone's attention again to the task at hand.

"Do not be afraid, Farishta," she laughed, holding a mirror close to my face. "Close one eye, then take the applicator between your fingers."

I drew the silver tip once above and once below each eye just where the lashes sprouted, leaving a smoky line across the inside of my upper and lower lids.

"Let us celebrate Farishta's new eyes with more tea and sweet biscuits," Grandmother said, clapping her hands for the servant girl to bring us more refreshments.

A loud crash in the courtyard and the sound of screaming frightened the returning servant, who dropped the tea tray and ran out of the room. Little Farishta's older brother, Aziz, ran into the women's quarters, his face white and his lips quivering.

"Mother, soldiers have broken through the outside door." He

was almost in tears. "I am the only man here, and I think the soldiers are going to take me away. Some of them have gone to the roof where Grandfather is drying our harvest of marijuana."

"You grow marijuana?" I shouldn't have been surprised at this. Eight-foot cannabis plants grew in profusion alongside the roads and irrigation ditches of Balkh and every other province in the north.

"All families in this district have produced hashish for generations, Farishta-*jan*," said Grandmother, who seemed surprised at my ignorance. "It is our custom."

The door to the women's quarters flew open, and an armed Afghan soldier pointed at Aziz, who cowered next to his mother. "The boy must come with me," he ordered.

There wasn't time to radio Captain Baker and his men at the bottom of the hill, but I knew that Afghan soldiers in this part of the country did not conduct presence patrols without American advisors. I found it hard to believe that Colonel Tremain would authorize his men to allow their Afghan trainees to break into a family compound.

I stood up and faced the soldier. "Take me to the American who is in charge of this training mission."

He was momentarily stunned that a woman would make such a demand, but when I didn't blink or back away, he released the boy and walked out of the women's quarters. I followed him through the partially smashed wooden gate. Fifteen Afghan soldiers stood outside the compound with their rifles drawn. Several yards away, I could see an American soldier watching us. His rifle was also pointed at the khan's fortress.

He shouted in Dari at the Afghan soldier who had come through the gate in front of me. "Muhammad, why did you bring that woman out here?"

"I brought myself out here," I shouted back in English. "What the hell are you doing authorizing these soldiers to break into a family compound?"

"Are you American?" asked the astounded soldier who lowered his rifle.

"Who authorized this operation?" I demanded.

"Who are you?" he replied. "And what are you doing here?"

I explained who I was, and he informed me he was on a special training mission and did not report to Tremain. More than that, he would not reveal. He barked a command in Dari to the Afghan soldiers, who followed him at a trot down a dirt road and away from the khan's fort.

I switched on the radio to alert Captain Baker.

"This isn't the first time your Yanks have led patrols into our AO without advance warning," he muttered. "I knew I shouldn't have let you stay up there."

"I'm fine, Tim," I assured him.

"Right, I'll report this incident to the PRT and let the colonel sort it out with Tremain."

They picked me up an hour later. "Angela, if you ever go on a patrol with my MOT again and you ask to sleep overnight in a family compound, please remind me to say no," Baker pleaded as we drove out of the khan's village and headed back to Mazār-i-Sharīf. Fuzzy nodded in silent agreement.

"I promise."

Four days later, our tired convoy rolled up to the gates of the PRT just before sunset. Driving with the windows down had turned my hair into a tangled, windblown mess. My dust-caked skin was deeply tanned, and the freckles across the bridge of my nose were more prominent than I liked.

But Grandmother's kohl had not faded, and she had been right about its effect. I passed a mirror in the hall, and the eyes that looked back at me had never been a more luminous green. I shouldn't have looked any closer. When I did, I instantly regretted not having used sunblock on the patrol. Buried under the grime were the unmistakable cracks and furrows of my emerging crow's feet and aging neck. On the other hand, surrounded by a hundred men who didn't really care what I looked like, what did it matter?

I knew that Mark was still in Helmand, and although I silently regretted he wouldn't be returning to Mazār until the end of the month, I was also glad he wouldn't see me in my current condition or hear about my encounter with the American soldier.

As I passed the officers' mess, Sergeant Major stepped out to greet me. "Welcome back, Angela. Look who else returned early," he said, pointing through the door. Mark was standing alone looking out the window. He turned when he heard my name, but I had already started up the steps to my room.

FORTY-FIVE

August 21, 2005

By late summer, Stefan was coming to Mazār at least once a month for meetings with the Russian consulate staff. He would usually call me with an invitation for an early dinner at the one restaurant in town frequented by expats. It had a small garden, candles on the tables, offered a mediocre Indian menu, and served beer and wine, although only to foreigners.

Occasionally we would go for drinks at the UN guesthouse, where the expat members of the Mazār Social Club gathered most nights. This was not a venue I would have frequented on my own, but my evenings with Stefan were a wonderful escape from the confines of the PRT, and they were useful for getting to know some of the UN staffers on a more personal level.

I found myself counting the days until Stefan's next invitation. He had never made an improper approach, nor had he probed me for information about sensitive topics. There were no romantic overtones to our encounters, just two diplomatic colleagues who really enjoyed each other's company. I had even stopped objecting when he insisted on picking up the tab for dinner. My embassy had been formally notified that I was socializing with him and that it was a completely platonic relationship.

On those rare occasions that I left the PRT after dark, the colonel insisted on knowing where I would be, with whom, and when I would return. I felt like a teenager with a curfew, but I willingly complied. One night after dinner, when I stopped by the ops room to sign out for an evening with Stefan, Mark was there, updating the daily intelligence summaries with the ops officer.

"Going out with your Russian again, eh, Angela?" teased the ops officer while I completed the trip sheet.

"Just a few hours at the UN guesthouse," I replied, glancing over at Mark, who was shaking his head in silent disapproval.

I was surprised to find him waiting for me several minutes later in the narrow passageway just inside the gate as I was exiting the PRT.

"Hello, Mark," I said, recoiling at his simmering anger and wondering if I had done something to offend him. "Is there anything wrong?"

"You're a fool going off like this with the Russian at night, Angela," he said, blocking my way with one hand pressed hard against the metal door that led to the road in front of the compound. "You know full well that Daoud's armed thugs cruise the streets after dark. I, for one, do not understand why the colonel allows you to do this."

He moved closer to me, breathing hard as though he had run to occupy this spot before I arrived. I backed against the cold brick wall of the archway.

"There's an armed bodyguard in Stefan's car with us," I argued.

"Irrelevant! There's a good reason they lock their women up at night in this country," he snarled.

"You can't be serious, Mark," I shot back. "I'm sure you wouldn't come here and say this to a male Foreign Service Officer."

"I'm completely serious, Angela. And yes, I don't think it's safe for any of us to be joyriding around in this country after dark without protection. Look at what happened when you left the MOT in Sar-e Pol and went off for a sleepover with the ladies. You almost got yourself shot by one of your own soldiers."

I hadn't been able to quash that story, which got more exaggerated each time it was retold in the pub by Captain Baker and his men, but that was my concern and not Mark's.

He stared intently at me for several seconds without speaking. "What have you done to your eyes?" he asked.

"Oh, it's just some kohl one of the village women had me put on—while I was having my 'sleepover with the ladies,'" I added, echoing his sarcasm. "It takes several weeks to wear off."

He continued to stare. "I hope your Russian likes it."

"Jesus, Mark," I snapped. "You really should mind your own business."

"Angela, you really shouldn't . . ." he began, his voice dropping to a whisper, which was interrupted by the honking of Stefan's driver.

Unlatching the gate, I brushed by him, moved by his concern for my safety but irritated at his tone, which felt to me like a patronizing effort to control my movements.

"I'll be fine, Mark," I called over my shoulder.

As I slid across the soft leather backseat of Stefan's official car,

I could see Mark standing in the shadows of the passageway. His final "Don't go" rang in my ears.

Stefan was as unaware of Mark's concern—he didn't even know Mark existed—as he was of the colonel's requirement that I provide in writing my destination and precise time of return to the PRT whenever I went out after dark. Mark had never come up in our conversations—even that night in Kabul at the NATO bar, when Stefan had barely missed his awkward approach and hasty retreat.

Stefan and I had a delightful evening at the Mazār Social Club—a few drinks and a great discussion about disarmament with some UN weapons experts we met in the bar. When Stefan dropped me at the PRT just after nine P.M., we agreed to meet again when he returned to Mazār the following week. I went down to the ops room to sign in and Mark was still there reading reports. We exchanged polite nods, but no words.

The next day, I was pleasantly surprised by a last-minute invitation to accompany the soldiers from the Danish MOT, who worked out of the safe house in Aybak, on a three-day horseback patrol into a roadless part of Samangan Province. Their terp was sick, Colonel Jameson couldn't spare any of our terps, and the Danes asked him if I could go along as their interpreter since they knew I could ride. I accepted immediately. Jameson announced my trip during the ops room briefing while Mark leaned against the wall, shooting disapproving looks in my direction, certain that my presence on that patrol would not be worth the problems I was likely to cause.

He was wrong on all counts and I felt vindicated. It was an outstanding trip. A local warlord, who let us use his best stallions, had them saddled and waiting for us at the canyon entrance where the road ended. The Danes inaugurated a new police station at a remote mountain outpost. I demonstrated one of my solar ovens to the policemen, who asked if they could keep it so they could make their tea without building a fire.

It was so warm at night that we slept without tents under the stars in a high valley carpeted with lemongrass and alpine sage. To top it off, the village men treated us to a wild, no-holds-barred *buzkashi* game on our last day. I couldn't ride in the game, of course, but I took lots of photos.

"Angela, I'm back in town. Are we still on this evening for a drink at the Mazār Social Club?" It was Stefan calling, punctual and cheery as always. I was back at work in the bullpen. The week had passed so quickly, I'd forgotten about my promise to join him.

"Of course, Stefan," I said. "I'll be out at the gate at seven. I have some fantastic *buzkashi* photos to show you."

"Excellent," he said. "See you tonight."

I signed out in the ops room as required and laughed at the jokes of the younger officers, who teased me about spending so much time with the Russian. I didn't see Mark, who was barricaded inside his int cell processing reports.

The warm summer air in the garden of the UN guesthouse—thick with the perfume of the jasmine vines that covered its walls—was almost as intoxicating as that second gin and tonic Stefan handed me just after nine P.M.

I showed him the photos I'd printed from the *buzkashi* game and wanted to tell him more about my trip, but he insisted on changing the subject to Afghanistan's burgeoning opium production, a significant portion of which was making its way into the veins of Russia's youth. I was normally able to hold my own with Stefan during these discussions, but my words were having trouble keeping up with my thoughts.

I had foolishly skipped dinner at the PRT and was starting to feel lightheaded. That second drink had definitely been a mistake. My guard was down. Would I never learn?

"If we can't offer these farmers something that will make them as much money as poppies, then the opium should be legalized and bought up by the Afghan government," I declared loudly.

I was now totally out of line, expressing my personal opinions instead of those of the government I was supposed to be representing. I babbled on and Stefan did nothing to stop me.

"I see no other way to bring this mess under control." I was starting to slur my words as I tried but failed to focus on Stefan, who was observing me with an intensity I had never noticed before. "There's a serious global shortage of medical morphine. . . ."

I closed my eyes and sucked in a lungful of air.

"Stefan, I'm not feeling very well. Could you take me back to the PRT? I'm so sorry to cut our evening short."

Without a word, he rose, took me by the arm, and gently led me to the consulate vehicle, which was parked just outside with its engine running. My head was spinning, and I didn't resist when he slipped his arm around my waist to keep me from pitching against the car door.

The next thing I recalled was blinding lights outlining the

hulking shadows of soldiers in full kit, their rifles drawn, surrounding Stefan's car.

Someone was banging on the window, ordering him to hand me over. We were on a dark street, hemmed in by four vehicles, their engines running and their headlights—all on high beam, illuminating the interior of the Russian consulate car.

"Let Miss Morgan out of the vehicle now, and we will let you proceed without incident. There will be no report made of this to your embassy or to the Americans." It was Mark.

"Stefan, where are we?" I asked—confused by the lights and the sound of a familiar voice, but too far gone to be frightened. "Why is Mark here?"

"Well, my little one, it appears that this is where we must part company," said Stefan, addressing me in Russian. His words tumbled in my direction as though flung from the far end of a tunnel.

"How unfortunate—this business of ours, Angela. It's all such a sad little game." He placed one finger under my chin and tipped it up until our eyes met. Mine were barely open.

"I know you can't understand anything I'm saying," he added, "but it's just as well."

I could in fact understand every word. It was just too difficult to respond. I seemed to be floating in a vat of novocaine. My body had gone completely numb.

He was about to move in for a kiss when he pulled back suddenly to prop me up with a hand on each shoulder. I heard the locks snap up and a sharp exclamation from Stefan's driver as all four doors were pulled open by the soldiers. Mark dragged me out and shoved me roughly into the backseat of a PRT vehicle.

I held my head erect with great effort, my inhibitions now buried many layers beneath whatever had been added to that second gin and tonic. Falling across the seat, I leaned against Mark's shoulder.

With my eyes at half-mast, I gazed into the face of this darkly handsome but very angry man. "Did you know you have little flecks of green in your eyes, Mark?" I mumbled, trying but failing to raise the corners of my lips into a smile. When he didn't respond, I plunged ahead. "And here I thought they were just that gorgeous Paul Newman blue."

"I believe you Yanks have an expression," he said, ignoring my slurred attempts at flattery and snapping the buckle of my seat belt to keep me upright.

"Yes," I whispered slowly, no longer able to keep my eyes open. "It's 'I told you so.'"

Even through the fog that had enveloped me I was dimly aware that 1) I had to stop talking before I said anything else I might regret; and 2) A diplomatic incident and the probable loss of my security clearance had been narrowly averted.

Colonel Jameson called me into his office the next morning to discuss the previous night's events. I had no memory of the return trip to the PRT or how I got to my room, but I awoke with a splitting headache, still wearing last night's clothing—my shoes squared neatly on the floor next to my bed.

"One of your UN friends at the guesthouse saw the Russian helping you to his car. Never having seen you the slightest bit intoxicated, he had the foresight to call our ops officer, describe the situation, and let us know that you were leaving."

The colonel shook his head. "I should never have authorized you to leave the PRT after dark without a military escort. Thank God our patrol arrived before he got you inside the Russian consulate."

My chagrin at having been the cause of this mess made me uncharacteristically silent.

"Angela, are you all right?" asked the colonel, concerned at the blank look on my face. "Shall we have the doctor check you? One of our medics took your vitals last night after the major got you up to your room. Everything seemed to be normal."

"I'm fine and grateful to everyone," I said, silently panicking because my fingers, toes, and the tip of my tongue were still numb. What had Stefan put in that drink? "But I'm mortified that I've caused so much trouble."

"Actually, my dear, the trouble was minimal on our part. The evening patrol was getting kitted up to leave camp just before Mark took a cell phone call in the ops room from your UN friend. Mark went along with the patrol to plot the most direct route from the UN guesthouse to the Russian consulate, where he presumed your diplomatic colleague had planned to take you for a brief—and if I may put it delicately, unsolicited—photo session. We believe that Mr. Borosky must have—as you Americans say—slipped you a 'mickey' in order to get you into a compromising position and then blackmail you."

Covering my face with my hands, I moaned, more to myself than to the colonel, "I'll have to report this to my embassy."

"That is entirely up to you, Angela. We promised the Russian that as far as we were concerned, the incident was closed once we had you back under our protection."

Even though Stefan hadn't successfully carried out his plan, I felt violated and betrayed. I had trusted him and really believed we were friends. The colonel's reassuring words did little to lessen the anger I felt at myself for being so gullible.

"Nothing actually happened that would stand up in a court of law, Angela. You did nothing wrong, and the Russian, who of course has diplomatic immunity, can claim neither did he. You had one drink too many on an empty stomach, and he was giving you a ride home. Period!" The colonel downed the last of his coffee and continued.

"We kept the duty interpreter out of this, and the soldiers on last night's patrol have been sworn to secrecy. I'm quite certain you will not be hearing from that fellow again. It appears that the 'Great Game' is still alive and well," he said, laughing.

"You might want to thank Major Davies for his quick thinking and excellent map-reading skills," added the colonel, rising from his chair to indicate that our discussion was over. "We might not have gotten to you in time without his help."

FORTY-SIX

September 1, 2005

After my dramatic rescue from Stefan, who did turn out to be a Russian intelligence agent, I could no longer deny the fact that Major Mark Davies was on my mind constantly. I tried hard to dismiss my feelings as the impossible longings of a lonely middle-aged woman. But I could not. I knew only that I had to extinguish this flame while it was still manageable and before I said anything more to Mark that I would regret. My drunken mumblings about his blue eyes the night he pulled me out of Stefan's car were embarrassing enough, even though he had never mentioned the incident again.

Was it the difference in our ages that kept my behavior in check? I presumed but didn't know for certain that Mark was ten if not fifteen years my junior. Was it the fishbowl nature of life inside the walls of the PRT, where there was no privacy at any time anywhere? All of these might have contributed to my uncertainty, but there was really only one thing that had kept me from making a total fool of myself in Mark's presence. It took me far too long to admit it, but I was terrified of being hurt again.

For a decade after Tom's death, I had sought comfort in the

arms of other men. In my desperate search for solace, I had not only failed to bury the anguish of losing my husband and child, I had gone out of my way to find the worst sort of men, as if I were trying to punish myself for not finding another Tom. The stunning end to what I thought had been a genuine friendship with Stefan made me even more wary of the feelings I had for Mark. But he was different. I knew I could never replace Tom, but I seemed to be reaching a level of trust and friendship with Mark that I had not experienced with any other man. I was stronger now. I had survived Stefan's betrayal. And I was falling in love.

After the incident with Stefan, Mark and I found ourselves once again lingering over coffee following the evening meal in the officers' mess, engaging in spirited arguments about the pacification of Afghanistan or the propriety of females in war zones. We had even begun to share stories about our personal lives.

Although I finally felt comfortable enough to talk to him about Tom, he had never mentioned his ex-wife except once in passing. He was visibly upset when she came up one evening during our conversation in the officers' mess. Colonel Jameson had interrupted us with an offhand remark while Mark and I were deep into a heated discussion about my impulsive gallop across the *buzkashi* field in January.

"I say, Mark, your wife, Edwina, is quite the equestrian, is she not?" The colonel had twisted around in his chair but was staring directly at me as he addressed the major.

Mark stiffened imperceptibly, and his face darkened as he turned to face the colonel. "Actually, sir, no. My ex-wife never showed the slightest interest in riding. You must be thinking of Mitchell's wife, also named Edwina. She's a champion dressage rider."

"Oh, yes, of course," said the colonel, clearing his throat and returning to his conversation with the ops officer.

Mark stood quickly and picked up his dinner tray. "You'll excuse me, Angela," he said, glancing back at the colonel. He paused as though about to speak again, then left the room without another word.

Mark avoided me for the next several days, approaching only to bid me a safe journey as I climbed into a PRT Land Rover and rolled out the gates with a patrol of British and Swedish soldiers. We were off on a two-day trip into Jowzjan Province, where we would be purchasing several horses for a police outpost that had turned down the PRT's offer to buy them jeeps.

The grateful Afghan police chief had insisted that horses would be far more useful for patrolling than jeeps since, unlike diesel fuel, grass was free and available everywhere. He and his men knew how to take care of horses, he told us. They had no idea how to maintain a jeep.

"Don't let Angela on any of those horses, Peter, or you'll never see her again," Mark shouted to the Gurkha captain who was commanding our patrol as we headed out the gate. "And take care she doesn't set any brush fires with those solar cooking boxes of hers."

"Yes, sir," the captain replied with a laugh and a casual salute out his open window. I waved and Mark gave me a thumbs-up as our convoy rumbled off, chased down the road by a pack of mangy dogs and a rolling cloud of ochre dust.

FORTY-SEVEN

September 5, 2005

"Angela?"

I was cooling down after a hard run on the treadmill, but I could hear Mark's voice through the music on my headphones. I punched the STOP button. We hadn't spoken since I'd returned from the patrol to Jowzjan Province.

He was standing in the doorway in his uniform. The rest of the soldiers who had come to work out after dinner were streaming out of the gym and heading for the pub to watch a major international soccer match that was about to start. Mark waited until we were alone.

"I'm sorry I've been avoiding you. I've missed our after-dinner chats."

"So have I, Mark. Was it something I said?" I asked as I wiped the perspiration from my face and neck.

"No, it was the colonel, when he mentioned Edwina in front of you." He looked down and pressed his lips together.

"Most of the men know that she left me last year for a senior officer, but Colonel Jameson apparently did not. His comment took me by surprise and I reacted badly. I just don't like being reminded of the whole messy affair. It was painful and embarrassing. Nothing like what you experienced, I know, but it's still fairly fresh and I . . ."

"It's okay, Mark," I interrupted. "I understand."

"Would you like to join me in the pub? It may be a bit noisy with the boys watching their game, but . . ."

"I'd love to."

We switched out the lights and walked together down a narrow cement path that led to the back entrance of the pub. Mark stopped halfway down the walk and turned to face me. Taking my hand in his, he brushed his thumb over the back of my fingers and raised them to his lips. I was suddenly out of breath, and it wasn't from the three miles I'd just run.

We stared at each other in silence under the glare of the halogen security lights until a scraping latch signaled that someone was about to exit the pub. Mark quickly released my hand and nodded formally at the sentry who opened the door. The young soldier, oblivious to what had just happened, greeted us both with a nod and a smile. We entered the pub just as another goal was scored. The boys were all cheering wildly. I was dazed and confused.

Mark ordered two Strongbows, and we stood together at the bar discussing inconsequential matters until the game ended and the pub closed. I went back to my room, and he went off to his. There was no place inside the PRT that could provide the privacy we needed, and leaving the compound was not an option. When I saw him the next day, he made no mention of what had happened the previous evening. And neither did I.

A note from Jeef was delivered to the PRT the following morning by one of the guards from his dig. Rahim brought it to the bullpen and waited attentively while I read it. I was still distracted by what had transpired between Mark and me, but I forced myself to focus on Jeef's message.

His cell phone was not working, so he had sent a handwritten invitation to join him and Fazli the next afternoon at their dig in Balkh. There was a postscript urging me to bring Rahim along.

"Will you take me, Farishta-*jan*," Rahim asked when I looked up from Jeef's note. "I have some questions to ask Professor Mongibeaux about the archaeology books he sent me last month."

"Have you already read this note, Rahim?" I asked.

He nodded shyly. "I'm sorry, I thought it might be . . ." He stopped speaking mid-sentence and paused. "I thought it would be . . . interesting to go along."

Rahim was keeping something from me, but I decided not to pursue it.

"The Romanian MOT is going to Balkh City tomorrow to meet with the new police chief. I'll ask them if we can ride along."

"Thank you, Farishta-*jan*. I will send a message back to Professor Mongibeaux and tell him to expect us."

The Romanians dropped us the following morning at Jeef's dig, which had grown deeper and wider since our last visit. Rahim was strangely subdued as he and I climbed down the bamboo ladders to the lowest level, where Jeef and Fazli were examining a tunnel crammed with fragments of Greek columns that the workmen had recently uncovered.

"Angela, Rahim, welcome to our newest hole in the ground," shouted Jeef as he crawled backward out of the tunnel and switched off his flashlight.

Fazli waved at us both and motioned for Rahim to join him at the mouth of the tunnel. I noticed that Fazli was smiling and slapping Rahim on the back.

"So, are you ready to hear Rahim's good news?" asked Jeef, his eyes dancing with excitement.

"What good news?" I asked, glancing over at Rahim.

"A jury of French and Afghan judges has selected Rahim's design, over a host of professional submissions, for a proposed Bactrian Cultural Center that will be built near here using traditional building materials."

Rahim overheard our conversation and approached me with downcast eyes and an embarrassed grin. "I didn't want to say anything until I was certain."

"Rahim, this is wonderful news. Congratulations. I had no idea!"

"A licensed architect will have to draw the actual construction plans," Rahim added.

"Yes," said Jeef, "but the design is yours."

"Are you angry that I kept this from you?" Rahim asked me with a worried look.

"No. Of course not," I assured him. "I'm so proud of you."

"There's a prize, too," Jeef added before exchanging another guilty look with Rahim.

"I have been offered a scholarship to study architecture and archaeology in Paris," said Rahim, looking oddly despondent at such wonderful news.

"And he is guaranteed a job for life when he returns to Afghanistan from his studies," added Jeef. "Fazli and I will have to retire someday, and we'll need capable hands and educated minds to carry on our work here well into the twenty-first century. We both agree that Rahim is the perfect candidate, and we said so to the committee."

"But you don't speak French, Rahim."

"That is not a problem, Farishta-*jan*," Rahim replied. "They will give me a year of intensive French language training and, like you, I learn foreign tongues fairly quickly. I am the main support of my family, but even my mother is urging me to take this scholarship."

I didn't push him for more information since I already knew the reason for his lack of enthusiasm despite this wonderful news. His sad brown eyes betrayed the agony he was feeling at having to leave Nilofar behind and give up all hope of marrying her.

FORTY-EIGHT

"Need any help, Angela?" asked Fuzzy, as he walked into the atrium after supper with several Gurkha soldiers.

"Come on in, guys. I can always use some extra hands," I said, smiling at these marvelous young soldiers who were giving up their free time in the pub to help me build more solar ovens. This group had been up here before and they knew the drill. Within a few minutes, they were chatting quietly about an upcoming rugby game as they measured and cut squares of cardboard.

"Sergeant Major told us that more of the MOTs are taking these things when they go on patrol," said one of the Gurkha corporals as he spread glue over a piece of foil, "and the Romanians saw a shepherd in the foothills near Marmol heating water with one of your solar ovens while he watched his flock."

"When do we get to try more of your solar-cooked food, Angela?" asked Fuzzy, who was carefully marking a large square of cardboard using one of my templates.

"My cooking experiments are over, Fuz," I replied. "My goal now is to get as many of these ovens as possible into the hands of Afghans before I go home in December."

The screen door creaked open again. It was Mark with two MOT commanders. The Gurkhas jumped up and stood at attention. Fuzzy nodded in their direction but kept on with his work.

"As you were, men," said Mark. "We've come to lend you a hand, Angela."

My pulse jumped when I heard Mark's voice, but I kept my eyes down and continued cutting cardboard. He sat down next to me and pulled a knife from his pocket. "Perhaps you should start charging a few dollars for these."

"Great idea," I replied, still too flustered by his unexpected appearance and his proximity to make eye contact.

Sensing my discomfort, he added in a loud and formal voice, "Right, Angela, tell us what to do. We're ready for our marching orders."

During the next two hours, my little band of helpers managed to produce six more small solar ovens that the MOTs could take with them on patrol to demonstrate and give away to village men, who would hopefully share them with their wives. They all stayed to help me clean up, but Mark was the last to leave.

"Come outside, Mark, the sky should be spectacular tonight," I said, after we had stacked my supplies in the corner of the empty atrium.

I opened the balcony door, and we stepped outside into a balmy late summer evening. The power was out again all over Mazār, and there was no moon. The sun had set almost an hour ago, but a sliver of sky along the western horizon still glowed a deep indigo blue. The Milky Way shimmering in the blackness overhead, arched like a ribbon of lace over the Hindu Kush.

"Beautiful, isn't it?"

He didn't respond and I didn't press him. We scanned the sky and avoided each other's eyes, until he broke the silence.

"I'll be going back to Basra in less than two months, Angela. Perhaps we could meet somewhere after you've finished here in December." He hesitated, his voice rising into a question as though he were uncertain about my response.

My heart jumped, and I inhaled so sharply that it actually hurt. I remained mute, staring out at the dark shapes of the mountains until I felt his hand on mine. I turned to face him, my eyes flooding with tears.

"I'd like that, Mark," I replied avoiding his gaze, "very much, but . . ."

"What?"

"I'm too old for you," I whispered, choking on my words and feeling like an idiot as soon as they had escaped my lips.

"There are a few things about you that do bother me, Angela," he said, brushing away my tears, "like your refusal to stop encouraging a certain illicit romance and your impetuousness, but I promise you that your age and mine are of no consequence whatsoever." He kept his impossibly blue eyes trained on mine.

Although I was melting inside and was aware at that moment of little other than Mark's eyes and voice, his reference to Rahim and Nilofar still pained me.

"I'm forty-seven years old, Mark, and you're what . . . thirty-three?"

"I'm thirty-six and I believe I have fallen in love with you, so does it really matter?"

"I don't know. It shouldn't matter." This difference in our ages, the last line of defense I felt I could raise to protect myself from being hurt again, was crumbling fast. "I don't want it to."

"Then tell me it doesn't," he said.

I was about to reply when footsteps in the atrium interrupted our conversation. A member of Mark's intel staff pushed open the screen door.

"Sorry to interrupt, sir, but the colonel needs to speak with you urgently. One of the boys said you were up here helping Angela build her stoves. Sorry, Angela," he added with an embarrassed laugh since it was clear we had long ago finished working on the stoves.

"Thank you, Corporal. I'll be right there," said Mark crisply.

"Sir," he said, spinning smartly on his heels.

"To be continued," Mark said as he took my hand in his and kissed it before vanishing into the atrium.

Mark and I struggled to conceal our growing affection, but it was difficult. We took meals together as often as we could, but found it impossible to be completely alone for more than a few minutes without being interrupted. In the presence of the interpreters, we were always excessively formal, but I'm sure that even they could see that something had changed between us. Inviting Mark into my tiny room next to the communal loo on a floor I shared with twenty men was out of the question. He shared a room on the other side of the compound with two Gurkha officers. Anything more than our daily conversations would have to wait until we were both out of Afghanistan.

———

I had continued making sporadic visits with Nilofar to the neighboring Hazara camp throughout the summer, but Rahim was still the only one who knew about these unauthorized trips. My method of getting back into the PRT seemed foolproof. When I got within a block of the compound, I would call Rahim's cell phone, and he would wait just inside to open the gate when I knocked.

My secret excursions came to an abrupt halt a few days after Mark and I had declared our feelings for each other on the balcony.

Nilofar had hired a taxi to take ten solar ovens to a newly established Hazara displaced-persons camp on the other side of town. The women in our neighborhood camp had told their Hazara relatives about what we were doing, and the newcomers wanted a demonstration.

Nilofar could have made this trip on her own, since she knew as much as I did about solar cooking, but I wanted to see the camp and meet the women.

It was foolish of me to think that no one would notice us leaving the PRT and loading so much equipment into a taxi that morning, but I had grown careless in my subterfuge. It had been so easy all summer to slip out of camp and return unnoticed.

Unfortunately, Mark was speaking to one of the Gurkha sentries on the ramparts just as Nilofar and I got into the taxi. As he watched us drive away, there was no doubt in his mind who was hidden under the two burkas.

.

He went immediately to speak to the Afghan sentries and learned for the first time about my many forays outside the PRT and about Rahim's complicity. Rahim was ordered to notify him as soon as I called.

The taxi dropped me back at the PRT five hours later and drove off with Nilofar, who was late for her class at the university. I was elated at the enthusiastic reception we had received from the women in the camp. More than fifty had gathered to watch us boil water and cook rice with the sun. A caravan of Kuchi nomads had camped nearby to trade with the Hazaras, and several of their women who came to watch our demonstration offered to trade their bracelets for my solar ovens. I gave them three and told them to keep their bracelets.

I made my usual call to Rahim, who sounded uncharacteristically annoyed when I told him I was ready to be let in. He hung up before I could ask him what was wrong. Was he upset because Nilofar had left without coming in to see him? I knocked three times on the heavy metal gate and waited. When it swung open, a very angry Major Davies was standing alone in the passageway.

"Good afternoon, Angela."

"Mark! What a surprise!" I stammered as my eyes adjusted to the darkness.

"How long have you been doing this?" he asked, slamming the gate shut, throwing the bolt, and blocking my exit with his arm.

"Doing what?" I replied in a hopeless attempt at innocence.

"Leaving the PRT without authorization and protected only by the thin blue silk of the burka you have just stuffed into your rucksack."

"Look, Mark, I . . ."

"Angela, I have the greatest respect for your efforts to help the women of Afghanistan cook with sunshine, and I wish you were getting more support from your embassy. While you are assigned to this PRT, however, the British Army is responsible for your safety."

"I know that, but . . ."

"I'm not finished," he snapped. My pupils had widened and I could just make out the sharp contours of his face in the dim passageway.

"Are you aware that there is a war on in Afghanistan? Are you also aware that there are many people who would love to get their hands on an American diplomat, especially a female?"

"Of course, I am, but under the burka . . ."

"Are you out of your fucking mind, Angela?" He ran his fingers through his dark hair and grabbed my shoulders. "I thought last month's episode with your Russian friend had knocked some sense into you. Apparently, it did not."

I tried to pull away, but he tightened his grip. If Mark was this angry at me, what had he said to poor Rahim? I'd had no right to implicate my young friend in my decision to break the PRT's rules about travel outside the wire. How could I have been so thoughtless? No wonder Rahim sounded angry when I called.

"The colonel, Sergeant Major—all of us, including you—are about to be overwhelmed with security preparations for the provincial elections, so I propose we keep this discussion and Rahim's involvement between us as long as you agree to the following condition."

At least he was going to leave Rahim out of it.

"What condition?" I asked, my eyes narrowing.

"Give me your word that you will never leave this camp again without a military escort."

I stared at Mark in silence, seething at his veiled threat. I knew he was right, and I had no defense for my actions, but I resented being treated like a child.

"You really have no choice, Angela. Your only other option is to have me report this incident to the colonel. And in that case Rahim *will* become involved."

"You win, Mark," I said, fighting back tears of frustration.

"Angela," he said softly as he released his grip, "I don't want anything to happen to you. Please understand why I'm doing this."

"I do, Mark," I said lowering my head in defeat. He glanced behind him and seeing no one in the courtyard, wrapped both arms tightly around me. I tensed and tried to push him away, but he wouldn't let go. My anger drained away, replaced by fatigue and resignation, and I slid my arms around him, resting my head against his shoulder. We stood quietly holding each other until a horn honked outside and the guards began to slide the barriers away from the gate.

FORTY-NINE

September 12, 2005

As Mark had predicted, everyone was overwhelmed with meetings in preparation for the upcoming provincial elections. He and I saw very little of each other the week following our encounter at the front gate. I was also too busy to spend much time with Nilofar, who wanted to continue her regular visits to the PRT. They were ostensibly to brief me on her solar cooking and women's rights activities, but they were also the only way she could spend time alone with Rahim.

Nilofar's attempts to interfere in arranged marriages were angering some of the most powerful warlords in the northern provinces. Her clandestine relationship with Rahim was also very close to becoming public and was even more dangerous for her now that her parents had forbidden her to see him. I worried about her constantly, awed at her courage but fearful that she was about to run afoul of the conservative Afghan society, which could so easily crush her spirit.

I was unaware that Rahim was also starting to worry about me until he stopped me one morning on his way to breakfast and hit me with another of his off-the-wall questions.

"Farishta-*jan*, are you a CIA agent?"

I looked directly into his eyes and tried to keep my voice steady.

"No, Rahim, I'm not, but why do you ask?" Where the hell had that come from? During our morning staff meetings, a few of the officers occasionally teased me about being with the CIA, but I'd always assumed that their remarks were never repeated outside the secure vault of the ops center.

"One of the terps heard the soldiers talking about you. It is very dangerous for you if the Afghan people know about this."

Had the soldiers been discussing my rescue from Stefan's car last month? But that was impossible. The night patrol had been sworn to secrecy. "Please tell the interpreters that I do not and never have worked for the CIA. I give you my word on that, Rahim," I responded in a firm voice.

"I will do that, Farishta-*jan*," he replied, looking relieved as he trotted off to the mess hall to load his plate with eggs and toast.

"Colonel Jameson, there's something I'd like to say before we begin," I announced as we assembled for the officers' morning staff briefing.

"Go right ahead, Angela," he said, noting the concern in my voice.

I looked slowly around the room to ensure I had everyone's full attention.

"I know there has been some joking about my being in the CIA at these meetings, and I haven't said anything as long as I thought it stayed in this room. Outside this room, however, it's no joking matter," I continued.

"This morning, Rahim told me that one of the other terps overheard some of the soldiers talking about me being a CIA agent."

The officers remained silent and I pressed on. "Any gossip that implies that I am a member of my government's clandestine intelligence service can put the lives of our interpreters, especially Rahim, in danger. The covert officers in my government's CIA and in your MI6 have difficult and dangerous jobs, but I am not and never have been one of them. I am simply little old boring Angela Morgan, the diplomat."

"There is certainly nothing little, old, or boring about you, Angela," teased Mark. There were a few knowing nods and snickers from the other officers around the room, but after that the rumors about my affiliation with the CIA ended.

I joined Mark that evening for dinner and coffee in the officers' mess. "It's wonderful to know that you don't find me old or boring," I joked.

"It just came out," he said squeezing my hand under the table. "I hope I didn't embarrass you."

"On the contrary, Mark. I think we all needed some comic relief after my grim little speech."

FIFTY

September 16, 2005

My NATO colleagues and I were enjoying some of the French major's espresso and sharing stories about our preparations for the upcoming elections when Colonel Jameson appeared in the doorway of his office and cleared his throat to silence us.

"The police training center was hit last night," he announced grimly. "One rocket passed completely over the compound and exploded harmlessly in the desert. Another landed inside near the trainees' barracks. It woke everyone up when it exploded, but none of the Afghan cadets or instructors was harmed. The third rocket appears to have been a dud."

Although the entire country of Afghanistan was officially designated a "war zone," it hadn't really seemed like one in the north since I'd arrived in January. Except for that one trip with Mark to the Pashtun village when I'd been required to wear my body armor and helmet, the relative freedom we enjoyed here was extraordinary compared with my colleagues in Kabul and at U.S. PRTs in the south. I silently prayed that this incident was a fluke and not a trend.

"This is the first attack on foreign forces in more than two years," said the colonel, looking in my direction. He had read and concurred with a message I'd recently sent to my embassy describing the growing resentment of foreign forces in the north. Although our MOTs continued to maintain a low security profile, the same was not the case with the other foreign forces in the area.

Colonel Tremain's men in their new up-armored Humvees, the Germans who traveled over from Kunduz in their armored personnel carriers, and the Dutch who had been sent in to provide extra security for the elections were speeding around Mazār, with top gunners concealed behind sunglasses and bandanas, their machine guns aimed at pedestrians. Many locals had begun complaining to us about this, since as far as they were concerned all foreign military personnel were part of the PRT.

"There's not much more we can do to protect ourselves here since we're surrounded on all sides by family compounds," added the colonel with a resigned shrug, "but I urge you to keep your eyes and ears open."

"Colonel, perhaps we should invite the local mullah and some of his followers to the PRT for a meal," I said.

I had often seen the old man from my window, standing under the pistachio tree in front of his mosque, gazing up at the antennas and guard towers of our compound.

"With our high walls, razor wire, and the military convoys rumbling in and out of the gates, we don't present a very welcoming appearance. The neighbors might be more willing to share information with us if they knew us a little better."

"Excellent idea, Angela," the colonel replied. "I'll get Sergeant Major and Rahim to set something up."

It took another month to organize, but eventually the old mullah and seven neighborhood elders accepted the colonel's invitation to come for breakfast. They walked through the gates of the PRT that morning with great trepidation, but were quickly disarmed by the warm greeting they received from the soldiers and officers.

The colonel gave them a tour of the PRT, which they seemed to enjoy as much as the orange juice, yogurt, and muffins we served them at a long table in the conference room. The mullah in his thank-you speech told the colonel this was his first invitation to visit the PRT since the U.S. Army had departed in 2003. I sat silently at the far end of the table, my hair wrapped in a scarf throughout the breakfast so as not to offend our elderly guests, whom I knew would probably be less than pleased to see a woman in this room full of men.

The American Embassy never responded to my report on the aggressive security posture of new foreign forces in our area. Nor did they have any comments about the attack on the police-training center. The looming parliamentary elections had overwhelmed everything else.

My British diplomatic colleague Richard Carrington had spent very little time in Mazār over the summer and as a result our professional relationship had improved markedly. He was about to be permanently assigned as the UK's representative at PRT Lashkar Gah in Helmand Province to prepare for the arrival of the British Army in early 2006. Helmand was far more dangerous than any of the northern provinces, and I made sure he knew how much I admired him for volunteering to go. He'd come back to Mazār to help plan our itinerary through the Sholgara Valley, where he and I would be serving as official poll watchers on Election Day.

"Right, Angela," he said, picking up his dinner tray and heading out the door of the officers' mess, "I'll be flying to Kabul tomorrow to brief my ambassador on our plans, and I'll drive back on election eve with my civilian security team. We'll be ready to follow you and your boys in the Beast at 0530 hours sharp Sunday morning."

"Safe flight, Richard," I replied, slipping my feet out of my sandals and curling up on the couch to watch the evening news on BBC. The room was empty. Every officer not at work had gone to the pub to watch another important sporting event.

"Angela, may I have a word with you?" Mark entered the officers' mess with a tray of food and sat down on the couch next to me.

"Sure," I said, slipping my feet back into my sandals. We'd both been so busy the past week that we'd hardly spoken.

"I've missed our dinners together," he said, "but my boys and I have been swamped with the elections approaching." He set his tray down without a sound and ran his fingers through his hair. He was upset about something.

"We'll have plenty of time later, Mark," I assured him. Since we were alone, I reached out and took his hand in mine.

"I understand that you and Richard will be traveling into the Sholgara Valley for Election Day," he said, squeezing my fingers.

"We are, but don't worry, we'll have plenty of protection,"

I replied, smiling up at his stern face. "I'm keeping my promise never to leave the PRT again without proper security."

"Are you aware that there is a single narrow road leading into and out of that valley with steep cliffs on either side?"

"Mark, you know I've been to the Sholgara many times."

"Have you read the intel reports from the MOTs about armed thugs threatening to invade the polling places and intimidate voters?"

"Of course I have, Mark," I said, bristling at his condescending tone. I silently forgave him because I knew how worried he was about my safety, but I hated it when he spoke to me like this. "I believe that's the very reason Richard and I have been asked to go there." My voice rose slightly, betraying my irritation. I didn't want another lecture from him on the dangers lurking outside the PRT. "The presence of foreign observers is expected to help deter that behavior."

"Of course, but if you manage to enrage enough of those fellows during the day, you'll offer them a very tempting target when you exit the valley through that pass late in the afternoon."

Rising from the couch, I snatched my tray from the coffee table and stared down at him. "I'm willing to risk it."

"I suppose we're all here to take such risks," he replied grimly, clearly wanting to say more.

"Mark, I'm not doing this to make some point about my desire for independence. This is my job! It's why I'm here." I knew it would be impossible to convince him, but I had to try to make him understand. "These elections are critical. You know that. Monitors are coming to Afghanistan from all over the world to help ensure that the whole process is run as honestly and fairly as possible. I'll be careful. I promise."

Mark clenched his jaw in silence as I turned and left the room. He departed the following morning with MOT Bravo, which by design or coincidence was off on a four-day patrol into the Sholgara Valley.

FIFTY-ONE

September 18, 2005

Election Day was chaotic, hot, and dusty. Weapons were not allowed in the polling places, which meant that Fuzzy and the embassy bodyguard could not accompany Richard and me to observe the voting. They had to stay in the vehicles at each stop along with Jenkins and Richard's civilian driver while Richard and I went into the voting centers, protected only by the oversized international observer badges dangling from our necks. I would inspect the women's sites on my own while Richard, accompanied by Rahim, who needed no badge, would observe the men.

Some of the more remote female-voting stations I visited resembled raucous teenage parties. The women, their burkas thrown back, laughed and joked and leaned into one another's cardboard voting booths as they searched the enormous full-color ballot sheets for the photo of their local warlord, provincial chief, or mullah. They knew whom they were supposed to vote for and would squeal with delight when they finally found the correct photo.

The concept of a secret ballot had not yet filtered down to this corner of Afghanistan. For these rural women, the novelty of going into a semi-public place where they could throw back their burkas for a few minutes was enough of a treat.

The last place I visited at the far end of the valley was quite a different story. Miriam, a local school principal, welcomed me warmly into her well-organized polling station. Her three assistants, who were also teachers in her school, handed the women their ballots, told them how to make their marks, and instructed them not to speak to one another until they were out of the tent.

This orderly procession of female voters halted abruptly when three armed men, scowling and brandishing AK-47s, lifted the back flap of the tent and marched in uninvited. I remembered Mark's warning about voter intimidation and prayed this would not turn into a violent confrontation. I was more angry than frightened, but I had no idea what to do.

The men didn't notice me at first, since the faces of all the women in the tent were uncovered. That lasted for less than ten seconds, when every one of the female voters pulled their burkas back over their faces and squeezed into a tight knot at the rear of the tent. Only Miriam, her three assistants, and I still had our faces exposed.

Miriam glared at the heavyset leader of the group, her wrinkled jaw twitching in anger. She was spitting mad and was having what Colonel Tremain would have euphemistically described as a Whisky-Tango-Foxtrot moment. The two younger men took several steps back to escape the heat of Miriam's anger and looked to the older man for guidance.

I remained with the female voters at the back of the tent, feeling like a coward next to Miriam's bravery. She stepped forward with her arms folded over her chest, and in her most authoritative schoolteacher voice, ordered the men to leave the premises immediately.

"I believe that false ballots are being added to the boxes, *honum*," the old man said sharply. "You must open them so my men can count the votes."

"These boxes will remained sealed until election officials deliver them tonight to the counting center in Mazār-i-Sharīf," Miriam replied calmly. The three female poll workers stepped forward and stood next to her, their faces still defiantly exposed.

I pulled out my camera and began snapping photos of their confrontation.

"Journalists are not permitted here," shouted the older man, glaring at me.

I informed him that journalists were indeed permitted in the polling stations, but weapons were not.

"And if I take your camera?" he said angrily, "what will you do then?"

His arrogance infuriated me and I foolishly threw caution to the winds. "I am here from the PRT as an official election observer, and I am accompanied by armed NATO soldiers who are waiting for me at the bottom of the hill. Shall I summon them?" I asked, pulling my cell phone from my pocket. I didn't mention that I was referring only to Fuzzy, Jenkins, and the two civilians from the British Embassy. I didn't even know if my cell phone would work out here. I prayed silently that my bluff would succeed. It did.

"You will pay for this," he warned before exiting the tent with his men.

After promising Miriam that I would report the incident to the election authorities in Mazār, I walked down the hill to find that Rahim had just cast his first vote ever. When my young friend saw me approaching, he waved his purple ink-stained finger in the air and shouted proudly, "Look, Farishta-*jan*, democracy!"

By late that afternoon, our little convoy was headed northeast toward the narrow cut that would take us out of the Sholgara Valley. I rode in the Beast with Rahim, Fuzzy, and Jenkins, and regaled them with the story of the armed gang that had invaded the women's tent.

Jenkins couldn't resist interrupting halfway through my story. "And you just stood there and said nothing, right, Angela? I don't believe that for a second," he snorted. Fuzzy nodded in silent agreement.

"I did take a few photos for the record," I admitted.

"Fuzzy, keep your eyes peeled until we get through this pass," Jenkins cautioned half in jest.

"Right, mate," grunted Fuzzy.

Since the Beast had no AC and its windows had to be left down so we wouldn't suffocate in this heat, we were in the lead as our little convoy entered the narrow gap that cut through the valley wall. Richard and his civilian bodyguards following close behind us were protected from our dust inside their air-conditioned, fully armored British embassy van.

We had been driving through the canyon for less than a minute when Fuzzy stiffened suddenly and shouted at Jenkins, "Mate, hostiles ahead!" I peeked out the open window and could see armed men on the cliffs ahead of us. Jenkins was traveling at a good clip, but he hit the brakes hard. Richard's much more heavily armored vehicle skidded to a halt, inches from the Beast's rear fender.

I stared up at the shadowy figures lining the ridge and prayed they were not allies of the man I had confronted in Miriam's polling station. If anything happened to Fuzzy, Jenkins, or Rahim because of my actions, I would never forgive myself.

Seconds later, our radio began to crackle with familiar call signs. "Delta two zulu, delta two zulu. This is bravo nine alpha. We are in overwatch north of your position. Bridge secure. Clear to move through to my location. Out."

"It's the fucking Gurkhas," said Jenkins, resting his head on the steering wheel and heaving an enormous sigh of relief.

He gunned the Beast and we exited the narrow canyon into a shaft of bright September sunlight. Standing on a rise near the bridge was the young Gurkha captain who commanded MOT Bravo. Next to him was Mark, as I had never before seen him—covered with dust, unshaven, deeply tanned, with a pistol strapped to his hip and a rifle slung over his shoulder. He waved solemnly as our little convoy passed safely out of the valley.

FIFTY-TWO

October 2, 2005

In early October, Rahim informed Colonel Jameson he would be leaving for France in January 2006 to begin his studies.

"Farishta-*jan,* he wasn't even angry," a surprised Rahim told me when he left the colonel's office. "All he wanted to know was who I recommended for the new head interpreter."

"Rahim, by early next year, the British Army will have moved to Helmand and the Swedes will have assumed command in their new compound by the airport. Since the colonel can't take you with him, he's probably not too concerned about who will do the translating for the next PRT commander."

"I have recommended my mother's brother-in-law, who has just finished medical school in Kabul," said Rahim, beaming. "His English is better than mine."

"A doctor! Why would you recommend a doctor, Rahim?"

"He can earn more as head interpreter at the PRT than he can working in a hospital."

"Have you told the colonel?"

"Not yet. I will bring my uncle tomorrow to introduce him."

Since the announcement of his scholarship, Rahim had been

spending as much time as the colonel would allow at the museum in Kabul with Jeef and Fazli. I knew he was also having clandestine meetings in Kabul with Nilofar, whose absences from Mazār usually coincided with his. I hoped they were being discreet.

Although Mark and I had agreed to disagree about my complicity in their doomed romance, I thought I had finally convinced him that there was no harm in their seeing each other until Rahim left for France. Nilofar would be spending the rest of her life in Mazār-i-Sharīf married to a Hazara businessman she hadn't even met. My two young friends deserved a few more months together before they were separated forever.

I was thrilled about Rahim's scholarship and had planned to suggest to Mark that we meet in Paris next spring. I'd skipped my workout to spend an hour at my desk answering an urgent query from the embassy after dinner. I headed over to the pub, where Mark and I had agreed to meet at nine, and ordered a cider. When the back door opened and he entered, still wearing his gym clothes, I waved at him from the bar.

"Mark," I called. "Come let me buy you something cold to drink."

"Angela, I need to speak with you, but not here," he replied, nodding toward the empty soldiers' dining hall. He was not smiling.

"What's wrong?" I asked as he motioned for me to follow him.

When I picked up my cider to bring it along, he grabbed it out of my hand and slammed it down on the bar. "Leave it!" he ordered. It was too noisy in the pub for anyone but me to have noticed his angry gesture.

I followed Mark into the dining room and sat down across

from him at one of the metal tables. "I don't even know where to begin," he said, his voice quavering. "A few minutes ago, I was taking a shortcut from the gym back to my room through the vehicle park when I heard a sound inside one of the empty shipping containers."

I knew what was coming.

"Thank God, it was me and not one of the armed sentries," he muttered through clenched teeth.

"I saw something red moving in the shadows and asked whoever was inside the container to come out and identify himself."

My heart dropped. Nilofar had been wearing a red shawl when she came to talk to me in the afternoon about one of the girls she was trying to help. I thought she had gone home hours ago.

"Nilofar?"

"Worse than that," he replied. "It was Nilofar and Rahim, and God only knows how long they'd been in there or what they'd been doing.

"I told them they were both out of their fucking minds. Do you know what they did then?" he asked.

I shook my head.

"They wrapped their arms around each other and laughed. Rahim's reply to me was that they were indeed out of their minds, but so was the whole country." I smiled inwardly at my young friend's courage.

Two soldiers walked through the dining hall, discreetly ignoring our conversation as they passed the table. Mark waited until they were gone to continue.

"I told Nilofar to call her brother immediately and explain that she had stayed at the PRT to have dinner with you," he said, his voice rising. "I hate all this lying you've been doing to protect them, Angela, and now I'm doing it, too! I told Rahim that if I saw him with Nilofar again, I'd go to the colonel."

"Mark, I had no idea. I thought she left hours ago."

"Angela, if anything happens to those two, you will be partly to blame," he said. His face was rigid with anger. "You seem quite willing to put yourself at risk, but you must understand that sometimes your actions involve others as well—with the Russian, with your little slumber party at the warlord's compound, your secret solar cooking outings, your election adventure in the Sholgara, but especially your rash encouragement of Nilofar and Rahim."

I was stunned at the intensity of his anger, but I was not going to stop those two from seeing each other. They had too little time left.

"Mark, you have no right to interfere with their relationship," I argued. "They're both adults and they know the risks. Once Rahim leaves for France, they'll never see each other again."

"And you have no right to encourage them, Angela," he replied.

He had gone too far. I stood and glared down at him. "I will admit that I was wrong about one thing. You and I really are far too different for anything to have worked out between us. You can at least be grateful that I had more sense than Nilofar and didn't do anything to embarrass you in public."

My eyes brimmed with tears as I walked out of the hall without another word.

Mark didn't speak to me the following morning. He wouldn't

even look at me. Nilofar called in the afternoon to apologize for causing any trouble. I didn't see Rahim, who had departed early for Kabul. This time, Nilofar did not try to follow him.

I begged her to come to the PRT so we could talk. She spent the afternoon with me in an unused conference room going over the previous day's confrontation with Mark and voicing her despair at Rahim's imminent departure. When I told her what had transpired between Mark and me, we briefly reversed roles as I burst into tears and collapsed into her arms.

With only three months left to my tour, and my brief relationship with Mark now at an end, I focused relentlessly on my work and began to prepare detailed briefing memos for my yet-to-be-named successor. Alone in my room at night, I would have plenty of time to feel sorry for myself, but I vowed that no one at the PRT would ever see that side of me.

I kept Fuzzy and Jenkins busy the following week with trips to all five provinces to meet the members of the new provincial councils. The PRT had already heard from council members in Sar-e Pol, who complained that they had nowhere to hold their meetings and were currently using one of the governor's storerooms. There were similar reports about a lack of resources from the other councils.

I was counting the days until I could leave this place and had with great sadness added Mark to my long list of failed relationships. I deeply regretted that our friendship had ended this way, and I still missed our after-dinner conversations, but he was avoiding me like the plague. Thank God, he would soon be gone.

––––––––

Rahim knocked on the door of my room the following Friday when he returned from Kabul. I hadn't seen him since the incident with Mark.

"Farishta-*jan*, I am sorry to bother you on your rest day. I had to come to the PRT today because I am the duty interpreter."

His face reddened, and he took a deep breath before continuing. "I am so sorry that Nilofar and I have upset the major and that you are now angry at each other."

"It's not your fault, Rahim," I replied. "The major and I just had a misunderstanding. We'll get over it. It's you and Nilofar that I'm worried about."

"Thank you, Farishta-*jan*, but Nilofar and I know we have no power to change our fate. All we can do is enjoy our last few months together as much as we can."

He turned to leave, then reached into his pocket. "I almost forgot, Professor Mongibeaux asked me to give this to you," he said, handing me a small box.

"Farishta-*jan*, I think Nilofar may be calling to schedule a meeting with you later this afternoon," he added with a sly grin. "I will let her in when she arrives. *Khuda-hafiz*, God be with you."

He was impossible, but I adored this boy.

Inside the box, nested on a square of dark blue silk, was a tiny silver medallion. It was a miniature replica of the Ai Khanoum plaque Jeef had shown me on my first visit to the museum.

FIFTY-THREE

October 15, 2005

"Angela, Fuzzy and I are making a quick mail run to the airport for Sergeant Major. I think there are some packages for you. Want to come along?" Jenkins had spotted me eating a late lunch alone in the officers' mess.

"I'd love to go."

"Rahim is coming, too. He wants us to drop him at the university. We know what that's for, don't we?" Jenkins said, pursing his lips and batting his eyelashes.

"He's going to meet Nilofar?"

"Bingo!" Jenkins replied.

It was so risky for the two of them to be seen together at the university. I warned them repeatedly about this and begged them to confine their meetings to the PRT. Too many people knew them there and word might get back to her parents. They refused to listen.

The afternoon was sunny and dry, and we drove into town enjoying the breezes blowing through our open windows. With the monthlong fast of Ramadan in its second week, it was quieter than usual at midday. Rahim babbled on to his captive audience about how Nilofar had insisted her arranged marriage with the Hazara merchant be delayed until she graduated from law school. Her parents had concurred even as they informed her that her future husband would not allow her to work once she started having children. Fuzzy and Jenkins agreed with Rahim that this small victory was a wonderful development.

Rahim had apologized profusely to Mark after the incident in the shipping container, and Mark had stopped avoiding me completely, but our conversations were strictly professional. I now had no one at the PRT with whom to share my concern about Rahim and Nilofar. They were deeply in love with each other, and it was difficult for me to imagine them calmly shaking hands in January and saying good-bye forever.

Fuzzy was for the first time in a long time in a good mood. He smiled at Rahim's story and waved at the children who ran alongside our vehicle.

Jenkins turned the Beast into the western entrance of downtown Mazār. As we approached the intersection in front of the Blue Mosque, he slowed for a small boy dragging two overloaded donkeys through the traffic.

A young man with a clipped beard, wrapped in a gray blanket—odd attire for such a balmy day—stared intently at us from the curb. Suddenly, with no warning, he threw off his blanket, pointed an AK-47 at the Beast, and began to fire.

Unbidden images of the black clouds billowing over the embassy in Beirut and Tom's body lying in the rubble raced through my mind as I watched this young man calmly squeezing off round after round in our direction. I was frozen in place, staring out the window and hypnotized by the muzzle flashes coming from his rifle. Less than five seconds had passed.

Fuzzy reacted instantly. He pulled his weapon from between his knees, shoved it out the window, and prepared to return fire. Jenkins stepped on the gas and laid on the horn. Rahim, with lightning reflexes, hit the RELEASE button on my seat belt, shoved me to the floor, and covered me with his body. Bullets from our attacker made staccato pings as they punctured the Beast's metal skin and shattered the front windshield.

Jenkins sped around the Blue Mosque and out of town, heading for the airport as fast as the traffic would allow until he noticed Fuzzy slumped over in his seat—his mouth hanging open. Fuzzy's rifle was lodged under his arm, which dangled out the window. A thin trickle of blood poured from his left eye and from a hole in the back of his head where a bullet had pierced his skull.

"Jesus Christ, Fuzzy's dead!" cried Jenkins. He was swerving dangerously, unaware that he had also been hit. Blood soaked his right sleeve as he struggled to keep the Beast from running into oncoming traffic.

I crawled back into my seat and pressed my fingers against the side of Fuzzy's neck to check for a pulse. There was none.

Fighting back the panic that was beginning to rise in my throat, I began to talk myself down. *You're alive, Angela. Get a grip. No one is shooting at you now. You have nothing to fear.* I could hear Mike's clear instructions and my response: *"Morgan, if this happens again, you'll know what to do?" "Yes."* I could either curl into a helpless ball on the backseat of the Beast, or I could help my friends.

Fuzzy was beyond help, but Jenkins was losing blood fast.

The three of us were in shock, but we had to get to the airport quickly where there were medics to care for Jenkins. Rahim didn't know how to drive.

"Pull over, Jenkins. I'll drive."

"I think you'll have to, Angela," he said as the Beast bounced across an empty patch of dirt at the side of the road. Jenkins radioed the PRT to report the ambush and crawled into the backseat, grimacing and breathing hard. He was growing weak from loss of blood.

Rahim wrapped Jenkins's arm with bandages from the first-aid kit and kept pressure on the wound while I drove the Beast to the airport with Fuzzy's bleeding corpse slumped against the window on the seat next to me. I resisted the urge to look over at him. There was no time to feel anything until we were safely inside the perimeter of the Forward Support Base.

Two medics pulled Fuzzy's limp body from the Beast. One of the doctors drove Jenkins to the Jordanian Field Hospital just down the runway. Rahim and I were taken to the mess tent and offered cups of tea before we sat down with three security officers to tell them everything we could remember about the ambush. I was surprised at how calm I had been during the attack—how calm I still was.

Before coming to Afghanistan, I had worried for months that this tour of duty might send me over the edge of the emotional precipice I'd been teetering on since losing Tom. But since the possibility of being kicked out of the Foreign Service had ultimately trumped my fear of suffering a complete mental meltdown, I had come. It now appeared that the events of this year had made me stronger—at least when I was faced with a crisis. Dealing with the reality of Fuzzy's death would be another matter entirely.

The morning after the attack, I was awakened from a deep sleep by an early call from a very excited Marty. "Ange, congratulations, I got you the London assignment, and you're not going to believe this next bit. PRTs are suddenly the flavor of the month! The secretary of state came back from her one-day visit to Kabul last week and said we need to have PRTs in Iraq!"

"Thanks for the news about the job in London, Marty," I replied after a long pause. "I actually thought you might be calling because of the ambush," I added, feeling no joy at learning about my dream assignment.

"What ambush? There were no attacks on the secretary, were there?" He sounded concerned.

"Marty, I'm talking about an attack here in Mazār. My vehicle was ambushed near the Blue Mosque yesterday. The guy who has been guarding me for the past ten months was killed, and my driver was wounded. I wasn't hit. I'm okay, just a little shook up."

"Jeez, Ange, I'm so sorry, but I'm glad you're all right. I hadn't heard anything about that. I'll have to check CNN."

"It won't be on CNN, Marty. No Americans were killed, and this is Afghanistan, not Iraq, remember?" My long-suppressed tears began to flow.

"Let me know if I can do anything, Ange," said Marty before hanging up. I buried my face in my pillow and wept long and hard for Fuzzy. Several hours later, I forced myself to get up and take an ice-cold ship shower.

Colonel Jameson and his officers had been preoccupied since the previous afternoon with implementing increased security measures and investigating the attack. After returning to the PRT from the Forward Support Base, I had stayed up until midnight filing reports to the embassy.

No one noticed in the morning that I was slowly sinking into a black hole—no one that is except Mark, who'd barely spoken to me since our argument about Rahim and Nilofar. I had been sitting alone for an hour at a table in the soldiers' dining room where Fuzzy, Jenkins, and I used to talk and joke at breakfast. My tea had grown cold. I was stirring it absently with a finger when Mark appeared in front of me.

"Have you eaten anything since yesterday afternoon, Angela?"

I shook my head silently.

He turned away abruptly, and I resumed stirring my cold tea.

Three minutes later, he set a tray in front of me. "Buttered toast, scrambled eggs, a bowl of fruit, and a hot cup of tea with milk and sugar—just the way you like it.

"Now eat!" he commanded. "I'm not leaving until you do."

"I'm not hungry," I replied in a barely audible voice.

"Angela, have you ever heard of PTSD?"

I nodded without speaking.

"Perhaps you should speak with someone . . ."

I looked into his glorious blue eyes and gave up trying to hold back the tears. "I've been dealing with PTSD since the year my husband was killed," I said, covering my face with my hands. "I have it under control now. I'm just really sad today, Mark."

He handed me a napkin to wipe my tears.

"It's perfectly normal to feel this way when you lose a good friend," I added, trying not to sound as miserable as I felt. "You don't need to worry about me. I'll be fine," I said with little conviction. "I'm going back to my office in a few minutes, but I do appreciate your concern."

"I'd really like to see you eat something, Angela."

I bit into the toast and scalded my lips on the tea.

"That's better," he said smiling. "Angela, I . . ."

A young corporal from ops rushed into the dining hall, interrupting whatever Mark had been about to say. "Major Davies, you have a call from NATO headquarters in Kabul. It's about the ambush. Sorry for interrupting, Angela," he added, his eyes avoiding mine.

Mark stood up immediately. "I'm on my way, Corporal. Angela, if you need anything, please let me know."

"Thanks, Mark," I murmured as he left the dining hall. I ate everything on the plate and went back for another cup of tea.

Jenkins had been flown to the military hospital in Kabul that morning. Since he was so close to the end of his enlistment and so devastated by his mate's death, he took the option to escort Fuzzy's body home and take an early discharge. When he called me from Kabul to say good-bye, we could barely speak through our tears.

The next few days were a blur of meetings as we tried to analyze what had occurred and more importantly—why. The assailant, who had been trained in Pakistan, was a young man from the Pashtun village Mark and I had visited in the summer. He had been chased down and turned over to the British soldiers by shopkeepers who had witnessed the ambush.

Colonel Jameson and Colonel Tremain strongly disagreed

about the handling of the assailant after he had been captured. I was working at my desk in the bullpen when Tremain stormed through and into Colonel Jameson's office two days after the attack.

"Are you bullshittin', me, man?" he said to Jameson in an agitated voice. "You turned that son of a bitch who killed one of your own men over to the Afghans?" I remained at my desk, but I could see Tremain through the open door. He was trembling with rage.

"I did," Colonel Jameson replied calmly. "British armed forces are in this province to build public support for a functioning Afghan police force. It is our duty to respect the laws of this country, Hugo. We had no authority to detain the man."

"Goddammit, Jameson, we would have thrown his sorry ass on a C-130 and shipped him off to Bagram for questioning. When and only when our boys got every bit of information they could squeeze out of the bastard, would we hand him over to the Afghan police at Pul-i-Charkhi."

It was painful to listen to the argument of these two men, both of whom I respected so much. They were fine officers, operating in a country and in a war with very few clear rules. They cared deeply for their men and their mission, but their approaches to this tangled web we had woven for ourselves in Afghanistan were dramatically different. My sympathies remained with Colonel Jameson. I was convinced that the less aggressive British approach would be more successful in the long run, but it was not my decision.

"Are you at least going to let your men and Angela start wearing body armor?" asked Tremain. He had lowered his voice.

"Of course I am, Hugo," Jameson replied, his voice still steady. "You know how much I value your opinions, but your army and my army approach things differently."

"I'll say we do," snorted Tremain.

"Angela, would you come in and close the door after you," called Colonel Jameson.

I stood and glanced back at my NATO colleagues. Their ears must have been burning, but their eyes remained focused on their computer screens. I went into the colonel's office, closed the door behind me, and spent the next hour with the two men as they discussed how they would cooperate more closely in the future.

Letters and calls of sympathy poured into the PRT from provincial governors and local officials, including the old mullah across the street. Even General Kabir sent his condolences. The only thing he and Governor Daoud still agreed on was their shared hatred of the Taliban and al-Qaeda.

The evening after the ambush, the colonel summoned everyone in camp who was not on duty for a memorial service in the pub.

"We pray for the family of Lance Corporal Fotheringham, a valued friend and a fine soldier," he said to the assembled troops. "We also pray for the swift recovery of Lance Corporal Jenkins." The officers and men bowed their heads. I had pressed myself into a corner and was staring at the dark stain on the wall where my giant, gentle, wonderful Fuzzy had hurled his beer that night.

"Today is a time to reflect on the tasks we must still accomplish in order to prevent further suffering in Afghanistan," said Jameson to the silent crowd of soldiers. "The people of this region have welcomed us during the two years of our presence in Mazār-i-Sharīf. We cannot let the actions of a single person affect our attitude toward or our respect for the Afghan people."

There was some muffled shuffling and grumbling at this comment until another officer began to read from the Field Service Book. I was sobbing. The officers and soldiers around me pretended not to notice.

When the men were dismissed, business as usual quickly resumed inside the camp. Not quite ready to go back to the bullpen and carry on as though nothing had happened, I went out to my rose garden, where a few hardy blooms were still showing off their colors.

"Doing all right, are you?" Mark came up behind me and rested his hand lightly on my shoulder.

"It was so fast. He was so young, Mark. There was nothing I could do."

"It's true that you could do nothing for Corporal Fotheringham, Angela, but there was something you could do for Jenkins, and you did it. You got him to the medics as quickly as possible," Mark said, "and probably saved his arm."

"Such a waste, losing Fuzzy like that."

"Yes," Mark agreed, "a terrible waste."

He kept his hand on my shoulder and stayed with me until my tears had dried.

FIFTY-FOUR

October 17, 2005

"Ange, it's Bill."

I leaned back in my desk chair, pressed the cell phone hard against my ear, and squeezed my eyes shut. It was so good to hear my brother's voice. I was still numb after the ambush and Fuzzy's death but I was handling it better than I had expected. After Mark's force-feeding at breakfast, my appetite had returned and the tears had stopped.

"Bill, thanks so much for calling. How did you hear about the attack? I didn't want to tell you and upset Dad, but I really appreciate the call. I'm fine, but my bodyguard was killed and our driver was injured."

There was a long silence on the other end of the line. For a moment, I thought the phone had gone dead.

"Ange, what attack are you talking about?"

"I thought that's why you called me," I replied, feeling confused.

"Ange, Dad passed away last night," he said, his voice choking. "It was a massive stroke. Happened right after he went to sleep. He just never woke up."

There was a time when this much bad news would have sent me to bed for days, sufficiently sedated to shut out the rest of the world. Not anymore.

"We scheduled his funeral for next Thursday. Think you can make it?" asked Bill. "His wife has already packed her things. She's leaving for her parents' place in Phoenix this evening. She said to contact her lawyer when the will is read."

"Of course, I'll come home," I assured him. "I may have trouble getting out of here with all this security, but I'll do my best."

"Okay, sis. Hurry home. I'm glad you're okay."

That night, Mark and I had dinner for the first time in weeks. When the pub opened at eight, he purchased two cans of cider for me, two cans of beer for him, and invited me to join him upstairs on the balcony. For the next three hours, we sat outside bundled in heavy jackets, baring our souls to each other under a bright October moon. The few officers who came up to smoke that evening retired to the far end of the balcony and tried to give us as much privacy as possible.

It had been a bittersweet but revelatory conversation. Mark started by offering his condolences for my father, although I made it quite clear that Dad's death had not been unexpected and that I was suffering far more from losing Fuzzy.

He apologized profusely for berating me the day he had discovered Rahim and Nilofar together in the shipping container. He confessed that he had been in agony during the two weeks when we'd barely spoken, but said his pride had kept him from approaching me.

"It wasn't so much your involvement with Rahim and Nilofar that upset me, Angela, although that was part of it," he said as we sat on the balcony in plastic chairs with our fingers laced tightly together. "It was your own impulsive risk-taking that was driving me mad. I was certain you would eventually get yourself into a situation you couldn't get out of, and I would lose you."

He squeezed my hand and brought it to his lips.

"I worried so much every time you went out on patrol it was impossible to concentrate on my work." He stared out at the dark peaks of the Hindu Kush and continued. "I was so angry the night I found Nilofar and Rahim that when I saw you in the pub, all my frustrations came pouring out—but not in the way I had intended."

In the end, we agreed that two emotionally battered grown-ups, thrown together in a war zone, with significant differences in age and temperament, could actually fall in love—and it might even last. I told him about my onward assignment to London, and suggested we get together there when he came back from Iraq in the spring. He was thrilled at the news and wanted me to meet his parents and sisters.

"Mark, you know that I'll be flying out in the morning to attend my father's funeral," I said, overwhelmed by this unrelenting sequence of bad news. "By the time I return, you'll be packing for Iraq."

"Please don't remind me," he said, his voice choking. "We've had so little time together here and now with my stupid refusal to speak to you these past few weeks, I've denied us even that."

"Let's focus on the future, Mark."

As we gathered up our cans to leave the balcony, he took me gently into his arms and kissed me on the lips for the first time. Even such an innocent gesture felt awkward in this fishbowl military environment, but the other officers had left the balcony before us, and I did not resist.

"Promise me you'll come back from New Mexico before I leave," insisted Mark on our way downstairs. "The Romanian MOT will be flying out with us, and they'll be throwing one of their parties the night before we depart. I hope you'll be there."

"I wouldn't miss it, Mark."

I don't remember much about the flights or the funeral. I was tired and completely detached from the scene in New Mexico. I had exhausted all my reserves of grief on Fuzzy, whose death had rocked me far more than the passing of my own father. I deplaned at the airport in Albuquerque with a crowd of young GIs returning from duty in Iraq. They were a silent and unsmiling bunch, and looked as exhausted and drained as I felt.

Ten days later, four Gurkha soldiers were waiting for me at the Mazār Airfield with two PRT vehicles. Unlike the silent, deserted place where Fuzzy and Jenkins had greeted me in January, our little airport was now jammed with cargo planes and trucks.

The Germans were unloading equipment for the construction of their new regional military facility just south of the airport. An enormous unmarked Russian Anotov was discharging cargo into several large vehicles parked at the eastern end of the runway. The C-130 I'd come in on had been packed with newly arrived American, Swedish, and German soldiers. A long line of Humvees, Land Cruisers, Range Rovers, and Jeeps drove right up to our plane to pick up their passengers.

"Welcome back, Angela," said Krishna, my Nepalese Gurkha

vehicle commander, with solemn formality. While our driver tossed my bag into the back of the Land Cruiser, Krishna held out my twenty-five-pound Kevlar vest, so I could slip my arms in. The two helmeted Gurkhas in the follow car, alert and scanning the perimeter of the airfield, nodded at me through the windshield of their idling vehicle. No one was smiling.

The casual air and floppy hats of the British soldiers were no more. Only two months ago, Fuzzy and Jenkins had greeted me with hugs on an empty runway and we'd stopped in town to feast on kabobs, flat bread, and sweet Mazār melons. I had felt then like I was coming home. It did not seem that way now. I no longer knew where home was.

"I'm very sorry for your loss," Krishna said with downcast eyes as he allowed the weight of the vest to settle on my shoulders. Pulling the Velcro straps tight across my chest, I hoisted myself awkwardly into the backseat of the vehicle.

"Thank you, Krishna." I was ashamed to admit even to myself that I missed Fuzzy more than I missed my own father. The mental picture I had of Dad expiring peacefully at home, his TV droning in the background, attended by his private nurses, contrasted starkly with my last images of the young freckled Fuzzy, laughing at Rahim's stories, then grabbing his rifle with split-second reflexes to defend the rest of us against our attacker.

"We dropped Rahim at the university on the way to the airport," Krishna announced as we turned onto the main road. "He said he had to get a book from the library. I hope you won't mind if we stop to pick him up on the way back to the PRT."

"Of course, I don't mind." It would be so good to see Rahim again, although I knew exactly what was meant by that "book."

We drove into town with the windows rolled up and the heater blasting. By late October, the afternoon air was chilly despite the cloudless blue sky. Rahim was waving enthusiastically as we pulled up to the main gate of Balkh University. He did not have a book in his hand and, of course, he had no body armor.

"Farishta-*jan*," he shouted as he bounded into the vehicle. "Welcome back! It is good to see you. I hope you and your family are not too sad, and I hope that the funeral for your father was well attended."

I thought of Bill and me sitting with Dad's five doddering neighbors in the wooden pews of our local church, listening politely as Father Perez droned his way through the requiem mass. "Yes," I said, "it was very well attended. Thanks, Rahim."

"Didn't the library have your book?" asked Krishna, turning back to look at Rahim before we pulled into a stream of traffic and were immediately trapped in an animal-vehicle gridlock.

Rahim shook his head at Krishna and then glanced over at me with an apologetic grin. "No, Krishna, someone else had already checked out the book I wanted."

I rolled my eyes at his little white lie and resumed our conversation, this time in Dari. "Rahim-*jan*, you must be careful when you meet with Nilofar. Someone is going to see you and tell her parents."

"I know it is dangerous for us to be together," he said with pleading eyes, "but I must see her. We will not stop seeing each other. Soon I will leave for France, and she will be forced to marry that old Hazara merchant. May he be deprived of Allah's blessings forever!"

There was nothing I could say or do to comfort my distraught young friend or to convince him to be more careful.

"You are the only person I can talk to about this, Farishta-*jan*. Even my own mother does not understand how I could love a Hazara woman."

I believe I had shed more tears since arriving in Afghanistan than I had in the past two decades. Initially, I'd been embarrassed by my crying jags, which I feared the soldiers and terps would perceive as weakness on my part—but now I didn't care. I had bottled up my emotions for far too long, and it felt good to let them out.

Rahim had been around me long enough to know when the spigot was about to open. "Farishta-*jan*! I am sorry to upset you," he whispered, so as not to attract the attention of the two Gurkhas in the front seat. "I didn't mean to make you cry."

I smiled at him, wiped my eyes with my head scarf, and tried to think of something reassuring to say.

"It's not you, Rahim. It's everything."

FIFTY-FIVE

October 31, 2005

Just after sunset the day before Mark's departure, my vehicle and a follow car pulled up to the gates of the PRT following an exhausting eight-hour round-trip to Sar-e Pol. I was still recovering from jet leg after my return from Dad's funeral and I hated making these marathon drives wearing body armor, but the colonel had asked me to make the trip on behalf of the PRT to meet with a distraught provincial governor.

Tonight was the Romanians' party, and I wanted to have at least a few moments with Mark before he and the rest of the Gurkhas departed in the morning.

Although it was almost dark when we arrived, I could see Nilofar standing under a security light, arguing with the Afghan guards. Her head scarf was thrown back.

"Angela, I must speak with you," she called out when she saw me. "I've been waiting here for an hour, and the guards have been threatening to summon the police if I don't go away."

I signed her in and brought her with me to the dining hall, which was about to close. "Let's get some supper and we can talk," I said, handing her a tray.

"Where is Rahim?" she asked with an urgency I had never heard before. "I have been trying to call him on his cell phone, but he doesn't answer."

"He's in Kabul with Professor Mongibeaux. He left yesterday afternoon. Perhaps his phone is broken."

"Angela, men have come to my parents' house to threaten me again. They said I must not try to prevent the marriage of their cousin to a young girl from Chemtal. She is only twelve years old! She is threatening to kill herself if her parents force her to marry this man. My parents have told me to stop interfering, but how can I do nothing?"

"Nilofar, you can't solve the problems of every young woman who comes to you. You must understand that each time you help these girls avoid forced marriages you are angering some very powerful people." I envied her courage, but I was terrified that something might happen to her.

"I know this, Angela, but I must do it! Soon I will be forced into marriage myself, and then I will be the prisoner of my husband—forever. Until that time, I will continue to help others, because I know that no one is going to help me."

"Nilofar, you know there's nothing I can do," I said as I looked into her angry but innocent eyes. "I'm begging you to stop this before you get hurt."

She was defiant. Clenching her jaw, she muttered, "If they want to stop me, they're going to have to kill me."

Her phone began to buzz. "My brother is here to pick me up," she said with a sudden smile, as though this life and death conversation had never taken place. "I will call you tomorrow, Angela. Tell Rahim to get his phone fixed."

I walked her to the gate, watched her drive away with her brother, and went upstairs, hoping to be able to forget everyone's troubles except my own for just a few hours.

All the younger officers were looking forward with great anticipation to this evening's party because the new Swedish contingent that had just arrived in camp was coed. I was no longer the only woman at the PRT, and they would finally have women their age to dance with.

The electric outlets in the atrium were not working that night, but the Romanians, with their flair for the dramatic, had loaded their CD player with fresh batteries and placed flickering tapers in glass bottles on every flat surface in the room. The atrium glowed in the soft buttery candlelight.

I was anxious to see Mark, even if he only came for a few minutes.

The colonel had just poured me a glass of wine when Mark appeared in the doorway scanning the room. I raised my glass in a friendly salute and tried to appear blasé as he approached. It was impossible. I swallowed hard and was overcome by the reality that he would be leaving in the morning. He walked quickly in my direction.

The colonel greeted him, but his eyes never left mine.

"If you'll excuse me, Colonel," Mark said with a polite nod.

"Angela?" He stood in front of my chair, took my wineglass, and set it on the table next to me. "May I have this dance?"

"You want to dance?"

"Yes, with you," Mark said as he took my hand. The colonel

and the chief of staff next to him rose to their feet as I stood and was led by Mark to the center of the atrium.

I noticed he wasn't the only one with this idea. The Romanians had replaced their polka with a slow Eastern European tango and immediately claimed the most attractive female Swedish soldiers for themselves, leaving the other young officers to battle for the attention of the remaining few women.

As the warm strains of violins and concertinas filled the air with that most sensuous of all dances, Mark slid his hand around my waist and pressed his fingers into the small of my back. Tipping me like a glass of champagne and throwing me slightly off balance, he began to lead me in slow-motion circles around the room.

"This is a tango, isn't it?"

"It is," he replied, pulling me closer.

"I don't know how to tango, Mark."

"I do," he said as he skillfully changed direction, tightening his grip and leaving no daylight between us. I was barely breathing.

"I was afraid you wouldn't be able to come tonight," I whispered as his lips brushed against my hair.

"This I would not miss," he replied as he led me into another slow turn. "I've given my successor enough reading material to keep him busy until at least midnight."

"I'm going to miss you terribly, Mark."

"And I you," he said, guiding me between the Romanians, who were clinging tightly to their Swedish partners.

My pulse was racing, but tonight it was for a good cause.

"Angela, we have so little time left," he murmured. "Let's go outside." He took my hand and led me to the balcony.

We walked to the far corner, and Mark brought my fingers to his lips.

"You know that I'll only be in Basra for six months," he said, sounding desperate to get this information out as quickly as possible. "I want you to know that I've asked for an assignment near London when I leave Iraq."

"Mark, that's wonderful," I said, shivering in the frigid night air. He put his arms around me and I reciprocated. It didn't really matter anymore who saw us.

"You know, when I first saw you in Smythe's office last December, I thought you were his secretary," he said, laughing, "but I couldn't keep my eyes off you."

"And I thought you were one of the rudest people I'd ever met."

"How could I have known it was you that Smythe was referring to when he told me a female American diplomat was being sent to Mazār? You have no idea what was going through my head, Angela, when I followed him out of his office and we were formally introduced."

I reached up to touch his face, and he placed his warm hand over mine.

"When did you first change your mind about me?" he asked, stroking my hand.

"I'm not sure when it began, Mark," I said. "Perhaps when I first saw you dancing."

"You mean tonight?" he asked, looking confused.

"No, last summer at Ahmad's wedding," I replied, laughing.

"The interpreter's wedding? But the men and women were in separate rooms."

"Nilofar showed me a hole in the curtain where the women could spy on the men without being seen. She wanted me to see Rahim, but there you were in your uniform at the center of a crowd of singing, shouting men. Nilofar had to drag me away."

"Violating yet another taboo, eh, Angela?" He laughed. "You'll never learn, will you?"

"It was worth it, Mark."

We kissed, this time long and deep.

Mark reached into his pocket and pulled out a packet of "blueys," the pale blue onionskin airmail letters that had been used for decades by British forces for personal correspondence when on deployment. These handwritten letters were a vanishing tradition that was rapidly being replaced by e-blueys, but Mark didn't trust e-mail.

"I meant to give these to you yesterday," he said, pressing them into my hand. "I've included my military postal address. Will you write to me while I'm in Basra?"

"Every day, Mark."

We remained in our corner of the balcony, planning our reunion in London, until Sergeant Major announced that the colonel was going to bed and the party was over.

The other officers on the balcony collected their beer cans, stubbed out their cigarettes, and gave us a few moments alone to say our final farewell.

FIFTY-SIX

November 2, 2005

I had survived my first day without Mark and was already counting the days until we would meet in London. It was almost midnight. I was snuggled in bed under three blankets, rereading some of my favorite Rumi poems and thinking about Mark, when the cell phone began to vibrate on my desk. Late-night calls still got my adrenaline pumping. By the time I threw off the covers and my bare feet hit the floor, my heart was pounding so hard it hurt.

Calm down, Angela, I told myself. *Maybe it's Marty calling to say you got promoted. It's almost lunchtime in D.C. Or it's Mark since he's not flying out of Kabul until tomorrow morning.*

"Hello, this is Angela Morgan."

"Farishta-*jan,* please you must help us!" Rahim's voice was frantic and pleading.

"Rahim, where are you? What's the matter?"

"I'm in a taxi with Nilofar. We are almost at the PRT. Please, Farishta, I beg you—tell the guards to let us in. Nilofar is bleeding ba . . ."

"Rahim!" I screamed. "Rahim!" His cell phone had gone dead.

In three minutes, I was at the gate, wrapped in my robe. One of the officers on my floor had come running when he heard me calling Rahim's name. He notified the duty ops officer, who had ordered the guards to open the gates and admit the taxi. Rahim lifted Nilofar carefully from the backseat and carried her limp and bloody form into the dispensary, where the camp doctor, also in his robe, was waiting for them with a medic.

"What happened to her, Rahim?"

"She was attacked by three men, sent by a warlord who accused her of interfering with his plans to marry a twelve-year-old girl. They took Nilofar from the university as she was leaving class. No one did anything to stop them."

"I mean what did they do to her, Rahim?" the doctor demanded sharply as he began to cut away her blood-soaked clothing. Rahim turned away and began to sob. "They beat her. They tried to rape her, but when they saw that she was already bleeding . . . that it was her time of month, that she was . . . unclean to men, they . . . they violated her with a . . . a . . . a Kalashnikov rifle," he said, burying his hands in his face.

"Jesus Christ," muttered the doctor. "Angela, get Rahim out of here while I try to stop the bleeding. We've got to get this girl to a hospital fast."

"Not the hospital in Mazār, sir, please," begged Rahim. "They will find her and kill her."

"Sergeant, tell the duty ops officer we'll need our ambulance and two escort vehicles, ready to go to the Forward Support Base in ten minutes. Tell him to have the FSB inform the doctors at the field hospital that we're bringing the girl. They have blood supplies."

"Yes, sir," replied the medic as he rushed out the door.

I led Rahim into the frigid night air. "Where are her parents? Why didn't they come with her?"

"Her father wouldn't let her in when the men left her on the street in front of her house. He said that she had shamed her family by her actions and that no one would ever marry her now because she had allowed herself to be violated. She called me on her cell phone before she fainted. I came with a taxi and found her still lying in the street. I didn't know where else to take her."

We went back into the dispensary, where the medic was inserting an IV into Nilofar's arm.

"The Jordanian doctors at the field hospital will be able to help her, Rahim," the doctor assured him.

"Will she die, Doctor?"

"She is young and strong and she's a fighter, Rahim. She won't die."

As I wrapped my arms around Rahim, he buried his face in my hair and wept uncontrollably.

Nilofar was quickly stabilized at the field hospital. The young surgeon said her wounds would heal but warned that she might never be able to have children. Two days later, I escorted her on a military flight to Kabul, where she could recover from her wounds and her surgery.

She and Rahim had a tearful farewell at the Mazār airport. She would remain sheltered inside the compound of an international NGO for several weeks until they could locate a country that would give her asylum and a temporary residence visa. Nilofar could not return to Mazār. It was dangerous for her even to remain very long in Kabul.

FIFTY-SEVEN

November 4, 2005

I spent my first day in Kabul with Nilofar, who was still drowsy from pain medication. Just before sundown, I returned to the embassy and, after an early dinner, settled in for an evening in my hooch with a favorite mystery novel and a glass of sherry for company.

It was hard to concentrate on the book. I was still worried about Nilofar and was also agonizing over my own encouragement of her recklessness. Perhaps I could have prevented this tragedy if my warnings to her had been more forceful.

And then there was Mark, who was constantly on my mind. I reviewed to the point of obsession every detail of our last evening at the Romanian party. Was it only five days ago? I was worried about his being in Iraq even though I knew he had a desk job and would rarely go outside the wire. I was also making plans for our reunion in London.

My phone rang at six P.M. "Sorry to disturb you, Miss Morgan, this is the guard at Post One. You have a visitor, who must be signed in before I can admit him. I'll start filling out the paperwork and have it ready for your signature." He hung up before I could ask who it was.

Switching off my phone, I wondered who could be coming to see me so late in the day.

I stepped into the guard shack expecting to see Rahim, who I knew was trying to get down to Kabul to see Nilofar. I thought I was dreaming. Mark was handing his NATO ID card to the guard.

"Hello, Angela," he said in a voice that told me he wasn't certain I'd be happy to see him.

"Mark, I thought you left for Basra three days ago," I said, choking on my own words and grabbing the sleeve of his uniform to make sure he was real.

"I was, I mean we were, but the plane had engine trouble. We're now expected to leave tomorrow. I didn't know you were in Kabul until I called the PRT this afternoon and asked to speak with you. Sergeant Major said you had brought Nilofar here. What happened?"

"She was attacked and badly hurt, but she's stable now. She's in seclusion until a host country can be found for her. It's not safe for her to stay in Afghanistan."

His face darkened. "I knew it," he said, growing suddenly angry. The guard handed him a visitors badge and waved him through the metal detector.

"You knew what?" I asked, surprised at his tone.

"That you shouldn't have encouraged them to continue seeing each other," he said as I led him into the walled embassy compound.

"What are you talking about, Mark? This had nothing to do with Rahim. Nilofar was attacked because she was defying one of the warlords."

"You could have stopped her," he said, grabbing my arm. "What if that had been you?"

"Mark," I said, taking his face in my hands, "look at me. It wasn't me. I'm fine, and Nilofar will be fine. It was Rahim who rescued her."

He nodded without speaking.

"Why didn't you call me earlier to say you were still in Kabul?" I asked.

"I couldn't bear to say good-bye to you again, especially over the phone."

"Are you angry with me, Mark?"

He reached for my hand. "No, I just want you out of here as soon as possible and safely assigned to your embassy in London so I won't have to worry about you anymore."

"You don't think I'll be worrying about you in Iraq?" I asked.

"Is there someplace we can go to talk privately, Angela?" He was starting to look quite desperate. "I only have a few hours. My driver will be back at nine forty-five to pick me up."

"There's really no place on this compound where we can have any privacy except for my hooch," I said, feeling uncertain about what to do next until he put his arm around my waist.

"Shall we?"

We walked between the long rows of white shipping containers and entered my hooch in silence. I motioned for him to sit in my only chair.

"May I offer you a glass of sherry," I asked, forgetting for a moment that I only had one glass. "You take the glass. I'll just drink out of the bottle." I laughed as I began to remove the cork.

"Angela." Mark rose from the chair, took my hands in his, and brought them to his lips. We moved into each other's arms and were one breath away from kissing when a key slid into the lock, the knob turned, and there was DEA special agent Sally Dietrich wearing her black body armor, black uniform, and combat boots. A black pistol was strapped to her hip and a black duffel bag and semiautomatic rifle slung over her shoulder.

"Angela! Oh, shit! I'm so sorry," she cried at the sight of the two of us staring at her and moving apart with our arms dangling at our sides.

"They didn't tell me I was sharing, or I would have knocked. Hell, I would have asked for another hooch. Christ almighty, what horrible timing," she moaned, then added with an embarrassed grin, "but I suppose it could have been worse."

"Sally, what a surprise," I stammered, looking from her to Mark as they both stared at each other and then at me.

"This is Mark Davies. We worked together at the PRT in Mazār. He's on his way to Iraq tomorrow morning. Mark, this is Sally Dietrich. She's with our Drug Enforcement Administration and is training Afghan counter-narcotics squads. We shared a hooch when I arrived last December."

Mark and Sally shook hands, and the three of us stood in awkward silence not knowing what to say or do next until Sally took control of the situation.

"Listen, I have an early call tomorrow and have got to get some shut-eye tonight, but you two look like you really need some alone-time. Here's the deal. I'll head over to the cafeteria for dinner and join my boys for a beer, but at 2200 hours I'm coming back. I swear on my mother's grave, Angela, I will not step through this door one minute earlier or one minute later than ten P.M."

Without waiting for a response, she tossed her rifle, pistol, and duffel bag on the unused bed and was out the door.

"So now we have privacy," I laughed. "Almost four hours, and you're not leaving this room, Mark Davies, until I've finished with you," I said as I grabbed the collar of his uniform and pulled him into my arms.

Mark buried his face in my hair, which, untouched by scissors for the past eleven months, now fell in dark waves below my shoulders.

"I'm glad you haven't cut your hair," he murmured. "It smells like the roses in your garden at the PRT."

"It's only shampoo," I whispered as my lips parted and we became one sweet, sensuous tangle of teeth and tongue. He began to kiss me with an urgency that was frightening in its intensity. My response was equally violent.

"What are you thinking about, Mark?" We were resting quietly in each other's arms. An hour had passed since we'd spoken and there was a sadness in his eyes I hadn't seen before.

"I'm thinking about my biggest regret of the past year," he replied, brushing his lips down my neck and across my shoulder.

"And that was what?" I asked after catching my breath.

"That it took me so many months to acknowledge my feelings for you."

We kissed again and all conversation ceased. When I next looked at the clock on my desk, I sat up quickly.

"Sally will be back in less than an hour, Mark."

"A few more minutes?" he pleaded.

"We really can't have her walking in on us like this." I laughed, throwing back the blankets. "I made her a promise. We'll have plenty of time in London."

As he began to rise, I grabbed his shoulder and ran my fingers over the delicate indigo script that curled around his bicep. "Mark, your tattoo," I said. "It's in Arabic."

"Yes," he replied. "Can you read it?"

"Never give up," I murmured as he pulled me into his arms again.

We dressed quickly when we saw how late it was and walked hand in hand to the main gate, where I signed him out. A British Army truck, idling in the road under the halogen glare of a security lamp, was waiting to take Mark back to Camp Souter for his early morning departure. I stood on the street watching until his vehicle vanished around a barrier of sandbags and barbed wire, shivering in my light jacket, until one of the Nepalese guards touched my elbow.

"Ma'am, you should go back inside," he said gently.

When I awoke the next morning, Sally and her weapons were gone.

FIFTY-EIGHT

November 5, 2005

"Here it is! Your new chariot," announced an embassy staffer from the motor pool. "It's only 'lightly armored' so you can still roll down the windows and of course you'll have to wear body armor," he added. I didn't bother to ask what he meant by "lightly armored."

We were in a parking lot behind the motor pool. My shiny white "lightly armored" Toyota was parked next to a fully armored embassy vehicle, which the day before had run over an IED on a road just outside Kabul. Although the front was a burned-out, spaghetti-like tangle of twisted metal, the passenger compartment, including windows, was completely intact.

"How are you planning to get your van back to Mazār?" he asked as I continued to stare at the blackened vehicle next to my white one. "If you want it flown up, it will be weeks before I can get space on one of the C-130s."

"The PRT sent some of our soldiers down to Kabul this morning," I replied. "They'll be driving my vehicle and several new British Army vans back over the mountains. I'll be riding with them."

"I don't think that's allowed," he said, scratching his chin.

"They're picking me up tomorrow morning, and I've already signed all the papers for this Land Cruiser, so unless someone stops me, I'll be driving away with the Brits at 0800 hours."

"Suit yourself," he said. "It's your neck."

I went to say good-bye to Nilofar that afternoon. Two burly Afghan guards posted outside the high, unmarked walls of the compound where she was in hiding greeted me by name as I climbed out of an armored American Embassy vehicle. I'd been spending all my free time with Nilofar since bringing her to Kabul.

The Norwegian director of the center led me to a small garden where Nilofar was sitting alone in the sun. "Her parents haven't called," she said with resignation, "and I don't expect they will. We've had many girls staying here who were disowned by their families after being raped."

The day was cold and the cloudless sky a deep cerulean blue. Nilofar was wrapped in the red shawl she'd been wearing the night Mark found her with Rahim. A cup of tea sat cold and untouched on the table next to her.

I cleared my throat so as not to startle her. "Nilofar, how are you feeling today?"

She turned toward me. As always, I had to force myself not to flinch at the sight of her bruised and swollen face. "I am much better, Angela-*jan*, thank you." Her expressionless voice mirrored the psychological pain I knew she would bear for months if not years to come.

"I'll be going back to Mazār tomorrow morning, Nilofar. I wanted to say good-bye to you and make sure you have everything you need."

Her eyes filled with tears. "You are leaving?"

"I have to go back to work," I said, kneeling next to her chair and taking her trembling hands into mine.

"I'll call you every day. I promise." I struggled to keep from crying in front of her. "You're safe here."

"I know that. The women are very good to me and the other girls," she said, her eyes glistening, "but I will miss you, Angela-*jan*."

It broke my heart to see this strong, smart, brave young woman—an asset to her country and her people—reduced to a battered, frail shell of her former self. She squeezed my hands and stared at the mountains in the distance. "Rahim called me this morning," she said. "He calls me many times every day."

I nodded but was now choking on my own tears and unable to respond.

"He will be leaving for Paris very soon," she continued. "I may never see him again."

"You will see him, Nilofar," I said, stroking her hands. "Professor Mongibeaux and Professor Fazli are working hard to find an Afghan family in France to sponsor you."

Her eyes brightened but only for a second. "How will Rahim ever want me now after what those men did to me? The doctors say I will never be able to have a child."

"Nilofar, Rahim loves you very much, and nothing those men did will ever change that," I assured her.

After one of the servants brought us fresh cups of tea and a tray of biscuits, Nilofar and I sat quietly together in the fading afternoon light until the embassy driver called to say he was waiting for me outside.

I was anxious to cross the eleven-thousand-foot Salang Pass by car, even though it would be painful to make the trip without Jenkins behind the wheel and Fuzzy riding shotgun. My driver and vehicle commander were as young, polite, and competent as my boys had been, but it wouldn't be the same without the familiar banter we had developed after so many long patrols.

It was a grueling fourteen-hour slog with heavy snows and several accidents on the road slowing our progress. The snow was even heavier when we emerged on the much colder northern side of the Hindu Kush from the long, unlit Salang Tunnel.

When our convoy arrived at the PRT, the new Swedish troops and the British officers from the regiment that had replaced the Royal Gurkha Rifles welcomed me back and insisted I attend every meeting they held. I was now the PRT's éminence grise on Afghanistan.

It was a sad commentary on our knowledge of this country that someone like me, who had spent less than a year in country and had traveled—almost always—under heavy security restrictions, was now considered an expert. I was far from it. How could any of us really know what was going on in the minds of the tribes, sub-tribes, clans, and families of this feudal land. We couldn't.

I resisted forming any new friendships. My remaining time here was too short, and my emotional well had been sucked dry. I was counting the days until Mark and I would be together in London.

FIFTY-NINE

November 17, 2005

"Promise you'll write nothing personal in an e-mail, Angela," Mark pleaded during one of his infrequent phone calls from Basra. "Use the blueys."

The onionskin blueys, he repeatedly assured me, were the most secure and private way for us to communicate. Each letter would take up to ten days to reach its destination, but only he and I would see the contents.

His first bluey arrived with the British Army mail call only three days after my snowbound trip back to Mazār. He had sent it the morning he left Kabul for Basra.

His next one arrived as predicted ten days later. Three of mine had passed his traveling in the opposite direction—the great disadvantage of snail mail—but we had e-mail for short notes. Nothing personal and nothing long, just: "I'm fine. Miss you" or "First snowstorm in Mazār, roads closed." "Heard about new bombings in Basra. Be careful."

I had been asked to stay in Mazār for an extra six weeks until my replacement arrived. Since Mark would be in Basra until March, I agreed. The promotion list would be out in a few more days, and

I was optimistic that after this year in Afghanistan, I would be on it and guaranteed three and perhaps even four years in London.

As the weeks passed, Mark's letters began to paint a seriously worsening security situation in southern Iraq, but they all ended the same way.

> . . . I am counting the days until we are together again in London . . . wearing out your letters from carrying them in my pocket and rereading them to the point of obsession. I long for each one to arrive and I long even more to hold you in my arms again.

> I love you, my darling.
> Stay safe.
> Mark

SIXTY

November 25, 2005

Colonel Jameson departed for Kabul early Friday morning to meet and brief his successor, who was scheduled to fly up on Sunday and assume command. The new Swedish chief of staff, who had come just a week earlier, would be in charge until Jameson's replacement arrived.

I had given up trying to take Fridays off and was tapping away at my computer in the bullpen when Rahim appeared at the door.

"Farishta-*jan*, today is Friday. You are supposed to rest."

"And do what, Rahim? Sit in my room and read books I've already read three times?"

"No, you should go to a *buzkashi* game. Some of the soldiers are going, and I am no longer on duty. The Swedes will go to the airport after the game, and they have promised to drop me at the bus station. I have two days off and will go to Kabul to see Nilofar."

He stood beaming in the doorway of the bullpen. I hadn't seen him this happy for a long time.

"Perhaps you will be invited to ride by one of the *chapandaz*," added Rahim. "I have never seen you on a horse, but everyone knows you rode in a *buzkashi* game many months ago."

"It'll be a little hard for me to climb up on a horse wearing twenty-five pounds of body armor, Rahim, but I wouldn't mind watching one more game before I leave. Tell them I'll join them."

"We're leaving in thirty minutes. See you downstairs, Farishta-*jan*."

"Right, Rahim. Thanks for the invite," I said, smiling to myself at this resilient young man. He had come to the bullpen earlier in the week grinning from ear to ear to announce that friends of Jeef had found a sponsor for Nilofar in France. They had even arranged for her to continue her law studies once she was fully recovered from her injuries. After all their trials, they would finally be together.

"Angela, we're short one driver and one vehicle for our outing to the *buzkashi* field. More of the fellows want to come. I understand you're allowed to drive your shiny new State Department vehicle," said one of the new British officers. "Would you mind?"

"Not at all," I replied with a smile. Although the Gurkha Sergeant Major had refused to let me drive the Beast, his replacement didn't seem to mind if I made short trips into town in my new lightly armored Land Cruiser as long as I wore my body armor and was accompanied by someone with a weapon.

It was sunny but cold as our vehicles pulled onto the berm that lined the northern side of the *buzkashi* field. Several thousand cheering Afghan men had gathered to watch the game. The ones on our side of the field made way for our vehicles and welcomed us into their midst with the usual smiles and greetings in broken English.

I wore a long wool head scarf and a heavy winter jacket over my Kevlar vest. There was no longer any point in hiding my identity.

I didn't mind that I couldn't ride. I was happy just to have one last chance to watch this magnificent pageant of horses thundering across the open desert. It had been almost a year since I'd mounted that black stallion and galloped down this field. That ride—my boldest, most impetuous, and most exhilarating act in years—had been my first step in emerging from the shell in which I'd been hiding from life for far too long.

The entire scrum of more than one hundred horsemen had raced to the far side of the field where I could see a small caravan of Kuchi nomads passing silent and unnoticed behind the crowd. They were moving south into the foothills of the Hindu Kush where they would pass the winter in a protected valley. Four men in Biblical garb led seven camels carrying women, infants, tents, cooking utensils, and a child's bicycle. A small flock of goats and sheep trailed behind them. Several Kuchi children and their huge dogs kept the animals moving in the right direction. On the back of the last camel, a square of foil glinted in the late afternoon sun. I looked through the telephoto lens of my camera and zoomed in to confirm that it was as I had expected—the reflector of one of my solar ovens.

The Swedish MOT with Rahim parked their vehicles next to ours and pulled out their cameras. They were on their way back to Stockholm after having served six months at the PRT's safe house in the neighboring province of Jowzjan. This would be their last chance to photograph a *buzkashi* game.

After two hours, the wind picked up and the sky darkened. When it began to rain, the senior officer in our group announced that it was time to leave. We drove off the field in single file with the Swedes in the lead.

Our vehicles would follow theirs into town until the road forked and they headed east to the airport. As I maneuvered into a sharp turn around the Russian bread factory, I noticed that there was no one on the street except for a sickly stray dog—odd for midday even on a rainy Friday afternoon.

Without warning, a blinding flash of light and a deafening explosion transformed the lead Swedish vehicle into a fireball. The vehicle behind it was knocked onto its side, spraying gray mud into the air as it slid off the road and punched through the mud-brick wall of a family compound. The shock wave from the blast hit my Land Cruiser, and I pumped the brakes to keep from ramming the vehicle ahead of me. The British soldiers reacted instantly.

"Angela, are you all right?" shouted the corporal who was next to me in the passenger seat. He had been thrown with his rifle against the windshield, but had suffered only mild cuts on his forehead. As always, I had been the only one wearing a seat belt.

"I'm fine," I muttered as I stared at the carnage in front of us.

"Get in the backseat and stay down," he shouted as he and the other soldiers grabbed their weapons and a first-aid kit and rushed toward the Swedish vehicles.

One soldier radioed the PRT for help while others formed a defensive perimeter around the blast site and the wounded men.

I obeyed the order to stay put until I remembered that Rahim was in one of those vehicles. My heart sank. I couldn't bear to lose my friend. Not when everything had been so bright for him.

When I raised my head, I could see Rahim lying in a pool of mud on the side of the road. He had been thrown clear of the second vehicle when it rolled over. The one medic in our group was busy stabilizing the most seriously injured Swedes. I jumped out, ran to Rahim, and was overjoyed when I saw him push himself into a sitting position. He was dazed and unhurt, but lying near him was another badly injured Swede who had also been thrown from the vehicle.

"Angela, get back in the vehicle now!" ordered the Royal Marine, who was the most senior officer present.

"This man's hurt. I'm staying with him until someone can help," I shouted back as I knelt next to the soldier and began to tick through my first-aid checklist. He was still breathing but unconscious and in shock.

His face had been lacerated by broken glass, and a thin shard of metal protruded from his stomach. He had not been wearing body armor and was rapidly losing blood. I wrapped my head scarf around the metal to stabilize it and gently pressed the ends of the scarf into the gash to staunch the blood.

When he awoke and began to moan, I took out the morphine pen I had carried with me for the past eleven months and pressed it hard against his leg. The spring-loaded needle penetrated his skin and the morphine quickly took effect. He closed his eyes and began to breathe softly.

Despite the cold rain, a crowd of Afghan men began to gather in the street. The British soldiers, running now on pure adrenaline, pointed their weapons at the men and ordered them to move back. Rahim stayed with them to translate.

Within forty-five minutes, British and American soldiers had widened the security perimeter around the blast site. Medics from the Forward Support Base took over the care of the wounded, loading them into their vehicles and heading for the airport.

In the pouring rain under a darkening sky, the Estonian EODs gathered up the remains of the bomb for analysis. Other soldiers started questioning the neighbors about what they had seen before the explosion. I was unhurt and wanted to do something to help. Since Rahim and I were the only Dari speakers present, I offered to stay and assist with interpreting. There was not an Afghan policeman in sight.

We learned nothing that evening. Every man, woman, and child we interviewed claimed to have seen no unusual activities before the event.

The PRT was in a state of controlled chaos when we returned after dark. We were once again in lockdown except for those still out investigating the attack. I called the embassy to report the details we had gathered and let them know I was unharmed. The Swedish major and I scheduled a meeting with Governor Daoud early the following morning to request his support for the investigation since the Afghan police were refusing to cooperate.

The new American contract police trainers who had arrived in Mazār a few weeks before the attack were now in lockdown inside their well-fortified compound south of town.

"We're going to need their help investigating this, Angela," insisted the Swedish major. "The Afghan police are doing nothing."

"I called the Americans last night and asked them to join us at today's meeting with the governor," I replied. "They have orders from their headquarters in Kabul to stay inside their compound. I'm afraid we're on our own, Major."

"Damn it!" he muttered, slamming his fist against the wall. "All right, let's go. Governor Daoud, whom I've not even met, is expecting us in twenty minutes. You're going to have to do the talking. I hope you're all right with that."

"Let's do it," I said as we strapped on our vests and climbed into the PRT's only fully armored vehicle.

"Farishta, please tell the major we are truly sorry about the attack on your soldiers," said the governor, his face as impassive as granite and his voice as smooth as silk. "Two attacks in two months. This is extremely troubling."

He slipped his amber prayer beads slowly through his fingers, making a soft clicking sound as he spoke. I didn't know if Daoud had actually ordered the attack, but I suspected he knew exactly who had planted that IED.

"My chief of police is doing everything necessary to find the perpetrators."

"Sir, with all due respect, your chief of police is doing nothing," I replied, doing my best to keep my voice flat and calm. I translated our conversation for the Swede, who sat ramrod straight in his chair watching my tense exchange with the governor.

"As I told your colonel recently, Farishta, just as our president cannot control everything that happens in this country, I cannot control everything that happens in my province." Daoud's dark eyes narrowed.

"Governor, the PRT has been a peaceful presence in this province for three years. We lost one man last month and sent another one home injured. Yesterday we lost three more."

The wafer-thin veneer of civilization beneath which the real Afghanistan simmered had cracked open again and three young Swedes had tumbled through. Daoud knew where the fault lines were. We foreigners did not and never would.

"You must help us," I pleaded, knowing my words would have no effect.

"We will do what we can," he said, rising from his chair to indicate that the meeting was over.

Fully armored vehicles with electronic countermeasures were now required for all trips out of camp. My brand-new Land Cruiser was relegated to the back parking lot, where it sat unused next to the rusting skeleton of the Beast.

Jeef stopped by the PRT a week after the attack and invited me to join him for a trip to Balkh to inspect his winterized dig. He was traveling in a battered green Honda van that would attract no attention. I couldn't resist his invitation and slipped out of camp without telling anyone. I was breaking the promise I'd made to Mark, but I knew this would probably be my last chance to see the towering walls that surrounded that ancient city.

"I'm sorry you won't be around to see what we turn up here, Angela," Jeef said, looking sadder than I'd ever seen him.

"I must confess I have very mixed feelings about leaving," I admitted.

"I'm certain you must. There's something about this place that doesn't let you go."

When I told Jeef about my London assignment and my plans to see Mark when I got there, he didn't seem at all surprised.

"Angela, my dear," he said, taking my hands into his, "I always suspected there was a special attraction between you and the major. I know that your first love was tragically cut short in Beirut long ago, and I wish you both all the happiness you deserve."

SIXTY-ONE

December 10, 2005

On Saturday morning, an e-mail from Marty arrived with the disappointing news that I had not been promoted and would be forced to retire in one more year. His message did contain a cheery postscript:

> Because of your service in Afghanistan, personnel has authorized you to take an abbreviated one-year tour of duty in London if you so desire.

After replying to Marty that I would take the year in London, I sent an e-mail to tell Mark about my new situation. And then I began to worry. I would be out of a job in a year. What would I do then? What if things didn't work out between us in the real world? What if our relationship turned out to have been only a wartime fling that would evaporate under the pressures of normal life?

Mark's answer, which flashed on my screen within minutes of my message, erased any doubts I may have had about my decision.

A week later, a request arrived from the embassy that would further complicate my life. The U.S. Army command in Kabul had heard about my work with solar ovens and was inviting me to stay in Afghanistan for another year to start solar oven projects at several of their PRTs in the south.

I decided to hold off sending a response to that request until after Christmas, and didn't mention the proposal to Mark, whose letters were growing longer and more passionate each week. I was intrigued by the idea of working with our military to spread this technology into southern Afghanistan. If Mark and London had not been in my immediate future, I would have jumped at the offer without hesitation. This new dilemma caused me several sleepless nights as I wrestled with the fact that I would be unemployed in London a year from now while so many people here desperately needed this technology. I would try to find someone in the expat community in Kabul to take on the project.

SIXTY-TWO

January 1, 2006

For the past several days, I had watched from my bedroom window as workmen disassembled the small mud-walled mosque across the street brick by brick. The old mullah had proudly announced his plans for the construction of a new mosque the day he came to the PRT for breakfast. He had continued to pray five times a day under his pistachio tree throughout the demolition. Early on New Year's Day, I was awakened by the sound of chopping from the now bare plot of land where the mosque had stood.

Three burly men with axes were cutting down the pistachio tree. Two other men stood guard at either end of the road. I watched in horror as the gnarled old tree fell to the ground with a loud crash.

As the men began sawing the trunk into logs, swarms of neighborhood children appeared and began crawling through the top of the tree that now lay in the dirt. Like vultures on carrion, they snapped off branches and stripped the tree bare. There was enough wood to provide each of their mothers with cooking fuel for several days.

This magnificent tree, which had taken decades to grow to its impressive size and which had nourished the mullah and his visitors with its sweet nuts season after season, would by the end of the month be reduced to bags of charcoal and windblown ashes in the cooking fires of Mazār-i-Sharīf.

I was transfixed by the destruction below my window, and overcome with sadness knowing there was nothing I could do to stop it. In less than an hour, the men had loaded their rough cuts of lumber onto a truck and driven away. More children came running to the site to fight among themselves for the remaining twigs.

At eight A.M. after the last child had left the scene, a bright winter sun lit the bare patch of earth where the pistachio tree had stood. I could see the old mullah walking down the main road toward the site of his new mosque with a round of fresh baked *naan* tucked under his arm. He was coming to sing the second call to prayer. When he turned the corner and saw the raw stump of his beloved tree, he sank to his knees and began to weep.

SIXTY-THREE

January 14, 2006

A week after his uncle the doctor arrived at the PRT in early January to take up his position as head interpreter, Rahim left for Kabul to prepare for his departure to France.

Nilofar would travel with him, as would Professor Fazli, who wanted to be sure they were both settled with their respective sponsors in Paris. I hopped a Saturday morning military flight out of Mazār and met them at the airport in Kabul that afternoon.

"I will miss you," said Rahim, hugging me with such force I could barely breathe. "Thank you for being my friend, Farishta-*jan*. Nilofar and I will look for a reunion with you and the major next summer."

"We will definitely make plans to see you both, Rahim," I promised.

Nilofar had dissolved in tears and was unable to speak. The swelling on her face had gone down, but purple bruises were still visible around her lips and eyes where the men had beaten her. She wrapped her arms around me and held on until Rahim and Fazli pulled her gently away and led her out of the terminal and up the steps of the plane.

Nilofar turned to wave just before entering the cabin. "*Khuda-hafiz*, Farishta-*jan*! *Tashakur*," she shouted over the roar of the jets on the runway. Jeef and I waited until their plane was in the air. Before we parted, we promised to see each other in February when I left Kabul for London.

Following a day of meetings at the embassy with U.S. military officials to discuss the solar oven project and suggest some local expats who might be able to help, I was back at my hooch, packing for an early morning flight to Mazār, when there was a knock at my door.

Deputy Chief of Mission Paul Plawner and my dear friend Jeef stood side by side in the slanting afternoon light. They both looked unspeakably sad. I froze, unable to breathe, until one of them spoke.

"Angela, we've just received word from the PRT," said Plawner, swallowing hard and pausing to take a deep breath. "A British Army helicopter leaving Basra for Baghdad was shot down this morning. All personnel on board were lost. The PRT commander wanted us to inform you that Major Davies was on that flight. I am so very sorry, Angela."

I don't remember much about what happened next or how long I stood mute in the doorway, shaking my head in disbelief with tears running down my cheeks. At some point, Jeef put his arm around my shoulder, led me back into my hooch, and let me cry until there was nothing left inside.

I would receive no formal notification of Mark's death. I was not next of kin, and we had no attachment other than our love for each other. Plawner asked the embassy doctor to provide me with a sedative, which I accepted gratefully. Jeef stayed with me until I fell asleep and returned the following day to take me to lunch.

Early the next morning, stretched out on my cot and staring at the molded white ceiling of my hooch, I began to tick off the emotional milestones of the past year: my anxiety about coming to Afghanistan, my initial anger at Mark's arrogance, my affection for Rahim, my awe of Nilofar and her incredible courage, my betrayal by Stefan, Fuzzy's death, my profound love for Mark and his for me, and now this.

When I lost Tom, I'd been an expectant mother married to the first man I'd ever loved. My inability to deal with that loss had put my life on hold for far too long.

Losing Mark so suddenly had punched a painful new hole in my heart, but I could not afford to wallow in self-pity for another two decades. I no longer had the luxury of time that I'd had when I was twenty-seven.

"I'm going back to Mazār tomorrow," I told Jeef as I picked at my lunch in the embassy cafeteria.

"Perhaps, my dear, you should stay in Kabul for a few days so the doctor can look in on you." He patted the back of my hand with his gnarled fingers.

"Thanks, Jeef, but I have to finish my work in Mazār before I start here in Kabul."

He looked up in surprise at my statement. "Kabul? What do you mean?"

"This morning, I accepted an offer I received last month from the U.S. Army to initiate several solar oven projects in southern Afghanistan. No point in going to London now."

"No," he said with downcast eyes, "I suppose there's not."

Jeef watched in silence as I fingered the tiny Ai Khanoum medallion he had given me. It hung from my neck on the filigreed chain Mark had sent me for Christmas.

"Jeef, you can't know how much I appreciate your friendship and your support," I said.

"You will always have it, Angela," he replied with a sad smile.

Everyone at the PRT had heard about the helicopter crash in Basra and the loss of British soldiers. It was a major story on BBC for several days, but there was nothing on CNN. The British officers and soldiers all mourned the deaths of their comrades, but only our new commanding officer, who had known Mark when they were posted together in Northern Ireland, was aware of the tremendous loss I had suffered.

The others, even those officers who had seen us dancing that night in the atrium, had no idea of the enormity of my grief. As soon as I returned to Mazār, the colonel invited me into his office.

"Angela, if there is anything I can do, you will, of course, let me know," he said. "Mark was a fine officer and a good man. Would you like me to say something to the men?"

"Thank you, Colonel, but I'd prefer to keep this to myself," I replied with my head up and my eyes dry.

"As you wish," he said, rising and walking me to the door.

A week after my return to Mazār, a rosy-cheeked corporal

stopped me in the hall outside the mailroom. He was a newcomer to the PRT.

"Nice stack of blueys in the box for you, today, Angela," he said, smiling brightly and placing the packet of letters into my outstretched hand. "I see you have a friend in Basra. Looks like you'll be needing a few hours to read all of these, eh?"

"Yes, Corporal, I probably will," I replied, squeezing the fragile blue onionskins between my fingers.

I went to my room, flipped through the stack, and found Mark's last letter.

SIXTY-FOUR

January 21, 2006

"Hi, Marty. It's Angela Morgan."

"Hi, Ange. Isn't it the middle of the night in Afghanistan?"

"It's three A.M. but I wanted to catch you in your office so we could have this conversation in person."

"How are you doing? I'm so sorry about the whole promotion thing. Really a shame."

"Thanks, Marty. I'm going to make this quick because I'm almost out of minutes. I don't want the London job."

There was silence at the other end of the line and I thought I'd lost the connection.

"Marty?"

"I'm here, Angela. So you want to spend your last year in D.C. instead of London? Makes a lot of sense. Much easier to job search from here."

"Marty, I don't want to transfer back to Washington. I'm going to stay in Afghanistan."

There was more silence but this time I waited patiently for Marty to recover and reply.

"You're kidding, right?" he said, laughing. "You've been lobbying for that London job for more than two years. What happened?"

"It's a long story, Marty. I've been given the opportunity to manage a project in this country that I think might actually help some people. This is where I belong right now."

"Suit yourself, Ange. I'm sure personnel will be delighted to give you an extra year in hell if you really want it."

"Thanks for your support, Marty."

The phone beeped twice and the line went dead. Marty would have to handle the rest from his end.

SIXTY-FIVE

March 30, 2006

I remained at the PRT until early spring when the last British troops headed south to Helmand and the arriving Swedes abandoned our ramshackle compound and moved into their heavily fortified facility in the open desert east of Mazār.

My replacement arrived the same week the British Army handed over command of the PRT to their Swedish counterparts. He was a young diplomat, with the great advantage of having served a three-year tour of duty in Stockholm early in his career. His Swedish would come in very handy with the new guys in charge.

After spending three days introducing my colleague to my most important contacts, I decided to make a final solo call on Governor Daoud. Despite his early insults and as much as I disliked and mistrusted the man, I knew that he and General Kabir were the only real power brokers in the north. Under the watchful eyes of NATO troops, these two aging warlords would be keeping the lid on the kettle up here for the next few years.

In the provinces they controlled, they had as much of a political balancing act to manage as did the Afghan president in the rest of the country. With the exception of the two attacks on our soldiers and the rocketing of the police-training center, there had been relative peace in the five northern provinces for the past year and a half. Much of that was due to the uneasy truce and iron-fisted rule of these two men.

"God be with you, Farishta-*jan*," said the governor, hobbling slowly and supported by a wooden cane as he walked me to the door of his office, where we had met alone for almost an hour.

"You must bring us some solar food driers the next time you come to Balkh. Our farmers will be growing fruits and vegetables from now on since you won't allow them to grow poppies," he added with a crooked grin. "They will need a way to preserve their produce unless the Americans will be giving them refrigerators and diesel fuel along with seeds and fertilizer."

As I exited his office and climbed into a waiting PRT vehicle, he called out to me, "Farishta-*jan*, your Dari has improved amazingly in a very short time. Congratulations."

On my final morning at the PRT, I covered my hair with a scarf and walked out the front gate unescorted, with no body armor and no burka. I wanted to say good-bye to the old mullah across the street and congratulate him on his new mosque. I didn't know if he would remember me from our breakfast, or even if my very presence would offend him.

"Of course, I know who you are, *honum*," he said, greeting me on the pitted dirt road in front of his compound.

"You have been showing the poorest people in this neighborhood how to cook with your sun boxes. Everyone knows what you have done."

He looked up at the razor-wire-covered walls of the soon to be abandoned British PRT and smiled to himself. "*Honum*, I also know it was you who asked the colonel to invite me to breakfast inside your fortress, and I thank you for that."

I acknowledged his gratitude with a nod, but was distracted by the ragged stump of the pistachio tree that jutted from a muddy patch near the edge of the construction site.

"Imam, I was so sad to see your beautiful tree cut down in January."

His face darkened momentarily and then brightened into a wrinkled smile. "Come, *honum*," he said leading me into his small courtyard and behind a half-built wall.

"I received these yesterday from a friend in Samangan." He pointed at three large clay pots, each of which held a healthy, young, four-foot pistachio tree. "Every tragedy must have its new beginning," he said, touching the branches of one of the saplings.

"*Khuda-hafiz, honum*," he called as I walked back to the PRT. "God be with you, lady."

My last official acts at the PRT were to give my roses a final pruning and say a quiet farewell to the rusting, bullet-scarred carcass of the Beast, which had carried Rahim, Fuzzy, Jenkins, and me all over northern Afghanistan. I sat alone for a few minutes in the torn and duct-taped driver's seat of this inanimate and heavily cannibalized hunk of machinery that was about to be hauled away and cut up for scrap. "Thanks, Beast," I murmured, patting the filthy dashboard. "It was quite a year."

My trip back to the United States for consultations involved multiple transfers and several cancellations due to bad weather. I ended up being booked through Frankfurt and was put on a commercial flight home with some Army personnel who had been treated at U.S. medical facilities in Germany for minor wounds they'd received in Iraq. The more seriously injured troops were being flown out in military hospital planes.

I sat next to a tall, freckle-faced U.S. Army Ranger, who reminded me of Fuzzy. His arm had been broken when his vehicle struck an IED near Baghdad. His cast was off and he assured me he was fine. He was going home for R&R in Ohio before returning to duty. He didn't ask where I had come from and we didn't speak for the rest of the flight since he had put his headphones on to watch movies as soon as we took off.

When we landed in New York and I opened the overhead compartment, he noticed the "Enduring Freedom" patch sewn to my backpack.

"Have you been in Afghanistan, ma'am?" he asked as we made our way down the narrow aisle.

"Yes, I've been up north for the past year. I'm going back next month for another year."

"You a contractor?"

"No, Foreign Service Officer—Department of State."

"What's that thing under your arm, ma'am?" he asked, staring at the folded square of foil-covered cardboard that I'd stuffed in the overhead with my backpack.

"It's my weapon of choice," I said, "a solar oven."

"What's that for, ma'am?"

"It cooks food and boils water with sunshine. There's a lot of sun but not much wood in Afghanistan."

"Same deal in Iraq, ma'am. They could use a few thousand of those things over there."

"I'm working on it, Corporal," I said with a smile.

"Hooah," he replied as we parted and headed for our connecting flights.

ACKNOWLEDGMENTS

My daughters, Jennifer and Sabrina, encouraged me to take the assignment in Afghanistan, which provided the inspiration for this novel. Thanks, girls. You know I wouldn't have gone without your permission. Thanks to my good friends Kitty and Owen Morse, who urged me to write about my experiences when I came home, and to the friends and family members who were my faithful readers: Penny Hill, Martina Nicholson, Pat Currid and Jeane Stetson (who also provided ideas for the map), Mildred Neely, Rita Sudman, Judy Maben, and my daughter Jennifer. Two thumbs up for my remarkable editor at Riverhead Books, Sarah Stein, whose firm hand made *Farishta* so much better. My sincere gratitude goes out to the officers and soldiers who were my friends and protectors during the year I spent in Mazār-i-Sharīf, with a special thanks to the three British Army colonels who commanded the PRT while I was there, and the five officers who patiently responded to my questions during the writing of *Farishta*: Tom Barker, Daniel Bould, Ross Carter, Harry Porteous, and Hugo Stanford-Tuck. Since *Farishta* is a novel and not a documentary, I do hope you fellows will forgive the artistic license I took with your detailed guidance on all things military. Thanks to poet and scholar

Coleman Barks for introducing me to the magic of Rumi's poetry during his visit to Mazār-i-Sharīf in 2005. My highest praise is reserved for our brave young Afghan interpreters, especially one who will remain unnamed—but you know who you are. *Tashakur.*

My passion for solar cooking began during the year I spent in Afghanistan, where I saw children everywhere hauling piles of brush home for their mothers' cooking fires. With the exception of the time I spent writing *Farishta*, I have dedicated the last four years of my life to promoting awareness of this remarkable technology. I plan to continue.

Patricia McArdle is a retired American diplomat. During her career, she was posted in northern Afghanistan, among other locations.